For Austin and Stella
I hope you will enjoy –

THE HOUSE BY THE SHORE

with love and
best wishes –

Joy Martin

('Mary Joyce')

April 1998

THE HOUSE
BY
THE SHORE

Mary Joyce

HEADLINE

First published in 1997
by HEADLINE BOOK PUBLISHING

10 9 8 7 6 5 4 3 2 1

British Library Cataloguing in Publication Data

Martin, Joy
The house by the shore
I.Title
823.9'14[F]

ISBN 0 7472 2111 1

Typeset by
Letterpart Limited, Reigate, Surrey

Printed and bound in Great Britain by
Mackays of Chatham PLC, Chatham, Kent

HEADLINE BOOK PUBLISHING
A division of Hodder Headline PLC
338 Euston Road
London NW1 3BH

My thanks to the following for the assistance they have given me in writing this book: John Redmill MRIAI RIBA, the Oakley and Levie families, Julie Leahy, Peter Carr, Ruth Isabel Ross, Gordon D'Arcy, and all the people of Whitegate village, County Clare.

For Christine Green, with my gratitude and affection.

One

Sunday morning. Leonard and I were still in bed. He'd finished coffee, read the papers, watched the news on television. He stretched out on the rumpled sheet as I planned the week ahead.

'Tuesday's dinner with the Wilsons. Wednesday's free. We could see *The Cherry Orchard*. Supper at Quaglino's maybe?'

Leonard yawned. 'That sounds like a good idea.'

'Thursday's down for dinner here. Let's have Saturday in town. What about Modigliani?'

Leonard, with his dark brown hair and his liquid brown eyes, looked a lot like Modigliani before absinthe got hold of him, though he'd been a 'pale and ravishing villain'. Leonard had a healthy tan.

He grimaced. *Not* Modigliani. I racked my brains. Definitely not the Craft Show. Not the Kirov Ballet, either.

'There's something on the EEC. A seminar that Saturday.'

'Get the tickets,' Leonard said.

He was getting slightly restless.

I said, 'I think I'm going to change my image. Shall I become more elusive?' I hid my face beneath a tissue and peered over it at him.

'More erotic?' I reached out for a pair of earrings, held them up against my nipples.

'Or,' I peeled off a pillowcase, turned it into an ice-cream hat and posed as a reclining nude, 'elegant and *very* sexy?'

Leonard laughed delightedly.

'Idiot!' He reached out and grabbed the hat.

'You've ruined my elegance!' I shrieked.

He grabbed me. We tussled, tickled, teasing, giggling, working towards the inevitable. That was when she rang.

'Caroline, is that you speaking? This is Marie-Rose.'

'Who?'

'Marie-Rose Keane.'

A figure appeared on memory's screen. The woman Olive called

1

'the girl'. Pasty-faced and overweight. Dressed in clothes cast off by Constance who was also on the fat side.

'Marie-Rose! How are you?'

I wondered if she was in London – in Kilburn maybe, with relations. Before I could ask she spoke again.

'I have bad news for you,' she said. 'Your Aunt Constance is after dying.'

This was not the unpleasant shock it once might have been. I hadn't laid eyes on Constance since leaving Ireland long ago. Our contact had whittled down to scribbled news on Christmas cards. But she'd been my mother's sister, my only surviving relation on that side of the family.

'That's awful,' I said. 'What happened to her?'

'She was poorly these last few months.'

'I didn't realise . . . What exactly—?'

'It was The Usual,' Marie-Rose said.

It must have been cancer, I thought – not a subject people in County Clare would be eager to discuss. I should have been told about her illness. Marie-Rose had continued to work for my aunt even after Constance had moved out of Carrigrua into a smaller house. She should have let me know.

But maybe Constance had been touchy. People with cancer often were. Marie-Rose might have been warned not to mention it to me.

'Will you be coming over for the funeral?'

'When is it?' I asked, stalling, leaning back against the pillows.

'The removal is on Wednesday. There'll be Mass at eleven in Mountshannon. The burial will be in the new cemetery over in Scariff. I have it all arranged.'

Mountshannon. Scariff. Place names out of the distant past. The memories rushed out at me. The road winding through the villages and round the lake. The low stone walls and the hawthorn hedges. The animals grazing in the wet green fields. The blue hills. The long avenue through the wood that led to Carrigrua. It was May and the bluebells would be out and the leaves on the birch trees turning emerald. The whole of nature would be conspiring to draw attention to the house.

Tears came into my eyes. They were not for Constance.

'Are you still there, Caroline?'

'I'm sorry. I was thinking. Yes, of course, I'll come over. Is it all right if I stay with you?'

She didn't answer at once. She waited just long enough for me to wonder if we'd been cut off. Then—

'That will be all right. I'll make up a bed for you.'

'What was all that about?' Leonard inquired as I put down the phone.

He'd never been to Clare, never met any of my relations, apart from my father and his second wife. Even after Olive's death, I'd not been invited back. Not until now.

I explained.

'Will she pick you up at Shannon?'

'She didn't suggest it. In any case, I'd prefer to hire a car.' So I could drive around alone. Explore that place that used to be mine. Follow the road round the lake . . .

'You're miles away,' Leonard complained, accurately enough. He eased himself over to my side of the bed, to take up where we'd left off. But I was getting up.

'Yes. We must talk about this – what we're going to do. I'll go down and make more coffee.'

Leonard blinked. 'Oh, all right.'

I padded down to the kitchen on bare feet. Our modern, two-storey house in Wentworth was designed round a central courtyard and looked over a brick-built barbecue on to an acre of well-trimmed lawn. The year before we'd put in a heated pool.

It wasn't at all like Carrigrua.

Carrigrua, I said to myself, reaching for the coffee beans. The Wentworth house paled by comparison, became insignificant, super-ficial, rather vulgar. Like a grey sun, the graceful, blue-grey Georgian manor in which I had spent my childhood rose over my mind's horizon.

Carrigrua was a perfectly symmetrical, classic Irish house, with a walled garden to one side and a cobblestoned yard and stables and utility buildings adjoining the rear; a two-and-a-half-storey, six-bay, limestone symbol of status and gentility. It stood on a lake shore on the edge of a small wood and it was typical of the early eighteenth century in all ways but one.

The man who designed Carrigrua fell in love with the lake. He travelled in his coach through the lush green countryside of County Clare and he came upon the glory that was Lough Derg and he got an idea in his head.

From the beginning Carrigrua must have given the county plenty to talk about. Built in the days when the preservation of valuable tapestries and rich curtains took precedence over a view and when other houses were turned away from the ravages of the sun, Carrigrua

3

stepped boldly out of a mantle of silver birches to face the lake. Its harbour drove deep into the lake waters and its lawns ran wantonly down to the wild shore to merge with bedstraw and bog rush and reeds.

Carrigrua. The image of it stayed with me. But another perception was gradually dawning. Waiting for the coffee to percolate, I considered the implications of my aunt's death.

Constance might have moved into a smaller, more manageable house, but she hadn't sold Carrigrua. I was her niece, her only close surviving relation. A Conroy in all but name. The last of the line.

That could only mean one thing. Carrigrua must have been left to me.

I left the coffee bubbling away and wandered through to the living room. Its new look was quite austere, despite the rich dark red of the kelim cushions, the red hand-painted chest with the African carvings on it and the red and salmon Portuguese rugs laid out on the stripped lime pine floor. The walls were beige, the pre-cast concrete fireplace was unpainted and the curtains were swathes of cheesecloth I'd draped over fitted poles.

In fact, the walls were *always* beige, but no one ever noticed that. 'You've changed the decor *again*!' people would marvel, as they so often did, not realising that I never made drastic or structural changes, that I only switched and swapped, taking paintings from upstairs and hanging them in the living room to tone with the colours I'd introduced, tacking fabric over sofas, alternating cushion covers.

I used to be a window dresser. I was up to all the tricks. Take the fireplace, for example. It didn't work – it wasn't meant to. Its purpose was to hold ceramics. It was fun, I'd enjoyed making it, but it was not a fixture. Sooner or later it would go, find a place in another room, or maybe outside in the courtyard where it could be used for pots, and I'd chop and change again.

I couldn't do that at Carrigrua. Carrigrua was constant, immutable; its identity too definite, too long-established to tolerate my tricks and whims.

But was it still the house that I remembered or had it gone to rack and ruin? If it had been standing empty it must be in need of some attention. Restoration could prove expensive. Leonard was generous but he would see the house as a business proposition and ask if it was worth renovating.

And if it was not? I caught sight of myself in the thick sheet mirror I'd used to alter the room's perspective. I looked like my grandmother, Olive Conroy, though I was a few inches taller than her and my hair

4

was not a natural blonde. But Olive, too, had been small-boned, her face heart-shaped, her eyes large and grey like mine.

Right now, my eyes were wide with alarm at the notion that Leonard might advocate selling the house. Sell Carrigrua? No, I thought. That must never happen.

'What happened to coffee?' demanded Leonard, looming up in the mirror in his dressing gown.

'Oh, yes . . .'

He followed me back into the kitchen.

'How long will you be away?'

'I don't know. A week or so.' As long as a thorough inspection of Carrigrua would take. An estimate made of what precisely needed to be done in the way of restoration.

'A *week*?'

'Or so.'

I'd have to unpick some arrangements. Not the Wilsons. Leonard could go on his own. We'd defer *The Cherry Orchard*. Thursday – dinner. Not a problem. I'd phone up the caterers. Ask our cleaner, Mrs Langley, if she'd set and clear the table. Which left a rather long weekend. What could I set up for Leonard?

'What day are the gardening service people coming?'

My God, I thought, the garden. What state will it be in? The grass in this garden needs mowing once a week in spring. What height might it be at Carrigrua, where the growth is so luxuriant? The roses in the walled garden should have been pruned last November or December. Someone should be cutting the foliage off the daffodils, trimming back the shrubs, the japonica and forsythia. But in the orchard the blossoms on the apple trees will have set into tiny fruits. The fear of frost will be gone. The bedding plants should be laid down.

'Friday,' I answered automatically.

'Maybe we should put them off for a week. Unless they're prepared to wait for their money until you get back.'

'Can't you be here to deal with them?'

'I suppose so. Did Emma say if anyone else has been asked to lunch?'

'Lunch?'

'You are switched off. Today. At Hugh and Emma's.'

I tore my mind away from Carrigrua.

'I think it's ten of us,' I said.

I put on my red New York jeans, a matching body and my brand new scarlet boots. They pinched, but it was worth the pain. I wasn't going to walk that far. I tied my hair with chiffon scarves – an orange and a purple one – and tried on my gypsy earrings.

'You look gorgeous,' Leonard said. 'Why don't we go back to bed?'

'Delicious thought.' But it was nearly one o'clock.

Hugh and Emma lived down the road in Sunningdale in a quiet residential cul-de-sac.

'Ah, finally – the artist and the entrepreneur,' said Hugh, ushering us in.

Leonard and Hugh had been at school together. Leonard was the daring one; he had his own shipping and freight forwarding company, with offices in Staines and warehouses in central Africa stacked with motorcar tyres, crates of whisky, perfume and smoked salmon, in exchange for which he bartered anything legal, from cotton to flowers. Hugh was a merchant banker.

'There you are, at last,' said Emma.

Emma was a teacher before she got married. Unlike me, she had children, twins, a boy and a girl. Getting what she and Hugh wanted in one fell swoop typified Emma. She was kind but patronising; slim, confident, stylish and a superb cook. That day we ate sauteed John Dory with stuffed courgette flowers. The place settings exactly matched the yellow of the blossoms – each one carefully filled with creamy mousse – and the rich red of the sauce.

The twins, having eaten in the breakfast room, were playing outside in the garden when we took our places at the table. I was conscious of eyes checking out my jeans and boots; of Leonard revelling in the impact of my get-up.

'Caroline,' said Lizzie Baxter. 'How's the exhibition going?'

My pottery and co-ordinating poppy paintings had gained me a better reputation than I felt the work deserved. My oils on paper were quite facile – I dipped newsprint into paint to create a blobby background on to which I painted flowers – but they were little money-spinners.

'It's just over, actually. But I have another project.' I couldn't wait to break the news – to tell them about Carrigrua.

'Oh? What's that?' Lizzie asked.

'The house in Ireland. Carrigrua.'

They knew about Carrigrua and about my life in Ireland. To them, it was all part of Celtic Caroline's intriguing mystique, the ongoing saga of a child who, when her mother died in childbirth and her father went to England, fell into the clutches of a Draconian grandmother, a

6

frustrated aunt, an angst-ridden housekeeper and a dumpy, callous maid.

As they leant forward, avid for a new instalment, I explained about the phone call, imitating Marie-Rose.

'Caroline, is that you speaking?'

They roared with laughter at the accent.

'Not so fast with your laughter,' I said, playing with them. 'She rang to say my aunt is dead.'

'Aunt Constance?'

They had the lowdown on Aunt Constance. They loved what Norah said about her – that she took after my grandfather Lawrence, 'a lovely poor man with a neck on him like a bull and big thick legs like trees'.

'Aunt Constance. But it means the house is mine.'

'That's – wonderful,' said Carol Hunter.

'What condition is it in?' Trust Bob Baxter to ask that.

'It's bound to be rundown,' said Emma, worriedly, 'if it's been left standing empty. Especially being by a lake.'

'The Lake of the Ruddy Eye.' Carol always got it wrong.

'The *Bloody*, not the Ruddy Eye!'

I'd told them the legend about Lough Derg, a gruesome tale of a malicious poet who, offered whatever he wanted in life, demanded the king's remaining eye. The doleful monarch cast it out and washed its socket in the lake.

'That's why the lake is red,' I'd said.

As a child, I'd been sickened by this story. Later, I was relieved to learn that an underwater seam of iron oxide gave the lake that rosy hue. From this seam, too, came the name of the house, Carrigrua, the red rock.

'How long has it been standing empty?'

'Since Olive died,' I told Bob Baxter. 'Eight years ago, I think it was.'

'Quite a while. I wish you luck.'

Quite a while. The spectre of Carrigrua despoiled rose up again to haunt me. I looked at Leonard for support. Bad timing. Emma had got up to fetch dessert and Leonard's eyes were roving appreciatively over her pert bottom, shown to advantage in white clingy pants.

I reminded myself, as I had done on previous occasions when he was getting up to mischief, that Leonard was like a Lamborghini, superbly designed for the open road but too finely tuned for suburban use.

Anyway, Emma was the faithful type. Emma wasn't Carol Hunter. And that was over long ago . . .

Emma returned carrying a tray stacked with tiny pastry baskets. In each were six fat strawberries, exactly the same size, with a blob of cream on top.

'Look at those!' said Leonard.

'I never think of it as empty,' I said. 'Haunted houses never are.'

That got everyone's attention.

'There's a *ghost* at Carrigrua?'

'The Grey Lady,' I said, breaking the handle off my basket, crumbling the pastry into the fruit, so the effect wasn't quite so perfect.

'The who?'

I explained in Norah's voice. Dear, sweet-faced, anxious Norah. They were very fond of Norah.

'That's what we call our ghost – the Grey Lady. Haven't I told you about her before?'

The Grey Lady was gentle and fair and for ever nineteen. The daughter of the first family to live at Carrigrua, Protestant settlers who came to Ireland during the time of the Penal Laws, she fell in love with a Catholic, a younger son who had no prospects.

'Every night, she climbed out of her bedroom window to meet her lover in the wood. Until the young man went to France, to become a mercenary. He was killed at Fontenoy. No one ever told her that, so she's still waiting in the wood, in the hope that he'll come back.'

'Go on. Has she actually been spotted?'

'Not in Olive's time,' I said. 'I think Olive drove her out.'

I mimicked Olive, nose in air. 'Meeting in the wood indeed. But then she was a *Protestant*! What else could you expect?'

Howls of laughter this time round. Leonard laughing with the others. Olive would have been outraged.

Olive. They knew exactly what she looked like. Olive the unusual, whose style was drawn from several eras. Her hair severely cropped in the mode of the 1920s. Her long, narrow tweed skirts and high-necked, lace-trimmed Edwardian blouses. Those plain, sculptural, untrimmed hats which were sent to her from London. And the shoes that were her passion, hopelessly impractical for the country but right for her, with their low vamps and high stiletto heels.

She haughtily dismissed the ghost.

'Norah, kindly bring the muffins. The ladies will be here for tea.' I jumped up, stuck out my feet as Norah did, bringing in the muffin dish.

'The ladies sat like this,' I said, perching on my chair again. 'Their

8

scarves had hunting prints on them.'

They lapped it up – they always did. When I did the ladies for them – spiking cake with silver forks while balancing their cups and saucers – tears were streaming down their cheeks.

Then I became myself for them, plaguing Olive with my questions.

'Grandma, does a nun have legs?'

'*What?*'

'Is her body a triangle with her feet attached to it?'

'Pull yourself together, child. Just remember you're a Conroy.'

I followed with the Conroy creed.

'Conroys don't wear dirty clothes. They take pride in their appearance. A Conroy doesn't mind the dark. A Conroy's not a scaredy creature. A Conroy should add up much better. You're no good at sums at all.'

'What a dragon,' Lizzie said. 'How did you put up with her?'

I didn't satirise the house. Carrigrua was too precious to let people laugh at it.

Carrigrua, I kept thinking. How would I feel when I saw it again? Was it the house that I had known? Had its colour scheme been changed?

'Black or white?'

'What? Oh, sorry. Black, please, Emma.'

'So sad for you,' said Jenny Heron. 'I mean, it will be, when you sell it.'

'Sell it? I'm not selling Carrigrua.'

Emma frowned. 'But you can't live over there.'

'Partly here and partly there.'

'What about Leonard's business?'

'Ireland has the latest in digital telecommunications now. He can operate from Clare. Can't you, darling?'

'Possibly.'

Possibly . . .

'Two big houses. Still, if anyone can cope, you can, Caroline. I can't keep up with you. Painting. Entertaining. Rushing into and out of London.'

'That reminds me,' I said, 'Modigliani's at the Tate. Shall we go? Make up a party?'

'Girls' day out? No good bringing Hugh along. OK. Phone when you get back from Ireland.'

'Emma is a bit pedantic,' Leonard said, on the way home. 'But her cooking is to die for.'

9

'If you ask me, she overdoes it.'

'How do you mean?'

'Strawberries are perfect on their own. They don't need to go in baskets.'

'Actually, you're right,' said Leonard.

We made love on the living-room floor. For me, love with Leonard was a psychedelic trip. Not that I was into drugs, even when I was at art school.

It was sweet and strange and satisfying, as it always was with Leonard. But even then I was distracted, thinking of that graceful house in its wrap of silver birches, gazing out across Lough Derg.

The flight to Shannon was fifteen minutes late taking off. It gave me the chance to catch up on myself and draw breath after speaking to Mrs Langley.

Our cleaning lady was a reluctant worker. She was grudging with her favours and she had perfected the technique of inducing guilt in others. I felt bad because she lived in a council flat; because she had to earn her living; because her son was out of work. On Thursdays, I was conscience-stricken.

This week, she had proved elusive. I finally got hold of her just before I left for Heathrow.

'I'm off to Ireland, Mrs Langley.'

'Oh, you're going on *holiday*?' She sniffed.

I told her that my aunt had died. 'I'm going to the funeral. There's the house to see to, too – the one I lived in as a child. It seems that it's been left to me.'

'Is that so?' said Mrs Langley, sounding unimpressed, as usual.

Irritating. I became slightly imperious, in spite of asking her a favour. 'Could you work on Thursday evening? I'll pay you double if you can.'

'It's not convenient,' she said, 'but I *suppose* I could do it.'

'Terrific. You're going to need a key.'

'You'll drop one round?'

'I'll hide one in the garden for you.'

'You never know who might be watching.'

'In the courtyard then,' I said. 'Nobody can see me there.'

Now I worried lest they had. I thought, the Wilsons' house has just been burgled. Crime's increasing. Thieves do keep a watch on houses.

Oh, stop it. Stop worrying.

I tried, but it was difficult.

10

I thought, I'm just as bad as ever, as over-imaginative, as neurotic as I was nearly thirty years ago.

When I got on Olive's nerves.

When she got rid of me.

When I failed the Conroy test.

To me, the Conroys were quasi-divine. As noble as the British royals. As golden as the Kennedys. Gorgeous just like Michael Caine and Terence Stamp and Princess Grace.

Olive was one of Them, the Saintly, Fearless, Clever People. She was proud of being a Conroy.

'I was one by birth,' she'd say. 'My maiden name was also Conroy. Lawrence was my second cousin.'

Beyond emphasising that, she hardly ever spoke of Lawrence, only of the Conroy family.

'We were always powerful people. Before the Normans came to Ireland we owned all the land round here.'

'What happened that we lost it, Grandma?'

'Our land went to the Protestants. But then we got it back again, and the house along with it.'

The house. That was the thing that interested me. Even then, I was in love with Carrigrua.

Olive loved the house as well, but she loved the Conroys more.

I didn't make it as a Conroy. All I could do was draw and no one was impressed by that. I was a failure; second-rate. I knew that, and so did Olive; you could see it on her face. When I saw her looking at me with what seemed like sheer contempt, I feared I wouldn't last the pace. I thought, one day soon she'll kick me out.

When that happened I was wretched. I prayed that she would change her mind, but I was certain she would not.

In a way, I sympathised. I understood that she was right. I just wasn't up to it.

'We're sorry for that delay which was due to air traffic control congestion,' the captain said, bringing me back firmly to the present. 'We'll be taking off for Shannon within the next couple of minutes.'

An hour later I was less than thirty miles from Carrigrua. We landed in heavy rain. As I walked to the hire car, visibility was nonexistent. I took off through the downpour and soon found myself on the wrong road, heading for the county town of Ennis instead of the lake.

As I turned back, the rain suddenly stopped and the sun came out. A short distance further along the main Shannon–Limerick road I came to a travellers' site, saw their washing spread out on the bushes and the signpost I was seeking. It directed me into a stretch of conventional farmland where traditional dwellings had been replaced by modern bungalows and pastiche period houses.

Then, as if exchanging a civilised lover for a bit of rough, the countryside changed, became more unruly, the hedgerows delightfully unkempt, the cottages tumbledown, the fields more verdant, the gorse bushes gaudy on their perimeters. The cowslips were out, along with primroses, heartsease and kingcups. The sun was highlighting my return, glorying in it.

I rolled down the car window, felt the sun's heat on my arm and thought I'd never been so happy. Death had brought joy into my life.

Lord, I thought, poor Constance. I shouldn't be so callous. But my memory of Constance the woman was indistinct. I could recall the physical Constance very well. Pudgy, pale. Clumsy, uncoordinated. And no dress sense whatsoever. Those shapeless trousers, shirts and jerseys. They drove Olive up the wall.

Still, she did have one redeeming feature. Her beautiful hair, rich auburn with golden lights, thick and curly, transformed my unastonishing aunt into Stevenson's red-haired Queen. In my memory of her, she was sitting on the lawn at Carrigrua with the wind blowing her hair about her face.

'I really must have it cut,' she sighed, as if the mere thought of contemplating a visit to the hairdresser would overtax her waning strength.

It was difficult now to pinpoint her personality. She was rather passive, I thought, rather lethargic. The kind of person who would always take the easy way out. Not in the least like Olive. Funny how I could recall my grandmother so clearly and yet be so unsatisfactorily hazy when it came to my aunt. Maybe at the funeral my mind would clear and I'd weep for the person she had been.

But the charm of the land and the heat of the sun and the knowledge that I was moving closer and closer to Carrigrua put auburn-haired Constance right out of my mind. Drugged by the clean air, I drove happily on along the twisting road, towards my destination.

Two

Every mile took me a step backwards and each bend carried me further from the rational world into one ruled by the senses. Now and then the hedgerows and the trees that grew out of them soared up and reached out for each other to form verdant arches over the grey patchwork road. I drove through those tunnels bubbling with excitement, hyper-sensitive to smell and sight and sound.

After the rain the white wild garlic and the young grasses were at their most pungent and their scents led me into the boreens and meadows of childhood.

With those memories came another – of that day, the last day, when I'd travelled in the opposite direction.

It was Constance who saw me off. Olive did not come to the airport with us. It was a Sunday and that would have meant missing ten o'clock Mass, something she never did. Not that Constance and I missed Mass that morning. We were in the church at seven, after which I came home to a breakfast I couldn't eat.

On the way to Shannon we dropped Olive off at the church, along with Norah and Marie-Rose. I kissed Olive on the cheek. Like Marie-Rose, her eyes were dry. Norah was the one who wept and slipped a holy picture into my hand.

From the car window I watched them walk in single file into the porch, Norah valiantly blowing her nose and the other two staring straight ahead, not looking back to return my wave. It can't be happening, I thought wildly. Under my breath, I prayed to Saint Jude, the patron saint of hopeless cases, asking him to intervene.

Now, finally, someone *had* interceded. I *had* been summoned home. Constance had given me a second chance.

When I reached the outskirts of Scariff the odour of peat smoke transported me into cottages I had long forgotten. Out of the past came people, too. Men with wind-whipped faces and earth-stained trousers smelling of cattle and damp. Women who gave me soda bread hot from the oven and buttermilk with fat yellow globules floating on top. Each a study for a painting. When my studio was ready – the one I'd have at Carrigrua – I might paint those men and women.

No, perhaps I'd better stick to flowers. No more poppies. Maybe kingcups. Something yellow anyway.

I might convert one of the outbuildings into a studio. Leonard could set up an office inside the house, perhaps in the bedroom that used to be mine. He'd find amusement in the lake. He might even buy a yacht.

I got to Scariff. This was territory close to home where, on one of her afternoons off, Norah and I had fallen in love with Sean Connery at the Astor cinema. A sign pointing right, to the harbour, tugged the cord of memory. The Scariff River was down there, on its way to join Lough Derg.

I crossed a bridge and followed the village up a hill, between rows of terraced houses with pebble-dashed exteriors and a smart new Bank of Ireland. The Astor cinema had closed. A modern health-food shop had opened and the square at the top of the hill was doubling up as a parking lot.

The sign for the harbour and the thought of the river flowing into Lough Derg had given me an appetite for the lake. Soon, it would come into view. I rounded a bend and was taken aback by the sudden sight of it – shimmering, silver and surprisingly serene.

My hands tensed on the steering wheel. On the shore of that lake was the house. My house. My beloved Carrigrua. I stared wildly to see if I could catch a glimpse of it. I couldn't, of course. You can't see it from that point. But I was drunk on expectation and furious when a cluster of silver birches and after them a whitewashed stone cottage blocked my view of Lough Derg. I was only mollified when the bell tower of Holy Island rose up like a too-tall chimney and I could feast on the lake again.

Just before Mountshannon, purple rhododendrons were in full bloom and a young wood was flourishing. More signs welcomed visitors and informed them that Mountshannon had won the Tidy Towns competition.

I was trembling all over by then, seized by the temptation to go home in the real sense. If I continued straight on instead of turning left after the parish priest's green house, I could be at Carrigrua in less than ten minutes. The compulsion to give way was so overwhelming I was shocked by the strength of it. I'd never longed so intensely for anything before – for any person, Leonard included. What was happening to me?

On the right side of the road was a stone church with a wrought-iron gate painted a cheerful burnt orange. I pulled in just beyond the church, turned off the engine, buried my face in my hands and tried to come to terms with my feelings.

A voice inside me said, 'Don't bother. Just drive on to Carrigrua.'

I was about to throw caution to the winds and abandon the dead when a black Nissan stopped a few yards up from where I'd parked. Another car drew in beyond it and after that a third. Out of the cars stepped three girls of ten or maybe twelve wearing pretty summer dresses and carrying prayer books in their hands. Confirmation day, I thought.

Parents followed, suitably attired for the solemn occasion in sober suits and floral outfits. Then a lone father appeared. He was slightly built, fair-haired, pleasant-faced but too thin. He looked familiar. He had with him a pretty, dark-haired child, the pearl of the bunch, a princess in a lace-trimmed dress.

These two stopped beside my car.

'Where's your prayer book?' the man asked the child.

'*You* had it for me at the house.'

'I did?'

'Aw, Daddy, but you're really hopeless!'

I peeked out in time to see the child smile up at the man, her deep blue eyes with their long black lashes hazy with adoration for him. Touched by that, I glanced again at him. I thought – but I know you from somewhere. And then I shivered, for with recognition came unease. All of a sudden, I felt threatened.

The man did not look menacing. The expression on his fine-boned face was serious, rather than grim. There was nothing brutish about his demeanour. His tie was crooked and he was distractedly running his hand through his hair so strands of it were sticking up.

'I can't imagine where I put it. Would Father Clery have a spare one? Where are Grandpa and Mrs O'Grady?'

'They've gone in the church already.'

The man brightened. 'Maybe Grandpa picked it up.'

They drifted on. Other cars arrived, with boys as well as girls in them. Their advent broke the spell that had taken hold of me. The psychic path to Carrigrua was obstructed for the moment.

I moved on and, instead of heading for the house, I did as Marie-Rose had said and drove up a deserted road until I got to a bright red gate with the name 'Conroy Keane' emblazoned on its right-hand post.

Leaving the car outside on the grass verge, I walked up the gravelled driveway. The lawn had been freshly mown and there was not a weed in sight, not even a single dandelion. Olive would have been impressed.

The house was a re-converted stone farmhouse. There was bedlam when I rang the bell – chimes and barks, a woman's shout, a door being slammed. I was still waiting for Marie-Rose to materialise on the threshold when a trim, brown-haired woman came round the side of the house.

'It's yourself so, Caroline.'

'Marie-Rose!'

I wouldn't have known her. She was in her late fifties but she looked younger than her age and she was wearing good clothes – linen trousers, a T-shirt and an over-blouse.

I heard myself describing her to our friends in Sunningdale. *'No more hand-me-downs from Constance. Mind you, they made Marie-Rose housekeeper after Norah got beyond it. Maybe then she got ideas and took an interest in her appearance . . .'*

'Lord, but Olive was right,' she said. 'You're the image of what she thought you'd be.'

'Using Olive's name like that! Olive would have died of shock . . .'

Fighting off hysteria, I hastily put a hand over my mouth to suppress a giggle. 'Oh, good . . .'

One of her eyebrows shot up. 'Come round to the kitchen. It's easier than traipsing through the hall.'

As I followed her, a canine cacophony broke out and she shouted to it, 'Whisht! Take no notice of the dogs. They'll get used to you. 'Twould suit me better to be without them but they're needed for the security. I have your tea ready. There's plenty of time yet before the church.'

'I didn't realise we'd be going to the church this evening.'

'It's customary. But you wouldn't know that. You weren't over when your grandmother died.'

'No. I didn't hear until we got back. We were skiing in Switzerland.'

'Switzerland.'

To her, it might just as well have been Neptune or Uranus. She pushed open the back door. In the kitchen two mongrels were panting and salivating.

'Give me that and I'll put it up for you,' said Marie-Rose, taking my case. 'Your bed is made up in the visitor's room. Sit down at the table. I'll be back in a minute.'

I thanked her and obeyed. The larger dog eased himself under the table to inspect my feet. I cast my eyes about the kitchen. Everything looked new. If Constance had bought pots and pans over from Carrigrua they were not on show, only gleaming stainless steel utensils, Pyrex ware and labelled containers. The floor was covered by functional, rather nasty speckled linoleum and the windows hidden by net curtains as white and crisp as frost. Squares of muslin, weighed down by blue beads, were draped over plates of sandwiches and currant cake. There was a pink rose pattern on my cup.

'Maybe Aer Lingus fed you?' Marie-Rose was back.

'I just had a cup of coffee.'

She bustled around, switched on the kettle, set down a glass mug on the table, in which nestled three sodden tea bags, one of which she fished out and popped into my cup.

Great stuff for my ongoing saga . . .

'You like it strong, do you?'

'Not really.'

The tea bag was retrieved and replaced in the mug.

'Aren't you having anything?'

'I'm not hungry.' Her expression was impassive. Strange, inscrutable creature, I thought.

She watched me devour a second slice of currant cake.

'We'd better be getting ready,' she said then.

I asked if I could use an iron and went upstairs to rummage in my case for the black suit I had brought to wear at the funeral.

My room was like the kitchen. The carpet, the two single beds and the chest of drawers all seemed quite new. The room itself was spotlessly clean but as impersonal as an hotel bedroom. I sighed, and mentally refurnished it. I removed the carpet (more fleck, brown and rust), leaving the floorboards bare, threw out the beds along with their flower-patterned duvet covers and installed a Clare bed with a moulded canopy and a white-fringed spread. I replaced the chest of drawers with one from another age, set a china basin and jug on it and put a crucifix up on the wall. That was how the room should look.

Again it was strange that there was nothing of Carrigrua here, in the way of a picture or an ornament. Surely Constance hadn't left every single thing behind? If so, robbers and vandals would by now have had a field day.

Alarmed at the thought, I asked Marie-Rose.

'Constance sold most of it when we came here. There's a few things still there. Not much.'

17

'Why did she do that?'

'The money came in handy. And Constance didn't want anything that reminded her of the past.'

'She must have been devastated when my grandmother died. I wish I'd known. I could have come over.'

'The iron is on.'

I took the hint and went to work on the black suit, chastened by what I'd learnt. The news that Constance had sold the furniture was a body blow. The loss of my grandmother's effects added up to another kind of tragedy. The longcase clock that used to stand in the hall. The china cabinet. The polished mahogany table and matching chairs. The Irish silver. Constance, what have you done? I thought.

I changed, upset that Leonard and I had not been given the chance to buy what Constance had flogged off.

Marie-Rose was in front of me coming down the stairs, chic in a green suit with a straight skirt that ended below the knees. She had good legs. I wondered fleetingly why she had never married. Lack of opportunity, I supposed; too many eligible men forced to emigrate from the district when she was young.

I nearly bumped into her when she stopped at the foot of the stairs. She nodded to what I presumed was the parlour door.

'She's in there.'

'Who?'

She opened the door and gestured for me to go ahead of her. What I saw sent me into a cold sweat. Constance was in the room, or what remained of her, lying in an open coffin lined with blue satin. Her body was wrapped in a white shroud and someone had put rosary beads into her folded hands.

Apart from the sight of her dead, I was unnerved by the fact that her once-beautiful hair was now snow-white. Cut too short, it stuck up punk-like from her head. Between that and her yellowish skin she reminded me of a half-plucked daisy.

Around the coffin were six lighted candles and, on an adjacent table, half a dozen wreaths and a little basket containing Mass cards. I swallowed and caught Marie-Rose watching my reactions.

'It's come as a jolt to you, I suppose, seeing her laid out. It was always the way, you know. The parish priest will be here in a minute and there'll be people coming from all around to pay their respects.'

I said weakly, 'I did get a bit of a fright.'

'It helps you face death. You know when you look at the body that the person is gone from it. You were always soft, Caroline. The rest of

18

us can't afford to be that way. Your kind think a wake is a party but mine know better. The real purpose of the music and the dancing in the old days was to keep the rats from eating the corpse. That's why someone had to stay up all night with the body – like I did, last night.'

She made me feel seven years old. When I was that age Constance's hair had been red-gold. Once, when she was down with flu, I'd gone to see her in her bedroom. Her hair, long then, was spread out all over the pillow.

She'd said, to no one in particular, 'Isn't it *odd* how we all had such beautiful hair and Caroline's is so dull,' touching me on a raw nerve, so I wished I'd kept my distance.

But now the beauty was gone for ever from my aunt's hair and I was saddened that her one good point should have been taken from her.

'I suppose you would have preferred the English way,' Marie-Rose said. 'The coffin closed and no need to think what would be in there. Or I could have let her be taken to the mortuary. Forty pounds that would have cost me, but it wasn't that. She was better off here, with me.'

Before I could answer, a car came up the drive and the dogs began to bark again. Marie-Rose went to the door. I averted my eyes from the coffin and dabbed at them with a tissue that came away streaked with mascara. The opportunity to slip off and repair the damage was lost when Marie-Rose ushered a priest into the room.

'Father, this is Constance's niece, Caroline Tremain. You won't have met her before.'

'No, I don't think so. You're from England, are you?'

'That's right,' I said, longing to have another dab at my face. 'I've just arrived today from London.'

'Well, now, I'm sorry it's not under happier circumstances.'

He seemed a nice man and so did the undertaker who came in next. As I was greeting him I noticed the priest looking sourly at Marie-Rose.

Then the doorbell rang again and more people arrived. As they came in they took my hand and said they were sorry for my trouble. Each one dipped his or her finger into a small font and shook holy water on to the remains. Then they blessed themselves and said a short prayer before taking one last look into the coffin.

When the room had almost completely filled up, the priest said the rosary. I had difficulty remembering the Hail Mary at first, but it soon came back to me.

Marie-Rose hadn't told me what would happen next. We were at opposite ends of the room and I didn't get the chance to talk to her before the parlour began to clear. Eventually, the only people left were the undertaker and us two women.

The undertaker gave me a gentle tap on the arm. 'You'll want to say goodbye to her before I put on the lid.'

I did so with closed eyes. Afterwards I slipped out of the room and fled upstairs to clean my face. The coffin had already been loaded into the hearse by the time I returned and Marie-Rose was waiting for me by the back door.

'Will you drive?'

'You don't?'

'Not if I can help it.'

In the car she was silent and withdrawn, a mole gone underground. We followed the hearse to the church where the priest was waiting. He came over to me.

'The custom is for the coffin to be walked up the aisle with distant relatives on either side of it and close family behind.'

'I understand.'

I didn't bother telling him that there was no distant relations present and I was the only close one. He probably knew anyway. Marie-Rose was standing beside me, lost in thought, and she was still next to me as the coffin was carried into the church on its way to the altar. Not that I minded.

The coffin was placed in front of the altar and the priest said the rosary again. There was more sympathising and hand-shaking before those who had not yet given Mass cards and wreaths came forward to do so. The body was to be left to rest overnight in God's house while the other mourners came back with us to have refreshments.

It was after midnight when the last of them left and by then I was exhausted. Marie-Rose also looked worn out but there was no way she was going to bed without tidying up the place.

As she cleared the dishes, I went into the kitchen, took off my rings, laid them beside the draining board, and ran the water to wash up.

'Don't bother about that,' she said. 'I'll do it. You go on up to bed.'

'It's no bother. I tell you what, though. Could I quickly phone my husband?'

'The phone is out there in the hall.'

Our number rang and rang. Ten times . . . fifteen . . . seventeen . . . nineteen. Eventually Leonard answered.

'Did I wake you up?' I said.

'No, you didn't. I was showering.'

'How was it at the Wilsons'?'

'Not bad. Hugh and Emma. And the Baxters.'

'What did you have to eat?'

'Lamb. But we *drank* the chocolate mousse. How is everything with you?'

'Such a lot to tell you, darling.' I dropped my voice. 'But it's difficult to talk.'

'You're tantalising me again!'

'I know.' I giggled.

'How's the dumpy peasant then?'

'Think again. She's wearing Jaeger!'

'Tell me more.'

'Well . . .' I whispered. We sniggered like two adolescents. It helped me to get over Constance. 'Listen, darling, I must go,' I said finally. 'I'll phone you later in the week.'

I rang off and, still stifling my laughter, returned quietly to the kitchen where I caught Marie-Rose red-handed with my rings in her hand. Her glasses were on and she was inspecting my jewellery with the concentration of an expert assessing an uncut gem.

Then, as if she'd seen enough, she reached out for a dessert bowl and put the rings into it before setting the bowl down on the draining board.

Sensing my presence, she half turned. 'I didn't want your rings falling down the plughole. I'll wash and you dry, Caroline.'

All through the washing-up I could feel her wanting to make an announcement, even though she said very little, only, 'Don't worry about the spoons,' and, 'We can leave the rest to drain.'

At last, when every dish was back in its proper place, she said abruptly, 'There's something that I've got to tell you.'

'What is it?'

'Come on upstairs.'

I couldn't imagine why the announcement, whatever it was, couldn't be made where we were standing. Still, the nearer I could get to bed, the better it suited me.

Marie-Rose locked the back door and, leaving the dogs behind in the kitchen, we trailed wearily up the stairs. Suppressing a yawn, I asked what it was that she wanted to say.

For answer she opened the door of the bedroom across the landing from mine. Inside, a double bed was made up.

'This was our room,' she said clearly. 'Constance's and mine. We slept in here together.' Her eyes were defiant and wary, the eyes of a woman forced to divulge a secret.

21

I thought again of the half-plucked daisy. 'He loves me. He loves me not.' But the gender had been different. I remembered the look on the face of the priest. Were others as censorious? In that moment I felt sorry for Marie-Rose. I thought, wait till I tell this to Leonard.

Marie-Rose hadn't finished, I was sure of that. What more did she have to say? That she had loved Constance and was miserable now she was gone? Or was she just waiting for me to comment?

I was groping for the right words when she cut in, 'We were close long before that – when Olive was alive even. Not that we let her know what was going on, mind.'

'I'm sure you didn't.'

'And after . . . Caroline, Constance decided long since what she was going to do. Mind you, I might have gone first. Then it would have been different.'

At that, I did have a kind of foreboding. The central heating had gone off, the house had cooled down and I suddenly felt chilly.

'What are you trying to say to me?'

She fumbled for the door knob and held on to it. 'I'm telling you about the will, Caroline. It's all been left to me. This house and its contents. And Carrigrua with it . . .'

My whole body iced up. I was frozen to the spot, otherwise I would have caught her round the throat, shaken and throttled her, yelled out that it couldn't be true, that Constance would never have made such a will. That this house and its contents were nothing but Carrigrua was mine. That Marie-Rose was crazy to tell me this lie . . .

'It's best that you should know now instead of wondering why the solicitors didn't get on to you. It's always better to know where you stand.'

She waited for me to say something and when I didn't she babbled on.

'You must know full well that I would never want to live at Carrigrua or set foot inside the house again either. We were happy here, Constance and I, and this is where I belong. Carrigrua was your home, Caroline. It was never mine.'

For a glorious moment I thought she was going to be generous. That she would say Constance had been out of her mind when she made that will. That she would insist that Carrigrua was morally mine and that therefore I should have it.

'Go on.'

'So I've been wondering, do you want to buy the place? I wouldn't be asking a lot for it. To tell you the truth it would be hard in these times to dispose of a house that size. If it was Dublin now it would be different – Dublin or Wicklow or even Limerick. But we're very far out and most people who'd be wanting a house that big wouldn't want to live here.'

So much for my rights. Transfixed, in shock, I heard myself say in an even voice, 'How much do you want?'

She told me. It was a reasonable enough sum, a quarter of the price such a property would have fetched in Surrey.

I nodded and she took that for nonchalance, a sign that I was so well-off money wouldn't worry me.

'I thought you'd be able to afford it,' she said complacently.

Light dawned. That was why she'd been inspecting my rings. Trying to guess how much I was worth. She'd probably asked me to the funeral to interest me in buying Carrigrua from her.

Bitch. I became haughty. 'Well, Marie-Rose,' I said, 'I'll give it some thought. Obviously, I'd like to have a look at the place. As you say, it was my home.' More than that. 'Maybe tomorrow, after the funeral?'

'That would be all right.'

'Who has the keys? Is it on the market already? Should I phone the agents?' I was being too eager. I couldn't stop myself.

'I have the keys,' said Marie-Rose and for that alone I could have hit her. 'I've not put it up for sale. Constance is only after dying these last few days.'

'She never thought of selling it?'

'She did but, like I said, she knew there'd be trouble getting a buyer.'

Well, you're looking for one soon enough, I thought bitterly. Constance only just dead indeed. You're so anxious to dispose of Carrigrua you couldn't wait until the morning.

Marie-Rose was visibly drooping. She gave a huge sigh and put her hand on her head.

'All right, then,' I said. 'Let's leave it like that until tomorrow. We'd better catch some sleep.'

Maybe she did, but I stayed awake. I lay in one of the single beds begrudging Constance every minute of pleasure she had experienced in the double one in the room across the landing.

Once more, I had been cast out.

It was a miserable night. But somewhere in the middle of it I realised that I had unfinished business at Carrigrua. It's always easy to look back and say to yourself, that was when it began to make sense. In fact, it wasn't that clear-cut and I can't remember now whether I still held on to that thought when dawn finally broke.

One thing was certain. It would break my heart to look at the house, knowing that it wasn't mine. But I had no alternative. I had to retrace my steps. I had to go to Carrigrua.

Three

The road that led to Carrigrua had grass growing down the middle of it. Tall grey poplars and broad-leaved alders lined up on either side, solemnly, like guards of honour.

Alders were unlucky trees if you passed them on a journey. I thought ruefully that I'd already had my share of bad luck and, dismissing omens altogether, noted the familiar landmarks – a gate, a sloping field, a farmhouse set in off the road – that marked the route to Carrigrua.

I drove past a fine, yellow, L-shaped house with a double entrance to it. Williamstadt House, said the name on the gate.

Nearly home.

And then I was at the gates. My heart was racing when I reached them. Fashioned out of coiled wrought iron, painted indigo long ago but faded now to greyish-blue, they had a heavy padlock on them.

I got out of the car, clutching the bunch of keys which Marie-Rose had given me. The key to the padlock wasn't amongst them. Stupid, bloody, loathsome cow!

I scrambled over the moss-covered wall, tearing my tights in the process, scraping my lilac leather slingbacks and lambasting Marie-Rose.

The driveway stretched ahead of me, almost hidden under thistles, tangled grass and chunky clumps of purple clover. The land to my left, part of the original estate, must have been sold off, I thought, or rented in grazing to a local farmer because a herd of young Friesian bullocks came running down to the wire fence to take a look at me. Each was numbered with an ear tag and one had a ring with a plate and six rivets driven into its nose. Mooing plaintively, they followed my progress up the avenue until we were cut off from each other by brambles and scrub, and I entered the wood.

Then it began, the chorus of skylark and wood pigeon, the distinct 'tsip' of the song thrush, their unified calls making a humoresque for a homecomer. I could hear the lake lapping, but it was concealed from me by trees that huddled close together. Ivy and emerald-green moss had grown up over their trunks and interlocked branches, and between the fallen twigs was the fungus I had known as fairy candles. Flirty yellow butterflies darted over my head and beneath my feet were vivid purple orchids, wild violets, gentians and bluebells. I came across a badger's sett and heard a rustle as if some small animal was stealthily creeping out of my way and I knew that beady eyes were keeping careful watch on me.

Once, I used to hide out here and scrutinise the passers-by. If I didn't want to meet them, I could simply disappear. I did this sometimes with my father. It was not that I disliked him – no one did, I should imagine – but I couldn't make him out. On one level, he was pensive, vague and inattentive. Instead of being an irritation, this endeared him to most people, but my father's dreamy side only made me feel uneasy. He might float away, I thought, and take me off to England with him.

I found him cold, as well. We found each other heavy going; we never managed to make contact. Poor man – he was out of his depth with a young daughter. Campaigning for charity was one thing – he could persuade a school assembly to join him in supporting Oxfam – but he never knew what to do with me, either then or when I went to live with him.

When he visited from England he didn't stay at Carrigrua but with his cousins in Portumna, about fifteen miles away. They'd drop him off outside our gates and he'd meander through the wood, the way that I was doing now.

If I caught wind of his arrival, if Norah said, 'Mr Lacy's coming over,' I'd go in there to watch for him, in the vain hope that this encounter would be better than the last. Seeing him, I knew it wouldn't. A chill would come along with him, as if he was a ghostly presence, a person that I couldn't touch. I'd stand still behind a tree and let him walk away from me.

Half in the present and half in the past, I went on, skirting the debris and brambles. With all the rampant overgrowth, it was dark enough in the wood for the Grey Lady to have decided it was night-time. Ahead of me were fallen trees, the rotting branches of one arching low across the driveway. I ducked beneath it, my feet sinking into a carpet woven out of last year's leaves.

Soon after, my pathway home divided, one fork turning off towards the front of the house, the other towards the back.

26

I took the route towards the front. And there was the house, waiting at the water's edge.

At last I reached the granite steps that led up to the fanlight front door and the joy of looking again at Carrigrua outweighed my desolation. I drew my breath in. Hugged myself. Suppressed the urge to shout and dance.

It was not a crumbling wreck. The heart had not gone out of it. It was safe, whole. A living, breathing entity, wise and ancient, beautiful.

I paused at the foot of the wide steps, taking in every beloved detail of that fine facade. I counted the sash windows on the upper and ground levels and the four others which, like half-hidden moons, rose up from the basement. I checked the panels on the heavy mahogany door and the number of pewter arrows that splayed out into a semi-circle on the fanlight.

Perfect, I said to myself. Just as I remembered.

Excitement distorted my vision and blinded me to the legacy of desertion – to the white effloresence on the stonework where the gutters had failed, the broken panes of glass, the tottering chimney stack, and the missing slates on the sprocketed roof. I had waited so long to come back, nearly thirty years, and the child I had been when I last stood here demanded a perfect reunion, insisting that the dream I'd nurtured with such care should live up to expectations.

So intense was my love, so great my longing to re-enter the house, that a lump came up in my throat and I had to turn away from Carrigrua and look at the lake instead. It was tinged with red, as it so often was, so that, at any time of the day, the sun could seem to be setting, its radiance seeping like blood into the deep waters.

At that moment it was tranquil. But I knew it wouldn't stay calm for long, that sooner or later what was now a millpond would turn swiftly into a seething sea, as dark and as frothy as Guinness. Meanwhile the fisherman had gone home to tea and television, and the hire boats were moored for the night. The only ripples on the water were caused by the passage of a yellow-billed, green-headed mallard duck and a pair of mute swans with seven cygnets trailing along behind them.

Then I heard a curious cry. Something bright and brown flashed over the lawn and an otter disappeared rapidly into the reeds. I spotted the top of its broad, flat head as it broke the surface of the water and veered out into the lake.

It was all the same. The blue Tipperary shoreline in the distance.

The old stone harbour at Garrykennedy. The ruins of the O'Kennedy castles, there and at Dromineer. And nearer, half a mile or so out from shore, Hare Island, with its bushy-topped trees and perilous rocks, the landmark for crafts to change course from west–east to south–north.

I felt calmer then and able to look at the house again. When I did, it seemed to me that Carrigrua had fallen into a slumber rather than into a state of dilapidation. Now I was back, it would surely wake. Familiar hands would open the shutters, draw back the heavy curtains and unlock the massive door. The sounds of birdsong would be drowned out by jubilant cries of welcome and I would be embraced and kissed and folded back into the family circle.

Like the child I had been when I last stood at the foot of the steps, I waited for this to happen. When it did not, and from the wood the chorus of song thrush and skylark and wood pigeon continued unabated, I remained transfixed.

In that place there was no escaping the memories. And no escaping Olive, either. I could see her on the steps, as she was the day I left, wearing dark-grey shoes with almond-shaped toes and a grey winter coat with a hat to match. She'd always stuck to subtle shades. Grey, fawn, beige and dun she classified as ladylike. Red, green, turquoise, pink and peach fell under the heading of 'highly suspect'. Emerald was worst of all, especially on Saint Patrick's day. She wouldn't like my shoes one bit and she'd hate my wild print skirt.

Olive the uncompromising . . . I'd made fun of her in England. She was, I'd said, infallible, like the Pope but more effective. He was in the Vatican, so far removed from Carrigrua that he might have been in Heaven. Olive, on the other hand, was an ever-present factor, laying down the rules for life. More omnipotent than the Pope. As well-known as Julie Christie.

That made people shriek with laughter – that, and my impersonations. But they were just a part of it. A small part.

The truth is Olive was my idol and I longed to be like her. I didn't tell the others that. I did not confide in Leonard. I didn't say she was my anchor. I never said how much I loved her.

Now, seeing her up there on the steps, there was no escaping what I really felt about her. I couldn't run away from it. I wouldn't get away from her when I went inside the house. Olive might be dead and buried, but I knew that she'd be present, the way she was when I was young, in every room in Carrigrua.

I'd have known at once if Marie-Rose hadn't given me the front door key. It was unmistakable, a huge brass key made to fit into the best brass lock.

I thrust the key into the lock. The soft sound it made turning was the sweetest note I'd heard that day.

I'd thought that I was well-prepared to step into an empty house. But I was wrong. It was disturbing. The hall had always been sparsely furnished, but that little made a difference. With the silk firescreen gone, and the bellows and the fire irons, there was a sadness in there – as well as a fetid, musty smell. Loose twigs, looking as if they might have fallen from a rook's nest, were strewn about on the black and white marble floor.

But it could have been far worse. The chimneypiece – white marble with an inlaid relief of blue and yellow, decorated with scrolls and shells and two reclining angels – was its old ornate self. The white Dutch tiles of the surround hadn't been cracked and the basket grate and the metal fireguard hooked to its top bar were still there in their rightful places.

The drawing room was on the right, the dining room and library on the left, and at the far end of the hall the staircase swept up to the bedrooms and crept down to the kitchen, scullery, store and servants' bedrooms.

I went into the drawing room first. It had been a lovely room with a panelled wainscot, painted yellow, the wall above papered in a Chinese bird and tree pattern, the doors and skirtings chocolate brown. Today, it was as dark as the wood in there. I opened the shutters and the windows and the sun streamed in, highlighting the atrocities of desertion and neglect.

The Turkish-style carpet had been taken up and the bare boards, white with dust, were dotted with bird droppings. The wallpaper was hanging off and the yellow velvet curtains were rotted and stained. But the sash windows that reached from the floor to the cornice were intact and so were the carved and gilded pediments that adorned the six-panelled door. The fireplace with its stucco surround and the gilt-framed mirror that hung above it weren't broken, only grimy.

I was determined to look on the bright side. After all, I told myself, a price had to be paid for closing the shutters and keeping the vandals out. Having had no ventilation, the house was damp so the wallpaper glue had liquefied. Not a catastrophe. And no need, either, to get uptight about the droppings and the dust.

The dining room was in much the same condition. The stencilled floor was in need of waxing and the sky-blue paint on the main wall planes had aged better than the flock multicoloured paper.

Sadly, the dumbwaiter with its three circular trays was missing and, of course, the dining table. I had been expecting that, but all the same it got to me.

No table. No Olive at the head of it, presiding sternly over meals, her back set straight and her face made up.

There were sets of rules for meals. Children had to be good neighbours and to keep an eye on plates. The person on one's other side should never have to ask for salt – not if Someone was well-mannered.

In her attitude to eating, Olive was Victorian. There was lots of food for us, but she ate very little of it. Remaining hungry after meals was part of being self-disciplined, very necessary to Olive. Children, though, were meant to eat, including food they didn't like. Under the table was a ledge where I put unwanted scraps – cabbage and fat off mutton, queen of puddings, crusts of bread – when the grown-ups weren't looking. This technique (mouthfuls transferred into napkins before being dumped upon the ledge) demanded skill and expert timing.

In due course, the ledge filled up. I faced the unappealing fact. I'd have to clear a space on it. I waited till the coast was clear, armed myself with a plastic bag and sneaked into the dining room.

Under the table, it was dark. The food had turned to mildewed mould, grey, with little hairs on it. I couldn't touch it – yes, I could, or else I'd have to swallow cabbage.

I steeled myself and cleared the ledge. But just as I was crawling out, Olive came into the room. After her came Bishop Hickey. I shot back beneath the table.

'Where's the child?' the bishop asked.

I couldn't stand the sight of him. Despite my having such dull hair, he liked to run his hands through it. 'Come over here, my child,' he'd say, and then he'd start to stroke my hair, breathing deeply as he did it.

Another reason to be hiding.

'Outside playing,' Olive said, thinking I was in the garden.

'Have you told her?' said the bishop.

'No, I haven't, for the moment. I must tell her father first.'

'I hope he'll do his duty by her.'

That was when I should have known that I was leaving Carrigrua. Later, when I heard about it, I remembered what they had said and understood the situation. My father hadn't asked for me to go and live in England with him. That decision had been Olive's.

No more table. No more Olive. No more Bishop Hickey either. That, at least, was consolation.

I went into the library next. Constance used to curl up on one of the two brown leather chairs, reading the stories of Somerset Maugham. In a sense, she was still present, but the furniture was missing – the arbutus wood writing desk with the inlaid shamrocks on it and the leather chairs themselves. She had left the books behind. The ominous grey specks on their spines told me a depressing tale.

'You silly, gullible, neglectful bat!' I said to the figure on the chair. 'How could you have let this happen?'

In disgust, I turned from Constance to confront the other ghosts. Marie-Rose when young was there, but I soon got rid of her. In the basement I met Norah.

'The state they've let this place get into. Muck like this on my fine floor, and grease all over the kitchen table.'

'Your chair's still over in the corner. See, the patchwork cushion's on it.'

'The dresser's gone. My tray's not here. And where's the Oriental china?'

Outside in the cobbled yard there was much to placate Norah. The minute I opened the back door, the scent of thyme, rosemary and lavender drifted in from the herb bed that ran beneath the scullery window. There was lichen on the horse troughs and the earthenware pots in which the marigolds had grown had been turned over by the wind. But in the two flowerbeds bordering the yard itself, purple sage and creamy foxgloves sprouted up beside the weeds.

Marie-Rose was in the yard, hanging clothes on the line. These were mostly underwear. Olive's corsets, all-in-ones, and the roll-ons worn by Constance. Olive's corsets were designed to flatten and compress the bust. She deeply disapproved of breasts, implying they were vulgar things. I felt sorry for my aunt, who was very well-endowed. Her bras with their, to me, enormous cups were also hanging on the line.

In the far corner of the yard was the wooden famine tub in which soup was made for starving people during the potato blight. Beside the tub was the well. I used to think that it was holy, that its clear, sweet water had a special healing power. I was a firm believer in wells. If you had sufficient faith, their waters could cure anything, from loss of sight to aching heads. It all depended on the saint with which a well had been connected.

'What saint is looking after our well?' I'd asked Norah and Marie-Rose.

Neither of them seemed to know.

'But the magic always stays, even if the well dries up,' said Norah, trying to comfort me.

'Where does it stay if the well's gone dry?'

'In a tree,' said Marie-Rose. 'The one that's nearest to the well.'

Cobblestones are hell to walk on if you're wearing high-heeled shoes. I tottered in my once-smart slingbacks to investigate the well. There was water there all right and the rope that held the bucket hadn't rotted like the curtains.

I hauled the bucket up, scooped some water out and drank it. It was just as sweet as ever – champagne with a peaty flavour.

A charge went through me. I turned to look at the house again, back in the dream of owning it. It was – it *must* be possible. I reminded myself that Marie-Rose wasn't asking all that much. Once Leonard saw the house he would say that I was right, that we had to buy it from her.

I drank again – a toast to coming home this time. How could Leonard not say yes? He'd go mad about the stables and the harness room and sheds. The stonework would appeal to him, that soft, warm greyish-brown that was near to cinnamon.

In England, people would convert such buildings – turn them into voguish homes. I didn't like the thought of that. It would ruin the atmosphere to have several houses here.

I went on to do a quick tour of the outbuildings, starting with the harness room. There were cobwebs everywhere, trailing over the saddlery, which was in a sorry state, leather cracked and bridles broken. Not worth selling, I supposed. A horseshoe dangled from a nail, a legacy of bygone days. The sheds and stables were deserted. Everything was gone from them but the faint smell of manure.

That left the garden and the orchard. The walled garden had been one of the original features of the house. The urns and classical statuary typifying the eighteenth century had vanished from it before I was born, but it remained a formal garden, mostly used for growing roses, the paler ones preferred by Olive – damasks and the double whites and Madame Lauriol de Barny.

The garden had a gateway to it. The gate, blocked by decayed leaves and twigs, didn't want to open for me but I pushed it with my shoulder and it did so in the end.

There was a jungle on the other side. The roses wouldn't bloom this year. They'd been choked by grass and weeds. And Olive's hothouse had been damaged. Panes of glass were missing from it. I groaned aloud, thinking of the time and money that the garden would be needing, remembering how things had been before anarchy took over.

I had a clear recollection of the garden as it was in Olive's time. It was very pretty. The roses, pink and white and delicate, added to the overall impression that she had employed a potter, an expert in fine porcelain, to create a work of art of which a lady would approve. There'd been a hedge of double whites. Borders of the rounded damasks. And growing over by the shrubs . . .

All of a sudden, my mind went blank. I couldn't see the garden in it. Couldn't see the roses growing. Couldn't visualise the borders.

How weird. I'd remembered it precisely a minute ago. I'd always had an image of it.

Then something even stranger happened. My mind was no longer blank. I saw another image in it which superseded Olive's garden. Another garden.

No, not another garden, *this* one, but without the roses in it.

The same garden but with different flowers blooming. Brilliant colours. Lots of reds. Begonias and red-hot pokers. Stonecrop. Mallow. Dahlias. The recollection of each flower was every bit as clear to me as the water from the well. Star-shaped blooms and trumpet shapes. I saw them all from memory.

But what memory was that? A memory of a painting maybe? Or a dream that I'd had once?

A dream, I thought. A dream in which the garden I remembered became one with colour in it. Amazing the way that it came back, and the detail that was in it.

Soon, too soon, the dream began to slide from me, leaving just a happy feeling, as the best dreams tend to do. I felt invigorated by it, more optimistic than before. The garden in its present state wasn't really so chaotic. It was simply overgrown, not beyond control at all. I could easily put it right.

On the other hand . . . Olive's garden was too pretty. Too delicate. I preferred the other garden. The red garden. Maybe I would re-create it.

I walked on slowly, making plans. Behind the garden was the orchard. It, too, had walls round it, and a door that wasn't locked.

The orchard was laid out in the grid system. Paths made from old paving stones ran between grass squares on which apple trees were growing, and narcissi and daffodils. Further along were rows of raspberry and blackcurrant bushes, and the beds for strawberries, not that I could see them now, with all the weeds on top of them.

The far wall had ivy growing on the top. For me, that wall had been

33

a sanctuary. A child could lie down flat up there, pull the ivy over her and disappear from view entirely. If she felt adventurous, the wall could be a sailing vessel. At other times it was a castle; now and then a grand hotel, or a look-out point. From that position there was a view not only of the house and yard but also of the tradesmen's entrance.

I won't go up there now, I thought, but when I bring Leonard here I'll show him my sanctuary.

I turned back and retraced my steps through the yard and went inside the house again.

With the shutters and windows open, the smell of must was almost gone. Upstairs, though, it would be stuffy.

I remembered upstairs clearly. The bathroom and what had been my mother's bedroom were on the right-hand side. Swinging round towards the front was the bedroom Constance used, followed by my smaller one. Olive's big bedroom, looking out across the lake and also on to the wood and yard, was on the left-hand side. It ran over the drawing room.

The oak staircase, with its cut strings and delicate balusters, had not been damaged by the furniture removers. Pleased by that, I ran upstairs, reached the landing – then drew back.

The French cupboard was still there, against the wall of Olive's room. My stomach did a somersault.

It was a tall, blue cupboard with a lattice front to it. Though it used to be a bookcase, when I was young it was a store where Norah put the excess linen – eiderdowns, ageing towels, sheets that were in need of turning. As a child, I'd been terrified of that cupboard. Someone – Marie-Rose, I think it was – told me fairies lived inside it.

'They'll put a hump on to your back if you try to climb in there.'

Climb into that cupboard, *me*? What she said about the fairies added to my fear of it but it didn't instigate it. The fear was already there before I heard from Marie-Rose.

It was still there. I could feel it closing in. There was something about that cupboard. Something – sinister, I thought.

Ridiculous. Illogical. Embarrassing. I felt my face go hot with shame.

But – that cupboard made me nervous. More than nervous, really frightened . . .

Suddenly there was a raucous cawing sound. A shaggy black rook flew out of the bathroom and over my head. As startled by me as I was by it, it panicked, circled, and flew back inside the bathroom.

Guessing that the bathroom window must be broken or left open, I went inside to check on it. The window was open and the rogue rook had disappeared outside, leaving feathers in the bath, which was stained and full of droppings.

I closed the window and went back on to the landing. Just above where I was standing there was a trap door in the ceiling, giving access to the attic. As a child I'd imagined that a hangman lived up there. On my way to bed at night I never walked beneath that door in case his noose should drop on me.

You see, I said to myself now, you were always scared of something. First the cupboard. Then the noose.

But the trap door didn't scare me now. I wondered what was in the attic. Olive, although very tidy, had been something of a hoarder. There could be treasures in the loft. Pity there was no ladder.

The door to my aunt's room was shut. I say it was my aunt's but I never really felt that it belonged to her. Although Constance slept in there, to me it was the Grey Lady's bedroom. I saw in it a set of steps leading to a curtained bed. A feather quilt spread over it. A wardrobe for the lady's gowns. And (naturally, discreetly hidden) a flowered porcelain chamber pot.

There was nothing in the room, not a feather, only dust. No surprise in that, I thought. Constance would have cleared it out and taken her possessions with her.

Logic told me that my own room would also be empty. Illogically, I hoped to find something of the child I'd been kept for me inside that room. A memento of myself. A drawing glued to the wall, or a photograph of me.

But Olive wasn't sentimental. The plain brass bedstead in which I'd slept wasn't in there any more. The drawings that I'd made were gone. There were no pictures in the room, or any other items either.

Outside, it was getting dusky. There were shadows on the lake, and no sign of the swans and ducks. If I hung about the house, I'd soon be stumbling in the dark.

In my hurry to be going I nearly missed out Olive's bedroom. In the end, temptation proved too strong for me. I'd never been inside her room. In the old days, I'd no more have ventured in there than into a lion's cage, but I was aware that mysterious rituals, to do with face and hands and hair, were carried out behind that door.

Of course, the furniture was gone, which should have made the room seem bigger, but it didn't seem as vast as I'd thought when I was young. That didn't strike me as being strange – dimensions change when you grow up – but the fact that it was empty left a sense of anti-climax. Where had all the face creams gone, and the powder puffs and potions?

I didn't linger there for long. I felt that Olive was still present and outraged by my intrusion.

On the landing the blue cupboard loomed up in the semi-blackout. I swallowed, ran quickly downstairs.

But the blue devils followed me out of the house, and they cast shadows on my path as I walked across the lawn into the darkness of the wood.

Four

Marie-Rose was hovering. She pounced as I walked in the door.

'So what did you think of the house?'

'It's – not as rundown as I'd expected,' I said nonchalantly, not wanting to show too much interest in case she put up the price. It's a bargain, I kept thinking. I must get Leonard over here.

'But do you *want* it?'

What a question! 'I wouldn't rush into it. I'll mull it over with my husband.'

That squashed her, a bit. But she soon recovered.

'You being such travellers, it's a wonder the two of you never came here on a holiday. Or even you on your own.'

'No. I – we – never seemed to get round to it.'

'Your husband is too busy, is he?'

'Both of us are always busy. But we'll talk about the house when I get back and I'll keep in touch with you.'

'I'll be waiting to hear from you.' She hesitated, thought. 'Maybe if you didn't want Carrigrua yourself, you might know someone else that would?'

'It's a possibility.' I thought, why did I think I could stay here a week? I've got to get out of this woman's house. I'll leave tomorrow. In the morning. There's a flight going back at lunchtime.

'Do you fancy a fry, Caroline? It won't take me a minute to make rashers and eggs. And black pudding. You used to like black pudding when you were young.'

The funeral and after it the visit to the house had put food out of my head. I hadn't eaten all day. Now I realised I was starving.

'I still like black pudding.'

'Two eggs or one?'

'One's fine.'

I should phone Leonard, I said to myself. Not from here. I'll call from Shannon.

37

Marie-Rose started frying the black pudding. My thoughts returned to Carrigrua. I'd talk to Leonard over dinner. When he'd had a drink or two. I started to rehearse my speech.

'Leonard, darling, about the house. Constance has done something crazy . . . But Carrigrua's wonderful and it's in superb condition. She's not asking all that much . . .'

What if he doesn't agree with me? What if he thinks that I'm the mad one to consider buying it?

He must agree. I must persuade him that I'm right. We'll come back to Clare together. Maybe in a week or so. As soon as I can get him here.

'Do you prefer fried bread to toast?'

'Fried bread?'

'Or will I make a piece of toast?'

'Toast? Yes. I'd like toast, if you don't mind.'

I must succeed, I went on thinking. Leonard has to be persuaded. I continued my rehearsal.

I overslept and very nearly missed the mid-morning flight. I didn't have time to phone Leonard from Shannon, but I wasn't worried.

After Clare, Heathrow was an alien, dissonant world. The noise rasped on my nerve ends. People meeting incoming passengers looked at me with weary, dispassionate eyes. I pushed my way through the crowds and, thankful to be out of the terminal, lined up in the taxi queue.

Speeding along the A30, I went over my lines again, highlighting the virtues of Carrigrua.

'It's elegant, it really is. And wait until you see the view.'

We turned left into West Drive. Our house was a short way along on the right, approached through an iron gate and across a circular pea-shingle driveway.

Leonard's car was parked in the front. How odd, I thought. Leonard's not normally home in the afternoon. Don't tell me that his mother's here. We need a quiet evening.

I paid off the taxi and went indoors. The house might have belonged to somebody else. I'd travelled far from it these last few days.

'Leonard?'

There was no reply. I investigated. Leonard wasn't downstairs. He must be ill in bed, I thought. Concerned, I dumped my suitcase in the hall and, anxious not to disturb him if he was sleeping, crept upstairs and quietly opened our bedroom door.

Leonard *was* asleep in bed, but he wasn't on his own. A dark-haired woman was beside him. Her face was obscured by her tangled hair.

She lay with her back to him. His arm was round her shoulder.

I numbly registered the half-empty bottle of Moulin-à-Vent on the bedside table. The corkscrew and glasses. The fact that the woman was lying on my side of the bed.

I stood there, blinking. Leonard stirred, waking the woman in the process.

'Oh shit, what time is it?' she said worriedly. 'I've got to get back before Ron.'

She wriggled into a sitting position, revealing ripe bare breasts, and saw me standing in the doorway. Our eyes met. She was Sue Wilkins, the woman who ran the gardening service.

Of course, I thought, it's Friday and yes, Leonard did agree to come home today to pay her. I wondered if she had washed the soil off her hands before getting into my bed.

The colour had drained from her face. Her eyes were huge. She gaped at me open-mouthed, speechless.

Leonard, who hadn't caught up yet with what was happening, said lazily, 'Can't be that serious,' before he, too, spotted me and realised that it was.

For what seemed like an eternity, none of us spoke. I watched them, coldly noting their reactions. Sue began to cry. Tears streamed unchecked down her healthy, suntanned cheeks. Leonard, one eye on his discarded clothes lying in a clump over near the window, was in the classic dilemma of a man who, totally uninhibited in the presence of any one woman to whom he makes love, is mortified at the idea of being seen naked by two at a time.

'I'm sorry, Caroline,' he began, obviously praying that I would be graceful enough to exit and allow them to dress in privacy before attending the postmortem. 'I didn't mean—'

'Get out,' I said to Sue Wilkins.

She obeyed at once, walking like a robot round the bed to where, in happier mood, she had left her jeans and T-shirt and socks. But I was too quick for her. I snatched them up. Opened the window.

'Get out,' I said and, still quite calm, I threw the T-shirt and socks out over the azaleas on to the lawn beyond.

Sue yelped, stumbled over her shoes and, without stopping to pick them up, fled naked down the stairs, unaware that her jeans were in my hand.

I watched her run into the garden, pull her T-shirt over her head, look desperately around for the rest of her garments, retrieve only one of her socks.

'God Almighty!' said Leonard softly.

I remained in icy control. Sue was sobbing. From my vantage point at the window I could hear her quite clearly. She gave up the search for her missing jeans and headed bare-bottomed for the back of the house where she usually parked.

I heard an engine start up. Leonard say, 'Caroline, darling. Listen.'

Darling . . . Leonard was still in bed. Like Sue, he was not quick enough. In an instant I was across the room. I screamed obscenities. I clawed at his face. I drew blood before he could defend himself against my frantic hands.

He caught me by the wrist. I pulled myself away, knocked over one of the glasses, grabbed the half-empty bottle.

'Put that down!'

I struck at his head with the bottle. He ducked, so it hit his shoulder instead. Wine trickled like blood down his arm.

'Christ!'

He was bigger and stronger than I was. He caught me by the wrist again. I still held tightly on to the bottle.

Leonard forced me backwards. I spat into his face. He winced but didn't relax his grip. I screamed at him to get out, to follow that whore. He hissed back that he might just do that. He pushed me into the bathroom. I kicked his shins and bit his hand. He overpowered me. He got me on to my knees and held me there with one hand while he reached out with the other. Then he leapt back, slammed the door and locked it from the outside.

As a stratagem for calming me down, it failed. I screamed, again and again, beating with my fists at the door. Half-blinded with fear, I began to hit out indiscriminately, knocking over bottles of foam bath and Fenjal and shampoo. I broke a soap dish. I shredded the toilet paper, tore at the shower curtain, at my own underwear which I'd washed and hung up on the drying rack before I'd gone to Ireland. I keened with pain, as if there'd been a death in the house.

The wine bottle had rolled into a corner. I picked it up, intending to hammer on the door, and, straightening, caught sight of my own panting, sweating reflection in the bathroom mirror.

'You're nothing – nothing!' I shouted at that weeping, perspiring non-person, lashing out at the mirror.

There was the sound of glass breaking. Panic as I fought against what was buried deep inside me. Waves of terror as I felt myself losing the battle.

Then the floor rose up and I thought that I was being sucked through it, into the bowels of the earth. I tried to say so – to explain. But I was already losing consciousness. The words would not come. I stopped struggling and someone – or so I believed – placed a blanket over my head.

My hands were stained with my own blood. There were shards of glass in the basin. The bathroom was a disaster. I stepped through the ruins, trying to remember what I had done.

I wasn't sure how long I'd been unconscious, whether I'd fainted or simply fallen into an exhausted sleep. Gradually, horribly, things started to make sense.

I called out tentatively, 'Leonard, are you still there?'

No answer.

The bastard, I thought. He's run off with her and left me here.

On the off chance, I tried the door. It opened on to an empty bedroom.

'Leonard?'

Still calling, I went downstairs. No Leonard. No car, either. I returned to our bedroom and checked the cupboards. Leonard's clothes were gone.

I felt hollow – sick and sore and singed inside. Instinct told me to get into bed, pull the duvet over my head, hide until my wounds had healed.

But I couldn't go near that bed again.

Flinching from it, I shuffled out of the bedroom and on to the landing. Unsure of what to do, I stood there indecisively.

Eventually, instinct took control again, guiding me into the larger guestroom where Leonard's mother always slept when she came to stay with us. She usually left things behind. Books and nighties. Magazines.

And her sleeping tablets. They were in the bedside drawer, along with a handful of one penny coins. The phial that the pills were in had a safety lid on it. It took an age to open it. I was shaking from the effort by the time I conquered it.

I shook the contents into my palm. There were only two pills left.

I swallowed both of them, twice the prescribed dose, lay down on the guestroom bed, and let sleep come.

I woke the following afternoon, dazed and groggy from the pills. Clad in yesterday's crumpled clothes, I wandered aimlessly round the house, conscious of how quiet it was.

The door to our bedroom was ajar. I shut it, tried to close my mind as well, and drifted back downstairs again, concerned, not about my future life, but about the next half-hour. I turned on the television news. Images of war and wreckage made me turn it off again.

Where had Leonard gone? I wondered. Were he and Sue shacked up together, or had he moved in with his mother?

I checked the time. Three minutes had gone by since I'd switched off the television. I was raw with loss, scalded by grief. One more minute and I'd surely scream. I willed the phone to ring – and then prayed it would stay silent. I didn't want to talk to people. They'd know from my voice that something was wrong. Once they knew what that thing was, they'd despise me for losing Leonard.

I didn't change my clothes that day. I didn't bath or brush my hair. I didn't sleep that night at all.

In the immediate aftermath of Leonard's departure, I didn't leave the house. There was no need to shop for food. There was plenty still in stock and, anyway, I wasn't hungry.

No one called and no one rang. I lost track of time. Minutes seemed more like days. Seconds turned into hours. As the days wore on, the loneliness began to kill me.

One day, claustrophobia drove me into the garden. I walked around, disliking what I saw out there. The garden was too flash. Too showy. Too affluent. Designed to impress rather than to provide pleasure. Not like the garden at Carrigrua.

Carrigrua!

For the last few days, I hadn't thought about the house. Now it dawned on me that I had suffered another loss. My hope of buying Carrigrua had gone out the door with Leonard.

Digesting this, I went indoors. In the hall, I stopped and tensed. I sensed a presence. Someone else was in the house.

I listened, not moving. I'd been right. I wasn't alone. Someone was moving around upstairs.

It's Leonard, I thought. He's back. He's home. He's up there, waiting in our bedroom. My heart was beating very fast.

I had two coherent thoughts, one concerning Carrigrua. If Leonard had come back for good, he might buy it, after all. Then I thought it was a pity I'd not tidied up the bathroom before Leonard saw the mess.

I dashed upstairs.

Yes, our bedroom door was open. There was a figure inside the room. Except that figure wasn't Leonard. It was Mrs Langley. I'd forgotten it was Thursday. Of course. I'd left a key for her. She must have come in by the kitchen door while I was walking round the garden.

She gaped at me, dumbfounded, shocked by the havoc inside the bathroom, supporting herself with the vacuum cleaner.

'Mrs Langley,' I began, before I ran out of words.

It seemed important that I explain but it was beyond me. I had an almost irresistible urge to ask Mrs Langley to give me a hug, to confide in her, to ask for her advice. If she'd given me the slightest encouragement, asked what had happened to the bathroom, I'd have poured the story out.

But Mrs Langley went into herself. She said, 'I must be getting on. There's a lot to do in here.' She plugged in the vacuum cleaner. It rumbled into life, cutting out the need for speech.

She was safe. I left her to get on with it.

We kept out of each other's way until she had a coffee break. I filled the mug she always used and she opened a packet of chocolate biscuits. She added sweetener to her coffee, sipped it and set down her mug.

'Have you heard about Sue Wilkins?'

My stomach churned. 'No.'

'Her husband beat her up. They say she's black and blue. And it's not the first time, either. That Ron Wilkins has a temper. Mind you, there've been rumours about her.'

'Really?'

'Driving round without her clothes on. That could be why he beat her up. But then again, you never know.'

'No,' I said, 'you don't know, do you? Would you like another coffee?'

'I haven't finished this one yet.'

I felt naked, too. Sue getting her just deserts wasn't that much consolation.

Mrs Langley resumed work and we didn't speak again until just before she left. Then she said, 'I got the money from the drawer.'

'Yes?'

'That was for the cleaning last week. You have to pay me for the ironing.'

'I know. Can I pay you with a cheque?'

'If you haven't got the cash.'

When she left, I faced the facts. Leonard was gone for good. I'd have to plan my life without him. Make arrangements about this house. Find somewhere else to live. How was I going to cope?

The house, I thought. Start there.

Only – I couldn't make arrangements. Not without consulting Leonard. I'd have to phone him at the office. I squirmed. I couldn't bring myself to do it. I'd have to find a go-between.

But who? I couldn't think of anybody. All our friends were Leonard's friends. I couldn't make demands on them. They wouldn't want to intervene.

Who?

I let another week limp by before admitting to myself that what I needed was a lawyer.

Five

Helen Mitchell was in her early thirties. She had long legs, short red hair and a formidable manner. Her eyes bored into me.

She said, 'Do you know what you want?'

I did. I wanted Leonard back. A reformed and adoring Leonard, who'd do anything to make amends.

Fat chance.

'A divorce, or a judicial separation?'

I hesitated.

She expanded. 'Are you a Roman Catholic? If so, you might have a problem with divorce. Going for a judicial separation would still give you the right to make the necessary financial applications.'

'I don't have problems on religious grounds.'

'Then we know where we stand. How are you fixed financially?'

I told her.

'And your husband?' she went on. 'Tell me what his assets are.'

'I don't know. I really don't.'

'You must have some idea. What does he do for a living?'

She dragged the details out of me, then told me what I'd have to pay before she could proceed any further – her fees, on account of costs, and a fee to the court.

'I'm not sure I can afford you.'

'You can. We'll apply for legal aid so those aspects can be covered.'

'What does that involve?'

She shrugged. 'Form filling. In theory, the whole exercise is fundamentally that. In practice, battle commences once the respondent has been served with the petition.'

'I don't think I'm up to battles.'

'Not at the moment, maybe. One thing at a time. First, we must select the grounds.' The piercing eyes were on me again. They were grey. They matched her suit. 'You definitely want to go ahead? You don't want to wait in case he comes back?'

There was no way out of it. 'I don't think that's likely to happen.'

She shrugged again. 'Look, when you go home, I want you to write down all the ghastly things your husband has done to you so I can build a case against him. Don't start thinking that you're mean. That would weaken your position. Don't go *floppy*, for Heaven's sake!'

'No.'

She narrowed her eyes. 'You probably will. So many women do. They start thinking of the good times.'

There were *other* women like me? 'They do?'

'One of my clients wrote pages castigating her husband. He was an unfaithful bastard. He always kept her short of money. He criticised the way she dressed, made her feel inadequate. Then she added a postscript saying he was really nice! See what I mean? Mind you don't give in.'

I swore I wouldn't go floppy on her and emerged on to the bustle of the Strand with my head buzzing. I walked towards Trafalgar Square. Another woman was approaching, with a briefcase in her hand. She was young, in her twenties, and everything about her – her clothes, her swinging hair and her confident stride – showed she knew where she was going.

That was how I used to be. When I knew where I was heading. When I was sure I knew myself. When I hoped that I'd keep Leonard.

Now there were no certainties. I'd not only lost my husband, I'd mislaid myself as well. I was a nonentity, not a sparkling entertainer. The liveliness was gone from me. I couldn't make a baby laugh.

Still, I could try to dress the part. Make-believe that I was me.

At home again, I braved the bedroom. I sidled in, delved into the wardrobe and backed out carrying a rose Kenzo sweater, the yellow skirt that went with it, my midnight-blue velvet hipsters and my Walter Steiger snakeskins. Then I saw the dressing gown hanging up behind the door. Leonard's red silk dressing gown. For me, it was part of Leonard, synonymous with love and sex. Evoking warmth and small delights. Chilled white wine on summer evenings. Watching videos in bed. Snuggled up with books and papers. Sunday breakfast on a tray, cooked and carried up by me.

I laid the clothes on the floor and edged closer. That dressing gown was made for Leonard when we visited Hong Kong. It still smelt of him, I realised, of his sweat and aftershave. That made me conscious of being sexless, neutered by the loss of Leonard. All I had left was the smell of him and that would fade in the washing machine.

What was I thinking of, washing Leonard's dressing gown? I should rip it up instead. Tear it to tatters and post it to Leonard.

Bastard.

In the morning, there was that report to write. Compiling it was nauseating. I had to go back to that first affair – the first one I found out about. I couldn't remember the woman's name, only that she'd been a nurse. Leonard met her on a plane coming back from Africa. I discovered what had happened when I found a letter from her.

One year later, there was Hazel. She had worked for IPC. Leonard said they were just friends. He had condoms in his pocket. I'd been on the pill for ages.

The next one was a ski instructress whom we met in Lenzerheide. The fourth, a woman called Diana. She was with the BBC, researching a religious programme.

Carol Hunter, I thought grimly. Why did I forgive that cow? I should add her to the list. And what about Vanessa Harding, whose husband used to work for Leonard? Not to mention Sue Wilkins . . .

Writing about what went on meant re-living all the pain. And then there was that other factor. The ones I didn't know about. The ones who must have laughed at me and said they'd got away with it.

It made me very angry, too – with myself as well as Leonard. To think that I had bust a gut trying to hold on to him. The way that I sweated blood keeping him entertained. The effort that I'd had to make to do the other women out.

It hadn't worked. I'd lost the fight. And I'd been humiliated.

When I finished the report I felt demeaned and dirtied by it. I wrote a note for Helen Mitchell and rushed upstairs to have a bath. I scrubbed myself. It didn't help. The residue of dirt remained. Posting the envelope later on, I thought how shoddy the contents were.

That done, I drove to the supermarket. Wheeling a trolley round the aisles, I ran into Hugh and Emma. They were at the bread counter, waiting for their order to be put into bags.

'It's our fair colleen,' said Hugh. He didn't look at me. He stared at a chocolate log instead.

'Hello, Caroline,' said Emma. 'Have you tried the *paesano*? We think it's rather good. Well, Hugh likes it. Don't you, darling?'

'Not bad. We're running short of mixers, Emma. I'll go and get some Slimline tonics.'

He sidled off, leaving Emma to collect the bread. I thought that I should make an effort.

'Sorry I've not been in touch. I mean about Modigliani.'

'Oh, yes, of course – Modigliani,' said Emma. 'All right, Caroline.

Phone me and we'll make a plan. I must rush. We're in a hurry.'

She disappeared amongst the shoppers. I saw them in the car park later but they didn't notice me. Then it struck me – they must know where Leonard was. That was mortifying. It made me furious again. I took off for the shoe repairers, brooding about Hugh and Emma.

Mr Dixon, the shoe repairer, was a rather surly man. He nodded, but he didn't smile.

I produced my lilac slingbacks. 'Can you save these shoes for me?'

'Hmm.'

'You usually work miracles.'

Flattery was wasted on him. 'Leave them there,' was all he said.

I took the docket and was about to leave when he called after me, 'What about your husband's shoes?'

I swung round.

'Your husband's shoes,' said Mr Dixon. 'You left them here four weeks ago. You owe me nine pounds forty for them.'

It was as much as I could take, being asked to pay for Leonard's shoes.

'*I* don't owe you anything.'

'Nine pounds forty's what I said.'

I was sure I would explode. I turned, stumbled over a yellow wellie and fled to the car. My hands were shaking. I couldn't control them to open the door.

It mustn't happen again, I thought. I must keep my cool. I mustn't let my anger out.

'Wonderful stuff!' said Helen Mitchell.

I might have written a prize-winning novel instead of that report on Leonard.

'It is?'

'Think what the tabloids would make of it if Leonard was a public figure! You haven't seen him, I suppose? No idea where he's living?'

'He could be with his mother. Honestly, I just don't know.'

'We'll serve the papers at his office.'

'Wouldn't that embarrass him?'

'Hopefully he'll die of shame and you'll inherit all his assets. Stop being so considerate. Don't you want to start again? Rebuild your life? Have a house you call your own?'

Of course. Carrigrua.

'Let me tell you what's likely to happen when we serve Leonard with the papers,' Helen said. 'He'll be asked to disclose details of his assets. He'll refuse to do so. This is routine strategy.'

'What will you do if he refuses?'

'He'll comply – in due course. He'll become more accommodating as the date for the court hearing approaches. Most men do in his situation. It gets to them, the notion of those romantic encounters being portrayed as sordid. Everything spelt out in open court. The fear of being ridiculed.'

'OK. Do what you think best,' I said.

Carrigrua, I thought again. Once more, I retreated into the dream of owning it. I planned exactly what I'd do if I got my hands on it. The colours that I'd introduce.

It was all a kind of game, making plans for Carrigrua, but it really saved my life. Over the next few weeks, I toured the local fabric shops to see if there were any bargains. I kept an eye on junk shops, too, and made a file for colour schemes.

All this while, we heard nothing from Leonard. Months passed. I endured a lonely Christmas.

Then, two weeks before the court hearing, the phone rang and a familiar voice said tentatively, 'Caroline, it's Leonard here.'

I forced myself to say hello.

'Caro, you and I should talk, you know. Don't you think it would make sense? Why don't you come here? I'm at the Royal Berkshire.'

He was living in the hotel. He'd been there all along, a couple of miles away from me. That emerged later, when I drove over there to meet him. First, I spoke with Helen Mitchell.

'Am I right to go?' I asked.

'It won't do any harm to talk. Just make sure that's all you do. Be noncommittal when you see him. You mustn't let yourself be tricked.'

I also went to see the doctor. He put me on Valium. It was only half effective, as I discovered when I walked into the foyer of the hotel and saw Leonard waiting for me.

'Caro!'

My heart lurched. I was woozy, vulnerable, and I reckon Leonard noticed.

'You look awful,' he said. 'Worn out. Poor darling. Sit down and I'll get some tea.'

It was like being in a play. Helen Mitchell was the playwright. When the waitress brought our teas, I let Leonard speak his lines.

'Caro, this business of adultery . . .'

I helped myself to a chocolate biscuit. While I munched and drank

49

my tea, Leonard tried to win me over. He proposed we live apart, do nothing for the next two years, then I could sue him for desertion.

'Don't you think that would be best?'

'You know how I feel about it. You've read Helen Mitchell's letters.'

Leonard was bewildered by this response. He said uncertainly, 'Helen Mitchell's quite a force.' He paused, then continued purposefully, 'Of course, *I* know you're not the avaricious, grasping bitch that she makes you out to be. And *you* know I'm not mean by nature.' He paused again, expecting me to take this up.

I reached for the teapot, poured myself another cup, but I didn't say a word.

Leonard sighed. 'Well, what are *your* proposals, Caro?'

'Helen Mitchell has explained them.'

'But Caroline . . .' He leant forward. Stretched out his hand to cover mine. I removed my hand. I looked at him coldly.

I said, 'I have to go. Deal with Helen Mitchell, Leonard.'

The dazed expression on his face gave me the courage to rise from my chair, say goodbye, and quickly walk away from him.

'Congratulations!' said Helen Mitchell. 'Didn't I tell you he'd give in?'

He hadn't only given in. He'd been more than generous. Helen had outlined the details. I was to have an initial settlement. The house in Wentworth would be sold. The proceeds from the sale of it would buy another house for me.

Not just 'another house', but my beloved Carrigrua. With the money from the initial settlement, I'd be able to restore it.

I made a call to Marie-Rose. 'Is Carrigrua still for sale?'

'It is. Is someone keen to see it then?'

'I'll be in touch again,' I said.

It was there, waiting for me. Soon, it would be mine. The dream I'd had was coming true.

In my euphoric state, I thought I'd get in touch with Emma. 'About the Modigliani . . .'

'Isn't it over?' Emma said.

'Yes. Ages ago. Sorry I haven't phoned. Shall we go and see the Bonnard?'

'This week isn't good for me. Wednesday's out and so is Thursday. Friday I've a dinner party.'

'Never mind,' I said to her, 'I know how it is with you.'

That must have hit home. A few minutes later she called me back.

'Caroline, I've just checked my diary. It's no one important for dinner on Friday. Just Hugh's parents and my uncle.'

'Thanks,' I said. 'But Friday's difficult for me.'

I don't need her, I said to myself. I don't need anybody here. It's Carrigrua that I need, and the house needs me as well.

I'll be happy over there.

Six

The loose ends were tied up by June. I painted poppies in the meantime – fields of poppies, acres of them – lived frugally and saved more money for the house.

'You should replace your car,' said Leonard.

Leonard and I were friends again – that is, he tried to be friends with me and I tried to act composed. In fact, our infrequent meetings were a source of torment for me. The good times would keep coming back. The holiday we'd spent in Grasse, the smell of jasmine in July. The trip we'd made to Africa, the skies, the veld, the animals. The simple things that we had shared, the laughter and the company. And, of course, the love we'd made.

Some couples go on making love, even after breaking up. Out of habit, I suppose. Or maybe they cling on to hope. That wasn't how it was with us. Not that Leonard didn't try to make me go to bed with him. He did. He did it automatically. I managed to resist him – just. Leonard couldn't understand it. He did his best to regain control. He kept giving me advice and I took no notice of it.

'I'm not spending money on a car,' I said.

'Yours is nearly eight years old. It's going to give you trouble, Caro.'

'I haven't run up that much mileage.'

'It's that house,' said Leonard sagely. 'You're obsessed with Carrigrua. It's not normal, Caro darling.'

'I wish you wouldn't call me darling.'

'It's all you ever think about. I know you're mad about the place—'

'I am.'

'But have you thought it through completely? You'll be on your own in Ireland. Are you sure you'll be all right?'

'I've been on my own for months. That didn't seem to worry you.'

'If I were you—'

'You're not,' I said.

'I'd take it very slowly, Caro. This is an ambitious project. You're getting in an architect.'

The Irish Georgian Society had given me the phone number of an architect, a Dubliner who specialised in period restoration. The day Carrigrua was finally transferred to my name, I got in touch with him about it.

'Leonard, *please*!'

'A house like that can eat up money.'

'I don't need your warnings, Leonard. I know exactly what I'm doing.'

My plans included driving to Clare without stopping overnight. Once there, I wouldn't stay at Carrigrua, not until the house was ready. Marie-Rose had offered me the use of her house, provided that I fed the dogs. She was going to New York, to spend the summer with relations.

Leonard said, 'That's a lot of driving, Caro.'

'Eleven hours. I've worked it out.'

'Take a cabin on the ferry. Try to get a few hours' sleep. Otherwise you'll be exhausted.'

In defiance of this counsel, I didn't bother with a cabin. I arrived in Ireland feeling just as Leonard had predicted. Between Dublin and Kildare, he was proved right again. I had trouble with the car – the engine started to cut out. The journey south was hazardous.

Somehow or other I got to Clare and was just counting myself lucky when, on the outskirts of Scariff, the engine cut out one more time. I tried to coax it back to life but it stubbornly resisted.

I got out and looked around, wondering what I should do next. The back seat was loaded up with my possessions. Dare I go to look for help?

The car had stopped at the end of an incline. The path to the harbour was off to my right. I was still hovering in a state of indecision when I saw a figure coming towards me from that direction. It drew nearer and evolved into a thin, fair-haired man. The father of the pretty child I had seen the year before on her Confirmation day. Once again, he looked familiar. Why? And why did I think he might be threatening?

He drew level, stopped and summed up the situation.

'There's a garage up the road. Do you want me to get help?' He had a beautiful speaking voice, mellow, cultured, reassuring.

'Yes. Please. If you don't mind.'

'Not in the least,' said the fair-haired man.

He returned, bringing a mechanic with him. The bonnet was opened and judgement pronounced. The car would have to be towed back to the garage. It would be ready in a couple of hours.

'A couple of *hours*!' I wailed.

'It's the quickest we can do it.'

'Where are you going?' asked the fair-haired man.

'Mountshannon.'

'I came over here by boat. I could take you to Mountshannon. But then you'd have to fetch your car.'

'I'll stick around and wait for it.'

'Or we could take you for a cruise. I'm waiting for my daughter to come out of school. We live just across the lake.'

'I don't want to be a nuisance.'

'You wouldn't be a nuisance to us.'

I hesitated, thinking of a two-hour wait, of the luggage in the boot, and of my inexplicable fear. But the fear was surely ridiculous?

'Your car will be OK with Danny. Nothing will be stolen from it.'

Danny looked dependable. Two whole hours, I thought again.

'If you're certain you don't mind?'

'I'm certain,' said the fair-haired man. 'I'm Bob Studdart, by the way.'

'I'm Caroline Tremain.'

While Danny went to get the tow car, Bob and I continued talking. He mentioned that he was a writer and I remembered the name Robert Studdart and a novel I'd enjoyed. I managed to dredge up its title and asked if he had written it. He nodded.

'You set it in South Africa.'

'I lived there before independence.'

'And now you're living – where exactly?'

'Just past the harbour at Williamstown.'

'But that's near *my* family home. I mean, it's not far from Carrigrua.'

There was an infinitesimal pause before Bob Studdart said, 'Carrigrua? I thought you said your name was Tremain. Oh, I see, of course, you're married. You must have been a Conroy then.'

'My mother was. She was Olive Conroy's daughter.'

'I remember Olive Conroy,' he said in a neutral voice.

'I've bought the house. That's why I'm here. I'm about to renovate it.'

'Someone told me it was sold. So you're going to renovate it. Is your husband going to help you?'

'My husband won't be living with me. We're in the throes of a divorce.'

'Sorry. That was tactless of me.'

'I don't mind at all,' I said, even though that wasn't true. 'Tell me about you instead. Is your wife a writer too?'

'My wife died five years ago.'

Talk about *his* lack of tact. My remark was still dangling in the air when Danny drove the tow car down.

Almost immediately afterwards a noisy gang of schoolchildren turned up and crowded round the three of us.

'Has there been an accident?' asked a boy, rather hopefully.

'Afraid not,' said Bob cheerfully. I thought he looked like one of them, tousled after being at school.

'We thought that she ran into something.'

Bob laughed. 'Too bad we have to disappoint you.' He rummaged in his pocket and produced some coins. 'Here you are. For consolation. Go and get yourselves an ice cream.'

The gang pushed off, leaving just the one behind, the girl I'd thought of as a princess. We were introduced by Bob.

'This is, eh, *Miss* Tremain, Francesca. She's coming for a cruise with us.'

Francesca frowned. She swung her school case to and fro.

'Cheer up, pet,' her father said. 'Life's not all that bad, I promise. You didn't want to go for ice cream?'

'Not with them,' Francesca said. She stared into space, not looking at me.

'Then let's get moving,' said her father. He gestured to the right. 'The harbour's just along that road. It's on the river, not the lake. But I forgot, you know all that. You know this place as well as I do.'

'I don't. Not the river. Not the lake. I was a child when I lived here and we didn't have a boat. I wasn't as lucky as you are, Francesca.'

But she was having none of it. She stayed silent, ignoring me. We set off together past more terraced houses until we came to a small harbour. Beside it was a little park. Solemn black-headed gulls, searching for food at the water's edge, took no notice of our arrival.

Four cruisers were moored in the harbour, three of which obviously belonged to the same line, with the names *Limerick Castle, Dromoland Castle* and *Dublin Castle* engraved on their sterns and bows. The fourth boat was a different configuration. It had a central cabin with a sliding roof and was called simply *The Helen*.

'That's ours,' Francesca announced in a clear voice with the faint overlay of an English accent. 'It's a Broom. Helen was my mummy's name.'

She climbed aboard *The Helen* and we followed her. She made her way to the prow where she sat cross-legged, divorcing herself from the two of us.

Bob took the wheel, started the engine and reversed. At that point the river was narrow and passengers on the other cruisers, concerned for their welfare, sprang to attention, anxiously watching his manoeuvres. When he finally straightened out, a man from the *Dromoland Castle* applauded, the others joined in and the gulls flew off in consternation.

The river, brown as toffee, was sharded with silver and green. The sky was darkening and the hills to our left had turned into blue-black velvet.

As we left the harbour there were still reminders that this was farming country: boundaries marked off by barbed wire; muddy hoof marks left by cattle; black-faced sheep with legs to match. By a wooden stile, a chestnut pony whisked the flies off with his tail. But already there were signs that we might be entering a less predictable environment. On the banks, amongst the meadowsweet and the white blackberry blossoms, the star-like flowers of the stitchwort and the green, feathery triangular stems of Queen Anne's lace, stout-stemmed reeds were growing up. The water lilies had olive-green leaves. Their flowers were a glorious golden yellow.

'Will we be going past your house?' I really meant near Carrigrua.

'It's actually my father's house. He was on his own as well, so we came back to live with him.'

'So there are three of you. Or do you have live-in help?'

'No. Someone comes to clean the house. My father does the cooking.'

I had a vision of his father. He'd be larger than his son. Plump and jolly. Sociable. Santa Claus without the beard.

Bob said, 'Look, would you make some tea for us? The wherewithal is in the galley.'

The galley was three steps down. I put the kettle on, unearthed plastic mugs, found a carton of low-fat milk and a packet of shortbread biscuits.

Coming back, I saw Bob's socks. One was brown, the other navy. The brown one had a hole in it.

He shouted to Francesca and she came in from the prow, her hair damp and her cheeks moist. Her mood was as grey as the sky above. I told myself to disregard it. All the same, she got to me. I saw in her something of the child I'd been, but I didn't warm to her.

57

She took her biscuit and mug of tea and huddled into a pile of cushions thrown on to the long seat that ran down one side of the cruiser.

I sat opposite her, staring over her head at the sights on the right bank. Trees covered in holly and wild roses. A red life belt slung over a post. A sign encouraging us to visit the Church of Saint Cronan's, 200 metres away. And, in the water, a wrecked and rotting lake boat, upside down and three-quarters submerged.

We were now in a veritable fever swamp. Out of it rose conifers, blue-green sitka spruce and tall firs, their long, new, pale-green needles fringing the edges of their brown branches. The dark cylindrical stems of the bulrushes and the strap-like leaves of the yellow irises grew higher out of the water. The grass on the banks was olive-green and the flowers on the thistle clumps a rich, deep purple.

On and on we drifted into the jungle. We saw a svelte grey heron, heard the whinnying call of a noisy dabchick, and my exasperating journey south and the car's subsequent collapse slipped into perspective as minor irritants. I felt as if I was being massaged. Even Francesca seemed to be soothed by the motion of the boat.

Hm, I thought, when I'm settled at Carrigrua I might buy a boat. Not a big one like the Broom. A small one with an outboard engine.

'When are you moving into your new house?' asked Bob.

I wasn't mad about his choice of words – 'my new house'. I felt very strongly that Carrigrua had always been mine by rights. But I let that pass and explained my arrangement with Marie-Rose.

'So what are your plans for Carrigrua?'

'I've got an architect coming from Dublin to assess its overall condition. I'm holding my thumbs, as you can imagine. It seems OK to me, but then I'm not an expert.'

Francesca cut in. 'There's a curse on Carrigrua,' she said darkly.

'Don't be so ridiculous!'

'It's true, Daddy. Bad things happen to the people who live there. No one at school would go near that place.'

'That's enough,' said Bob, annoyed.

Francesca's cheeks were pink with rage. She got up and stood between Bob and me.

'I'm not telling stories, Daddy. Mrs Farrelly was talking to Mary Bugler about it the other day after geography. She said wasn't it amazing that anyone in their sane senses would be buying that house. Mary said it must be some old fool over from England that Marie-Rose Keane had been able to con.'

'That's more than enough. You'd better say sorry to Miss Tremain.'

The red mouth set into an obstinate line. 'I can't say sorry. That would be lying.'

'Don't worry about it,' I said hastily, concerned in case our cruise was spoilt.

As for the rumours Francesca had heard, the Grey Lady and her lover must be at the back of them. Ireland had always been awash with tales of curses and haunted houses. Francesca was impressionable. And Mrs Farrelly and Mary Bugler should be more careful what they said when there were children listening in.

'Go down and wash the mugs,' Bob said. 'And put the biscuits in a plastic box.'

Francesca obeyed and I leant against the cushions, trying to coax back the psychic masseurs.

'As you were saying, about the house.'

'Yes. The architect that I've got coming—'

I was stopped in my tracks by a chilling sight. In the water, by the reeds, was a dead swan. Stuck in its neck was a fishing hook. Gone in a flash was my rational self. In Ireland, the swan was linked with mystery, with magical powers and beauty and passion. In folklore, the killing of a swan was tantamount to the taking of a human life. To see one dead was a bad omen.

In the swampland the foliage grew taller and coarser. In the water, two discarded bottles floated. A sense of foreboding came over me and with it a dreadful suspicion that I was going out of my depth, that what I was facing might leave me broken, like the graceful creature drifting dead in the toffee-brown water.

I must have shivered because Bob said, 'It makes your blood run cold, doesn't it? Can you imagine the mentality?'

'Guard O'Hagan knows who did it,' said Francesca, coming up from the galley. 'That's what I heard today at school.'

School was obviously a hotbed of information and surmise.

'Let's hope he has some evidence.'

Their indignation dispelled my demons. We moved out of the fever swamps. The reedbed plants gave way to shimmering grasses, tangled honeysuckle and gorse that was more brown than gold.

Soaring white gulls heralded our arrival at the mouth of the river. Lough Derg spread out before us, less tranquil than when I had seen it last. There was more traffic on it, too – cruisers, fishing boats and yachts. The round tower of Holy Island was visible. Ahead was the Tipperary shoreline and, nearby, the tip of a submerged tree on which a pair of gulls was perching.

The feeling of space was exhilarating, as if our cruiser had been lifted up into the stratosphere. Like a glass of sparkling water, life bubbled up in me.

Bob must have sensed my feelings because he glanced sideways at me, smiled and said, 'Freedom!'

'Yes.'

'You won't be sorry you came back here.'

'I'm even glad my car broke down.'

'There's praise for you.'

Another cruiser went past ours. Two of its passengers, men in yellow jackets, waved to us and we waved back.

'Must have been fun to have been here a hundred years ago,' I said, 'when the canals were working and there were steamers on the lake.'

'Not as much fun as you might think. No weather warnings. Not the kind we have today. Winds were always causing problems. Flooding caused enormous damage. And people used to complain about the lack of navigation marks. But you can still go to Dublin today by canal. It's something that I'd like to do when I get around to it.'

'When you take a break from writing?'

'Which I'm just about to do. My current book is nearly finished.'

'Are you going on holiday?'

'No. I tend to do that in the winter. Spend a few days in London or Paris or Rome. Less often to New York, although I like the place. I enjoy a change of pace.'

He steered the boat round Holy Island, keeping a fair distance from the shore in order to avoid what he described as lethal rocks. The island, I knew, was the site of an ancient monastery. The Romanesque ruins could be seen from the water but not the Lady's Well where pilgrims used to pray before throwing coins down into its depths.

One of the ruined churches had scaffolding round its walls. A workman on his tea break raised his mug in a toast to us.

'That's Patsy Flynn's father,' said Francesca. 'And, Daddy, Naoise Nolan's there! That's the fellow Guard O'Hagan – well, that's what Mary Bugler says.'

'Let's wait until we get the facts. Shame I didn't bring the dinghy, then we could have gone ashore,' Bob said. 'The water here is much too shallow to bring a cruiser any nearer.'

So we didn't go ashore. We cruised away from Holy Island, my distrust of Bob forgotten. In its place there was attraction, liking, gratitude. So peaceful and relaxed, I thought. So carefree, wandering round the lake like this. Fun.

With the object of turning north, we cruised round Hare Island. Then I spotted Carrigrua. It was the first time I had seen it from the water. I was entranced.

Carrigrua. The minute I laid eyes on it, I lost interest in Bob Studdart. I thought, I mustn't waste any more hours out on the lake with this man and his child. Too many years have been wasted already. We must turn the cruiser round. I must head for home.

Seven

I'm almost sure that Bob walked back to the garage with me. But my attention was elsewhere and the other details of that encounter soon faded, like the gorse that had turned from yellow to dun.

Marie-Rose had arranged for a cousin of hers to be at the house when I arrived. The cousin, a woman in her early twenties, was lumpy and friendly and well-intentioned. She helped me carry my luggage in and explained that, when neighbours switched on their milking machines, the subsequent sudden surge of power sometimes affected the water pump.

'If that happens, go out to the garage, Mrs Tremain, and just press the start-up switch.'

'Will you show me where it is?'

She did. She gave me the instruction book so I could work the washing machine. Then she said, 'She was fierce lucky that you bought the house off her.'

'Maybe. But I've always wanted to come back.'

''Twas a long journey you had in the car. Did you stop off along the way?'

'No. I was in a hurry.'

'There's not many that can come back. Not much chance of a job round here. You'll be doing the place up, will you?'

'When I know what will need doing.'

'There's good builders in the district.'

'Yes, I know. I've made inquiries.'

'I have an uncle who's a builder.' She wrote down his name for me.

'Thanks,' I said, knowing that I wouldn't use him. For one thing, the architect in Dublin had already recommended a local builder. For another, there was no way I wanted to hire one of my enemy's relations. Over my dead body would another penny go into the coffers of the Keanes. If Marie-Rose saw herself as a pathway to opportunity, Lady Bountiful to her family, she was about to be disappointed.

There were definite signs of ingratiation. The fridge and the freezer were stocked with food and the cousin urged me to help myself.

When she'd gone I did just that. I poured myself a whiskey, too. I drank and thought of Carrigrua and again of colour schemes. In London, I'd spent hours leafing through various pattern books and I'd wheedled enough samples from English Heritage, Zoffanys and Colefax and Fowler to fill a cardboard box full of possibilities.

I tipped these on to the kitchen table and found that my sketchbooks, paints and brushes were underneath the samples. Packing them, I'd seen myself on the lawn at Carrigrua, recording the scene as the house was restored. No wind blew in this idyll and it wasn't raining either. In the real world, it *was* raining. Still, I didn't have to be on the spot to make a drawing of Carrigrua.

A surge of energy went through me. Sitting at the kitchen table, I drew the house from memory, as I'd seen it from the lake. I sketched in trees around the house. Pencilled in the little harbour. Drew the outline of a boat.

Then, bewildered, I sat back. A *boat*? What made me add a boat? I wondered. We'd no boat at Carrigrua. There's not one in the harbour now. It must have been our cruise today. That was why I drew a boat. But I hadn't drawn Bob's Broom. The boat I'd sketched was squat and snub-nosed. I thought, I must have seen it on the lake. Except I don't remember it. Strange.

It worried me what I'd just done. And it made me restless, too, unable to think about colour schemes, let alone unpack my cases.

The dogs were sleeping on the floor. Every so often, one of them snuffled. The only other sound was rain.

I pushed the drawing away from me and tapped my pencil on the table top. The rain on the windowpanes answered back, as if in response to a coded greeting.

Although wet, it was light outside. This is my first evening home, I thought. Why on earth am I sitting indoors when I could be outside exploring? There was the village to inspect, not to mention the world of boats.

Like Scariff, Mountshannon had its own harbour, larger and with good moorings. This, added to the fact that the pier wall was not directly exposed to the south-west winds, made it an attractive overnight stop for the hire boats and yachts.

That wasn't what attracted me. It was the lake that was my draw. The water's link with Carrigrua. The house coloured all my actions. Now, it sent me out in the rain and leaping into the car again. The dogs woke up as I started the engine and howled in protest at being left behind.

The village seemed deserted. Not a person was in sight. The two spinning wheels leaning against the weaver's cottage, Mountshannon's memorial to its once-active flax trade, weren't being scrutinised by tourists. No prayers were being said in either of the Christian churches. But there were cars parked on both sides of the main street and people were inside the pubs.

The rain turned from a soft patter into a very definite downpour. I drove past the Mountshannon Hotel and made my way towards the harbour. It was crammed with all manner of boats, moored two and three up, with lines stretched from deck to deck. The water-side scene was lively and noisy. I heard music blaring out, and roars of laughter from the yachts and cruisers.

The people inside the boats took no heed of my arrival. I envied them, but then I thought, out there, past Hare Island, Carrigrua is waiting for me. Furthermore, the house is mine. It's not rented, like these boats. It's going to be my home.

But my visit to the harbour wasn't hitting the desired spot. I left the boat people to their levity, drove back to the village and turned to the right, away from it.

I wasn't going to Carrigrua. So I told myself. Not that evening, at any rate. I was just driving in that direction. I'd only go as far as Whitegate.

Carrigrua was two miles further on from Whitegate. This village had origins far older than the Protestant estate settlement of Mountshannon. The monks who lived there in pre-medieval times had followed the Celtic custom of painting their gateway white, an indication to a traveller that he could stay there overnight. All that was left of the gateway now was in the name of Whitegate village. And the village itself had undergone a transformation, as I soon found out. When I went to our old church, the one I'd attended when I was young, I just couldn't believe my eyes. Instead of one church, there were two – two the same, joined at the side like Siamese twins.

Why build a dyadic church? I could make no sense of it. I left the car to investigate. There was a sign outside the building. 'Whitegate Fitted Furniture', it said. It looked like a successful venture and no doubt the design of the new extension had been dictated by the council.

'Outrageous!' Olive would have said. All churches were divine to her and the sight of the new, modern church, which I spotted across the road, wouldn't have compensated in the least for the concept of commerce moving on to hallowed ground.

I crossed the road to Kate and Paddy's where pub theatre was in progress and put my head round the door. The interior was jam-packed with people of all ages, children and women seated in rows and the men standing up beside the bar.

The play had long since started. One of the central characters, an old crone armed with a walking stick, was ruining the sport of a fine pair of would-be lovers, and bringing the house down as a result.

But I hadn't the hang of the central plot and the pub was over-crowded. I retreated to the car.

Carrigrua, I kept thinking, and, swinging out, nearly ran over a freckle-faced boy practising his hurling skills in the middle of the street. I swerved on to the pavement.

The boy watched as I almost hit a lamppost. I saw him check my registration. He wasn't in the least repentant. Light dawned. Thinking that I must be English, he was sending me a message, telling me that he was carrying on the great tradition of the Gaelic Athletic Association, the vehicle on which so much republican feeling rode and thrived in the past.

I waved a hand at Master Freckles. Determined to be serious, he solemnly reciprocated.

Olive would have slated him – and looked down her nose as well. To her, hurling was a common sport, not a game for gentlemen. Rugby was a different matter, a sport for the sons she hadn't produced. Or for her non-existent grandsons . . . Leonard hadn't wanted children. I'd gone along with that at first, unaware that the time would come when I would fret to have a baby. But Leonard remained adamant, reminding me of the conditions he'd spelled out when we got married.

I turned the corner. I said to myself, I'm not going to Carrigrua. It's far too late to go into the house. I'll just drive along that road. I'll stop at the gates for a couple of minutes and bask in the glory of ownership.

Of course, I had the keys with me.

I was driving fairly slowly, which was why I saw the fox. He was an old fox. His reddish coat was streaked with grey and there were thistles in his fur. The sight of him made me feel sick. It made me think about the kill.

Now and then, when I was young, the hunt would meet near Carrigrua. Along with the men in their smart pink coats there'd be children of four or five, sitting on their long-haired ponies, hoping that they would be blooded. I knew all about this ritual before I ever saw a kill. When the hounds had caught the fox, the master cut its mask and brush off. He threw the carcass to the hounds, called the youngest rider forward and smeared him with the fox's blood.

On the day I saw this happen, we – Olive, Constance and I – were watching from the car. They expected me to cope, not to fuss about the kill. Conroy children always coped, even when the blood was flowing. But I wasn't like the Conroys. I was sick inside the car, which reeked of vomit for a week.

Olive thought it was the kill that had affected me adversely. I let her think it was the kill. In fact, it was much worse than that. More shocking and, for me, more shaming because, in those seconds as the hounds closed in, I felt that blood lust in myself and I was excited by it. Afterwards I was disgusted. Sickened not by what I had observed but by what there was in me.

I was still like that, I thought, remembering how I'd gone for Leonard and the way I'd wrecked the bathroom. I shuddered at the memory, sickened and repelled again.

When I reached the wrought-iron gates, delight took over from disgust. I wasn't going to open them, let alone drive through the wood. But of course I did.

Even then, I didn't intend to go into the house. It was different when I saw it and when I noticed what had happened.

Somebody had mown the lawn.

Tears welled up in my eyes. This gesture was a way of saying 'welcome home' to me. And indeed I *was* home. Why had I thought it would be easy to come and go from Carrigrua? The minute I laid eyes on it I knew I had to go inside.

In any case, I thought, why not? It's still light and it's my home. I can be here whenever I like. What's more, I know it's safe in there. I see no muggers on the steps. Rapists won't be pouncing on me when I go into the bedrooms.

But something was waiting for me. A box was lying on the steps. A round tin box. With biscuits in it?

I picked it up and opened it. Inside, carefully wrapped in cellophane, was a freshly baked fruit cake.

The tears spilled over on to my cheeks. Wiping them off with the back of my hand, I thought how kind my neighbours were. Whitegate, I knew, was a caring community, partly because, if you live in the country, people depend upon each other. But it was more than common sense. Grace grew in the people here like maythorn growing in the hedgerows.

I went indoors, taking the cake with me. John O'Donnell the architect was coming down from Dublin the following morning. I thought I'd share the cake with him.

I set the box down and looked around, as I'd done on my previous visit. The house was just the same but there was a difference now: *I* was the owner.

The thought of Carrigrua having been in Marie-Rose's name for even a short while was unbearable. I banished it – and opened the shutters to let in the air.

I wasn't going to stay long. But of course I did stay. I went from room to room, mentally refurbishing.

Carpeting. When this house was built, I thought, the floors would have been covered by rush and straw and grass mats. Persian and Turkish designs were wrong, too ornate, now I looked around again. Seagrass would be fine for warmth and for keeping down the dust. But maybe I should go for Tintawn, which had a peaty, tweedy look. The walls? The house might have a cool facade, but inside it should be sunny. Curtains. Cream or white or gold or yellow? Should I paint on them or not?

This kind of thing can take an age. I was vaguely aware that the rain had stopped, and of the failing light outside. But I hadn't been upstairs.

It was darker on the landing. The French cupboard loomed up out of the shadows like a blue banshee.

Silly to be nervous of it. It was only a piece of wood. But the fear was back with me.

Ah, come on, I told myself. Are you frightened of a *cupboard*?

The answer was, well, yes, I am.

It's *your* cupboard now, I said to myself. If it frightens you that much, you can move it out of here.

But that only made it worse. Suddenly, I couldn't breathe. I thought, I'm going to suffocate. Gasping, I staggered into my old bedroom and leant against the windowsill.

After a while, the sensation receded and I was able to breathe normally again. I opened the window, grateful for the rain-washed air.

The light had gone. The night sky was as grey as charcoal but a red sheen, like a gaping wound, was running right across its belly. 'Red sky at night, shepherds' delight.'

But red was also the colour of danger. The colour of magic in popular folklore. The colour of passion and anger and blood. The colour of suffering. The colour of the shoes that danced away with the heroine's feet in Hans Andersen's famous tale.

68

Red. That dream. That image of a different garden. All the flowers had been red.

The sheen from the sky was streaming down into Lough Derg. The night and the fiery arc and the volatile lake seemed united in a chorus of warning. Telling me to run. To go before it was too late. Telling me I had no business coming back to Carrigrua.

'But this is where I belong!' I cried.

And I heard the old house sigh with relief on hearing me reply like that.

But maybe it was just the wind. Either way, I straightened my shoulders, tilted my head back and walked with a straight back along the landing, the way Olive would have done.

I went past the cupboard and I made a vow. I swore that, whatever the future might hold, whatever the pressures on me might be, nothing and no one would ever again drive me out of Carrigrua.

Eight

John O'Donnell the architect was a grey-haired man with a crumpled face and arms too long for his small, lithe body. He was early for our appointment. I found him leaning against his car, a silver Rover with a ladder on top, waiting for me to open the gates.

He was always early, he explained. Before he inspected a client's house, he liked to walk around the district and soak up the ambience.

'I've been looking at the harbour.'

I thought he meant the old Williamstown harbour, less than half a mile away, but he told me there was another one now, even nearer to Carrigrua.

'Dromaan harbour. It's handy from your point of view but badly sited in my opinion. Not much shelter from the wind. I wouldn't fancy mooring there, not if it was blowing a gale.'

'Do you sail yourself?'

'We do. We have a yacht. Have you got mooring at the house?'

'Yes, but no one's ever used it. Not in my time, anyway.' Except in my imagination. Why on earth did I draw that boat?

'Who knows, maybe you will yet.'

'Maybe. The house will keep me busy, though.'

'I'm looking forward to the house.'

'It's *wonderful*! A paradise.'

John O'Donnell looked concerned. I shouldn't gush so much, I thought. Leonard's right. I *am* obsessive.

Opening the gates, I wondered how the person who'd mowed the lawn had gained access to the grounds. Had he or she got there by boat? Or was there a hole in one of the hedges through which good fairies crept, hauling mowers in their wake?

Driving in convoy through the wood, I was nervous about the house. Would John O'Donnell find fault with it, or go into rhapsodies? Would he say he could restore it, or discover hidden problems?

The first thing he did was to stare at the roof.

'What's the matter with it?' I said.

'Hm?'

'The roof. The house. What's your reaction to it?'

'My reaction? I'm surprised. I was expecting a horror story.'

'I couldn't have given you that impression!'

He laughed. 'You didn't. But then people never do. They tend to be optimistic about older properties. Romance and ruins go hand in hand. That is, till the bills come in. In this case, though, I'd say you're lucky.'

'*Really?*'

'That's a superficial judgement. I'll tell you more when I've been inside, but it seems in good condition.'

That called for an instant celebration.

'Wait,' I said. 'Do you like fruit cake?'

'It's my favourite cake,' he said.

I'd brought a flask of coffee with me. We had a picnic on the steps, my first meal at Carrigrua in nearly thirty years. It was a glorious day – just as the red sky had predicted.

I explained about the cake, and afterwards about the lawn. John O'Donnell loved that story.

'What a present, mowing the lawn! Sounds like you are on to something.'

I was relaxing, drinking a second cup of coffee, when he surprised me with a question.

'What kind of life will you lead down here?'

'What do you mean, what kind of life?'

'Do you like formal entertaining or are you very casual? An architect should have some insight into the way a client lives. It's relevant to the restoration.'

'I haven't thought about a lifestyle. Only about being here.'

'How does your husband feel about it?'

'I haven't got one any more. I mean, I'm about to be divorced.' About to be divorced, I thought. Put like that, it sounded weird.

'The children will be living with you?'

'No. We don't – we didn't have a family.'

Until then, I hadn't noticed the recorder, placed beside him on the steps. Our conversation was being taped.

'Is that the way you keep notes?'

'Yes. I hope it doesn't worry you.'

'No. It's fine. It doesn't matter.' But it did. Those notes would be typed back for him. Someone that I didn't know would learn about my family background.

John O'Donnell sensed my mood. 'I'll turn it off for now,' he said. 'Are you ready to go in?'

Once inside, he praised the hall, then asked about the furniture. 'You've put it into storage, have you?'

'I'm afraid it's all been sold.'

'Ah. A pity. Never mind. After all, you got the house.'

He thought it had been left to me. I didn't disillusion him.

'Look,' he went on, 'if it's all right with you, I'll start at the top and work my way down.'

I saw he had a sketchpad with him. 'Are you going to make some sketches?'

'Yes. On-the-spot drawings assist a report.'

He was becoming a bit abstracted. I knew he'd rather be alone. But I was determined to follow him round and was hot on his heels as he went upstairs.

He saw the cupboard. 'Not everything was sold, I see.'

'Almost everything,' I said. 'Let's start on the other side.'

I steered him firmly away from the cupboard. He switched the recorder on again – one sure way of shutting me up. But I was there when he paced out the rooms, when he jumped on the floors to test if they would bounce or not, and when he checked the joists to see whether or not they were the right size for the timber that had been used. I listened as he recorded impressions and I peered at the sketches that he was making.

At last, he completed his round, finishing in Olive's bedroom.

'Right,' he said. 'It's just the fifth bedroom now. Then we'll go downstairs.'

'The *fifth* bedroom?'

'Yes. The one next door. The bedroom opposite the bathroom.'

'There's no room opposite the bathroom.'

'Yes, there is. There has to be. This bedroom doesn't run all the way over the drawing room. It's not long enough. Didn't that occur to you?'

'I don't understand what you're talking about.'

'It's very simple,' said John O'Donnell patiently, guiding me out on to the landing. 'There's another bedroom on this floor. A small bedroom. The door leading into it must be behind that big blue cupboard.'

'Oh, no. Surely not,' I said.

'I can assure you I'm telling the truth. You mean to tell me you never suspected?'

73

'No.' But Olive's bedroom was smaller than I'd expected. Why hadn't I realised what that meant?

John O'Donnell was amused. 'You're in for a surprise,' he said. 'We'll move the cupboard. Then you'll see. I can do it if you help me.'

'*No!*'

'It's not *that* heavy, Mrs Tremain.'

'I don't mind helping you,' I said. 'It's just . . .' But I didn't understand what it really was, or why I'd cried out like that. 'Just a bit warm,' I ended lamely.

I could see him working it out. Of course, she has her period. She's feeling a little bit under the weather.

'We'll do it later then,' he said. 'I may as well inspect the roof. That was why I brought the ladder. I'll go down and bring it up.'

I eyed the cupboard in his absence. He's wrong, I thought. It's very heavy. The two of us will never move it. *Good*, said a voice inside my head.

John O'Donnell returned with the ladder and told me something about roofs.

'You'd be amazed how even the best householders neglect their roofs. Being the most exposed, slates and chimneys and gutters suffer the brunt of weathering. Because they're hard to get at, they receive the least care. I need to examine the structure of yours and see what condition the timbers are in. I can do that in the loft.'

He went nimbly up the ladder and disappeared inside the loft. I called after him, 'Has anything been left up there?'

His voice drifted down through the hole in the ceiling. 'Quite a lot, by the looks of things. Masses of junk. Boxes and pictures and God knows what.'

'Is that so?'

I left him to his own devices, went through to my old room and stood by the window, looking out. Like the cupboard, the lake was blue.

A fifth bedroom. Another room. More space. Why wasn't I delighted by that instead of being apprehensive?

'You won't have problems with the roof.'

'Won't I?'

I returned to the landing in time to see John O'Donnell's feet feeling their way down the ladder. Back on the landing, their owner informed me that there could be more surprises waiting for me in the attic.

'Papers. Documents relating to the history of the house. Details of the furniture and the craftsmen who made it. That kind of thing.'

'I must go up and mosey round.'

'Do. You never know what you might find.' He added, hopefully, 'If you want to go up now, I'll leave the ladder here for you. I'll be getting on downstairs.'

'I'll come down with you,' I said.

He had to go along with it.

On the ground floor, he went through his pacing and jumping routine before descending to the basement. There, he sniffed for damp and the characteristic smell of dry rot and checked the level of the floor against that of the yard outside.

'A difference of seven inches,' he informed the tape recorder.

'Is that bad?'

'No. We'd only worry if they were the same. Look at the floor. See? The stone is a similar tone all over. No dark patches to indicate damp. I'll check the rainwater pipes and the gullies that drain the external area, but I think your luck is holding.'

'No horrors to report at all?'

'Only minor ones. You'll have spotted them already. The basement door is rotting. We'll have to replace that in due course. The radiators are rusty and leaking. The heating system is antiquated. The boiler is a dreadful old contraption and the flue connecting it to the chimney has collapsed. But that's the kind of thing you expect in a house like this.'

After that, he toured the grounds and told me again that I'd been lucky.

'That's it, then,' he said eventually. 'Apart from the fifth bedroom.'

There was no way out of it without making a fool of myself.

'Right. Let's go up and have a look.'

'About that cupboard. Don't you worry. I can manage on my own.'

'No. Of course I'll help you move it.'

'You needn't kill yourself,' he said. 'It needs easing more than shoving.'

We took up stations on either side of the cupboard. Without difficulty, John O'Donnell coaxed his end of it out from the wall.

'See,' he said. 'There's the door.'

'Yes. Amazing. You were right.'

A bit more effort and the cupboard was well out from the wall. I was hot and sticky all over by then, and not just from my exertions. A voice other than John O'Donnell's seemed to be addressing me, warning me not to open that door. 'Put that cupboard back,' it said. 'And get out of Carrigrua.'

'Go ahead,' said John O'Donnell.

'Maybe the door is locked,' I said.

'If it is, you'll soon find out.'

He stood back, smiling and expectant. I reached out a tentative hand. The latch turned. The door swung open and the world capsized.

The bedroom we had found was wrecked. The floor was strewn with broken glass, overturned furniture and scattered belongings. The wallpaper, a pretty floral design, bore the marks of someone's nails. The windowpanes had all been smashed. A board was nailed across the frame. There were stains on the windowsill. Old, dry stains that looked like blood . . .

The voice inside me asked a question, 'Isn't this only what you expected?'

There was an overpowering smell in the room. The smell of scent, a sweet, floral fragrance that conjured up the vivid memory of a girl. A young woman with ash-blonde hair and grey eyes and a Meg Ryan mouth curving up in a smile. I could see her quite distinctly in my mind's eye. See the dress she wore. A strapless, rose-red evening gown made, I thought, of taffeta.

'Heavens alive!' said Mr O'Donnell, but he was thinking of the room.

It was simply furnished with a single bed, an old-fashioned Victorian wardrobe, a dressing table and a chair. The wardrobe door was hanging open. There weren't any clothes inside it but a number of personal items – a dried-up lipstick, satin-covered clothes hangers, a broken ashtray, an empty cigarette packet and a silver hairbrush – were lying on the floor amongst the debris of fallen pictures, littered bed linen and a pillow which had disgorged its feathery contents.

'What do you think went on here?'

'I can't imagine,' I said limply.

'I don't suppose we'll ever know. Better not to think about it.'

'Maybe not.'

But I *was* thinking about it. About *her*. Trying to remember more. She was slipping away from me. I might have been asleep, trapped in a dream where nothing is known, aware that knowledge is within one's grasp but unable to glean any more.

I bent down and retrieved the silver hairbrush. There were initials on the back.

CC. Constance Conroy? Or . . .

My mother's name was Charity. She had died when I was born. That was the official story. But was it true? I wondered now. Could this have been her room instead of the one they'd said was hers? Had she been attacked in here? Raped and murdered by an intruder? A story told to protect me so I wouldn't fret about her?

'Why don't you think of it like this,' said John O'Donnell, noticing my expression. 'We've found an extra room for you.'

'That part's wonderful,' I said.

'Yes . . . Eh, shall I get on with my inspection?'

'Yes. You might as well.'

John O'Donnell got on with it. As he paced out the room, I automatically tidied up, gathering the scattered items. I put the hangers in the wardrobe. Laid the linen on the mattress. Stooped down for a pillowcase.

There was something under the bed. Something small and glittering. I knelt down and fished it out.

It was a bangle. A curved gold bangle, about half an inch in width, probably dating from the early nineteen thirties. Since it had no tarnish on it, I guessed that it was valuable.

My reaction was entirely selfish. I thought, if this is my mother's bangle, I have a right to it. Not that I had any intention of handing it over to Marie-Rose if it belonged to anyone else. Still, I wanted to have that right, to feel that something out of the past had been handed down to me. Maybe it did belong to me. Maybe there was evidence. Had the bangle been inscribed?

I undid the safety clasp and the bangle opened out. Sure enough, it was inscribed. But not with the name Charity. And not Constance Conroy, either.

'Clemency Conroy', said the inscription.

Clemency Conroy? Who was she? I knew no one by that name.

Clemency Conroy, I said to myself. I slipped the bangle on my wrist and as I did so I saw her again. The woman in the rose-red gown. I could smell her fragrance, too. She was with me in the room, sanguine amidst all the wreckage. A sunny presence. Yet I was sure that it was she who had suffered in this room.

Who was she? Why did I feel so close to her? And why was her pain mine?

It was deeply distressing. Kneeling there, with the bangle on my wrist, and John O'Donnell incongruously jumping up and down on the creaking floorboards, I wept for her.

I hid the bangle under my sleeve. I said nothing about my find.

John O'Donnell's assessment was finished. He looked around the room again. Then he said in a thoughtful voice, 'You're going to need a second bathroom. This is the obvious room to convert, being next door to the master bedroom.'

'No,' I said. 'It wouldn't be right.'

'Not right? What makes you think it wouldn't be right?'

I wanted to preserve the room that belonged to Clemency, not to cast her out of it. But I could hardly tell him that.

'The thing is, Mr O'Donnell, bathrooms can be pretty chilly. And this bedroom faces north.'

'You'd have a radiator and a heated towel rail. You wouldn't feel the cold.'

I tried to gather my scattered wits. 'Why would I need a second bathroom? After all, there's only me. I want to modernise the kitchen. Then I'd like to convert one of the basement rooms into a studio.'

That diverted his attention. He began to ask me questions. So I was an artist, was I? Getting ready for a show? Did I plan to give some lessons?

Yes, yes, no, I answered dully, thinking about Clemency. 'Shall we talk about the kitchen?'

He talked, and I tried to listen. Then he talked about the house and told me to apply for grants.

'I can get a grant?' I said.

'You can try, at any rate. Write to the Irish Georgian Society and the National Heritage Council. I can give you their addresses. By this time next week you'll have my report and a covering letter. When you've had a chance to read them – say within the next three weeks – I'll be in touch with you again.' He checked his watch and looked surprised. 'Later than I'd realised. I should be getting back to Dublin.'

'Wait a minute.'

'Yes?'

'Could I borrow the ladder from you? Can I have it for a while, so I can inspect the loft?'

'But—'

'Can I buy it from you then? I can give you cash for it.'

He could have told me to be patient, to buy a ladder from a shop when they opened in the morning. He didn't. He wouldn't let me pay him, either.

'Hold on to the ladder, Mrs Tremain. You may need it more than I do. Just be careful when you go up.'

I was left with a sense of joy, and another of terrible sadness. The joy was connected to Clemency Conroy – her presence in the house, and my own inexplicable familiarity with her warmth and her love.

The sadness came on me again when I thought about her room. Something awful had happened there. There was no avoiding that. Wasn't there blood on the windowsill?

When John O'Donnell had departed, I rushed upstairs again, drawn up there by Clemency. The cupboard didn't bother me. Not any more. I edged round the back of it and went back into the bedroom.

My eyes misted over when I got inside – and I met Clemency again. She drifted towards me in a haze, wearing, yes, a rose-red dress. Then that image of her changed, not just once but several times. She appeared in other outfits. Trousers and a yellow jersey. A tennis dress. A petticoat. And she was there in bra and knickers, getting ready to go out. Spraying too much perfume on. The scent that I had smelt before.

The final image of her froze. I tried my best to keep her with me while I racked my memory. Who was she to me? But the image blurred, and it faded the more I tried to focus on her. I persisted. But Clemency had gone again and the memory that replaced her only surfaced for a minute.

That recollection was grotesque. Frightening and unbearable. I shuddered.

Then, mercifully, some other instinct, a guardian of sanity, intervened to blot it out and I lost the memory of it.

The mist cleared. I was alone again. But the mystery remained. Who was Clemency? If this had been her room, if she had lived at Carrigrua, the answer should have been a member of the family. But Olive had only two daughters, as I could confirm myself.

I remembered a conversation that we'd had when I was six. Most of the other girls at school came from big families. Just one, Ellen Maguire, was an only child like me. Ellen had explained to me that her mother had lost three babies. I thought her very careless to have mislaid so many children. By contrast to Mrs Maguire, Olive was sharp-eyed and vigilant, hardly the type to have lost a child. But, then again, you never knew, for Mary had lost track of Jesus when He was on His Father's business. I thought I should check it out.

'Grandma, did you ever lose a child?'

I shouldn't have asked her, I realised at once. I could tell by her eyes that she was cross.

'And what do you mean by that?'

I swallowed and explained the background. She thought I was impertinent.

79

'I only had the two,' she said.

So was Clemency a niece? Or the daughter of a cousin? Where did she fit into things?

I intended to find out. That was why I got the ladder. Maybe there were clues up there, waiting for me in the loft.

Nine

The ladder was one of those aluminium fold-up ones, light and easy to manoeuvre. I didn't have a problem with it. But the ceiling was higher than I'd remembered. Much higher. It soared way above my head, looking sternly over the stairwell and down to the hall below.

I very nearly chickened out. I told myself I must be crazy to think of going up that ladder. I didn't have a head for heights. What if I panicked halfway up? What if the ladder slipped and I was hurtled into space?

Leonard would be sorry then. 'Poor Caro,' I could hear him sighing.

The idea of Leonard grieving was a darkly pleasing concept. I toyed with it momentarily before admitting to myself that it wouldn't be like that. Leonard might well grieve for me but he wouldn't leave it there. Oh no. He'd carry on to Hugh and Emma, maintaining that he'd seen it coming.

'Poor Caro. She was *obsessed* with Carrigrua. I *told* her not to go to Ireland.'

Self-righteous bastard! Indignation lent me strength. Why would I panic climbing up? Why would I end up a victim and give Leonard satisfaction? Not me. Those days were over. I was going up that ladder and it wasn't going to kill me.

I slipped off my shoes and transformed the ladder into a battering ram to push open the trap door. Climbing slowly over the stairwell, resisting the urge to look down rather than up, I felt my forehead break out in a sweat. When I reached the last rung I flung myself into the space beyond, landing in a froth of dust. I crawled a few yards away from the opening before scrambling to my feet.

John O'Donnell had been right, there was a lot of junk up here. His reassuring footprints strode firmly between discarded pictures and mirrors, chipped ornaments, an ancient gramophone that was probably a valuable antique, pots and pans and the remnants of an abandoned tea service. Cardboard boxes, an old leather suitcase and a life-size, rather garish statue of the Sacred Heart with blood flowing freely out of His wound were bound together by tangled skeins of spiders' webs.

The statue was a childhood friend. Nothing much was known about it. Perhaps, at one stage, there had been a private chapel in the house and an altar for the statue. Olive wasn't keen on it, but superstition, and the suspicion that the statue might have been blessed, prevented her from throwing it out. She had kept it in the kitchen, standing on the windowsill where it used to block the light.

I was very fond of it. The kitchen was a cosy place and, though the statue looked so sad and was in a sorry state, for me it was synonymous with comfort, warmth and cooking smells. Seeing it up there in the loft, I found myself thinking of roast pork, crackling and home-made scones instead of blood and sacrifice. Garish or not, I decided, it must go back to the windowsill as soon as somebody could move it.

Before that, I had work to do.

I waded into the pile of debris, dragged one of the cardboard boxes out into the centre of the floor, ripped off the sticky tape sealing its lid and yanked it open, all keyed up about what I might find.

As it transpired, it wasn't much. Inside the box were shabby woollies, clogged and snagged, a shapeless skirt with a broken zip and two pairs of trousers so worn in the seat they were almost see-through. They'd all been rammed in any old how, sleeves and legs turned inside out.

Along with the clothes was a catalogue for the Dublin Horse Show 1972, three unopened seed packets and a folder containing yellowing stationery. No documents. No letters. Nothing relating to Clemency Conroy.

Still, there were those other boxes.

Delving through the second box sent me into near despair. In it was a load of trash, mostly rubbish from the kitchen – rusty strainers, blunt knives and plastic Tupperware containers without lids. Deeper down were aged dishcloths, a frying pan with scratches on it and the top of a pressure cooker.

The third box contained more jumble, including threadbare towels and sheets and loose leaves from a cookery file. Halfway through it I nearly gave up.

What could have got into Constance to hang on to all this junk? Why not simply chuck it out instead of hauling it up here? What a batty cow she'd been.

Then I wondered, was that fair? Some unhappy, disturbed people hoarded rags and other rubbish. Constance might have been distressed when she brought these boxes up. She'd lost Olive, after all. That could have destabilised her. She might have had a nervous breakdown. It would explain her other actions. Going to live with Marie-Rose. Leaving everything to her.

Perhaps they *hadn't* lived together – not as lovers, anyway. Maybe that was just a story Marie-Rose made up for me. A smokescreen, not a love affair, designed to put me off the scent. So I wouldn't guess the truth, that she'd manipulated Constance. Maybe other people knew, or suspected what was happening. The priest who'd glared at Marie-Rose? If only they'd contacted me before it was too late for Constance. Before Marie-Rose got her hands on Carrigrua.

I sighed. No matter what I felt about it, the fact remained, it *was* too late. It was pointless speculating. What mattered now was Clemency.

But there was nothing in the box with any relevance to her, and no files or loose papers lying on the attic floor which might be of interest either.

My last hope was the suitcase. In its day it was a good one and it had stood the test of time. The leather hadn't cracked with age and the clasps that fastened it hadn't buckled under pressure. Although I'd never seen her use it, I guessed the case belonged to Olive, to a period in her life when she was less distrustful of hotels and less rooted to the house. She never slept away from home when I lived at Carrigrua. Those who did, she intimated – commercial travellers and the like – were really Not Our Kind Of People.

It might not have been her case, but her belongings were inside it. On the top was a dramatic broad-brimmed hat trimmed with faded cabbage roses. It was sadly crushed. In an effort to restore it, I put it on the statue's head, back to front so it wouldn't offend Him. It was a marvellous hat, the kind that smart women wore on semi-formal social occasions way back in the nineteen fifties. A romantic, sexy hat . . .

Although Olive was so prim, to me she'd always been romantic. An essential part of the Conroy myth was the concept of my grandparents as passionate, besotted lovers. The hat, black straw with a swathe of tulle, was made to measure for the myth.

It was a hat to wear to lunch, to celebrate a big event. A wedding anniversary? That appealed to me no end. I half-closed my eyes – that way I couldn't see the statue – and saw Olive in the hat. Olive dining in a restaurant, looking gorgeous in the hat while Grandfather Lawrence made a fuss of her.

In this picture of the pair, he remained a hazy figure. Olive never spoke of him. I'd never met him in real life. I only knew he wasn't handsome because Norah told me so. But she'd said that he was lovely. That was good enough for me. So what if he wasn't handsome? A lovely man could be romantic, even if his neck was thick.

I left the hat perched on the statue and rifled through the case again. Amongst the layers of crumpled clothes, obviously packed by Constance, was a white high-necked blouse with lace edging on the front. I took it out and, just for a moment, it seemed I was holding not only the blouse but Olive in my arms, something I couldn't recall ever doing in real life.

I pressed my cheek to the blouse and caught a faint whiff of Chanel Number Five, which was Olive's favourite perfume until she found out about Marilyn Monroe from an article she read. Poor Marilyn was dead by then but Olive said that she was fast, telling people that she wore nothing but That Perfume when she went to bed at night.

The other clothes inside the case also smelt of Number Five. Lifting them out and holding them up – those well-remembered skirts and blouses and a cotton brocade corset – I was eight years old again.

I rooted out a brown leather handbag, three pairs of shoes, one pair of boots and another hat, a domed one with a grey silk flower. The shoes, two-toned with buckled straps, were decorated with elaborate punched holes, and the boots, trimmed with tiny bows, had zip fastenings on the side and spindly, high, impractical heels.

It was the footwear that fascinated me. Even more than the clothes and hats, those shoes and boots made Olive come alive. I lined them up on the attic floor. They were dainty, beautifully made. Irresistible . . . The temptation was too great. I just had to try them on.

I eased my feet into a pair of grey suede shoes. Soft as warm wax, they wrapped themselves round my feet. They might have been made for me. They weren't my colour, being grey, but they were so comfortable. Surely I'd find a use for them.

I walked to the far end of the loft, to test their flexibility. They were wonderfully pliant and, at the same time, firm, supportive and sustaining. The story of *The Red Shoes* flickered through my mind again but these shoes, I thought – *my* shoes – weren't like the ones poor Karen put on. These shoes were a joy to wear.

I twirled, did a little dance and, swinging round to face one of the discarded mirrors, saw my feet and ankles reflected in its sullied glass. It was an eerie sight, one that took me back in time. As a child, I was more familiar with the lower half of Olive's body than with the rest of her anatomy. Eyes downcast, staring at her feet and ankles, I used to wonder what I'd done and if she'd be annoyed with me.

84

Now I thought, that's *her*, not me. *Her* feet, *her* ankles in the mirror. Olive's here instead of me. Her persona has taken me over.

Confused, I backed away – and saw *my* legs and trunk and face rising up from the feet and ankles.

Not Olive. Only Caroline.

But I didn't feel like Caroline. I felt different. Transformed. Confident. As if I really was a Conroy.

Well, I was, in all but name. I'm a Conroy, I said to myself. I own Carrigrua. I am all that Olive was.

It was a triumphant moment. With elation went the feeling that it was the house that mattered, not the ghosts that lingered in it. The house and my position in it.

My quest diminished in importance. Clemency, who'd seemed so real, so vital, only a few minutes earlier, became insignificant. Something – a voice inside my head – insisted she was just a dream. A trick of light, an aberration, a lie.

I dismissed her from my mind. I thought, gloriously, that I was in Olive's shoes in another sense than the obvious one.

And then I spotted something that had belonged to me. Behind the mirror, in a corner, was a rickety shelf. On it was a pair of boots. Not smart leather boots like the ones that Olive wore but a pair of wellingtons that I'd worn when I was young.

I've always hated wellingtons. I don't like the new ones either, the short ones that are blue or yellow, but the ones on the shelf were the worst of the lot – the clumpy, black, old-fashioned kind.

As a child, I used to hide those wellingtons and maintain that they were lost. Not that Olive was deceived.

'You'd better find them,' she would say. 'Or there'll be Trouble for you, Miss.'

Seeing them up there on the shelf, it suddenly came back to me why I hated them so much. I'd left those boots outside one night, lying by the kitchen door. Next morning, when I put them on, there was a sickening crunching sound and, to my horror, I felt *things* – horrid, noxious, creepy things – crawling around inside the boots. I screeched and howled and made a fuss, trying to kick the wellies off. But they were tight and wouldn't budge. I screamed and shrieked and bawled again, convinced the *things* were eating me, starting with my toes and feet.

Then someone came to my assistance. Someone who smelt delicious. Someone warm and sympathetic, who managed to remove the boots.

85

'You poor pet,' she said to me. 'They're just black beetles. Don't be frightened.'

Who *was* that someone? I thought now. I was never Olive's 'pet', and Constance never showed affection. Nor, of course, did Marie-Rose. And Norah smelt of lunch and dinner, not of that specific scent.

The fragrance of crushed flowers. *Her* perfume. The scent that Clemency had worn.

'You poor pet,' she'd said to me before she carried me indoors.

What had I been thinking of, to dismiss her memory?

Sobered now, the confidence gone out of me, I took off the grey shoes and rummaged through the case again. There wasn't that much left inside it. Another skirt. A knitted jacket. Two silk scarves. A nylon nightie. And something hard, something round, wrapped inside a mohair stole.

The stole was definitely Olive's. It was a present from the bishop, the time he came to Christmas dinner. 'A small donation,' he'd announced. All smiles, certain he was doing right.

But the colour was all wrong. Turquoise blue. A suspect shade. Olive's face fell.

The bishop wrapped the stole round me. 'Isn't that a fine stole?' His hand lingered on my shoulder, the way that he could touch my hair.

'Very nice indeed,' said Olive but she never used the stole.

What had Constance wrapped inside it? A pot that didn't have a lid, or a lid without a pot? You just never knew with her.

It was the muffin dish. It was so tarnished, so blackened that I barely recognised it. It was a pretty thing when polished, about six or seven inches in diameter with a removable salver and a base designed to hold hot water so the muffins would keep warm. Naturally, I thought of Norah. The muffin dish, more than what I'd found downstairs, re-connected me with her.

Norah ... In England I'd made people laugh, imitating how she walked. How could I have been so cruel? Mind you, she was cruel to me. I thought I could rely on her. She wept when I was sent away. She gave me a holy picture. But she never wrote to me. Not so much as a Christmas card. Constance had at least done that, though only after Olive's death. In fact, to tell me she was dead. But she'd made an effort and she'd kept in touch thereafter, while Norah, who'd professed to love me, had dropped out of sight completely.

Was Norah still alive? I wondered. Marie-Rose would know the answer. But she was in New York, enjoying herself at my expense.

Bitch. Buying clothes in Bloomingdales while I was crawling round the loft, getting nowhere with my quest.

But then I thought, hold on a minute. Constance left her rubbish here but no documents or papers. She must have taken them away with her when she moved out of Carrigrua. They could be in the other house. And with them may be information which relates to Clemency. With Marie-Rose so expediently out of the way, I can nose around her house and find what may be hidden in it.

Ten

The house was so tidy that I expected to come across any cache of documents within minutes of beginning my search. I started in the parlour where, apart from the orange Dralon three-piece suite, the occasional tables and a stand holding pots of African violets, there was a small, low cupboard with the TV set on top of it.

The cupboard didn't contain papers, only magazines – back copies of *Hello!* and *Majesty*. Other than that, there was nowhere to look.

Next, I tried the dining room. With just a reproduction table, six chairs and a matching sideboard, it wasn't exactly over-furnished. The sideboard didn't have much in it either, only glasses, two dozen of the same size, all of them shining bright and each embossed with a little green shamrock.

In the unlikely event that Marie-Rose had acted out of character and allowed Constance to tuck files and boxes out of sight behind the gleaming pots and pans, I searched the kitchen thoroughly too.

Nothing. I remained undaunted. Snooping downstairs was merely routine. What I was after would be somewhere upstairs, most likely in the master bedroom.

I hadn't scrutinised that room when Marie-Rose revealed its secret. This time round, I noticed the romantic touches (pink roses on the linen and the curtains), the vanity unit running the length of one wall and the practical built-in wardrobes.

Hm, I said to myself, lots of room here to store documents and files. Thinking Constance might have stuffed her paperwork into a suitcase, I checked out the wardrobes.

There were no suitcases in the first wardrobe, only two smart suits, half a dozen shirts and three pairs of trousers hanging up on uniform grey plastic hangers. The hooks of the hangers all turned inwards and little sachets of sweet-smelling potpourri were tied to some of them.

The second wardrobe was jam-packed with musty-smelling clothes – Oxfam rejects by the look of them – suspended from wire hangers, the kind you get back from the cleaners. Most of the hangers were crooked and bent. Instead of keeping the clothes in shape, they'd created hummocks in them. On the floor, in disarray, was an assortment of heavy lace-up shoes, boots that smelt of their owner's feet and an empty shopping bag.

Elbowing aside a Viyella shirt with a hole in the sleeve and a pair of baggy trousers, I poked my head inside the wardrobe. But I couldn't see properly so I removed some of the clothes from the rail and several pairs of the boots and shoes.

There was nothing of interest in the wardrobe. I backed out rapidly, holding my nose. As I replaced what I'd taken out, I asked myself why Marie-Rose hadn't tidied out this cupboard. Constance – it was obviously hers – had been dead for ages, almost a year. The clothes took up a lot of space and it was unlike Marie-Rose to put up with such a muddle.

Another mystery. But I was distracted from it by the sight of a case on the ledge above the hanging space. I fetched a chair and stood on it. The case was so heavy that, as I pulled it out, it swung me along with it.

By luck, we landed on the bed. The impact unlocked the case. It was, I realised, lined with books, which explained why it was so heavy. Many of the books were old and several, including works by Rupert Brooke, dated from the First World War. There were books on circus life and a set of six beautifully illustrated travel books, entitled *People of All Ages*, which I remembered from my childhood.

Unlike the books at Carrigrua, these ones were in good condition. Why had Constance brought them with her and left all the rest behind rotting in the library?

God only knows, I said to myself. Still, these books must have meant a lot to her and if I found it hard to visualise Constance reading Rupert Brooke, glorying in the wartime sonnets, it must be because I'd never really known my aunt.

Trying to understand her now, I read a couple of the sonnets. Someone – I couldn't remember who it was – said that they were 'true' and 'thrilling'. They were, I thought, and deeply moving, but they seemed too idealised, too English in their essence, to have had appeal for Constance.

I'd thought the case contained just books, that there was nothing else inside it. But when I put the sonnets back I found an aged photo album, its cover faded from blue to grey.

I perched on the bed and examined it. The album contained several photographs of a burly, bearded man. He stood on the granite steps, staring fixedly out at the lake, not enjoying being a model but doing his best to be obliging. He leant against a bicycle. He sat on horseback, dressed for hunting. I guessed that he was Lawrence Conroy, my shadowy grandfather, dead before my mother. He looked a lot like Santa Claus but he resembled Constance too. There was a picture of the two of them; he had his arm round her shoulder. As Norah said, he wasn't handsome but he had a nice, kind face and I was left with a sense of loss because I'd been deprived of him.

All the same, I must admit that I was more interested in seeing photographs of Olive, especially when she was young. Pictures of her at a ball, or a photo of her wedding. But I was disappointed. There were no pictures of Olive. My parents, though, were in the album, and my mother on her own, and Constance as a little girl, and the sisters in the garden, diligently sweeping leaves. But there was no sign of Olive.

Some photos had been taken out of the album. Between the pictures there were gaps. And several snapshots had been cropped, cutting out the sitter's head but leaving in a hand or leg. The result was often comic. A photograph of Lawrence Conroy, who must have been talking to somebody when the picture was taken, showed him with an extra foot with a high-heeled shoe on it.

I didn't even ask myself why someone would have cropped the photos. It was one more thing beyond my powers of deduction.

What else was in the case? I chucked the books out on the bed and found there was a file among them. A black lever arch file. 'Personal correspondence', it said on the spine.

I was sure I was on the brink of a momentous discovery. In the file would be letters – *old* letters – which had to do with Clemency.

No such luck, I soon found out. Some of the letters in the file had been written years ago, but none of them in that connection. All the same, the file was reassuring. In it were all the letters that I'd ever sent to Constance. She'd actually kept my letters. Every single one of them. She'd cared enough about me to put my letters into her file.

I was moved to tears by what she'd done. It was as if she'd reached out from the grave to me and said, 'You see. I truly cared about you.'

It nearly made up for her later betrayal. And then she was ill, I said to myself. Out of her mind and near to death. And Marie-Rose put pressure on her, forcing her to make that will.

The books were scattered on the bed. Still thinking about Constance, I put them into the case again, along with the sonnets and the file. What to do about the case? I couldn't even lift it, never mind put it back on the ledge.

'Oh, to Hell with it,' I said and left it lying on the bed.

The vanity units still had to be checked. They were divided into two sections. The left-hand side belonged to Constance and the right to Marie-Rose. It was the story as before. Anarchy on one side – a hopeless tangle of scarves, incompleted knitting, F-cup bras and broken combs. A state of order on the other. But no documents. No paperwork of any kind.

I couldn't think where else to look. I sat down glumly on the bed, sure that I was getting nowhere.

Then, as I was sitting there, the sun came peeking round the curtain. The bangle sparkled on my wrist.

I thought, *of course!* I haven't looked beneath the bed.

I jumped up, knelt down and lifted up the valance frill. There was something there all right. A form. A bundle. A sleeping bag?

No. Not a sleeping bag.

What then? A parcel. Wrapped in plastic, by the looks of things.

It was beyond my reach. I lay on my stomach, crawled in underneath the bed and got hold of whatever it was. It *was* plastic. A dustbin liner tied with string. Very easy to tug out. It felt soft, pliable. Oh shit, I thought. Not more old clothes. More smelly rubbish.

Disheartened, I untied the string. Inside the bag was tissue paper. Inside that was something red. Something made of taffeta . . .

A rose-red taffeta evening gown. Clemency's gown.

I heard myself cry out, aghast. For, like her room, her gown had been wrecked. Someone had attacked it, slashed it with a knife or scissors. The skirt was in ribbons. The bones poked through the severed bodice.

I lifted it up as gently as if it was a sleeping baby and laid it on the brown fleck carpet.

I smelt perfume. Felt a presence.

Clemency, I thought again. What happened to you, Clemency, and why did someone destroy your gown?

Although strapless, it was modest. Laid out on the floor like that, it assumed a human form. Became Clemency herself. A woman who'd been violated . . .

I sat down limply on the floor. What happened to you, Clemency? What happened to you in that room?

Then I saw the photograph. It was lying face downwards on the floor. I picked it up and turned it round – and saw my own face smiling back at me.

My face. But my hair was up, not down. I'd never worn my hair like that. I'd never worn a strapless gown . . .

Clemency. I knew at once that it was her.

Our faces were the same, but her expression was quite different. She was how I should have looked. Outgoing, eager, full of chutzpah. Confident and positive. But not insolent, I thought. Not brazen. Clemency was not a tart. There was nothing in that face to provoke extreme reaction. Yet Clemency, if this indeed was she, had been branded and indicted, the verdict on her as a person spelt out right across her forehead.

Slut! proclaimed the slanted writing.

Questions whirled inside my head. Whens and hows and whys and whats. Who would tear a gown to shreds? Who would deface a photograph?

It wasn't Constance who'd done that. The slanted writing wasn't hers. *Her* writing was diminutive. Her pen had barely touched the paper. The letters shrank back from the reader into the safety of the page.

Not Constance. Who?

The gown was lying on the floor, pathetic in its shredded state. What *happened* to you, Clemency? *Tell me.* Why did someone tear your dress? Deface your image in this way?

I picked up the gown again and put it back inside the bag. I pushed the bag beneath the bed.

By then, my throat was dry and parched. I went downstairs and filled the kettle. The two dogs, snoozing in the summer heat, sat up in hope of being fed.

'In a minute,' I said severely.

Abashed, the dogs collapsed again, but I could feel their eyes on me, reproaching me as I made the tea.

What happened to you, Clemency? Why did that woman keep your gown?

I'd resented Marie-Rose. Grown to hate the sight of her. Now my loathing of her turned to fear. I thought, thank God she's miles away.

The dogs were getting really desperate. Their eyes were putting me to shame. Opening a can of Pedigree Chum, I cut my hand on the lid of it. Blood dripped on the kitchen floor. The dogs, delighted, licked it up while I tried to staunch the flow under the cold water tap.

There were bloodstains in her bedroom. Her gown was torn. Her image sullied.

The carousel went round again. Had she been attacked in there? Had her judge been her assailant? Was that why her room was sealed, because she was murdered in it?

I had no answer to these questions. I thought, I'm failing you. I know I am.

But why on earth should I feel that?

Who was Clemency? What happened to her in that room?

That night I dreamt of death. In the dream, I was a child, calling out for Clemency. I went to find her in her room.

There was a body on the bed. It was wrapped in a scarlet cloak, but it was on the wrong way round; the hood disguised the face.

Clemency, is that you there?

I crept nearer to the bed. The cloak had once been white, I noticed. Blood was oozing from the body. That was why the cloak was red.

'Look!' I said. 'It's dyeing the cloak. But you can see the seams are white.'

I said this to Marie-Rose. She was with me in the room, sweeping old clothes out of it, using a yard brush instead of a broom.

In a rage, she turned on me. Her eyes were huge and filled with hate. Her hands were dyed with blood as well.

'Will you get out of here!' she said. 'There's too much blood in here already. What happened to your wellingtons?'

My feet were bare and they were bleeding. I must have cut them on the glass.

'I hate these wellingtons!' I said.

'Get out of here!' said Marie-Rose. 'Go on. Get out of Carrigrua.'

'I'll die if I go out of here.'

'Then die,' she said. ''Twould suit me better.'

But when I tried to leave the room Marie-Rose caught hold of me. Her nails cut through the dress I wore, and there was blood upon the bodice.

Then *I* was the body on the bed. *I* was wrapped inside that cloak. I was helpless, just a child. She was going to smother me . . .

I woke with a start to find myself tangled in the bottom sheet, the duvet fallen on the floor. My heart was beating very fast. I couldn't credit I'd been dreaming and not on the brink of death.

When I got over that, I laughed. It wasn't true! I was alive. Safe! My feet had not been cut with glass. And Marie-Rose was in New York.

It wasn't true. It hadn't happened.

But *some* of it was true, I thought. There was a well inside my head. The truth was bubbling up from it.

What happened to you, Clemency?

The answer was inside the well. However painful it might be, I had to pull it out of there.

Eleven

That day, I heard the cuckoo call for the last time before his summer getaway.

'He leaves for Spain at the end of June. He's frightened of the bonfires here that mark the eve of Saint John's day.' So Norah used to say, quoting from a book she'd read. But where was Norah herself? I wondered. Norah, who might jog my memory and assist me in my quest. She must have known who Clemency was. Hadn't they been in the house together?

Who was Clemency? Why couldn't I remember her?

The dream I'd had the night before kept on coming back to me. I was haunted by the spectre of a maddened Marie-Rose. Those hands of hers, those capable hands, I'd felt them round my neck last night. Were they the hands of a murderer? Did Marie-Rose kill Clemency?

What happened to you, Clemency? I must remember who you were. I must unearth the truth about you.

Going out that morning to buy milk, I passed the green house where the parish priest resided and that gave me an idea.

I rang the priest when I got back.

'Father Kavanagh?'

'Yes?'

'This is Caroline Tremain. Constance Conroy's niece. We met last year at her funeral.'

'We did indeed. And how are you?'

I fibbed and said that I was well. Just in need of information.

'Come down to the house at a quarter past twelve,' he said.

The smell in the house was green as well. Leeks and cabbage were being cooked.

'Colcannon,' Father Kavanagh confided. 'My housekeeper is a grand cook. And I have the stomach to confirm it. What information did you want?'

'I'd like to see the parish records. There's someone that I want to trace. Someone who's – who *was* related to me. The thing is, I don't know when she was born.'

'What is your relation's name?'

'Clemency Conroy. I don't suppose you know about her?'

'Clemency? Isn't that unusual? I'd remember a name like that. But no, I haven't heard of her.'

'There'd be Conroys in your records. We go back for generations.'

'Is that so? I didn't know. I'm a stranger to these parts. I came over here last year, after having been in Tulla.'

The village of Tulla was less than fifteen miles away, but I let that pass.

I told him about Carrigrua. How the family lost the house, and how we got it back again.

'That's something else I should have known. Come into the office and look at the books. I'm sure you'll find your cousin there.'

Outside, it was warm and sunny. But there was a chill inside the office and patches of damp on the whitewashed walls. The parish records were lined up on shelves behind a mahogany pedestal bureau.

'Take a seat at that desk, Mrs Tremain,' Father Kavanagh said, 'and I'll try to help you out. You say you don't know your cousin's precise date of birth but do you have a rough idea?'

I thought of the style of the strapless gown and worked backwards from that time.

'But really, Father, I'm only guessing.'

Father Kavanagh took down a couple of books and laid them on the desk before me. 'There now. I've gone back a bit before that. So you have more leeway on it. I'll leave you here to do your research.'

'You don't want to use the office?'

'Not now.' He smiled. 'It's coming up to dinner time.'

It's got to be here, I said to myself. Not only the record of Clemency's birth but those of all the other Conroys. A thought came fleetingly into my head. How come I never met the others, all those cousins that I must have had? Where were they when I was young?

I countered the thought with a 'Never mind that'. I needed answers, not more questions.

I seized on one of the record books. Its spine and cover were damp and mouldy. Touching it, I stained my hands, the way you do with cheaper newsprint. The pages in the book were worse. The damp had seeped through into them. Every single page was smudged. I couldn't read the writing on them. The records were illegible, defaced by my country's climate.

The second book was just as bad. I could have wept with the frustration.

Father Kavanagh said it put him in mind of the Custom House fire in Dublin, which destroyed so many records in the early nineteen twenties. There was no colcannon left but, by way of consolation, would I like some baked rice pudding?

'No, thanks. But you're very kind.'

'Any time that I can help you.'

There must be other ways, I thought. Other people who could help. Other people who'd remember. Who'd lived here when I was young. But things had changed in thirty years. I knew no one from my youth. Except, of course, Marie-Rose. And Norah, if she was alive.

But then I thought, of course – the Studdarts. Bob had said he remembered Olive. Maybe he knew Clemency. And there was his father, too. I should speak to him as well.

I'd promised Bob I'd keep in touch. I had his number written down. I'd phone and ask if we could meet.

A voice inside me said to wait until Bob contacted me. 'If you get in touch with him, he'll think you're after him.'

And there was, too, that sense of unease I had about him. I dithered. Cringed. I thought, he mightn't want to hear from me. He could have phoned. He hasn't bothered. I thought again of Clemency and rang Bob's number.

He came on the line at once. 'Caroline! Telepathy. I was thinking about you.'

'You were?'

'The thing is, I mislaid your number. I thought of going to Carrigrua in the hope that you'd be there. How's it going with the house?'

'Coming along. The architect has just been down. I'm seeing the builder there tomorrow.'

'You sound pretty busy then.'

'Hopefully I will be soon. Now I'm in a state of limbo.'

'That makes two of us,' said Bob, without elaborating further. 'Have you the time to come and see us?'

'At your house or on the boat?'

'Whichever suits you. I don't mind.'

'I'd like to see the house,' I said, thinking then I'd meet his father. Two birds with one stone.

'Then come to tea. Tomorrow, when you've seen the builder?'

'OK. Tomorrow afternoon?'

'Tomorrow afternoon it is. Let me tell you how to get here.'

He gave me precise directions, all of which I jotted down, grinning like a cheerful clown.

Tomorrow . . . The smile faded from my face as I gave more thought to the builder. His name was Michael O'Meara. He was meeting me at Carrigrua. I'd have to take him round the house. Into the fifth bedroom, too. If he saw the mess in there, he'd talk about it in the village.

I must clean it up, I thought. Sweep up all the broken glass. Remove the litter on the floor. Wipe the bloodstains off the sill. Protect Clemency from gossip . . .

Next day we had a proper heat wave. I kept yawning in the car as I drove to Carrigrua. In the meadows, sweaty men were cutting hay. Drowsy cattle used their tails to swish the gadflies off their bodies. In the hedgerows, wild roses flowered pink and white, and ragged robin was in bloom.

I woke the house and went upstairs with my bucket and my brushes. The blue cupboard, reduced again to furniture, had lost its power to terrorise. I even thought it might be useful, maybe in my studio.

The room beyond it was the same. As before, it smelt of scent. I stopped on the threshold and sniffed again, wondering what the perfume was.

The smell worked on my memory. This time, though, it evoked a far less pleasant recollection. Of voices – women's voices? – raised in anger. The memory was indistinct and didn't stay with me for long.

Was it important? To do with the state that the room was in? Why couldn't I remember more? How much was I imagining? Not the condition of the room. Nor that Clemency was there, if not now then in the past. I had her bangle to prove that. I'd seen her photo. Found her gown.

And soon, *today*, when I was talking to the Studdarts, I might establish who she was and, perhaps, what had happened to her.

I started to clear up the mess. Within the hour, the fifth bedroom was just like the other rooms – shabby, in dire need of decoration, but with nothing odd about it.

Only that it smelt of perfume . . .

In due course, Michael O'Meara the builder arrived, a skinny man with steel-rimmed glasses who looked like an academic. But there was cement on his jeans and the hand I shook was rough.

Within minutes of our meeting, I'd learnt a lot about his life. He was forty-six, he said. He and his widowed mother lived together in Whitegate village.

'She remembers you, she says.'

'Really?'

'From the time you were a child.'

It was good to be remembered. Folded gently into the past, like flour being folded into batter.

'It would be nice to meet her sometime.'

'She'd be pleased if you'd call in.'

I showed Michael round the house. His interest in it won me over before we even reached the basement.

''Twill be grand when it's done up. You haven't heard from Dublin yet?'

'I'm sure I'll hear within the week. When I do, I'll contact you.'

He knew then he'd got the contract but he didn't comment on it.

'Leave a message with my mother. We're in the thatched house on the left-hand side as you're going up the street.'

'Opposite the hairdresser?'

'That's exactly where it is. I'd like to take her out of there. Put her in a bigger house. But she's happy where we are. She likes to know what's going on. She keeps a watch on everything.'

I smiled, thinking it was just as well that Michael hadn't seen that room before I got my hands on it. His mother sounded like a sponge, waiting to soak up the gossip.

Nearly time to see the Studdarts. I had Bob's directions on me. 'Go past the two harbours. The second one, the old Steam Navigation harbour, belongs now to the Shannon Castle line. They have their hire boats moored there. There's a cottage on the right which has roses on the walls. Turn right again just after that.'

I drove there with the window down, thinking about Clemency and how to introduce that subject. Opposite the hire boat base a minibus had just pulled up. Tourists were emerging from it, lugging fishing rods and luggage. Several children were amongst them and a baby in a pouch. A young couple from the Shannon Castle line was guiding them towards the boats.

I edged the car past the bus, found the cottage on the corner and turned into a narrow road.

'Our place is on the right-hand side. Watch out for a broken gate.'

The gate was hanging off its hinges and proved difficult to open. On the other side of it was a meandering driveway flanked by straggling flower beds which led to a solid foursquare house, typically Victorian.

99

As I pulled in at the front, Bob appeared at the door.

'Caroline. I meant to meet you at the gate. I should have opened it for you. Did you have a battle with it?'

'I conquered it eventually.'

He steered me indoors through a dark hallway into a frosty blue drawing room. The room had a forlorn air. The sofa and armchairs were covered in an old-fashioned Sanderson flower print. The cushions were the worse for wear. The Wedgwood vase cried out for flowers. The glass bowl with the silver brim needed to have fruit in it. The faces in the photo frames looked as if they belonged to ghosts. It was not a happy room. Not a room for children, either.

'Is Francesca here?' I asked.

'She's on a school trip to Kilkee. Wait here and I'll get our tea.'

Bob went through to the kitchen and returned pushing a trolley laden with assorted goodies.

'What a feast. Don't tell me that *you* baked that cake.'

'I can't bake to save my life. My father is the cook round here. He's a dab hand in the kitchen.'

'Is your father going to join us?'

'He—'

The phone rang in another room.

Bob said, 'I've been waiting for that call,' and shot off to answer it.

I waited while the tea grew cold, then got up to inspect the pictures. Marine prints, etchings from the nineteen thirties, a watercolour of wild flowers in an over-ornate frame.

Someone coughed. I swung round. An elderly man had come into the room. He was tall with deep-set brown eyes and a mane of thick, white hair. He gaped at me.

'Who are you?' he whispered hoarsely.

'I'm Caroline Tremain,' I said.

'Dad!' Bob was back. 'I thought you were going to Limerick.'

Dad? They didn't look much like father and son.

Mr Studdart senior swallowed. 'Yes,' he said. 'Yes, I was. I left my chequebook. I got as far as Sixmilebridge. Caroline Tremain, you said?'

'I told you about Caroline, Dad. She was with us on the cruiser. She's moving into Carrigrua.'

'You told me. But you didn't say—'

'Sit down, Dad. I'll pour the tea. Though it might be cold by now. Sally phoned. We talked for ages. Caroline, sorry I kept you waiting.'

'Don't worry. Please. It's quite all right.'

100

But it obviously wasn't.

'It *is* cold,' Bob said disgustedly, feeling the teapot. 'Give me two more minutes, will you?'

He disappeared again. There was a long pause.

Then Mr Studdart said severely, 'You're going to do the house up, are you?'

'With the help of an architect.' I launched into explanations. Mr Studdart listened politely, without saying very much. This is hopeless, I said to myself. Talk about being heavy going. But it was my chance to ask him about Clemency. The only one I might get. I decided to take the plunge.

'A strange thing happened at the house,' I said. 'When the architect was with me. We found another room in it. Another bedroom, actually. I never knew that it was there. It was blocked off, you see. The door was hidden by a cupboard. I . . .'

I stopped. The old man's face was grey as ash. He looked absolutely wretched. God, I thought, what have I said? Only that I found a room. Why should that be so upsetting?

Mr Studdart didn't speak. He sat there like a waxen figure. I wondered what would happen next, which of us would break the silence.

Then Mr Studdart stirred, turned his attention to the trolley and offered me a buttered scone. 'Or would you prefer the cake?'

'Could I start off with a scone?' I said, trying to fit in with the situation, wondering why he'd been upset. By now, though, he seemed quite composed. I re-assessed the situation. Had he really been so stricken or was I the excited one?

I decided to play safe and leave Clemency alone. For the moment, anyway.

'Bob tells me you baked the cake. Did you make the scones as well?'

'I did.'

He treated into silence. Bob came back, to my relief.

'Have you told Dad about the house?'

'I went on a lot about it. I tend to do that, I'm afraid.'

'I'm sure he found it fascinating.'

Bob was playing it safe as well. He kept the conversation going while I munched a piece of cake. Then we got around to boats.

'Had you thought of buying one?'

'A cruiser would be too expensive. But, yes, I'd like a smaller boat. Something with an outboard engine.'

101

'Someone I know has a lake boat for sale. I'll show it to you, if you like.'

'I'd like to *look* at it,' I said.

'I'll take you round there afterwards. We could go in the cruiser.'

'Great. Will you come with us, Mr Studdart?'

'No.' Bob quickly intervened. 'Dad doesn't share my passion for boats. He never goes out on the lake. A lot of country people don't, especially the older people.' And then he talked about Germans. They went wild about Lough Derg. A lot of them had settled here. And, of course, there were the French. They loved it over here as well.

It was all a little strained. Mr Studdart did not join in.

'Shall we go?' Bob said eventually.

I got to my feet. 'Thank you for the tea,' I said. 'Particularly for the cake.'

Mr Studdart smiled at me. He said, rather engagingly, 'I'm glad you liked the Dundee cake,' and I thought how irresistible he must have been when he was a younger man, and how handsome he still was.

'Where's this boat?' I said to Bob.

'It's in Dromaan harbour.'

'I'll have to come back for my car.'

'That's all right. We won't be long.'

I thought, I'll raise the subject on the boat. Ask him about Clemency.

We walked across the lawn to the Studdarts' harbour where *The Helen* had been moored. Two small figures were lying on the deck. As we approached they both sat up. One of them was Master Freckles. His green eyes went from Bob to me. I wonder what's going on, they said.

The other boy was more forthcoming. 'Bob, we cleaned the boat for you. You want to see how grand it looks.'

'Pay up is what you really mean!'

They grinned.

'That was why we waited for you.'

'Are you going on the lake?'

'We are. But only over to Dromaan.'

'Can we come out with you as well?'

Of course, Bob said that they could come. I cursed inwardly, thinking that my chance was gone. I couldn't speak of Clemency, not in front of these two boys.

There was no chance on the way over. But when we pulled in at Dromaan, Freckles and his trenchant friend leapt ashore and disappeared.

Bob hardly noticed that they'd gone. 'There's the boat,' he said to me.

It was an eighteen-foot open boat with a light outboard engine and it looked in good condition. The bodywork was cream and green.

'What do you think of it?' Bob inquired.

'It's – fine. It's just the kind of boat I want.' My mind was more on Clemency and when I could bring up that subject.

'You might get a bargain there. He's keen to find a buyer quickly.'

'Could you ask him what he wants?'

'If you like we'll go and see him. He just lives across the road.'

'You mean we'll go and see him now?'

'Yes, why not? If you've time.'

'Well—'

'Bob!' The boys were back with us again. 'Bob, you've got to come and see!'

'See what?'

'The goat. He's here! He's up there, waiting at the house!'

'He is?'

The goat turned out to be a wild one. *Very* wild. He had massive horns like scimitars. He'd taken up residence in front of a house with large windows. We watched him from a discreet distance. He was lying on the porch, his profile turned towards the road. He was shaggy, fierce but regal too, like a goat that had stepped out of a fairy story.

'Where on earth did he come from?'

'When you passed you didn't see him?'

'I didn't. No. I—'

'He's been around for several days. We think he swam here from an island.'

'Why would he swim over here?'

'Maybe a younger goat challenged his authority. Forced him to get off the island. He could be dangerous, Caroline. I think we'll beat it out of here. You'd better come with us, you two. Is there someone at the house?'

'No, there's not. The car is gone.'

The boys were goggle-eyed – subdued. They stuck like Super Glue to Bob.

'I'll have to phone around,' he said. 'See where they might be. Warn them that he's in the garden.'

Whoever 'they' were, he didn't explain and I didn't really care.

When we reached the Studdarts' harbour, he told the boys to fetch their bikes. 'Don't ride up that road,' he cautioned. 'Go to Tommy's, both of you. Caroline will take you home. You will, won't you, Caroline?'

'Yes.' I tried not to sound too disgruntled.

'Your bikes will fit into her boot. And remember what I said. Don't go near that goat.'

'No, we won't,' said Freckles' friend.

I took them home. I had no choice. Tommy lived in Whitegate village. We hardly spoke along the way. I thought of Clemency and when I could meet Bob again. He'd said nothing about that. Drat him! Drat the goat and drat the boys!

'Thanks a lot,' said Freckles' friend when I dropped them in the village.

Freckles said, 'Thanks very much then, Mrs Tremain.'

Mrs Tremain? They knew my name and I didn't know theirs. But that figures, I thought wryly. People here know everything – or, if they don't, they find it out. By comparison, I'm useless. I still don't know who Clemency was.

But I know that she was harmed. I suspect that she must have been murdered. I must go on. I must find out what happened to her. I've got to rack my brains again and find another source of help.

Twelve

It grew hotter by the minute. In the wood, the butterwort was pink and pretty but it oozed a sticky fluid, in the hope of trapping insects. A trap . . . I thought of the marks on the windowsill, of the shredded gown and the photograph. I shivered in the summer heat. I forced myself to make a list.

1. The family solicitor. He should know about Norah, if she is alive or dead. He might have heard of Clemency.
2. The people in the shops in Whitegate.
3. The garden centre. Owner, Mrs Alice Egan.
4. Bob again. (When I could get him on his own.)

I knew who the family solicitor was because he'd acted for Marie-Rose when I bought the house from her. He was in Scariff, I remembered. I looked up his number and called.

'Hello, it's Caroline Tremain. Could I speak to Mr Casey?'

'He's away on holiday. He's not coming back till August.'

On holiday. I might have known it. Don't despair, I told myself. Try the shops in Whitegate next. Someone is bound to be in the picture.

There weren't an awful lot of shops. One of them was closed that day, which gave me only two to call on.

I did some shopping in the first one and took my basket to the counter. The woman on the other side itemised the things I'd bought. Then I mentioned Clemency.

'Have you ever heard of her?'

To my chagrin, she didn't react. She went on counting out my change.

'There you are. That's two pounds forty.'

I tried a second time. 'I'm making inquiries about a relation. Her name was Conroy – Clemency. Does that ring a bell with you?'

Her expression was that of a patient person listening to a raving cretin. 'No, it doesn't, I'm afraid. Don't forget to take your butter.'

I left, but not before I'd dropped my bag. The contents flew around the floor and landed up in the potatoes. In an effort to retrieve them, I put my foot down on a lipstick.

'Here's your comb,' the woman said.

'Thanks. I'm sorry.'

'Don't worry. Did you drop this pound?'

The young man in the second shop had several customers to cope with. He didn't need the likes of me. All the same, he was polite.

'Clemency? I only heard of Constance Conroy and she died a year ago.'

'I know,' I said. 'She was my aunt.'

'Oh, yeah, that's right. Of course she was.'

He was wishing I would go and stop holding up the queue. He's too young, I told myself. An older person would remember.

I wanted to meet Alice Egan in connection with the garden. Carrigrua was a mess. The grounds were being choked by weeds. I couldn't clear them on my own. On the phone, Alice said I should employ a landscape gardener.

'I'm afraid that's too expensive.'

'I know.' Her voice was kind and sympathetic. 'You'd better come and talk to me.'

She was somewhere in her forties, a lean woman with rough hands and a weatherbeaten face.

'I knew the garden well,' she said. 'Quite Victorian, it was, when Mrs Conroy finished with it. Old-fashioned, highly scented flowers. Larkspur and hollyhocks. Delphiniums, lupins and sweet peas. Wild roses up the walls. The borders straight, with herbs in them. Different parts were different colours.'

'One part blue and one part pink. You know the garden *very* well.'

What about the other garden? said a voice inside my head. The garden that was mostly red.

But that was just a dream I'd had. Funny how it stayed with me.

'My mother told me all about it, not the once but many times. She's dead now, God rest her soul, but she was in the Wednesday Club when Mrs Conroy was alive.'

'The Wednesday Club?'

'You didn't know about the club? It was for the gardening ladies. They always met at Carrigrua. The first Wednesday in the month.'

Women in tweedy suits, I thought. Eating muffins with their tea.

'It was started long ago. In eighteen ninety-five, I think.'

'Really? Mrs Egan, you say your mother knew my family. Did she know Clemency as well?'

Alice Egan's eyes grew wider. She said uncertainly, 'Clemency?'

'Clemency Conroy. She must have been related to me.'

'Is that so?'

'Your mother never mentioned her?'

'I – can't remember, Mrs Tremain. It was all so long ago. That is, since my mother died.'

She was obviously nervous. Something's going on, I thought. But what? And would Alice Egan tell me? Her face had acquired a shell round it.

'You know, Mrs Tremain,' she said, 'the basis of your garden would still be there. If you'd like, I'll come and have a look at it.'

'I'd love it if you looked at it. To get back to Clemency, are you sure you don't remember?'

'No,' she said, 'I don't. I'm sure. About the orchard, Mrs Tremain. I'd say the cane fruit could be saved. The greenhouse – the orangery, they used to call it – might need attention from a glazier. I know a man who lives in Scariff.'

I gave up on Clemency. 'Could you get hold of him for me?'

'I will indeed. I'd be delighted.'

'And I'll need labourers as well.'

'I know three that you could use. Two of them have jobs already, but only on a part-time basis. Naoise Nolan would be fulltime.'

Naoise Nolan? What had someone said about him?

'You don't object to Naoise, do you? Guard O'Hagan does, I know. But we have different views of Naoise. Naoise's never been in trouble. I can recommend his work.'

'Then that's good enough for me.'

'I'll get them all to come and see you.'

We discussed the rates I'd pay and when I'd want them to start work. Then I tried another tack.

'By the way, have you come across Miss Keane? She used to work at Carrigrua.'

'You mean Marie-Rose, I take it.'

I nodded. 'Do you know her well?'

'She's a customer of mine. She used to come here with your aunt.'

'But you don't know that much about her?'

Alice Egan looked bewildered. 'She's a Keane. They live round here . . . I'm glad you're happy about Naoise. *I've* not had a problem with him.'

Then we were back inside the garden. We chatted about flowers and shrubs and bluebells overcrowding beds. Alice became animated. But I

107

knew that if I mentioned Clemency she'd put on her shell again.

Why? Why were the people to whom I talked so averse to opening up? Was there a conspiracy to conceal the truth from me? Like lettuce in a salad spinner, the questions tossed inside my head.

Clemency maintained the pressure to find the answers in a hurry. She was always with me now, in her rose-red evening gown, smiling, sunny, optimistic, relentlessly reminding me of what I had to do about her.

Pushing away my unease about him, I thought, I should try Bob again. But perhaps I'll wait a while. In the hope he contacts me.

But he didn't. No one did.

Then John O'Donnell's report arrived. Roisin Ryan came with it in her green post office van. By that stage, I was seeing everyone as a possible informer and I pounced on poor Roisin.

'Mrs Ryan, can you come in a minute, please? There's something I'd like to ask you.'

Which proved to be a big mistake.

'That would be against the rules.'

'Rules?'

'We're not allowed to enter houses.'

I'd offended her, I realised. 'Maybe when you're not on duty?'

But the damage had been done and Roisin had gone cold on me. 'Maybe.'

'Thanks anyway,' I said, and went inside to read my post.

From worrying about Clemency, I moved on to Carrigrua. Suppose the news is bad, I thought. Suppose John O'Donnell lied when he spoke to me in person. He'd seen me get one shock already. He might have thought another one would be too much. I'll tell her when I write to her . . .

The report was long. It started with an introduction summarising what Mr John O'Donnell had been asked to do by Mrs Caroline Tremain during his visual inspection of Carrigrua House on such and such a date. Carrigrua was described. A precis of its history given.

'Oh, get on with it!' I muttered.

I needn't have been so impatient. What I wanted was one page on – the condition of the house. 'Two of the gutters have failed,' I read. 'There are leaks in the radiators . . . Four slates are missing from the roof . . . The chimney stack will need attention . . .' And finally the magic words, 'But there are no major problems.'

'The darling man!' I told the dogs, as if John O'Donnell was the one who'd kept the house in good condition. Had he been here, I would have hugged him.

Unable to express my feelings, I went back to the report. The rest of it outlined his plans for the studio and kitchen, which we had discussed already, and the minor alterations. Nothing to upset me there. But on the final page there was. I read the words with disbelief. 'Plans for the conversion of the fifth bedroom into the master bathroom.'

'I *told* him that we won't do that!'

The dogs leaped up.

'Why's he doing this?' I asked them. 'I'm not going to change my mind. I don't need a second bathroom.'

I dashed off a quick note to John O'Donnell to acknowledge his report and suggest another meeting. Then I rushed up to the village to leave a message there for Michael.

I was barely at the door of the thatched house when it opened to reveal a stout, elderly woman with a halo of white hair and young, inquisitive blue eyes.

'Mrs O'Meara?'

'You'll be Mrs Tremain,' she said. 'I'd know you anywhere. You haven't changed a single whit, only that your legs have stretched. So you've come back to us at last. You poor thing. I hear you bought your house from her that had no rights to having it.'

'I'm afraid so.'

She took me by the arm and led me inside. A pine dresser formed a dividing wall between the parlour and the kitchen. By the window that faced the street, an armchair was strategically placed.

'Michael would have me move from here,' said Mrs O'Meara confidingly. 'And for what, may I ask? Come and sit here at the table.'

She fussed around, filling a kettle, setting places at the table. I might have been a child again, waiting for my buttermilk.

'About herself,' said Mrs O'Meara. 'What chance did your poor aunt have with one like that around the place? A divil she is and we all know it. She'd have Saint Peter swearing, only he'd know better than to cross her path at night!'

I hadn't passed on the message for Michael. As I listened to his mother, I was thinking how stupid I'd been. *This* was the person to whom I should talk. She had lived here all her life. She knew what went on. She'd remember everything. She'd surely know of Clemency.

She was still in full spate on the subject of the Keanes. ''Tis only to

109

be expected. Her father did everything dirty. And you know what they do be saying. "*Faoi bhun chrainn a thiteas an duillir.*" '

I'd forgotten all my Irish. I shook my head and she translated.

' "Under a tree falls its foliage." There's bad blood in all them Keanes. Do you take sugar in your tea?'

I shook my head a second time and got a few words in. 'What exactly did her father get up to?'

Mrs O'Meara told me a long and complicated story of a right of way between her family's land and that owned by the Keanes. The dispute which had arisen from it involved cattle trespass, gates deliberately left open on a wet day so an O'Meara cow had ambled out on to the road where a car ran over it, and the poisoning of milk.

'Not that he had to do that at all. Only to tell Marie-Rose. She'd put the *mi-adh* on the cows.'

The idea of Marie-Rose putting a curse on an animal matched my own perception of what she was like.

'That lot would kill you for the land. Land, or the money they'd get from it.'

It was frightening to think how close Mrs O'Meara might be to the truth.

'Marie-Rose would go that far?'

'Yerra, she might, though I'm not saying she did, and between the jigs and the reels, she'd get away with it, too. But you know that yourself.'

'I don't know anything. Not even— Mrs O'Meara, you're the one who knows so much. Can you tell me who Clemency Conroy was?'

I'd caught her by surprise, so much so that she lost her tongue. But not for long.

'Clemency, is it? Why would *you* be asking me that? 'Twouldn't be a subject I could discuss, not with the way that everything went. 'Twouldn't be fitting, in my opinion. Though there are others that wouldn't agree. Not that I would waste my breath on the likes of them.'

'But Mrs O'Meara—'

'What's wrong with them at all, at all, to be going on about it? The madam in Mountshannon is another matter. You could pass judgement on *her* all right. The Four Courts would agree with you, it's as clear as ice that's washed.'

Clear? I might have stumbled off a bog road on a misty night, so confused was I by her. I groped for direction, and seized on Norah.

'Do you know what became of her?'

'I do and I don't,' said Mrs O'Meara. 'She's not dead, for sure, though by now she may be near it. I think they put her away. You tell *me* something now, if you can. Did Guard O'Hagan get into his house?'

'I don't know. I don't know Guard O'Hagan either. What's the problem with his house?'

'With the goat in the garden, how could he get in?'

Light dawned. 'Guard O'Hagan. He lives over by the harbour and he has a boat for sale?'

'He does and he has. They've been stopping in his cousin's house. But maybe the goat is out of it now.'

'I don't know,' I said again. 'Mrs O'Meara, about Norah. What do you mean, they put her away?'

'Goats are that scatty. There was one that got into the church at Portumna more than twenty years ago, and didn't he fetch up half inside a confessional box?'

I couldn't but laugh. I was dying to ask what happened next and had to put a brake on myself. It was all too easy to follow Mrs O'Meara into a conversational blind alley rather than manoeuvre her on to a straight road. I reversed sharply and returned to Clemency.

'Mrs O'Meara, before you tell me about that, let's get back to Clemency Conroy. You said "not with the way that everything went". Won't you tell me what you meant?'

'I said that, did I? Do you know, I don't recall it. I'm not as young as I was, you know. When you're getting on, you remember well them things that happened when you were a child, and what you said ten minutes ago you don't recollect at all. Autisia, I think they call it. Mind you, with all that's going on in the world – the wars and the bombs and those poor black children swelled up with the hunger – a short memory could be an advantage as well as being a drawback, though Michael mightn't agree with me . . .'

In a country where giving a straight answer is generally regarded as a failure of imagination, Mrs O'Meara had raised evasion to the level of an art form. But why was she dodging the questions I asked? Pretending to be so forgetful when it seemed to me that she had a memory like a data bank?

Under the circumstances, it was a wonder that I remembered to pass on the message for Michael. Afterwards, curiosity got the better of me and I went along to Dromaan harbour to see what the goat was doing.

Others were curious too. The road by the harbour was jammed with cars. Bob was there, talking to a tall, grey-haired man and a

111

middle-aged woman in a floral dress. The man was clutching his head with one hand and gesticulating with the other.

I pulled up next to them and put down the window.

'Hi.'

'Hello, Caroline,' said Bob.

The grey-haired man said, 'What if he gets into the house?'

'What's going on?' I said to Bob.

'The goat brought down that long front window. No, don't get out of your car just yet. We don't want him charging you.'

'How come that he broke the window?'

'Saw himself reflected in it. Thought it was another goat. We tried to get him out of there but he went for us instead.'

'So what can be done about him?'

Bob grimaced. 'Somebody is going to shoot him.'

'That's horrible.'

'He'll wreck the house if he gets in. And he's dangerous as well. Look, Naoise Nolan's coming now.'

A young man was approaching – a handsome, dark-haired young man with a rifle in his hand.

'He's a brilliant shot,' said Bob.

'I'm not staying to watch this happen.'

'Don't.' He added as an afterthought, 'Are you going to Carrigrua?'

'Yes.'

I left, turning the radio up to full volume so I wouldn't hear the shot. Life in the country, I said to myself.

'It had to be done,' Bob said later that day when he and Guard O'Hagan joined me at Carrigrua. 'And Naoise didn't mess about. Even you'll admit that, Poirig.'

Guard O'Hagan's hand flew up to clutch his head again. 'I wasn't pleased to have *him* in it.'

'Best shot in the rifle club.'

'I know we had to use the rifle. A shotgun would have been too drastic and blasted goat all over the place. But, even so, I didn't like it. That fellow is sadistic, Bob. I'm still convinced he got that swan. He wouldn't have done it before I retired.'

'Maybe you're right.'

'I know I am. Mrs Tremain, I hear you've interest in my boat.'

I caught Bob's eye. 'I have. Depending on the asking price.'

The price was right. I bought the boat. We shook hands on the deal and Guard O'Hagan promised to teach me how to handle it.

112

'Fancy celebrating?' Bob suggested as Guard O'Hagan got into his car. 'Dinner? Tomorrow night?'

'If we don't discuss the goat!'

I had something more important on my agenda. As I saw the two men off I was thinking, good, Bob on his own at last. I'll quiz him about Clemency.

Thirteen

The Caroline who'd lived with Leonard was summoned to go out with Bob. I washed her hair, did her make-up, selected clothes and footwear for her. Her sandals were Manolo Blahnik's. He was into flowers that year and the ones I'd acquired had a narrow stem-like strap linked to a velvet rose. The dress I'd bought in Covent Garden in a vintage reject shop. It was only cotton velvet, but the colours, muted oranges and browns, were harmonious and rich. As a dress it was indecent, reaching just below the crotch, but it made a brilliant top which went well with mocha pants. Caroline the Clown was back.

The other Caroline was nervous. It was ages – years and years – since I'd been taken out for dinner by a man who wasn't Leonard. I reminded myself that it wasn't a date – not for me, at any rate. It was An Investigation. Inside, I remained strung up.

Bob, by contrast, was relaxed in his cords and yellow shirt. He'd lost a button from a cuff and made do with a safety pin, but he was tidy otherwise.

'I want to hear about the house,' he said as soon as we were in the car.

'We're starting work on it this week.'

'I hear you're using Mick O'Meara.'

Sensing my surprise, he added, 'I met his mother in the village. She told me that you'd been to see her.'

'She told *me* about the feud.'

'The feud?'

'Between her family and the Keanes.' I was fishing, I must admit. I wanted Bob to tell me more about the wicked, scheming Keanes, particularly Marie-Rose.

But he only grinned and said, 'She's hopping mad with old man Keane. Talk about the Unforgiving . . . About the house. How long is it going to take? When will you be moving in?'

Thwarted about Marie-Rose, I chattered on about the house until we reached the Lantern. The restaurant, perched upon a slope, looked down on a still, seraphic lake and across the water to the blue-tinged Arra Mountains. There were white lace cloths on all the tables and people talking German at them.

'The Germans love it here,' said Bob. 'The weather never puts them off.'

I was waiting for the appropriate moment to mention Clemency's name. But when our orders had been taken, Bob apologised to me. 'I'm sorry I've been so switched off. I was still resolving something.'

'What was that?'

'Just a state that I get into when a book has been completed. Limbo.'

There'd been a place that I called Limbo when I was a little girl. Its real name was Derrainy. It was a tiny triangle that lay between three parishes. It did not belong to any of them and it had Celtic origins. Nowhere Land. A children's graveyard. A resting place for babies that were not baptised. Olive hated driving past it. Funny how these things came back.

Bob told me about his Limbo. 'When you're certain that you've boobed and the book is a disaster. Sorry. This is very boring.'

'No, it's not.' Not boring, but unfamiliar, in my experience of men. Leonard never talked like that. He never said that he might fail. Perhaps he never feared he would. 'It's not in the least bit boring. So, tell me about Limbo.'

'Believe me,' said Bob, 'it's excruciating. But Heaven usually precedes it.'

Laughing at himself. Inviting me to join the mirth. As a matter of course, I fell in with his mood, as I always did with Leonard's.

'Tell me about Heaven then.'

'Heaven's when you stumble on it. The Idea. The Perfect Plot. A foetus for a masterpiece. But then I become conceited. I think, this one's going to win the Booker. Faulkner, move aside for me. Do you like this German wine? I'm afraid it's on the sweet side.'

'It's fine. So when do you move out of Heaven?'

'My agent boots me out,' said Bob. His agent's name was Sally Sears. 'An angel out of Hell,' he said. 'I don't know where I'd be without her.'

He spoke of her and of his work. He was self-deprecating, natural and unaffected. Quite the opposite of Leonard. Not godlike, either, but attractive.

'Anyway, enough of me and my neurosis,' he said as the waitress brought our orders – Dover sole with mashed potatoes. 'Tell me,

116

what's it like for you, being back at Carrigrua?'

'I'm picking up the threads,' I said. 'Starting off when I was eight.' Or maybe further back than that? I thought again of Clemency.

'It couldn't have been easy for you, growing up in Carrigrua.'

'I was happy there,' I said. 'I had Olive, after all. Of course, she was intimidating, but . . .' My turn to be the Entertainer. I did my imitations for him. I tried my best to make him laugh.

But he didn't laugh, or smile. He said, sympathetically, 'Was it better with your father?'

'Better?'

'Less lonely? All kids need their mothers, though. Francesca is still missing Helen. You've no memory of your mother?'

'No,' said Caroline the Clown. She was puzzled, lost for words. Bob's reaction to her act hadn't been what she expected.

'Either way, it's foul for kids. Were you possessive of your father?'

'I didn't have much feeling for him.'

'That's sad.'

No matter what I said, Bob seemed to be sorry for me. Where was Caroline the Clown to help me cope with his compassion?

Before I could find her he spoke again.

'Francesca has the opposite problem. She cares too much. And she's possessive. I get exasperated sometimes. Bad of me. Worse, because I've been through something similar and I understand her feelings.'

'*Your* mother died when you were young?'

'No. But in a sense I lost her then.'

'What happened?'

'She – cracked up. Became withdrawn. Incommunicado. An early menopause, I suppose.'

'Didn't she recover from it?'

'No,' said Bob. 'She never did.' He returned to the subject of my childhood. He asked at least a dozen questions. When I tried a flip reply, I didn't get away with it. 'No, tell me truthfully,' he'd say. Or, 'What did you really feel about it?'

Caroline the Clown was baffled. It was all too real for her. Halfway through my Dover sole, I realised she'd deserted me.

Bob continued drawing me out, asking why I'd cared for Olive. 'You don't make her sound endearing.'

'Not endearing, but so strong. An anchor. Well, I guess you can imagine.'

'Yes,' said Bob. 'I think I can.'

'Life wasn't all that easy for her. She was brought up by her cousins.

117

And she was young when she got married.'

'That doesn't sound so hard to me.'

'Her marriage wasn't all that happy.' Hadn't I heard that from Norah? Or was it from someone else? 'I think he used to hit the bottle. He was always up in Dublin. And she was down here on her own, with the girls – my mother and my aunt, I mean. So she was lonely, I suppose, and maybe she became in-turned.'

'Interesting,' said Bob thoughtfully. 'So that was life at Carrigrua. You must have been devastated when you left that – secure background.'

Was that a note of irony? Was he making fun of me? The look he gave me wasn't mean, but . . .

'I was,' I said. 'I hated it.' Without the other Caroline, I felt naked and exposed. I barely recognised myself. Who *was* this person who was talking? Clemency, I thought. Think of Clemency. She's the one who counts, not you.

At the pudding stage, I got the chance to mention her.

'Bob,' I said, 'there's something I want to ask you. Do you know who Clemency Conroy was?'

'*Clemency* Conroy?' echoed Bob.

'Yes. I've just come across her name. She was – related to me.'

'Clemency,' said Bob again.

'Does she mean anything to you?'

'How come you heard of her?'

Without describing its condition, I told him about the room, and that I'd found a bangle in it.

'That's astonishing,' said Bob.

'Her name was inscribed on it.'

'Hm.'

'I'm desperate to know who she was.'

'That's – understandable,' said Bob.

We weren't getting anywhere. All the same, I tried again. 'You can't throw any light on her?'

'No. I'm sorry. But I can't.'

Stalemate. As if to underline the fact that the subject was exhausted, Bob cross-examined me again about my life when I left Ireland.

'So you went to art school, did you? You turned down a two-man show? *Why?* You obviously had the talent.'

I edged away from that. It wasn't something I liked to discuss. I moved the conversation on to the work I hoped to do.

'Have you brought any paintings with you?'

118

'A few. I've done some sketches since I've been here.'

'Can I have a look at them?'

'If you like. They're nothing special. Faces that were interesting. Oh, and one of Carrigrua.'

That gave Bob the excuse to come into the house when he took me home. The minute he walked through the door, I realised how exposed I felt. Where was Caroline the Clown who might have protected me? The image of a threatening Bob returned to tantalise and torment. Why did I feel we'd met before? Why should I be nervous of him?

The dogs were all over me, adding to my agitation.

'Stop slobbering,' I said to them as I put on the coffee pot.

'Where are all those sketches then?'

I produced some flower paintings.

'You must do well from these,' said Bob, not saying they appealed to him.

'And there are these other sketches. This one's—'

'Mick O'Meara's mother. It's brilliant, Caroline. I love it. Can I buy it from you?'

'No. Just have it as a present.' I tore the sketch from the pad. 'There you are.'

'Thanks.' He laughed delightedly. 'It's marvellous. It's really her. Come on. Let me see the rest. Where's the one of Carrigrua?'

'Here.'

This time round, he didn't comment. He just stared at the sketch. He didn't look very happy with it.'

'I told you it was nothing special.'

'How come you drew *that* boat?'

'That boat?'

'Yes. That particular boat. You've made a very detailed drawing.'

I looked at the sketch again. I *had* made a feature of the boat – its squat shape, snub nose, open aft cockpit and foldaway hood.

'What made you include those features?'

'I don't know. I suppose it – the boat – was somewhere in my memory.'

Bob was looking troubled. I wondered what was on his mind. Whatever it was, it made him persist.

'Did you see that boat in England?'

'No. I must have seen it here. On the lake. That day when you took me out.'

'I doubt if it was then,' said Bob. 'You see, that's a Freeman 22. You seldom see them on this lake.'

119

'How peculiar, but I can't explain.'

Bob shook his head and lapsed into puzzled silence. I was perplexed myself. In an effort to cope with my confusion, I did what I had done before. I focused in on Clemency. That led me on to someone else.

'Bob,' I said, 'has Guard O'Hagan lived here long?'

Bob came back from wherever he'd been. 'Only all his life,' he said.

All his life. In which case he should have heard of Clemency. We'd be spending time together when I bought the boat from him. Another opportunity.

Bob was finishing his coffee. He gulped down the last few dregs and said, reluctantly, 'I suppose I should be off.'

'Thanks for dinner. I enjoyed it.'

'Let's eat on the boat next time.'

I muttered that it would be nice. Other things were left unsaid. Bob did not attempt to touch me. He didn't even kiss my cheek.

He said, 'That's good. I'll phone. I promise,' but he'd gone away again before he even left the house.

That's all right by me, I thought. Bed was not on the agenda. This was an investigation.

All the same. I felt rejected. And when he'd gone, I cursed myself. I thought, he could have helped me with that case. I'll have to put it back myself.

In the wake of his departure, I went up to tackle it. Stuffed with books, it was too heavy. I put it up without the books and tried to add them afterwards. That was a fiasco too. There wasn't room to lift the lid.

By then it was almost 2 a.m. and I'd had enough. I left the books strewn on the floor and closed the door on the upheaval.

Back in my own room, I removed the Clown's make-up and peered at the face behind it. Who *was* that woman in the mirror? What was she to do with me?

Until that evening, I'd known exactly who I was. I'd never harboured any doubts. I was Caroline the Clown. Caroline the Entertainer. I'd been her since I was young. Since I was a little girl, when she'd irritated Olive by overdoing the histrionics.

True, that Caroline had been half dead since the Sue and Leonard farce. But I'd known she still existed. Only a matter of hours ago, I'd brought her back to life again. Now it seemed she'd gone for ever. In her place there was a stranger.

Bob's doing. He'd seen off the Entertainer and conjured up this other woman. Someone I didn't know and wasn't sure that I would like. Who knew what she might do? I thought of what I'd done myself after finding Sue with Leonard. I thought of the wreckage in Clemency's room.

Who was Clemency? Why did I have this strange conviction that her identity and mine were as interwoven as the lace on the tables in The Lantern restaurant?

Clemency . . .

Bob had been no use at all in helping me to pinpoint her. But maybe Guard O'Hagan could. We were due to meet that week, the day before the builders came to start work at Carrigrua. The minute I got a chance, I'd ask him about Clemency.

Fourteen

The day I was due to take over the boat, temperatures soared up into the eighties. In the first week of July it was hotter in Clare than it was in the south of Spain. When I woke, the lake was sleeping, wrapped in a bedspread of the same cornflower blue as the cloudless sky. In the Keane kitchen, bees had got into the marmalade jar.

Later that drowsy morning, I listened to the low hum of heat as I sat waiting by the harbour. The land had turned into a purring green cat. The lake was a saucer of rich blue milk and the sun was a golden fire, inducing slumber in the land. But the change from the moderate to the Mediterranean had been almost too abrupt. The heat was using a gaudy palette to paint over a masterpiece. I was still undecided about the effect, trying to get used to the florid tones, when a family of swans swam up to the harbour. As I watched, a wily cygnet hitched a lift. As the family sailed past, it was perched on its mother's back and I was enchanted all over again.

Soon, the picture was retouched, and the outline of a vessel and a lone figure sketched into it. The figure raised a hand in greeting. I stood up and waved at it.

The swan family scattered. Guard O'Hagan pulled into the harbour and threw a rope for me to catch.

As I grabbed it, he made a suggestion. 'I've been thinking, Mrs Tremain. Would we go out to Holy Island? It's an interesting place.'

'I've been wanting to go there.'

I scrambled on board and we set off. It was no cooler on the water than it was upon the land. Guard O'Hagan was wearing an old Dalkeith khaki cap, the kind that Sherlock Holmes affected. The long flaps came down past his ears so he looked like a cocker spaniel. But he was wiser than I was. The sun beat cruelly on my head, stripping the colour from my streaks, turning them from blonde to orange.

Still, that was a small price to pay for the glorious view that I got of Carrigrua as we moved out from the harbour. The wood formed a natural shelter, curving round the lush land on which the house had been erected. It was a bejewelled setting. The diamond that was Carrigrua. The trees and reeds like emeralds. The lake and sky the bluest sapphires. I wished I'd brought my sketchpad with me.

'She's an easy enough craft to handle, as you can see,' said Guard O'Hagan, bringing my mind back to more practical matters. 'But you must tune in to the Munster Weather Line before you think of taking her out. And watch out for white tops on the waves. These lake boats weren't designed for rough weather, Mrs Tremain.'

'I'll only use it in the summer.'

'Winter or summer, Lough Derg is a treacherous place. Too many people have perished in it. You've heard of the clergyman's sons, I take it? Who lived over in the glebe house?'

'I don't think I heard about them.'

'A terrible story,' said Guard O'Hagan. 'A fine pair of lads, back down from the College of Surgeons. They had an arrangement to sail over to Garrykennedy to collect a friend. The mother told them not to go, that the lake was much too rough. But the father was conscientious. You made a promise. You should keep it. That was his philosophy. The lads took heed of what he said.'

'They were drowned?'

'Not only that. The very same moment their boat keeled over, didn't the maid call out to the mother to say she saw them alive and well, coming up the avenue. There's a memorial to the two of them in the Protestant church at Mountshannon. Mind you, that was long ago. But even in recent years we've had incidents you wouldn't believe. People won't listen. The tourists are worst. They come over here on their holidays and they think this lake is nothing more than a big pond in the middle of a field.'

He warned me about Parker's Point, where the turbulence caused by the confluence of the north–south and east–west winds whipped up into frequent squalls.

By then, we were almost past Hare Island. As islands go, it was minute, not more than forty feet long and less than that again in width. The few scraggy trees that had survived in the wind-blown terrain gave the island the appearance of a large shaving brush sticking up out of a massive bath. A dinghy was moored by the rocky shore. Two children were swimming in the lake, watched closely by their anxious parents.

When I was young I couldn't swim, Olive having vetoed bathing. A memory came back to me. A warm weekend when I was young. I'd had a friend, Cathleen, to stay. This was a rare treat. I didn't normally

124

have friends to stay, or play, at Carrigrua. But Olive said it was all right. Cathleen's father was a judge. And, unlike us, Cathleen's family spent their holidays in France. That made them sophisticated.

She was the instigator, the one who said, 'Let's put on our bathing costumes and lie over by the harbour. That way we can get a tan.'

'I don't have a bathing costume.'

'Wear your pants. It doesn't matter.'

I knew it did. I knew that we were doing wrong. I didn't want to tell Cathleen, who'd find it hard to understand the way things were at Carrigrua.

We'd just settled on our towels when Marie-Rose came rushing down.

'Mrs Conroy's raging mad. She's seen you out her bedroom window and she says you're very bold, lying around without your clothes on. Come back this minute to the house.'

Cathleen couldn't make it out. 'What makes her think that we're so bold?'

I tried to explain to her. 'She thinks that we're immodest. Girls should be – more covered up.'

'But we've got our pants on us.'

'That's not enough. A man might see us.'

Cathleen giggled. 'What man? There're only women in your house.'

'The parish priest might visit us.'

'He wouldn't think we're doing harm.'

'You'd stand no chance in a boat like this if the winds were to come up.'

That was Guard O'Hagan, not Cathleen.

'I know about the winds,' I said.

Norah told me all about them, in particular the terrifying and tragic tale of *Oiche na Gaoithe Moire*, the Night of the Big Wind, a cataclysmic tornado that struck Ireland in the last century on the night of Epiphany. The Big Wind caused many deaths, swept away tens of thousands of houses and trees, and convinced the population at large that the end of the world was surely at hand.

'It was the noise that was so awful,' Norah used to say to me. 'The wind howling and roaring. And the little children weeping.'

For me, as for those unhappy children, the Big Wind was a supernatural force. They who knew about such things insisted that the wind was red – the colour of the Otherworld.

'Did you hear that Germans have bought Illaunmore?'

Illaunmore was the biggest island on the lake, comprising 250 acres.

Every field once had a name. Norah used to recite them for me, reeling them off like decades of the rosary. The Fern Field. Hickey's. Gortnasillia. The Drill Field. Uncle Pat's.

'Is that so?'

'They've turned it into a shooting estate. That's where I'd say the goat swam from.'

'But that's *miles*. He must have been strong.'

I was waiting until we got to Holy Island before broaching the subject of Clemency. The rest of the way, Guard O'Hagan regaled me with local gossip. I learnt that Mrs Farrelly the teacher had won a prize in the Irish sweepstakes only to be done out of her money by a solicitor in Portumna. That Mary Bugler was giving private lessons in Irish at vastly inflated, deplorable prices. And that Michael O'Meara's second cousin was going to marry a widower against the wishes of her mother.

Then the high bell house for which Holy Island was famous came into view. Beside it were the ruined churches, a workman's hut, and a cell-like structure where Christian hermits used to worship.

''Tis nothing now but a home for cattle,' Guard O'Hagan said as we approached the shore. 'They swim them over from the mainland. But the looters have been here. Gravestones have been lifted out.'

'Who would do a thing like that?'

'There's a fellow I could name. But they haven't nailed him yet.'

'Who could that be, Guard O'Hagan?' I was pretty sure he'd tell me.

He did. 'Naoise Nolan. A fellow as crooked as the horns of two rams. And it's not even so much what he's done as what he's capable of doing. Watch the way I bring her in. The water's shallow and it's loaded here with rocks.'

A path of dried mud, indented by cattle hooves, led upwards from the tiny jetty. Skinny trees provided shade. Still talking, Guard O'Hagan walked ahead. I caught snippets of information.

'Stones over there – pagan origins. Maybe used for grinding herbs. The well – they say your sins will be forgiven if you see yourself in it.'

Eventually, he paused for breath, then suggested that we complete our deal by shaking hands through the centuries-old bargaining stone that lay before us in the long grass.

To me, the stone looked more like a clump of rocks than something of historical significance. But I crouched beside it, inserted my hand into the small aperture and our fingers met.

'Good luck to you,' said Guard O'Hagan. 'And don't forget, phone the Munster Weather Line.'

Now, I thought. Now. Here's my chance. Time to talk of Clemency.

'You've lived here all your life,' I said. 'I'm sure you knew my family. Did you know Clemency as well – Clemency Conroy?'

Guard O'Hagan didn't answer. Instead of saying yes or no, he got a nasty coughing fit. It went on and on, the flaps on his cap fluttering like two ineffectual distress signals.

'Will I bang your back for you?'

He shook his head and coughed again. There was nothing I could do. Eventually, the coughing stopped, but then he couldn't find his voice.

I waited, determined not to be put off. At last, Guard O'Hagan seemed like his old self and I tried again.

'Guard O'Hagan, as I was saying just now, does the name Clemency Conroy ring a bell with you?'

'The Conroys were a well-known family.'

'But *Clemency*,' I said, 'Clemency Conroy. Do you know where she fits in?'

'I never was asked to go into the house.'

Knowing Olive, that made sense.

'You never heard of Clemency?'

'I'm trying to remember now who was in that family. The father – what was his name again?'

'Lawrence.'

'Lawrence, yes. And the mother?'

'Olive Conroy.'

'I sometimes saw her at the church. Ah, yes . . . I'm just watching the time, Mrs Tremain. I'd say we should be heading home. I said I would be back by one.'

'I wouldn't want to make you late—'

'She's always punctual with the dinner.'

'—but there was one other thing. Marie-Rose Keane, Guard O'Hagan. Has she ever been in trouble?'

'In trouble? Her?'

'Yes. In trouble with the law,' I said. 'Or questioned, in connection with a crime.'

'She has not.'

He couldn't have sounded more definite. Investigation terminated.

I followed him as he walked tall through the high grass back to the muddy path where the cattle, after swimming from the mainland, had plodded past the grave slabs to the pastures by the bell house.

It was cooler going home. The sun sank slowly, as weary as the land it had savagely scorched. Swans coasted on the surface of the water, too worn out to search for dinner.

I dropped Guard O'Hagan off at Dromaan harbour.

'Thanks for the lesson.'

''Twas nothing,' he said.

Which more or less summed up what I knew about Clemency. Another dead end. It was much easier to clear the clutter from Carrigrua, I thought ruefully, than to solve the mystery that lay buried at the heart of the house.

Michael and his team arrived. There were only three of them but within minutes of their arrival I noticed that they had a knack of occupying every room.

Michael gave me a brief résumé of what they would be doing first. While he repaired the guttering and checked out the roof for leaks, Sean O'Higgins the plumber would install the heating system and Ger Kinead the artisan would begin to strip the walls.

After that, the Electricity Supply Board van pulled in and a red-haired man announced that he would be putting in a new fuse box so our power could be connected.

Then Naoise Nolan came.

'Mrs Egan sent me over,' he said. 'She says you want the garden cleared.'

Nothing threatening in that. And Naoise wasn't threatening either.

Or was he? There was something sly about him, I thought. Something mocking in those eyes. I felt that he was sneering at me. I wished I'd heeded Guard O'Hagan. 'It's not even so much what he's done as what he's capable of doing.'

I became brisk, authoritative. In fact, I behaved like Olive.

'I do,' I said. 'Are you ready to start work?'

Naoise Nolan dropped his eyes to the level of my thighs. 'I am.'

'In that case . . .' I hustled him towards the orchard, told him what he had to do and returned to find the other lads Alice Egan had recruited, Chris Malone and Bernie Fahy, waiting in the yard for me. I told them to clear out the paddocks and sat down with a pile of brochures to consider kitchen units.

Michael interrupted me. 'You're here all this time,' he said. Not wild about my presence, obviously.

'I will be in and out, you know.'

'I suppose you have to be.' He sighed, and added, 'Did you see those other brochures?'

128

'Are there other kitchen brochures?'

'The bathroom brochures,' Michael said. 'The brochures for the other bathroom.'

'I don't want a second bathroom.'

Michael looked aggrieved. 'He said you would be needing one.'

'John O'Donnell told you that? He's wrong. I meant to have it out with him. Anyway, it wouldn't do, to have a bathroom where he wants one. Over the drawing room. Suppose I overflowed the bath?'

'You wouldn't do a thing like that.'

'I might. The point is, I don't want a second bathroom.'

'I'd say you might regret it yet.'

'I promise you I won't,' I said.

Perhaps he didn't tell the others. Later, when I went upstairs, I heard a noise in Clemency's room. Water was being slopped around.

Inside the room, Ger, instead of stripping walls, was tipping water from one bucket into another and then reversing the procedure.

'Why are you doing that?' I said.

Ger jumped, splashing water on the floor. 'Himself said that I should do it.'

'Why?'

Ger blushed. He said in a muffled voice, 'Maybe you should talk to Sean.'

'Where's Sean?' I said, exasperated.

'Downstairs. Underneath this room.'

Sean was in the drawing room.

'What's going on up there with Ger?'

Sean was visibly embarrassed. 'We're, like, testing for the sound of water.'

'*Why?*'

Sean swallowed. I thought he'd never get the words out. 'For when you put the toilet in,' he said eventually. 'We thought that might be troubling you . . . The noise from when you're using it. Maybe that's what's stopping you from putting in the bathroom.'

'I see.'

'You can't hear anything from here.'

'Sean,' I said, 'that's not what bothers me at all. I just don't want a second bathroom.'

'He says you're bound to change your mind. I couldn't hear a sound myself, but we can insulate the floor.'

Honestly.

'Now look, Sean,' I said, 'get this into everyone's head. I don't want a second bathroom. I'll *never* change my mind about it.' Why did no one listen to me?

The house cried out for furniture. I wasn't sure what I could afford – what the prices might be like – but, next day, I went to Ennis on a shopping spree.

On the outskirts of the town, I came across an antiques shop. In the window was a fly leaf table and what looked like a rack for boots.

Inside the shop, a dark-haired woman with a scarlet bandeau round her head was sitting by a library table, nibbling a Toblerone and reading *The Clare Champion*. She raised her head when I walked in and looked at me inquiringly.

'Do you need assistance or would you prefer to browse?'

'About the table in the window—'

'That's a hunt or wake table. The perfect shape for holding coffins. It goes flat against the wall. And that's a rack for riding boots. They hung them upside down, you see.'

'And this table? The one you're sitting at, I mean.'

'Was used by landlords long ago. The leather top spins round, like this. And you have these little drawers for storing tenants' documents.'

That was when I saw the bed. It was a four-poster with a shaped tester on the top, designed to hold a canopy. The posts were carved with ears of wheat. It was beautiful, superbly carved. And, what's more, it spoke to me. 'Buy me,' it said. 'I belong at Carrigrua.'

I was done for. I knew that, even if it made me bankrupt, I just had to have that bed.

'Do you like it?' said the woman. 'It's a marriage bed. The wheat symbolises fertility. It's early Irish Georgian. That's why the mahogany looks so light. The red kind is Victorian.'

Her phone rang.

'Stay there,' she said. 'I won't be long.'

I kept staring at the bed. It was bound to be expensive. But it was so beautiful. I wondered what its history was. For all I knew, it might have been made especially for Carrigrua. Perhaps the Grey Lady or at any rate her parents had slept beneath the canopy.

Forget the tables, I said to myself. I'll just settle for the bed.

'The Georgian sideboard?' said the dark-haired woman into the telephone. 'The bow-fronted one with partitions for bottles?' She put her hand over the receiver and hissed at me, 'Sit down there and read the paper. I'll be with you in a minute.'

'Thanks.'

I sat on a Georgian dining chair with a ruby-red leather seat, perfectly shaped to fit the backside. The phone call went on in the background.

'. . . lined with zinc. To keep the food inside it fresh . . .'

My mind was really on the bed, much more so than on the paper. I vaguely registered the headlines.

'Fresh Talks to Resolve Health. Deepening Row Between Health Board and Irish Nurses Organisation.'

'West Clare Drama Festival Begins.'

'Clare Association of Chicago Holds Its AGM.'

'Tragic Death of Ennis Schoolgirl.'

And then it came to me. Of course, I thought. That's where I should be looking. In the paper. In back copies. If Clemency died a tragic death, there would have been a press report. Even a natural death would have merited a mention because her second name was Conroy.

'. . . weren't too house-proud in those days. Didn't trouble about dust . . .'

I thought, the paper's printed here in Ennis. They'll have back copies in the office.

'Sorry about that,' said the woman, putting the receiver down. 'So, do you want to buy that bed? I have the steps to it as well.'

'I do.' Mad. I hadn't asked how much it cost.

'Would you like to see the steps?'

I saw the steps. I bought them, and the bed as well, trying not to think of the money I spent.

'We'll deliver them to you. What's your address?' said the dark-haired woman.

She mentioned when they would arrive. But now I'd bought the bed and steps, my mind was back with Clemency.

Before I left the shop I checked where the offices of *The Clare Champion* were located. They were in Barrack Street.

The old town, with its thirteenth-century friary and narrow streets, was the gateway for travellers to the majestic Cliffs of Moher and the fertile lilac rocks of the Burren. The tourists were in town that day. Ennis looked like London's Oxford Street and I wasted precious time searching for a parking space. In desperation, I sneaked the car into the Old Ground Hotel car park and walked past the T-plan procathedral into Old Barrack Street.

The offices of *The Clare Champion* were abuzz with activity. Both receptionists were busy. I waited, filling in time by flicking through the

131

pages of the current edition, reading country correspondents' reports, details of farm produce and cattle prices, comments on the environment, the Gaelic football results, and news of the fines imposed on late-night drinkers 'found on' licensed premises by the vigilant Guards. I'd got to the wedding pictures when one of the receptionists freed herself and asked if she could be of help.

'Yes, please. I'd like to read through your back copies.'

'How far back?'

'More than thirty years,' I told her.

She shook her head. 'I'm sorry but we're putting those editions on to microfilm at the moment and that department isn't open.'

'I don't believe it!'

'Have you come far to see those copies?'

'Far enough.' Which was true. Indeed I had.

'You could try the Study Centre. They keep back copies there as well.' She gave directions. 'Up O'Connell Street to the square. On to the Queen's Hotel. Go over the bridge at the Franciscan abbey. That brings you into Harmony Street. The library's on the left-hand side. The Study Centre's after that.'

The Study Centre proved to be a peaceful haven. A long red table ran down the middle of the reading room. Hanging on the walls were photographs of the instigators of the 1916 Easter Rising, including one of an unusually jovial Eamonn de Valera when he was President of Ireland, along with Mrs de Valera.

The back copies of *The Clare Champion*, inside smart black leather covers, were laid out on adjacent shelves. Until then I'd not been anxious, only keen to see those copies. But now, for no obvious reason, I felt curiously guilty. I started reasoning with myself, justifying what I was doing. 'I'm only going to check the papers. Is there something wrong with that?'

The guilt stayed obstinately with me, a mean, incessant, throbbing guilt. My heart was pounding and my lips were dry. But I picked up one of the black files and carried it over to the table.

Clemency, I thought. Concentrate on Clemency. I started to go through the file.

'Dangerous Game of Tip-and-Run.'

'Bunratty Castle to be a Showpiece.'

'Ireland's Second Biggest Grotto.'

Nothing about Clemency. Not in that file, anyway.

I replaced it on the shelf and took down another one. The headlines varied in their content. Some were sad and some were funny. One said,

'Complained to Guard and Summoned. A man who, after a drink too many in a Kilkee public house, could not find his ass to go home called to the Garda station.' But there were no stories, not even so much as a paragraph, about anyone called Conroy.

That day I became an expert on the county as it was when I was young. I could have told you what the teachers were demanding, how Saint Patrick's Day was spent, how many break-ins were recorded and who lost their driving licence.

But nothing about Clemency.

January. February. I was back again in March. March the 5th. March the 12th. March the 19th.

Something wrong with this edition. It was missing its front page. Somebody had torn it out, leaving just a jagged edge, on which something had been written.

Black ink. Familiar writing. A single letter. 'S.'

'S' for 'Slut'.

'S' for 'Spell' and 'S' for 'Spite'.

God Almighty, I said to myself. *She's* been here. She's thwarted me.

'Excuse me?'

A young man had appeared at my side.

'Yes?'

'We're just about to close the centre.'

'Of course. I didn't realise it was so late.'

I left. I walked back along Harmony Street and over the bridge, moving zombie-like amongst people leaving work, carried along more by the momentum of their energy than by my own.

I thought, despairingly, I've been defeated. All I've found is further evidence of malice and madness. Otherwise, the trail is dead.

I was almost in Mountshannon before I recovered enough to work out that the Study Centre wasn't the only place in the British Isles where I could find back copies of *The Clare Champion*. The British Newspaper Library would carry those editions too, and what's more they'd be intact, for surely Marie-Rose (I had no doubt she was the villain) would not have gone across to London to tear out pages from a newspaper.

I couldn't wait to phone the library. When I did, my call was answered by a woman's voice.

'Thank you for calling the British Library. This automated service accepts numbers from your keypad if you are using a touch-tone phone. If you know the extension you require, key that number now.'

133

'Just a moment,' said another voice.

Finally, the newspaper library came on the line and I told it what I wanted.

'Write in with your request.'

'*Write in?* But that's going to take an age. Can't you look it up for me?'

'I'm sorry. Those are the library rules. We see if we can help you first. If we can, we ask for money.'

It was irrational to be incensed. The library wasn't at my beck and call. All the same, I fumed and raged. I was running out of patience. If only somebody could help me. Someone over there. Someone who was close to me.

That was when I thought of Leonard.

I hadn't been in touch with him since we'd said goodbye in England. I didn't want to think about him but, naturally, I often did. The way he saw it, we were friends. I didn't share this view of us. Friends don't cringe with pain in each other's company. I'd dressed the wounds that he'd inflicted but they hadn't healed. To think of getting Leonard's help was like lifting lint too soon.

But Leonard was in England. Less than thirty miles from London. And, as I knew to my ultimate cost, he was a fast mover. Once his attention had been caught, his imagination sparked, he acted like a flash of fire. Handled properly, Leonard would go to the library. Or get someone else to do so. It only meant a call from me.

No, I thought. I don't want to talk to Leonard. Haven't I had enough pain?

But then I thought of Clemency who had suffered more than I had. Loving, laughing Clemency, whose blood had stained the windowsill. It's only a phone call, I said to myself. For Clemency it isn't much.

Actually, it was a lot, but I got Leonard on the line.

'Darling!' he said, as if there was nothing wrong. 'Are you phoning me from Ireland?'

'Yes, from Marie-Rose's house. Would you do a favour for me?'

Leonard was too much of a businessman to agree to anything without checking on the facts.

'What is it that you want?' he said.

Without going into detail, I told him what I needed.

Leonard demurred. 'The British Newspaper Library's in Colindale. Right at the end of the Northern Line.'

'I know. But I need that information. In fact, I need it desperately.'

The 'desperately' got to him. He was intrigued, as I knew he would be.

I wound him up a little more. 'If I don't get that information, I could be at risk.'

'At *risk*? What are you talking about, Caro?'

'I can't tell you on the phone. It just means a lot to me.'

'All right,' Leonard said. 'I'll see to it within the week. What's your number over there?'

After that, I inspected my wounds and found that they were raw and sore. I was still a convalescent. As a curative, I poured myself a gin and tonic. It didn't work. I ached all over.

Knowing that I wouldn't sleep, I went outside and pottered around. The sky was a black velvet cloth on which the stars had been embossed. The moon was shining like the sun. It lit the garden like a spotlight.

In the hope of tiring myself, I walked to Mountshannon village and down to the shore, away from the harbour. The lake wasn't in the least bit red. The moon had gilded it and turned Holy Island gold. The bell house was a neon phallus, erect amongst the pious ruins.

I huddled under a tree, wondering about the newspaper cutting. When would Leonard send it over? When I got it, would I know any more of Clemency or would I still be in the dark?

It was so bright, I could see the beetles crawling in the grass. So quiet, I could hear the water lapping. To many of the local people, Lough Derg was not the lake but 'the river' – the River Shannon, named for the Lady Sinann, grand-daughter of the sea king Lir, she who had defied the law debarring women seeking knowledge.

I was a seeker too, I thought, the knowledge that I sought cut off by a dam inside my head. But maybe tonight, here in this peaceful place, that knowledge would come flooding back.

I stayed there in the hope it would. I thought about the Lady Sinann. She had met a tragic death, engulfed in Saint Connla's Well, as punishment for being so daring.

Clemency, what happened to you?

The night did not provide the answer. The sun was up when I got back and then, of course, I fell asleep and only woke again at lunchtime.

The dogs were dying for their food. I fed them first, then made a sandwich for myself.

Suddenly, the dogs gave tongue. They rushed towards the kitchen door.

The door opened. Alarmed, I backed away towards the hall. I thought it might be Naoise Nolan, that Guard O'Hagan had been right. Perhaps he had a gun with him.

But it wasn't Naoise Nolan. It was someone much more frightening. 'Marie-Rose!' I said, aghast.

Fifteen

Fondling the ecstatic dogs, she said, 'You didn't get my letter then? When you didn't meet my plane I told myself it never reached you. The post is terrible these days, especially from America. How are you, Caroline?'

I must have muttered some reply. She went on in a chatty way, as if she was a normal person.

'I'm not too bad myself at all. Just jaded from the flight I had. It's good to be at home again. I missed it here when I was gone.'

I tried to control myself, to speak in a voice as calm as hers. 'Was that what brought you back, being homesick over there?'

'Of course. What else? It's not as good as being in Clare, being in New York, I mean.'

'No,' I said. 'It isn't, is it?'

'My feet are swelled like two balloons. It's jet lag, Caroline, that's caused it. I don't think I'll fly again.'

'I don't like it much myself.' How normal did I sound? Could she sense my terror of her? I watched her discreetly, wondering how mad she was. Scared of what she might do next.

'I'll make myself a cup of tea. Do you fancy one?'

'No, thanks. Really. I'm not thirsty.' How unpredictable could she be? I was prepared for anything.

She filled her cup and, easing shoes from swollen feet, took her place beside the table.

'Are you sure you don't want some? Just to keep me company?'

Silently, I shook my head.

She gulped her tea, smacked her lips in satisfaction and said, in the same seemingly sane way, 'It was as well that my letter didn't come. Our flight was dead late taking off, and two hours late into Shannon. You'd only have been waiting for me. Though I suppose being travelled, you'd have thought of checking first.'

'I might have thought of that,' I said, thinking, had I known that she

137

was coming, I'd have fled in panic from her.

Marie-Rose finished her tea. 'I'm that jaded, Caroline. I never slept upon the plane.'

'Maybe you should put your feet up.' Anything to put distance between us.

'What time is it?' She checked her watch. 'A queer old hour to be going to bed.'

'Even so.'

'You're right. If I don't get on to the bed for a while I'll only pass out at the table.' She got up decisively. 'You wouldn't think that I am rude?'

'Not in the least,' I said, relieved to be getting rid of her.

'We'll have a chat tonight,' she said. 'I'll tell you all about my trip.'

She was nearly through the door when I thought, oh, Jesus Christ, those bloody books! They're still piled up there, in her bedroom. When she finds them she'll go mad. Madder than she is already.

'Wait there a minute!' I said to her, no doubt sounding mad myself.

Marie-Rose paused, looking surprised. 'But—'

'Hold on!'

She *was* weary, I suppose, and too tired to argue with me. At any rate, she sat down again at the table and I pelted up the stairs, wondering where to put the books. In my room? It was the only place. I couldn't hide them in her bedroom. I didn't have the time for that.

It took long enough, lugging them across the landing in three instalments, praying that she'd stay downstairs until the job had been completed.

A miracle, she didn't move! I came down, panting, red-faced, hot and bothered, to find her dozing at the table.

Not the best place for her, either. I wanted her asleep, in bed.

'Marie-Rose?'

'Hm?'

'Wake up.'

'Yes. I will. I am,' she said.

'You need to go and have a rest.'

She obeyed me like a child. Had she been another person, I'd have smiled to see how heavy-eyed she was as she tottered up the stairs. But she was Marie-Rose and I thought she was a witch.

I heard her bedroom door shut and afterwards there was a silence. Had she really gone to sleep or was she wide awake in there? Did she realise by now that I'd been inside her room? There might be indents on the carpet where I'd left the books piled up. I might have left a book behind. Suppose she checked beneath the bed. Was the anger mounting in her? She was a strong woman. A crazy woman. Mad people were supposed to be strong. Yes, she might do anything.

I must get out of here, I thought. But all my goods were in the house. I couldn't just abandon them.

I waited, still as Lot's wife after she'd dared to look over her shoulder. The silence remained unbroken. When fifteen minutes had gone by without sign of Marie-Rose, I took off my shoes and tiptoed upstairs. On the landing I heard a reassuring sound. I very nearly laughed out loud. The witch was snoring in her sleep!

Sleeping! Snoring! But slumber doesn't defuse anger. Inside my room I put a chair against the door, in case Marie-Rose woke up and came to see what I was doing. I packed frantically, hurling garments into cases, lumping shoes and shirts together, and make-up with my underwear.

On edge, terrified of treading on a loose board or making any other noise, I humped the cases down the stairs. I carried out the boxes last and loaded up the car again.

Then I thought of all those books that I'd dumped inside my room. When Marie-Rose discovered them, as she would be bound to do, she'd know I'd found them in her bedroom. That would really get her going. She might come after me. That was all I needed. Marie-Rose at Carrigrua . . .

I crept upstairs and fetched the books. I scribbled a note to Marie-Rose, saying I felt I shouldn't intrude on her any more but rather move over to Carrigrua. Then, trembling and sweaty, I was off and out of the house.

I locked the car when I got in it just in case the witch appeared. But she didn't. I'd escaped, in spite of her.

I was off! Earlier than I had planned, I was going home. Moving into Carrigrua.

The last two years at Carrigrua, I was sent to boarding school. Now, I felt a child again, returning for the holidays, even if I wasn't wearing a navy-blue tunic and a long-sleeved shirt.

Those holidays – Constance would have come to fetch me. She'd have checked my hair was combed before she let me in the car and made sure my tie was straight lest Olive got annoyed with us. Along the way, we would have stopped, first at Sparlings' to buy sweets (Olive wouldn't let me eat them so that had to be a secret), then at Carroll's butchery for the mutton I detested.

On the steps, when I got home, Norah would be standing waiting. She'd have a hug for me, then I'd have to change for dinner, into a Viyella dress.

Dinner at Carrigrua was at eight o'clock precisely. This ritual, with its emphasis on gentility and decorum, astonished the other girls at school, who had their tea at six o'clock.

'You're not allowed to talk?' they marvelled.

'She doesn't like it if I do. Only if I'm asked a question.' Answers had to be concise. I did not exchange opinions.

'You poor thing!' my classmates said.

But I was *privileged*, I thought. After all, I was a Conroy, and Conroys were superior.

It was very different now. For one thing, the only table that remained was the pine one in the kitchen. And when I got to Carrigrua, Norah wasn't waiting for me.

But Michael was. He didn't smile, as Norah did.

'Mrs Tremain,' he said portentously. 'A bed has been delivered for you.'

'Has it? That was very quick.'

'A huge big ugly thing with poles.'

Ugly? My bed?

'I was out when it arrived,' said Michael peevishly. 'Otherwise I could have stopped them.'

'Stopped them doing what?' I said.

'Taking it inside the house. Getting in the way of building.'

I was eight years old again. In disgrace with the grown-ups.

'Where's the bed?' I dared to ask.

'In the little middle bedroom. Ger is busy in the big one.'

I'd planned to sleep in Olive's room. I'd bought the bed with that in mind.

'Never mind. I'll manage in there for the meantime.'

'*Manage?*'

'Yes,' I said. 'I'm moving in. Today. I'm going to live here from now on.'

'*Here?* You mean inside the house? While the work's being done on it?'

'Yes,' I said again.

I reminded myself that I wasn't a child. I was the owner of the house. I had the rights that went with it.

'I've no alternative,' I said. 'And anyway I want to be here.'

Michael sulked. He pursed his lips and glowered at me. He didn't help me with the boxes. I staggered in with them, telling myself that it was childish to allow his attitude to spoil this momentous day. But it did. Even my beautiful bed looked wrong, squashed inside that little room. Still, it was a lovely thing. I stroked the carving. Marvelled at it. I thought how right I'd been to buy it.

'That could well have woodworm in it.' Ger was peering round the door.

'There's no sign of woodworm, Ger.'

'They could be in there all the same. And there's something else as well. Come out here and look at it.'

The 'something else' was a small damp patch on the landing ceiling, over the doorway of Clemency's room.

'I don't like the cut of that.'

'I suppose it's just a leak.'

'Michael checked the roof for leaks. We've not had a drop of rain.'

'So?'

Ger scratched his head. ''Tis hard to know.'

I didn't want to know. I wanted the patch to go away as mysteriously as it had arrived. I wanted a hassle-free life, one in which small problems, like the patch, and big terrors, in the shape of Marie-Rose, didn't play an active role.

I went back to inspect the bed. The sun was streaming through the window. It wouldn't do the bed much good. I'd have to put some curtains up.

I dug my sewing basket out and found a box on which to stand in order to measure the window drop.

I thought, the last time I perched up here I couldn't reach as far as that. I used to hide behind the curtains. I'd sit here on the window ledge and kid myself that I was safe.

The lake was as blue as milkwort. Still as milk inside a jug. The only cloud that I could see was a little blob of cream.

Then everything I looked at changed. The lake was no longer blue but an angry blackish-brown. Its waves were tipped with alabaster. And the sky was different too. It looked like it did at night but without the moon and stars, fused with a rosy purple light, just the shade of bitter vetch. Out of that nigrescent sky, violet lightning swooped and streaked. And I could hear thunder, too, or thought I did, and howling wind.

There was a boat out on the lake. I could see it very clearly. It was the boat that I had drawn in my sketch of Carrigrua, snub-nosed with an open cockpit. 'A Freeman 22,' said Bob. The waves were lashing over it.

141

I thought, it can't be true. It can't. It can't . . .

Then my vision cleared, my ears unblocked and I was staring at the view as it was before the storm. Blue lake and the cloudless sky.

I climbed down from the window, more sober than I'd been before I watched the storm develop, and more in touch with memory. I sat in judgement on myself.

Earlier, when I'd seen pictures in my mind (the garden that was mostly red, the images of Clemency) I'd wondered what was wrong with me. Wondered if I was unhinged. But now I decided that these memories and visions were not indicative of madness. They were nudges from the past, reminders of my early childhood, which was linked to Clemency.

Remember her, they said to me. *You have an obligation to her.*

I understood. I accepted that and yet, in doing so, I felt guilty. But why guilt? I asked myself. What did *I* do to Clemency? Isn't Marie-Rose the villain? I'm just the investigator.

Despite the presence of the builders, I felt lonely in the house. Determined to do something useful, I braved the ladder to the loft, intending to sort out the things that Constance had abandoned there. But it was worse up in the loft. More isolated. Muckier.

In the end, I threw the clothes down to the landing, carried them into Clemency's room and began to sieve through them. Some of them I'd keep myself. Olive's footwear, for a start. And maybe that romantic hat would respond to being steamed. Much of it was only rubbish. Most of the clothes that Constance had owned were too tacky for Clare Care. I'd have to take them to the dump. But that meant bringing down the boxes and for that I'd need help – which I wouldn't get from Michael. And Ger seemed just as negative.

Thinking of Ger made me think about the patch that he'd discovered on the ceiling. Glancing up instinctively, I saw the wretched thing had grown. It was on this ceiling, too.

Braving his petulance, I got Michael up to see it.

'That leak looks serious,' I said.

'It's not damp. I'll tell you that.'

'What else could it be?'

Michael hesitated, divided between his need to put me in my place and reluctance to admit he didn't know what caused the patch.

'I'll look into it,' he said. 'When I get the time, that is.'

With that, he took himself downstairs again and I went to inspect the grounds, to see what the lads had done.

The yard was looking very good. They'd cleared all the weeds away and left the herbs to breathe again. The whole place smelt of lavender. I picked a bunch of lilac flowers and put it on my marriage bed.

The day wore on. The workmen left. The harbour called me down to it. From there, I scrutinised the house. Although it was so old, it was more alive than I was, and cooler in the summer heat. Its cloak of trees was old as well. The bark was silver-white and peeling. Growths – the ones that we called witches' brooms – were forming on each blackened base.

The witch I knew had gone from there. So I tried to tell myself. But I was frightened of Marie-Rose, frightened that she'd come that night. Break in and catch me on my own.

I locked the doors when I went in and closed the downstairs shutters too. But I couldn't shut her out. With a sinking heart, I knew I'd dream of her that night.

Those dreams . . .

At first, I only dreamt of Olive. She was doing her tapestry, a picture of a hunting scene. The hounds were panting, running towards me. I could hear them giving tongue. The huntsmen had their pink coats on. Why do we call them pink? I thought. Those coats are red. We all know that.

Red. So red they might be dyed in blood, and look, the Master's hands are bleeding.

The tapestry became a wheelchair. I was sitting in the chair. My legs were numb. I couldn't walk. I was wearing adult clothes but I knew that I was young.

Marie-Rose was in the room. In her hand was a knife. Blood was dripping from the blade. Her hands were drenched in blood as well.

Everything I saw was red. I tried to scream, to call for help. I couldn't scream. I couldn't talk. The power of speech was taken from me. Marie-Rose had seen to that.

I woke in a cold sweat and couldn't go to sleep again – a pattern that was to be repeated over and over again that week. I dreamt incessantly of Marie-Rose.

In one dream, she was a bloated blimp, floating high above my head before becoming a balloon, a giant pillow which was going to suffocate me. Another time I couldn't talk because I was a baby still, a toddler who could not explain that Marie-Rose had hidden a stick behind the clock in the dining room. When she was on her own with me, I knew that she would beat me with it. In a third nightmare, I was running away from her along the shore of the lake, into water turned to blood.

In the mornings I felt demeaned because my dreams were so absurd. And, in the nights, I heard a voice.

'*Get out . . . The cupboard . . . Clemency . . . The headless horse will come and get you . . .*'

I tossed and turned. I tried my best to calm my mind. It didn't take much notice of me.

My marriage bed was not a help because I was alone in it. In the middle of the night, I thought about the other women who had shared it with their lovers. Had the motif worked for them? It wouldn't ever work for me.

That week, the days were bad as well. Carrigrua was a mess. Upstairs, Ger was knee-deep in the paper he'd stripped off. In the basement it was worse, with Michael working in the kitchen and tools and debris everywhere.

Being at home, where I'd longed to be, was like living in a club with 'Men Only' on the door. Signals sent out by the builders discouraged me from lingering.

Three days went by, four – that is, since I'd talked to Leonard. 'Within the week,' he'd said to me. I willed him to get on with it, to courier the information.

On the fifth day there was still no news from him and a glum-faced Ger came up the stairs.

'That damp patch on the ceiling there.'

'Yes?'

'Michael says that honey made it.'

'*Honey?*' I struggled, not with images of death, but with a vision of Pooh Bear eating honey in the roof.

'There've been loads of bees around.'

Now I came to think about it, there *had* been lots of bees about. I'd vaguely put it down to heat.

'I haven't seen a swarm,' I said.

'It would be up there in the eaves.'

'How could they have got inside?'

'Maybe through a crack,' said Ger. 'They'd only need a tiny hole.'

Oh Lord, I thought, another problem. At that moment, Carrigrua seemed the image of myself. Hollow, tattered and ill-used. But not, I hoped, beyond repair.

'How much damage can bees do?'

'They could bring the ceiling down.'

'*Bees* can bring a ceiling down?'

Ger nodded sagely. 'They could if there were thousands of them.'

'*Thousands?*'

'My brother studied bees at school. You can get,' he paused for dramatic effect, '*ninety thousand* in a hive!'

Ninety thousand! God, I thought. 'Can we get an expert in, to get rid of them, I mean?'

Ger looked dubious. 'The only fellow that I know of doesn't have a telephone.'

'Where is he?'

'Somewhere at the back of Scariff.'

'You don't know any more about him?'

'No,' said Ger unhelpfully. 'I have to check the floorboards now.'

That seemed like a safer subject.

'Are many of them loose?'

'A few. Some will have to be replaced. And some have fierce awful stains. I don't know if you'll get them out.'

'Glycerine will loosen them.'

When that was done, I was going to make a polish, a real Georgian polish, wax with garden herbs in it, and work magic on those floorboards.

Meanwhile, there were all those bees. You could see them from the yard, buzzing round that upstairs window. Ganging up. An army marching on the house. Ninety thousand in a hive . . .

'Mrs Tremain?' Naoise had appeared from nowhere.

'Yes?' I said, trying to keep the nervousness out of my voice.

'Marie-Rose Keane is looking for you. I met her over in Mountshannon.'

Fear put hands round my neck. I could barely nod at Naoise, let alone reply to him.

'She wants you to go round and see her.'

Before I could find my voice, I heard a howl inside the house.

Ger came running out the door. 'It got me on the hand!' he said.

'What happened to you?' Naoise asked.

'A bee. It hurts like Hell,' said Ger.

A bee . . .

Relieved, I found my voice again. 'I'll go and get some ointment for you.'

But Ger had more bad news for me. 'I think the power could be off.'

'What gives you that idea?' I said.

'That bee sting gave me such a fright, I hit the cable with a nail.'

So now we had another crisis. I had an almost overwhelming and completely childish urge to sit on the cobbles and scream out loud. Much good that would do me.

'Do you know an electrician?'

This time, Ger had the answer. 'Matt Murphy is your man,' he said. 'He works on shift. He could be home.'

I got the ointment for Ger's hand. I went in search of Mr Murphy and found his wife at home alone. Her husband, she said, was repairing a lighting circuit on one of the cruisers owned by the Shannon Castle line.

I thanked her and, fighting off that childish urge, drove to the marina. It was deserted except for someone in the office, talking German on the phone. I didn't like to interrupt him. All the hire boats were out except for one, the *Cloghan Castle*.

'Hello?'

But there was no one on the boat. Matt Murphy must have gone, I thought. Then I saw a flash of scarlet. At the far end of the old harbour a solitary figure in a red jersey was sitting on the ground.

I walked round the slatted jetty, overlaid with lattice wire to prevent a person slipping. Then, ignoring a danger sign, I climbed a wooden barricade and set off along a grassy path beside which a few sturdy alders had survived the winter gales. Rocks soon took the place of grass. Some were missing from the path. It was indeed a dangerous place.

The figure in the red jersey metamorphosed into a man of sixty or so, with faded sandy hair and freckles on his craggy face. He got to his feet as I approached.

'Are you Mr Murphy?'

'I am.'

We talked and he was sympathetic.

'It doesn't sound so bad to me.'

I nearly wept with gratitude. 'It doesn't? Ah, that's wonderful.'

His eyes had wandered to the lake. A cruiser had come into view.

'That's a Birchwood,' said Matt Murphy.

'How can you tell from so far off?'

'I just recognise the shape. I often come to watch the boats. Like a lot of other people. Not now, I mean, but long ago. Did you know this was the main embarkation harbour for emigrants from County Clare?'

'I didn't know. That's interesting.'

'I sometimes think, all the weeping and the wailing there must have been, with people going away for good. And now we have the pleasure cruisers.'

'You must see a lot of them.'

'Well, they're novel still, at this end of the lake anyway. Twenty years or so ago, they were all in Killaloe. I'm talking of the hire boats now.'

'And those in private ownership?'

'There were just a few of them. There still aren't all that many here. They're too expensive, I'm afraid.'

'I suppose they are,' I said. 'About the cable, Mr Murphy—'

'I'll come over later on. The minute that I've had my tea.'

I thanked him and went home to find a royal-blue BMW eight forty Ci parked outside the house. A familiar car . . .

A man was leaning on the bonnet. He was familiar too. Very familiar.

'Hello, darling!' Leonard said.

Sixteen

He was wearing jeans and a T-shirt, yet he looked too well-dressed, too exotic for the country. I was shocked rigid. I thought, I wish I'd washed my hair this morning and, oh my God, those orange streaks . . .

'What an amazing surprise,' I said.

'You didn't get my message then? I phoned to say that I'd be coming. I spoke to Marie-Rose about it. She promised that she'd let you know.'

'Oh, yes. I remember now.'

'You mean you actually *forgot*?' Being forgotten by a woman was unusual for Leonard.

'In a way. You'd better come inside,' I said.

Leonard went to the boot and took out a travelling bag.

'It won't get stolen if you leave it.'

'But I've come to stay with *you*. I must say it was a surprise to hear you'd moved in quite so soon. The house must be taking shape. The builders working overtime?'

'Not exactly. Leonard, did you bring that information?'

'I have it somewhere in my bag. My secretary got it for you.'

'So you have it. Can I see it?'

'Hold on. I've only just arrived. Let me adjust to my surroundings.'

He followed me up the steps, put down his bag and looked around him.

'Stunning hall – or will be, when you've done it up. Have you finished upstairs yet?'

'Not quite. Won't you fish it out for me?'

'Fish what out?'

'That cutting from the paper, Leonard.'

'Don't rush me, darling. I'm worn out. Coming over all this way. It's not just down the road, you know.'

'That makes two of us,' I said. 'I'm a bit knocked out myself.'

'Been overdoing it with the house? You always were a dynamo.'

149

'It's not so much the house as . . .' My voice trailed off. The story was too long for Leonard. Too long and much too complicated.

He didn't press me to explain. Not then.

'We both need a drink,' he said. 'I brought some wine. It's in the cool-bag. Get some glasses, will you, darling.'

'I don't have glasses, only mugs. And I haven't got a corkscrew.'

'I brought a corkscrew,' Leonard said.

We sat down on the steps and drank. Leonard marvelled at the view.

'What a place. It's wonderful. Now I know why you came back. We should have come here long ago.'

'Yes,' I said. 'I wish we had.'

'Me too. Anyway, we're here at last. Carrigrua. You'll have to show me round the house. Are the builders still inside?'

'They'll be gone by now,' I said, still grappling with the fact that Leonard had pitched up and was sitting there beside me.

Or was he? Maybe he was just a vision. If I pinched him, would he feel it?

'Caro, darling,' he said. 'I've been worried about you. You told me that you were at risk.'

'I only said I might be, Leonard. If you didn't get that cutting.'

'What *is* this all about? You're not depressed or anything?'

'Perplexed would be a better word.'

'What are you perplexed about? Here, let me refill your glass.'

The Leonard relaxation treatment. The trouble was, it worked on me. After two glasses, Leonard looked less alien and a lot more like my husband.

'Caro, darling, I should feed you,' he said when we'd polished off the bottle. 'Pity the shops are closed. We could have eaten here *al fresco*.'

But several of the shops were open. We went out in search of food and returned with enough provisions to satisfy six greedy people.

Was I awake or was I sleeping? True, Leonard did seem quite substantial, but he was behaving strangely. Being so considerate. For instance, when we bought the food, he'd thought of what *I* liked to eat. The Leonard that I used to know wasn't so solicitous. In the past, I'd tended to his every need but he hadn't cherished me – not as he was doing this evening.

What's going on with him? I wondered. Has he worked out what he's done? What he lost when he lost me? Is he trying to compensate? Is he saying take me back?

He must have come to make amends. That is, if he's here at all . . .

Vocally, it seemed he was. Leonard talked a lot that evening. It was

150

mostly about London, how he'd seen this show and that. He'd been to the Bush theatre to applaud *Saint Nicholas*, the new play by Conor McPherson. He outlined the plot for me, then moved on to 'London's Monets' and an evening at the opera. He made me feel I'd been with him, sharing what he'd seen and heard. I must say I enjoyed myself, being taken out by Leonard.

Halfway through the meal, I thought, we've changed parts, the two of us. Leonard's taken on my role. He's become the Entertainer.

This was a delightful thought. I laughed. I couldn't help myself.

'What's so funny?' Leonard asked.

'Never mind. I can't explain.'

Leonard frowned. 'There's something odd going on with you. You're in trouble, aren't you, darling? This business of the cutting . . .'

'Mm,' I said. 'Of course. The cutting. I can't wait to see what's in it.'

But that wasn't true. Not any more. I was affected by Leonard's arrival. I thought again how he had changed and become a different person. A better, more attractive person.

But he'd always been attractive.

Leonard unlocked his bag and took out an envelope. 'Here you are. What an intriguing business, Caro. I'm dying to know what it's about.'

'You haven't read it yet, I take it.'

'I thought I'd let you do that first.'

'Good for you,' I said to him – and put the cutting in my pocket.

'Aren't you going to look at it?'

'Not yet.'

'Caro, darling. Honestly. You're keeping me on tenterhooks. What is going on with you?'

I nearly spelt it out for him. What I knew of Clemency. The fear I had of Marie-Rose. But I had too much on my mind, most of it to do with Leonard, and I wasn't up to it.

'What's going on with *you*?' I said. 'Are you still involved with Sue?'

'Sue? Susie Wilkins, do you mean? I haven't seen her in an age. Not since—'

'I found the two of you in bed?'

'Darling, must you bring that up? It was a year ago, you know.'

And it wasn't serious.

But perhaps that was the point. It hadn't mattered much to Leonard. Just to me. Perhaps to Sue.

Had I been foolish? I thought now. Overreacted, gone berserk and lost out as a result?

151

Other women remained calm when their husbands were unfaithful. *They* thought it wasn't serious. Not a threat to their wellbeing. Because they were confident. Sure that they were more important, much more loved than their menfolk's passing fancies. *I* was the woman Leonard had loved. The only one, he often said. Was I stupid, missing out? Were these other women wiser?

It was getting dark. Above the lake, the dusk drew curtains on the sky. Where was Leonard going to sleep?

Not with me. But maybe in my room, I thought. Either there or in Clemency's room. There was a mattress on her bed. I'd removed the bloodstained linen and the blankets weren't marked.

Which of us should use that room? In theory, Leonard was the one. Why should I give up my bed to an uninvited guest? But that room was Clemency's. If I put a guest in there, he'd have to share the room with her.

I'll sleep in that room, I thought. She won't welcome an intruder.

'Aren't you tired?' I said to Leonard.

'Yes, you're right. It's time for bed.'

But when we went inside the house we found the power was still off. I'd forgotten about Matt. He must have called when we were out.

Leonard said it was romantic that the house should have no lights – then added that he had a torch, in his bag or in the boot. He rummaged around until he found it.

'Saved! Come on. Let's go to bed.'

The torchlight got us up the stairs but there was moonlight on the landing and my old room was well lit up.

'My God, that bed!' said Leonard promptly. 'Did you get it with the house? It must be worth a bloody fortune.'

'You see it all in terms of money.'

'I suppose I used to, yes. But everything is different now.'

'Why should things be different now?'

Leonard kissed me on the cheek. 'I'll tell you in the morning, darling. Sleep well. You're sure you're happy in that room?'

Of course I wasn't happy there. For one thing, I was feeling guilty. I had the cutting in my pocket and I knew that I should read it. But again I hesitated. I told myself I was too tired, that I wouldn't take it in. I was too dazed by what had happened. Tomorrow I'd feel differently. Tonight I'd try to catch some sleep.

But I couldn't get to sleep. It was too hot in Clemency's room. Too warm to have the bedclothes on. I kicked them off and lay awake. Was Leonard lying awake as well, sprawled out on my marriage bed? Was he thinking about me?

'*Everything is different now.*'

What did he mean when he said that? That he was different – more mature, a nicer person altogether? Or that he'd changed the way he viewed his relationship with me? In the morning would he say, I've had enough of straying, darling. I promise you that I'll be faithful. I have a new approach to marriage . . .?

We *were* still married, after all. The divorce had not come through. Under the terms of our arrangement, we had to wait another year until we got the decree nisi.

What would Leonard say tomorrow? I wrestled with my thoughts all night. They were mostly about Leonard. At least, I thought, it made a change from thinking about Clemency. She left me alone that night. I didn't dream of Marie-Rose.

I still meant to read the cutting when I woke up in the morning. Instead, I edged away from it. It would disturb me, I told myself. Maybe later on today . . . What I need now is an energiser. I'll go down and make some coffee.

But of course there wasn't any power. In the kitchen I found Leonard rooting around in search of milk.

'I've probably run out of milk.'

'That's not like you,' said Leonard, puzzled.

'Running out of milk, you mean?'

'Well, that and forgetting things. How long has this been going on?'

'Are you saying I've cracked up?'

'No, no,' said Leonard hastily. 'That wasn't what I meant at all. Now tell me what was in that paper.'

'I haven't read the cutting yet.'

'You haven't read it yet?' said Leonard. 'But you couldn't wait to get it.' He looked seriously worried.

I said that I would read it later. Somehow, I just didn't want to share this with him. 'First, I have to phone Matt Murphy. When are you going back to England?'

'I've only just arrived,' said Leonard.

And he had to tell me something.

What it was just had to wait. The builders interrupted us. They looked at Leonard, then at me, wondering what was going on.

Of course I had to introduce them. Ah, the husband, said their eyes.

'You didn't get the power back on,' Michael said accusingly.

'We'll have it back for you this morning.'

Leonard took control of things. The builders warmed to him at once, relieved to have a man in charge. What a bloody cheek, I thought.

153

Aren't I the one who owns the house? But I was relieved as well, glad to hand the reins to Leonard – for the moment, anyway.

I phoned Matt Murphy. He arrived and soon we had the power back on.

'Now show me round the house,' said Leonard.

Having something to explore, he was in his element. 'It's wonderful,' he said again. 'I suppose you've lots to do here – when the builders let you do it.'

'I have.'

The marble surrounds in the hall and drawing room badly needed skilful cleaning to bring back the splendour that lurked underneath.

'What potions will you use for that?' asked Leonard, just as curious as ever.

'Soap and quicklime and caustic potash.'

And then there were the bedroom grates. The ironwork was caked with rust.

'I'm going to scour it with white spirit. Then I'll blacken it with graphite.'

I had a dozen jobs lined up, not to mention making curtains.

'And then I'll have my studio.'

'The same old Caro, always busy.'

'Of course, I said. 'I haven't changed.'

But that wasn't true. I had. Caroline the Clown had gone. Had Leonard noticed she was missing? If he had, he didn't say so.

'We must go round the grounds,' he said. 'That is, if you have the time.'

I thought he would tell me then, while we were walking round the grounds. The walled garden was the perfect setting for a reconciliation.

Except that Naoise was there too, and Leonard stopped to talk to him. The conversation took an age. I switched in and out of it, catching part of what they said.

'I've a Purdy,' Leonard said.

'Is that so? You're lucky then. The one I have was made in Dublin.'

'Trulock and Harris? They used to be in Dawson Street.'

After that, they moved to shooting.

Naoise said, 'Did they fly well, the birds that day?'

'Fantastic. And the wind was good . . .'

'Fascinating,' Leonard said when the conversation finished. 'That fellow is so well-informed.'

'I find him rather sinister.'

'You do? But he's extremely bright.'

154

'Come and see the orchard, Leonard.' I walked ahead of him, trying not to see the brambles that were clogging up the fruit trees. 'Don't you love the smell of apples?'

'I've always loved being in an orchard.'

That sounded pretty positive. We were only strolling now. I let my hand fall by my side so Leonard could reach out for it before he launched into his speech.

But he didn't take my hand. He didn't break the silence either. Someone else did that for him.

'Mrs Tremain?' Bernie Fahy was beside us, with a cutter in his hand. 'The weeds are cruel wild,' he said. 'I never thought they'd be so bad.'

'Hello,' said Leonard cheerfully. 'We haven't met. My name is Leonard.'

Bernie Fahy was enchanted. They, too, struck up a conversation, with Leonard asking lots of questions and Bernie coming up with answers. It was all about the garden but I hadn't known till then that Bernie had such knowledge.

I stood by, half intrigued and half frustrated. Leonard wasn't in a hurry, but then he'd always been like that, letting life spill over him, luxuriating in its flow.

'Where's Chris?' I asked eventually, thinking, he'll be next in line to chat.

Bernie reluctantly switched his attention from Leonard to me. 'He's getting all the ivy down.'

'He's not!'

'He is. It's bad for walls. It strangles them.'

'I don't care,' I said. 'I love it.'

Abandoning the two of them, I ran towards my sanctuary – the nook I'd dreamt of showing to Leonard. My hiding place. My look-out point.

But Chris had got there long before me and the damage had been done. The wall was bare. My nook was gone.

Distraught and on the verge of tears, I told Chris he had ruined the orchard.

'You said we should get out the weeds.'

'I didn't mean to shift the ivy. You should have asked me what to do.'

'I did. You said—'

'He can re-plant the ivy, Caro.' Leonard had caught up with us. 'It grows in quickly. You know that.'

'I know,' I said. 'It spreads like weeds!'

Leonard sighed. He didn't speak on our way back. He didn't try to take my hand.

Back at the house, things were proceeding much more smoothly. There, I was more acceptable – Leonard's presence saw to that. Michael, in a benign mood, had some happy news for us.

'Pauky Driscoll's won a prize in the lottery,' he said.

I didn't know who Pauky was. I told him that was marvellous and he responded with a smile.

Ger had other news for me. 'Bob Studdart's been here looking for you. I told him ye were in the garden. He wouldn't stay. He left a note.'

'Who's Bob Studdart?' Leonard asked.

'Just a friend. He lives near here.'

I saw Michael glance at Ger. Was that a wink? I wasn't sure.

'I'm glad you're making friends,' said Leonard.

It wasn't what he should have said. I turned away to read Bob's note. It was brief and to the point. 'Free for lunch one day this week, or maybe dinner on the boat? What appeals to you, I wonder.'

'I feel like fish and chips,' said Leonard.

'We can get them in the village. I'll phone and order them for us.' Not romantic fare exactly, but they *were* brilliant fish and chips.

'This lifestyle suits you, does it, Caro?' Leonard said as we were eating.

'I haven't really got a lifestyle.'

'Are you seeing a lot of Bob?'

'I told you that he's just a neighbour.' Was he worried about Bob? Jealous that he was a rival?

'What other friends have you made here?'

What was in his mind? When would he reveal to me why it was that he had changed?

Not then. And not later on that evening. I willed him to get on with it but all he did was look at me and ask about my life in Clare.

Another night without much sleep, curled up on our separate beds.

The workmen thought we slept together – or, anyway, I think they did. We were a topic for conjecture, as I ruefully discovered when they gathered for their tea break.

Going down the basement steps, I heard their voices drifting up.

'The husband's got the lead on Studdart.'

'Studdart isn't in the running.'

'You're wrong in that. I'd say he is.'

I heard them taking bets on it.

'Would you put a fiver on it?'

'Would a cat take milk, I ask you!'

Of course this had its funny side. Another time I might have laughed. Then, I loathed being talked about – my sex life being analysed by the likes of Naoise Nolan. Particularly Naoise Nolan.

And I hadn't read the cutting. Frankly, I was dodging doing so. Leonard's presence was distracting me. It tempted. It said, do you have to be disturbed by the contents of that cutting? You will be, you know. But there could be another route – the one that you would take with Leonard.

The information in the cutting – Clemency's story – had to do with being there, with my life at Carrigrua. My relationship with Leonard belonged in another place. He might profess to love the house. He might feel he could move in. But he, and the life we'd shared, were poles apart from Carrigrua.

Leonard, meanwhile, remained silent on the change there was in him. He coaxed me out for a lakeside drive. He said how lovely the area was. How peaceful it was being here. An antidote to urban pressure – implying that it was all my doing. Leonard being his charming self. But then, that was Leonard for you. Charm was inborn in the man. He was such a sunny person.

I liked to think that Clemency was sunny, too . . . It seemed that I was at a crossroads, being asked to make a choice between Clemency and Leonard. On one side was the known road leading to my old existence. On the other was a tangled pathway which might lead me anywhere. I stood between them, hesitating, with the cutting in my pocket.

For two nights in a row, the nightmares hadn't bothered me. I thought I might be free of them. I wasn't. They soon came back. On the third night Leonard stayed, I dreamt of Olive and myself.

Olive wore an evening gown. Pale-grey chiffon. Very pretty. We were going to a ball – at a castle, so I thought. That night I was not a child. I was a member of the party.

Then, as it often is in dreams, we were not inside the house but in the tiny bay that lies beyond the little harbour to the right of Carrigrua. There, the trees thinned out and the grass crept down to the water's edge. Grass of Parnassus, white blossoms with dark veins, grew in that enchanted place, and the violet water flowers, lobelia and rare germander. Seal-heal crawled on hairy stems and the stamens of lilac-coloured mint stuck up from the soggy ground.

She was dressed but I was naked. On the ground there was a ballgown, lavender and made of silk, which had been laid out for me. I put it on and coiled my hair and wove the wild flowers into it.

157

My feet were bare. Olive, taking note of this, took her two-tone grey shoes off, the ones with buckled straps on them.

'Put these on,' she ordered me.

I put them on exultantly. I didn't want to dance in them but just to feel that I was her. To experience her power. To have the serum of her strength injected into me instead.

Then Olive left and Ger turned up. He was on his way to work.

'Those shoes are much too big for you.'

'They're not too big at all,' I said. 'She and I are both size three.'

'No, they're loose,' said Ger, annoyed.

He hammered nails into the shoes so that I could keep them on. The nails were sharp and very long. They pierced the soles. They pricked my feet. Blood speckled the grass and I began to cry with pain.

'But she and I are both the same.'

'You're not,' said Ger. 'You're not the same.'

Seeing him hold the hammer up, I screamed for Clemency to help.

'Darling?'

But that's Leonard's voice, I thought.

He was bending over me. 'What is it, Caroline? What's wrong?'

'My feet are wet. There's blood on them.'

'What?'

Leonard switched on the light.

'There's blood on me,' I said again.

'Let me see.' He touched my foot and smelt his fingers. 'That's not blood. It's honey, darling.'

'*Honey?*'

Leonard looked up at the ceiling. 'It's oozing down on to the bed. There's got to be a swarm of bees up there.'

Things were falling into focus.

'There is. Behind the water tank, I think. I didn't know what I should do. I—'

'You don't have to do anything,' said Leonard soothingly. 'I'll sort it out tomorrow morning. In the meantime, I'll move the bed out of the firing line. Get up for a minute, darling.'

Feeling foolish, I obeyed.

'Don't you want to swap with me?' said Leonard when he'd moved the bed. 'Or, more like it, share my bed? It's much more comfortable than this.'

But that was going too quickly for me.

'No,' I said. 'I'll be all right. But leave the light turned on for now.'

I could have read the cutting then instead of staring into space.

Instead of thinking about Leonard and the way he'd responded when I was in need of comfort.

We have to make it up, I thought. Should *I* be the one to introduce the subject? Start by saying, Leonard, look, I've forgiven you?

He'd be pleased by that. It would take his guilt away. Set the scene for him to tell me how much he'd been missing me. For him to ask me to come back.

Surely Leonard wanted that. He must love me still, or why else would he be here? He didn't have to bring the cutting. He could have posted it to me.

If I went back to him, I wouldn't have to read that cutting. I'd escape the pain that this house inflicted on me. If we were reconciled, I thought, I'd leave the house – leave Carrigrua and the mystery that was in it. Clemency would stay behind, remain for ever in this room. I'd have no more nightmares then.

'You had nightmares,' Leonard said when we met up in the morning. 'Poor Caro. You've got circles under your eyes.'

'I know.' I wished he hadn't noticed them.

'You've been working much too hard. And you're under stress as well. Tell me, what was in the cutting?'

'I'm afraid I haven't read it.'

'Caro, darling,' Leonard said. 'What *is* it with you? Something's preying on your mind. You told me that you were at risk. I'm more than curious. I'm worried. What's been going on?'

'I can't explain. Not yet. Not till . . .' I let the sentence hang.

Leonard gave up. He talked about the bees instead. 'Ger and I will deal with them.'

'But how?'

Leonard didn't answer that. He only said that Ger was out, buying things that they would need.

These turned out to be protective gloves, vapour strips and a roll of lattice wire.

'What's he going to do with those?'

Leonard turned vague. 'We have a plan,' was all he'd say.

In fact, I also had a plan. I had to go to Tuohys' store, which was several miles away, just over the Galway border, to pick up some goods I'd ordered. When I mentioned this to Leonard, he asked how long I would be out.

'An hour or so.'

'Take your time,' said Leonard sweetly. 'There's no need for you to rush.'

Tuohys' catered for the farmers, selling everything they needed. I pottered around the hardware section, re-examined all the paint charts, thought again about the yellows which I'd chosen for the house, and had a chat with Mr Tuohy.

I returned to Carrigrua to find Ger wearing a curious helmet made out of the lattice wire.

'We've killed the bees,' he said to me.

They'd found the swarm, drilled a hole, pushed some vapour strips inside it – then they'd filled it up again. That killed the bees inside the house. To block further access to it, they'd inserted some more strips in the crack beneath the eaves.

'It was simple,' Leonard said.

'Yes,' I said. 'But was it legal? It seems very cruel to me.'

'It's too late for ethics, darling. And the bees are gone for good.'

'I wish you hadn't done it, Leonard.'

'They might have stung you,' Leonard said. 'I gather that they went for Ger.'

I let it be. As Leonard said, it was too late. And he'd been protecting me . . .

Sometime later that same day, I tried to get my message over, so he'd know he was forgiven.

'I'm really glad you came to see me.'

Leonard said, more soberly, 'I just had to talk to you. To see you, not to use the phone. So I'd know the way you feel about the way it's all worked out.'

'I was very angry with you.'

'Do I know it!'

'I was hurt.'

'Yes. I'm sorry,' Leonard said.

'We used to be so close.'

'That's exactly how I see it.'

'It's not as if you're still with Sue.'

Which was Leonard's cue to say, 'Why would I be, when I love you?'

He didn't take it. He stayed silent. Feeling culpable, I thought. Soon, when it was dark again, I'd take the guilt away from him.

I waited for the night to come, more impatient by the minute. At dinner, though, there was a moment when I thought that he'd say something. But the moment passed, the chance was missed and Leonard headed for his bed.

I let him settle down in there then put my head round the door.

'Come in, darling,' Leonard said. He was lying on the bed, a graceful panther of a man underneath a cotton sheet.

'I felt we hadn't really talked.'

Another silence.

Eventually, Leonard said, 'You're right. We haven't. Sit down, darling.'

There was just the bed to sit on. I leant back against a pole on which that motif had been carved.

'I'm not angry with you now.'

'It's very sweet of you to say so.'

'I'm delighted that you're here.'

He should have said how glad *he* was to be in my company. He should have put his arms round me.

Instead, he said he'd been unhappy when the two of us broke up.

He's leading into it, I thought. He's going to say how much he missed me.

'I never fell in love with Sue, or with all those other women.'

'I know.'

'But, as I said, my life has changed.'

It wasn't the words that were so wrong. It was the way that Leonard said them. A cold hand reached out for my heart.

'In what way has it changed?' I asked.

'I've met someone else,' said Leonard.

'Someone else?'

Leonard sat up in bed and picked up a fallen pillow. He held it against his chest, as if the pillow was a shield. When he spoke again, it was in a studied voice, as if he had rehearsed his lines.

'Darling,' he said, 'after you and I broke up – a few months afterwards, that is – I went to a party and met this woman. Her name is Jenny Campion. She handles the PR for Lancôme. We – became involved. It just worked, for both of us . . .'

I closed my eyes and took a deep breath. I said, in an unsteady voice, 'Is that why you came to see me, to tell me you were screwing her?'

'You know that wouldn't be my motive.'

I could feel his eyes on me. 'Well, what *is* your motive then?'

'You and I, we're not divorced. We won't be for another year. But we could get it through much quicker – that is, if we both agree.'

Tears were welling up inside me, forming into a waterfall. 'What makes you want to rush it through?'

'Jenny's pregnant, Caroline, and I want to marry her.'

161

The waters that were in me broke. But there was anger in me too. Primeval rage. I hated, *envied* Jenny Campion who was going to have a baby. Grief engulfed me and I wept.

'Oh, darling, don't. Please.' Leonard let the pillow drop. 'I don't want to hurt you, darling. You know how much I care about you. That's why I found it hard to tell you – why I had to come and see you. To check on you. To make sure that you could cope. That you weren't . . .'

'That I wasn't cracking up!'

'Darling, come here. Get into bed with me.'

The offer of comfort undermined what was left of my dignity. I got to my feet.

'Don't go,' Leonard said.

But I did. I carried my pain away with me. I took it through to Clemency's room and sat there on the floor, hunched against her iron bed.

Pregnant.

Leonard hadn't wanted children. But in his voice there had been pride. Oh yes, I thought, he certainly has changed.

I worked out something else as well. I realised he wanted more than a speeded-up divorce. Leonard wanted my approval. My praise for making Jenny Campion pregnant.

There was no end to what he wanted.

When the tears were out of me and I was just a wrung-out rag, I used the sheet to wipe my face. It was pointless going to bed. I knew I wouldn't sleep that night.

The cutting was inside my pocket. To read it was to take the turning leading to the tangled pathway. But now I had no second choice. There was no going back to Leonard.

I reached out for the envelope.

Seventeen

I slit it open with my thumb and took the cutting out.

I laid it open on the bed. The story – her story – had been the lead that day. Into the silence the headlines screamed: 'Lough Derg Searched for Missing Woman. Crewless Cruiser Found on Rocks'.

Intensive dragging of Lough Derg by the Guards and civilians under Sergeant Dennis Mulvanney of Ennis continued yesterday in the search for Miss Clemency Conroy of Carrigrua House, Whitegate, after an empty cruiser was found on the rocks off Holy Island.

Miss Conroy went missing on Wednesday. The Guards say she may have been on board the cruiser that evening when a force nine gale hit the lake, though they admit that the boat in question is not the property of her family.

Sergeant Mulvanney said the Guards were not prepared, at this stage, to reveal who owns the boat, only that it was moored at the harbour at Carrigrua House within the last few days. He told our reporter that Miss Conroy was used enough to handling boats but may have over-estimated her ability to cope with a storm on the lake.

'But that is hypothetical,' the Sergeant said. 'We do not know for sure as yet that Miss Conroy was on board the boat.'

He went on to stress the dangers of the lake when a storm blows up and spoke of another accident, the year before, in which a fisherman had drowned.

I read on. The report added that a statement concerning the owner-ship of the wrecked boat would be made at a later stage.

I got to the last paragraph. The one that told me who she was. I had to read it over twice, and even at the second reading I couldn't credit what it said.

163

Miss Conroy, who is twenty-nine, is the daughter of Mrs Olive Conroy, and sister of Miss Constance Conroy, both of Carrigrua House. Another sister, Charity, wife of Mr Alan Lacy, previously of Portumna, died six years ago.

And still I couldn't take it in. But there it was, in black and white. Irrefutable evidence. Clemency Conroy was my aunt.

Olive said she had two children. *Just* the two, she'd said to me. Surely Olive wouldn't lie.

Then I came to terms with that. I thought, no, it wasn't so much that Olive lied as that she denied the truth. She wanted to protect the household. I only had to think of her on the day they dragged the lake to understand how it must have been.

We must all have been in torment. Omitting Marie-Rose, of course. Olive would have feared our grieving. Worried lest it was contagious, leading to her own breakdown. She was unselfish, matriarchal. She would have wished to keep her strength so that she could bolster us. In order to contain herself, she must have muzzled us as well, given instructions that no one was to speak of Clemency, then or afterwards.

Her own mourning would have been a private matter. She'd have wept alone, I thought, never letting others see her in those moments when she cried.

To me, the idea of Olive crying was both strange and awful. Olive weeping, just like me. It was almost beyond belief. But it must have been like that. She lamenting in that lonely fashion, all the years until her death. Living by that lovely shore. Hating to look at the lake where her daughter had been drowned.

But had it happened in that way? What about this room, the wreckage that I'd found in it? The bloodstains on the windowsill? My images and dreams of violence? What had they to do with drowning?

Except, I thought, there was the boat. My fingers knew there was a boat. But I knew very little else.

What the Hell was the matter with me? Why had I no recollection whatsoever of Clemency until I returned to Clare and re-discovered her?

She'd slept in this very room when I was six years old. Most people retained clear memories from that age. Leonard could recall being two, being bored in his pram. Once, he'd scrambled out of it and gone searching for his mother. He remembered doing that. What was wrong with me that my recollections should come and go? That I could sense

164

a presence, feel a warmth, smell a scent – and then suffer from amnesia?

Clemency Conroy was my aunt. We'd lived together in this house. I must have seen her every day. Shared meals with her. Sat beside her at the table. And then forgotten that she existed.

What kind of person could I be to blot out her memory?

Mad. *Was* I mad? As mad as the person that I feared? The vandal who had torn her gown? There was madness, certainly. At least I was not malicious.

I thought, she couldn't have had an accident. Her death and anger were connected. I am sure of that. Why can't I remember more?

But some things, a few, are coming back to me. That process began only after I broke up with Leonard. After I'd gone wild with rage and caused such havoc in the bathroom. When I came back for the funeral, I didn't hear or see things. True, I was frightened of the cupboard. But I was always scared of it when I was a little girl.

The real fears came later. The true images and scents. The truth, knocking on the door that was locked inside me. Saying, find Clemency. Find out what happened to her. When you do, you'll find yourself.

Leonard left in the morning. Before he did, we had a talk. I told him that I'd pave the way so he and Jenny could get married.

'Where are you going to live?' I said.

'In Sunningdale of course,' said Leonard. 'Oh, by the way, I rang Mrs Langley the other day to say that I'd be needing her. She said she wouldn't work for *me*. That she'd only work for *you*.'

'Imagine that.'

'She was always odd,' said Leonard.

He told me that he'd be in touch. But I knew he was going much further away from me than the few hundred or so air miles that separated Shannon from Heathrow.

''Bye 'bye, darling. Do try not to work too hard.'

The car roared into life, raced towards the wood, and he disappeared.

I'd been angry in the night and the minute he left I was angry again. Not with Leonard, though, but with all those other people – Guard O'Hagan, Alice Egan, maybe Michael's mother too – who had kept the truth from me. They would have known – they *must* have known that Clemency was my aunt. They must have heard about her death.

What game were they playing with me? One they had no hope of winning. I was about to make that plain. I thought, I'll call on all of them in turn and confront them with the cutting.

'Mrs O'Meara,' I'd start off, in an intimidating voice. 'Why did you try to hide the truth?'

'I'm not as young as I was, you know. Autisia, I think they call it.'

Perhaps I wouldn't start with her. Guard O'Hagan might be a better starting point.

'I never was asked to go into the house.'

But surely that was sheer evasion? He was from the area. He had been in the Guards. He'd have known about the boat. He might have helped to drag the lake in the search for Clemency.

I walked purposefully round to his house, to find that the gate was shut. There was no car in the driveway either, and the curtains were drawn. Still, I rang the bell.

Chimes pealed faintly in the hall. No one came. I rang again without success. That's it, I thought. They've all gone out.

Then, as I was about to leave, I heard a thumping sound coming from behind the house. Investigating, I found Freckles there, digging up a carrot bed. He wrinkled up his nose at me.

'Are you looking for my grandda? If you are, he isn't here.'

'Then where is he, do you know?'

'They've gone on their holiers.'

'On holidays? When will they be coming back?'

'They've gone a month,' lamented Freckles. 'Four whole weeks in Majorca!'

'When did they go away?'

'They went off on Wednesday morning.'

That left me with Alice Egan. I went home to fetch the car and, fuelled by my indignation, roared into the nurseries, intending to be tough with her.

Alice was serving a customer but she acknowledged my arrival, calling out, 'Oh, hello there, Mrs Tremain. I'll be with you in a jiffy.'

Several minutes – five, ten – ticked by while I stood there, simmering.

'Wait there a minute, Mrs Gleeson, and I'll take them to the car.'

'Thank you, Alice,' the customer said.

I had my anger under control. Alice, bustling back in my direction, didn't sense that I was raging.

'Sorry about that, Mrs Tremain. Mrs Gleeson's a bit slow-moving. How are things at Carrigrua?'

'The lads are doing their job all right. Including Naoise, I might add.'

Alice looked gratified. 'That's nice to hear.'

She waited expectantly, thinking, I suppose, that I'd come about the garden or was going to buy some shrubs. I didn't let her wait for long.

'I came round to tell you something.'

'Oh, yes, Mrs Tremain?'

'Do you remember the other day when I asked if you knew who Clemency Conroy was? I've just found out she was my aunt.'

I might just as well have hit her.

She gasped and said, 'You found out about her, did you?' in a disconcerted voice.

'Yes. And you don't have to pretend any more. I know all about her now. I know the gist of what went on.'

That contention seemed to shock her. 'You do?'

'More or less. I . . .' She had tears in her eyes. Surprised, I stopped.

In a shaky voice she said earnestly, 'Oh, Mrs Tremain, I must apologise to you. We didn't know what we should say. You caught us off our balance. You not remembering who she was. We thought, well, it's better left. Better not to talk about it. I'm sure you understand our feelings.'

'Not really, Mrs Egan.'

'You'd feel just the same, I'm sure. If you'd been in our position.'

In spite of vowing to be tough, I had an urge to comfort her. 'You don't have to be this upset.'

'But I do. I am. I feel terrible about it.'

'Don't feel terrible,' I said.

'And Guard O'Hagan feels the same.'

'You mean you've talked to him about it?'

'I did indeed. I see him often. "What could I say?" he said to me. Oh, Mrs Tremain, but it mightn't be true.'

I tried to make some sense of this. 'Mrs Egan, can you please be more specific? What do you mean, that it mightn't be true?'

'But you *know*,' said Alice Egan. 'And maybe it's as well you do. You poor thing. It's very sad.' She reached into her pocket, took out an embroidered handkerchief and dabbed the corner of her eyes.

Hoist by my own petard. I said cagily, 'Yes, it *is* sad. But I need more information. That was why I came to you.'

Alice Egan blew her nose. Her ruddy face grew redder still. 'Please excuse me, Mrs Tremain. It's so distressing, isn't it, and much good I am to you. The thing is, all I know is hearsay and I wouldn't pass that on in case she takes it out on me.'

'Who? Who would take it out on you?'

'Marie-Rose. Oh, I shouldn't have told you that! Of all the stupid things to say!' She was more upset than she'd been before. She blew her nose a second time and looked at me with watery eyes. 'I mustn't go on discussing this. It's better left the way it was. For everyone's sake. You do see that?'

'No, I don't. I want to know.'

'Maybe you'll come round to it. Oh, there's Mrs Gleeson back. She must have left some shrubs behind. I'd better go and see to her. But anyway, Mrs Tremain, please, if you don't mind, don't let her know that I mentioned her name.'

It was pointless hanging on; Alice had clammed up again. What had I got out of her? That it – the story of my aunt I still didn't know – might be hearsay, nothing more. That she'd talked to Guard O'Hagan and he felt terrible as well. That she was nervous of Marie-Rose. That was more significant. But what did the rest of her chatter imply?

Sighing, I drove home through the wood. The broken branches and fallen trees would have to be removed from it, and the bracken pulled away so the wild flowers could breathe.

Bob's bicycle was propped up against the steps and Bob himself was in the house, being updated on the bees.

Bob my ally. The only one left now that Leonard had gone.

But was Bob really on my side or out there on the other one? Should I pay heed to the misgivings that he aroused in me? Surely I should. Surely he, who'd grown up near Carrigrua, would have known who Clemency was.

'Hi!' he said cheerfully. 'I'm here to issue invitations. My father's turning seventy-five. I'm giving a party. Will you come?'

'When is it?'

'On the twenty-second.'

'So soon?'

'As usual, I've left things late but I hope you can come.'

A party? I wasn't sure I fancied going. Caroline the Entertainer wouldn't be around to help me. Without her presence I'd be bare. Exposed to strangers who would say, 'Isn't that the Tremain woman? Do you know, her husband left her . . .'

'I'm not sure that I can make it.'

'Try,' said Bob. 'There'll be quite a crowd.'

'I'll try but I can't be certain . . .'

'I promise you it will be fun. Think about it, anyway. It seems ages since I saw you. What have you been up to lately?'

I knew he'd heard of Leonard's visit. Everyone around would know, not only that he'd been to see me but the reason why he came. Walls have ears, and so do builders, especially the ones in Clare.

'*The husband's got the lead on Studdart.*'

But he didn't want to keep it . . .

'This and that. I've just come back from Alice Egan's.'

'Did she sell you stacks of plants?'

'I didn't go there to buy plants. I just went round to talk to her.'

'I'm glad you're making friends with Alice. She's a really lovely woman. Always thinks the best of people. She'll be coming to the party.' He looked at me quizzically. 'Go on, say you'll come.'

He talked me into it.

'Maybe I will,' I said.

'Good. Now, what about this other boat trip? Do you fancy lunch or dinner? Hang on, before you answer that, I have a suggestion. I thought of going to Gurthalougha.'

'Where?'

'It's up the lake. On the Tipperary side. It would mean staying overnight.'

'Overnight, on the boat?'

'Or at Gurthalougha House, if you prefer a proper bed. That would be up to you. Would you like to come or not?'

I was making calculations. The trip would give me lots of time to have a decent talk with Bob. He'd relax out on the water. I'd be more relaxed as well. In a better frame of mind to drag the story out of him. That is, if he knew the story. And if he didn't, if he was truly innocent, not part of a conspiracy, he might remember something, some small but important thing, which related to my aunt.

'It sounds like a fun idea. I don't mind sleeping on the boat,' I said to build an atmosphere of trust, conducive to my private mission.

Was I mad thinking that – thinking I could trust this man? But could I?

That feeling that I'd had about him. The conviction that we'd met before. That I should be nervous of him. Shouldn't I trust my intuition rather than my faith in him? I could be heading for dangerous waters, going up the lake with Bob.

I had to be mad, I told myself. Except – who knew what I might find out.

Eighteen

We didn't pick a perfect day for our cruise to Gurthalougha. Leonard took the heat wave with him and now rain was in the offing. The Tipperary hills had turned navy blue and the sun had run a lemon bath. But the rest of the sky, distinctly grey, had the look of a child with a grubby face bent on planning villainy.

Easing *The Helen* out from the harbour, Bob said, 'I'm looking forward to this break. It's been a hellish week.'

'What's gone wrong?'

'Francesca's playing up,' said Bob. 'I have to go to London shortly and she wants to come with me. I've told her several times she can't. It's not a holiday for me. I'm going across to see my agent. But that doesn't register. The trouble is, she's so possessive.'

'Is she fussed about today? Did she want to come with us?'

'No. But that didn't stop her sulking.' He made her sound a fearful brat.

'Oh, Lord.'

'Don't worry about it. It's not your doing. But I must admit that I was glad, though guilty too, to get away for a little while.'

'I don't see why you should feel guilty.'

'No? Why should you? But I do. Anyway, it's good to be here. I like sleeping on the boat, even when it's moored at home.'

'Do you do that often, moor at home and sleep on board?'

'Now and again. Francesca hates it when I do.'

'Don't you let her sleep on board?'

'Not as often as she'd like.'

'That sounds dictatorial. Are you a dictator dad?' I was trying to keep it light, not to think of the night ahead. But Bob took me seriously.

'I can be somewhat heavy-handed.'

He said no more about Francesca. A rock loomed up ahead, with a bust of a man on the top of it.

171

'What in Heaven's name is that?'

Bob chuckled. 'We call him Mr Benjamin. But that's because he's on top of the Benjamin Rock. Some pranksters put him there, stuck him on with cement, and he's become a beacon. Inevitably there's a gull standing on his head and crapping. Look, there's one settling down right now.'

At that, the hills changed out of their navy-blue shawls and put on grey ones instead. Rain in folds of silver chiffon swathed Lough Derg and the sky reached out for a pale-pink scarf.

'Take my place,' Bob suddenly said and went to fetch me a glass of wine.

There were no other boats in sight. The lake was ours, the whole expanse, and as if to confirm that this was a gift that Heaven gave, a curious icy light, pure and translucent, appeared above the hills on our right-hand side.

Bob was back at the steering wheel. I sipped my wine – chilled Sancerre, palest gold from a cool-box mine – and stared at creamy blobs of sheep grazing on the verdant hills. At huddles of trees from which houses peaked out like censorious aunts surveying our progress across the lake.

Rain fell, riddling the lake with ripples, transforming it into a honeycomb.

'Is that a tower ahead?' I asked.

'It's the Catholic church at Portumna. It was built from the ruins of the Clanricarde residence, after the landlords lost their power.'

'Lord Clanrackrent,' I said, remembering.

'Yes. The last Lord Clanricarde must have evicted more tenants in Galway and Clare than any other Irish landlord, yet he never came to Ireland.'

'Was he the villain, or his agents?'

'There wasn't much to choose between them. The agents were a rotten crowd. They didn't all get off Scot-free. I heard that in Whitegate the local lads all got together and pulled an agent off his horse. They clubbed him with their sticks until he was dead. And then the whole parish, including the priest, took a vow of silence. They kept it for over a hundred years. This talkative county of ours is well able to conceal its secrets if it's so disposed.'

A murder and a vow of silence. Had that pattern been repeated in the case of Clemency? Was Bob talking naturally, providing me with local history, or was there more to what he said? Was he passing me a message? Was he saying, look, we're too clever here for you. We know how to keep our secrets? Or was he threatening me in the nicest possible way? Reminding me of parish power.

He said no more about the murder and the vow of secrecy. Instead, he drew my attention to a wood away to the right of the Catholic church, to a clearing and a big white house with a steel-grey roof. It might have been a hunting lodge. I suggested that to Bob.

'I think it was. That's Gurthalougha, by the way. The hotel has a private jetty. We can moor there for the night.'

Behind us, the last of the sun was flowing away in a molten stream. The sky was sullen with rage, the hills charcoal and the ridge of trees that ran beneath them every bit as black as jet.

'See, there's a duck taking off.'

Stone markers like cairns were sending signals out to us, guiding us into the shaded harbour.

'Lots of jetty free,' said Bob.

I went ashore to tie up. Bob took over afterwards and I waited as he secured the rear warp, wishing I could record the scene. Bob profiled at the end of the slatted jetty, the long, blue, Caribbean-style boat moored alongside ours, the wood in its many green variations – olivine, lime, emerald, Lincoln green. The dark-green reeds and the darkening lake.

We walked through a tunnel of forest trees along a path fenced with logs, following the signs that read 'Reception through archway' and 'Welcome to Gurthalougha House. For attention call to door marked Reception'.

We reached a cobbled courtyard. A grey tabby cat was stretched out on a wooden bench. Fuchsias flowered in white stone troughs.

At the reception desk a pretty dark-haired woman greeted Bob delightedly.

'Nice to see you here. Go and join our other guests.'

In what might have been a family drawing room, a group of cheerful Americans, an English pilot and his wife and an elderly Irish couple were nibbling cheese straws and sipping sherry. Through one tall window I saw the sky. One part was the colour of milk and another blue, and the lake was indigo.

'It's good to see the rain at last,' said one of the Americans. 'We've been having New York weather. We wondered if we were in Ireland!'

Soon afterwards, dinner was announced. We might have walked into a wood instead of into a dining room. The walls were papered green and on one a naïf painting of a brown bull was cordoned off in a black frame. Eight tables had been laid. On each was a glass bowl containing

173

red peonies and a candle in a china holder.

The Americans sat on our left-hand side, the Irish couple by the window.

'Do people here *speak* Irish?' the New Yorker asked.

'It's taught in school but not that often spoken.'

'Didn't the Irish once speak French?'

'The aristocrats in Munster did, eight hundred years ago.'

'Like the Russians,' said the woman.

At the other nearby table, the Irish man was speaking softly. 'I want to take you on a day trip, lead you into real temptation.'

'Mm,' his wife said, smiling at him. 'I think I like the sound of that . . .'

'Bob,' I said, deciding that I'd be direct. 'I've found out who Clemency was. I've discovered a lot about her.'

It caught him right off balance. He gaped at me, his fork frozen halfway between plate and mouth.

'How did you manage that?' he said.

Not 'What did you find out about her?' but 'How did you manage that?' As if he'd known that there was something concealed.

I explained about the cutting. Told him what I'd gauged from it. 'It looks as if she might have drowned. People must have talked about it. Didn't you hear *anything*?'

His fork was still suspended in mid-air. He put it back on his plate, leaving the bite of food uneaten. He looked uncomfortable, unhappy.

He said uneasily, 'In those days, Protestants and Catholics didn't mix as freely as they do today. Our families wouldn't have socialised.'

'You wouldn't need to socialise to hear about a thing like that. I'm sure, deep down, you do remember. Rack your brains a little bit.'

'The older people would know more.'

'I've tried. They maintained they didn't know anything about my aunt. Doesn't that strike you as being odd? A place this size, and no one knows?'

'Who did you approach?'

'Mrs O'Meara – Michael's mother. Alice Egan. Guard O'Hagan. Wouldn't you think they would know?'

He didn't answer that. 'What did they say to you?'

'Guard O'Hagan was quite vague. Dodgy is a better word. Alice got worked up. Said it was better left. For everybody's sake. What do you think she meant by that?'

Bob sighed. 'Alice Egan is a love. She'd be thinking about you.

174

Anyway, I think she's right. The past is better left alone. You should go forward, Caroline.'

'I can't. Not until the past makes sense. Should I speak to someone else? To some other older people. Your father, for instance. He must have heard the story too.'

'Yes. I suppose he must have done.'

The blue eyes were miserable, willing me to drop the subject. Their owner's back was to the window. The sky beyond was changing colour, part indigo, part blue-black, with a line of cream beneath. It was neither day nor night. Nothing yet had been defined.

Where was Bob in all of this?

'I can't afford to lecture you. I'm obsessed with the past myself.'

'In what way are you obsessed?' The sudden sharpness in my voice induced a wry grin from him and an assurance that his particular obsession had nothing to do with my dilemma.

'Let's talk about something else. The positive aspects of our lives.'

'Like what?'

'I gather that your husband's gone. That would be positive for you.'

'I didn't know that you met Leonard.'

'I didn't. But if something isn't working you're better off when it's all over. And if what I hear is right, he sounds rather narcissistic.'

'Leonard *is* a bit self-centred.' Which was being kind to Leonard. Bob was right. I was better off without him.

Not that I accepted that. But it did occur to me that Bob was a different kettle of fish.

The sadness had gone out of his eyes. But why had he been so unhappy? Was it to do with his own past, with which he'd said he was obsessed? His childhood? His wife's death? Perhaps with his mother's breakdown? Perhaps they hadn't socialised, not because of their religion but because of Mrs Studdart. She'd become withdrawn. He must have suffered as a result.

Poor Bob, I thought. I must stop being so suspicious. It's obvious that he knows nothing about Clemency. He's not enemy, he's friend.

From then on, I let the sympathy build up. We talked of other things, mostly about work.

Back in the wood, Bob guided us by torchlight and we entered a world in which the night spoke to us in its own tongue. Not English or Irish or even French, but the one that's spoken in the natural world.

When the jetty stretched before us, Bob switched off the torch and held out his arms to me.

'Caroline?'

175

'No!'

The moon was shining on his face. I thought of the first time I had seen him. Of how threatened I'd felt then.

'Am I being insensitive? You're still in love with Leonard, aren't you?'

That was one way out of it. I told him, yes, it was too soon. 'And anyway—'

'Come on,' he said, and without further ado ushered me gently on to the boat, offered me a choice of cabin, said goodnight, and shut the door.

I was still nervous, still unsure, wondering if he might come back either as a would-be lover or – after all – as enemy.

He did neither. Eventually I got into my bunk, resigned to another night of frightening dreams and wakefulness. Instead, the boat became a cradle and I was rocked into a deep sleep from which I didn't wake at all.

The dreams I had were all of Bob. I dreamt that the alchemy of the natural world had gone to work on me, weaving spells and ridding me of inhibitions. In that night, reservations slid away. The smells and the sounds of the wood, the sensation that he was alone with me and the irrepressible need to protect had their effect on Bob as well. Loving him, I was as wet as the shore where the waves had swept. He parted my legs and drank from me. The boat swayed. The love we made was tangy as pine, pungent as sage, sweet as the lilt of the Irish harp. We were close in every sense, but we were not one, for our loving didn't require that I lose myself in Bob. And when it was over, the two of us laughed and used our bodies in a different way, curved together, side by side.

I woke, refreshed, to a silver landscape, to unseasonable touches of frost on the trees and reeds, and the breath of the lake in the form of mist. Four swans were taking flight just beyond the markers, a ray from the still-hidden sun flashing on their noisy wings. Bob had cooked breakfast for me.

After it had been devoured, we pulled away from the enchanted jetty into a fog in which, all too soon, Gurthalougha was lost to us. The rocks of Goat Island rose up like black icebergs out of the silver lake. Red-breasted mergansers, arrow-like with thin red bills, flew up out of the veils of mist. We passed an eel netters' boat, its crew in yellow dungarees.

Gradually, the fog lifted and warmer shades, peach and apricot, filtered into the lake and land.

'Who needs Majorca when there's this at home?'

176

'That's what I told Pauky Driscoll.'

'I was thinking of the O'Hagans.'

'But they haven't gone away.'

'Oh, yes, indeed they have,' I said. 'Their grandson told me so himself.'

'Their grandson?' Bob was puzzled. 'Do you mean young Brian? He's Guard O'Hagan's afterthought.'

'His *son*?'

'Freckles and a cheeky face? He was on the boat with us.'

'That's him. He was digging in the garden. He told me about Majorca.'

'Pauky and his wife are there. Pauky's a celebrity. He won the lottery, you know. His picture's been in all the papers. But they're the older generation.'

Ah-ha, I thought. So Guard O'Hagan's not away. Young Brian must have got confused with everybody chasing Pauky and thought I, too, wanted him. Well, now I know his dad's at home, I'll call on him when I get back.

'Caroline,' said Bob, 'you're coming to the party, aren't you?'

The party. Another opportunity. Bob himself had admitted that his father must have heard something about Clemency. The party was this very week.

'I'd love to come,' I said to Bob.

I went to Guard O'Hagan's. I didn't have to ring the bell. The front door was standing open and Guard O'Hagan, wearing his accustomed cap, was in the hall, talking on the telephone.

'Come on in,' he mouthed at me, gesturing with his free thumb towards another open door.

'No, it's not,' I heard him say. 'Pauky Driscoll's my father-in-law and he's away. He isn't here.'

The room I entered had pink chintz curtains and chairs to match. A ginger cat was fast asleep on one of the chairs and an elderly terrier with greying ears was sprawled on a well-worn rug.

Neither of them noticed me. It was only when Guard O'Hagan himself came into the room, muttering darkly, 'It's getting out of all proportion!' that the cat stirred, miaowed faintly, and lapsed back into sleep again.

'I'm sorry, Mrs Tremain, but that was Clare FM just now, looking for my father-in-law. His head will be swollen with all the fuss.'

'How much did he win?' I asked.

177

Looking gratified, he told me. It was an impressive figure.

It took a while to get away from lotteries and progress to Clemency, but we got there in the end.

'Guard O'Hagan,' I said, 'has Alice Egan been in touch?'

'She has, despite the press being on the phone. They've jammed the line all week, you know.'

'Then you'll know I've been to see her.'

He looked me straight in the face. I saw in his eyes what I didn't expect to see, a sadness and a sympathy.

He said, 'I'll tell you now about your aunt. You should know that she was drowned.'

'You're certain she was drowned?' I said.

'That was the official verdict.'

'Then that means they found her body.'

'After it had been washed up.'

'Why didn't you tell me that before?'

'I thought Alice told you why. You'd *forgotten*, Mrs Tremain. We thought that it was better left. That it would be bad for you if we talked to you about it.'

He must think I'm unhinged, I thought, to forget what happened here when I was a little girl. And no doubt he has a point.

For a moment I wavered, wondering if it was that simple from Guard O'Hagan's point of view. But then I thought, that isn't so. Something has been covered up. And yet there was his sympathy.

'Mrs Tremain,' he said, and he sounded so sincere, 'I can only say one thing. It might be consolation to you. There was no *evidence*, you see. Nothing we could pin it on. No witness that came forward then.'

'Do you mean that there was talk?'

'A lot of talk was going on. But there was nothing that would show that she might have harmed the girl. That's the point you must remember.'

'Harmed the girl? Harmed Clemency? Was that what they said round here?'

'There's nothing that I can repeat. Nothing that I should have heard. I can't move from that position. The verdict was that she drowned.'

The phone rang again. Muttering, 'The BBC now I suppose!' he went off to answer it.

From where I stood I heard him shout, 'He isn't here. I told you that.'

I trailed through the hall and waited till he'd finished talking.

'That's the end of it,' he said eventually and, replacing the receiver, swung round to find me there. 'The intrusion drives me wild. Let me see you out of here.'

'Wait a minute, Guard O'Hagan. I haven't asked—'

'There'll be others phoning up. We get no peace around this house. And there they are, enjoying the sun, not knowing that we're being plagued.'

Still muttering about the press, he shooed me out of the open door. But the visit had been worth it. I knew now that Clemency's body had been found. That the verdict said she'd drowned. *And* that people had been talking, meaning that they'd been suspicious.

The signs, added to what I knew already, led the way to Marie-Rose. With that conclusion came relief. After all, I wasn't alone. Others had followed a similar path.

Yet they'd lied to me. The past was better left, they said. Thinking of my state of mind. Fearing that I couldn't handle hearing of the tragedy. That did not ring true. There was something more behind it. Something that they wouldn't say. Not to me.

What did they suspect went on? What did they know that I did not? Did anybody know for certain?

I thought, surely Norah must know? Where was she when Clemency died? In the house? She must have been. I didn't remember her ever going out, not at night, at any rate. Her day off, on a Wednesday, never took her very far – no further than the cinema – and she was always home by seven. She must have been at home that night. And Mr O'Casey the solicitor, who might throw light on her whereabouts, must be coming home himself after his prolonged vacation.

I rushed to the phone when I got home and dialled his offices in Scariff.

'He told us on the twenty-first.'

That was the day before the party Bob was giving for his father.

'Would I be able to see him then?'

'He's no appointments free. Not until the twenty-seventh. Can you make it in the morning?'

'Oh, but—'

'I'll put you down for half past ten.'

'All right,' I said reluctantly, reminding myself that I had the party in the meantime and, with it, the chance to talk to Mr Studdart.

I couldn't wait to get to it.

Nineteen

Dressing up was always fun, the kind of challenge I enjoyed. But that was when I thought I knew the woman who was going out.

The day of Mr Studdart's party, I dithered over what to wear. Nothing seemed appropriate until, rooting through my crushed belongings, I found a pale-grey chiffon slip, a converted lining from a ballgown. It was full and ankle-length, more of a skirt than a petticoat. Added to a white silk T-shirt and a decorative belt, it became a party outfit – with another slip beneath it, a black lace one for preference.

The skirt, however, needed ironing. Arriving in the kitchen with it, I ran into Ger and Michael.

'There's not much room to iron down here,' Michael said, accosting me.

I backed off, knowing that since Leonard had left, I was in disgrace again.

'I've just come down to get the iron.'

Then Ger got in on the act as well. 'What room are you ironing in?'

I told him. It was Clemency's. 'I'm going to use that room for storage. I'm tidying out the loft, you see.'

'The room that has the perfume in it? That perfume's fearful strong,' said Ger. 'I'm sneezing all the time from it.'

'What about those books?' asked Michael.

'The books?'

'The ones that have the mildew on them. Are you going to throw them out? They'll be getting in our way when we're working in the library.'

'Some of them will have to go. I must go through them, shelf by shelf.'

I left them to get on with it. I ironed the skirt and put it on and searched for Olive's grey suede shoes. They were perfect with the skirt. But they were curiously sexless. The whole effect was achromatic, as if I'd been decolorised.

Suddenly I was annoyed – with the builders, with myself for letting them walk over me, for looking like a washed-out clod.

I dug inside my case again and found a rose-pink velvet jacket dating from the 1940s and marked down at the Cancer Shop because it had a hole in it. Covered by a beaded rose, you couldn't see the hole at all. Costume jewellery added colour – glass earrings and a matching necklace. I put Clemency's gold bangle on as well.

Time to go. But, coming out of the kitchen door, I found a cow was in the yard, a strange-looking creature with an auburn hide and a fringe of matted hair that gave her a coy appearance. I glowered at her through narrowed eyes. Amusing as she was to look at, I knew what damage she could do to my newly tidied yard.

'We'll have to get you out,' I said, wondering how she had got in. Through that hole in the fence, the one I hadn't yet discovered? Perhaps she'd find her own way out.

She seemed rooted to the spot. I shouted at her to get out. She stared at me reproachfully. I waved my arms around like windmills but she didn't get the message. Finally, I fetched a brush and whacked her on the rump with it.

'Go on. Move off, you stupid creature.'

Sure enough, she lumbered off, crapping on the cobblestones. I found the hole and shooed her through it.

That left me with the hole. It would have to be blocked off. I did it with the folding ladder. By the time I'd done all that, precious moments had been wasted and I knew that I'd be late.

It was hot inside the car. I rolled the windows down for air and the smell of cloves drifted towards me from the wood. By the gates, white foxgloves, rarer than the purple ones, were growing in profusion. Across the lake, the hills exposed their soft blue breasts. In the field the corn was ripe, a paler and less fulvous gold than the bangle on my wrist. You could hear the black rooks cawing. Hear an automatic gun. See the rooks disperse and soar, hover, swoop and then re-settle.

Outside Guard O'Hagan's gate, I saw Freckles and his friend, leaning on their bicycles. They were obviously bored. As I waved at them, I thought how different it used to be, before I was a child myself, when there were country entertainments. Norah used to talk about them. The fun that went with 'pattern days'. The visits to the holy wells. The songs and the pipers and the gooseberry fairs. And, of course, the story-telling. Now there were no summer fairs for the likes of these two boys. The Studdarts wouldn't have a piper and we wouldn't do the cake dance, as they did in days gone by.

The road, following the lake, curved in a Cupid's bow. A bull appeared round the bend. Massive, black, obscenely fat, it looked like a rubber toy blown up to bursting point by a giant's child.

The bull came strutting towards the car. As I pulled away from it, I noticed that it was untethered. I feared that it might gore the boys, but then I saw that a man was coming after it, a swarthy fellow with a scarlet cap and a heavy blackthorn stick. As he swaggered past the car, I thought that they were potent symbols, man and bull as proud as chieftains, kindling thoughts of minotaurs.

Opposite the Studdarts' gateway, two almost identical cottages stood side by side, one with a tiled roof, the other thatched in the old-fashioned way. A small, slim woman was coming out of the tiled cottage. She had a parcel in her hand. She crossed the road and turned into the Studdarts' gateway. When she was halfway up the drive, I parked my car outside her house.

Walking up the avenue, I heard the sounds of talk and laughter. I squeezed between cars, carelessly parked, and stopped for a while to get my bearings.

On the lawn, small groups of people, amongst them Guard O'Hagan, Father Kavanagh, Alice Egan and Michael O'Meara, were catching up on local news, too engrossed to notice me. Weaving my way between the throng, I caught snippets of their conversations.

'He got *inside* the house, you say. Did he get away with much?'

'Just the clock. Noel Lynch saw him on the street and got ahold of Guard O'Hagan.'

'The stuffy weather's killing me.'

'It isn't natural to us.'

At the top of the steps, Frank Studdart was standing with his shoulders back, greeting guests as they arrived. As I approached, he smiled benignly. Encouraged, I held out my hand.

'Happy birthday, Mr Studdart.'

Instead of saying I was welcome, Mr Studdart seemed struck dumb. His expression quickly changed from benign to melancholic. My good wishes might have been a malediction designed to plummet the birthday boy into suicidal realms.

Approaching was another misery, munching on a chicken leg. Francesca. She saw me and her eyes grew darker. Grimacing, she looked away and sidled past me down the steps.

Then someone tapped me on the shoulder.

'Hello, Caroline,' she said.

Oh no, I thought. It can't be her.

183

'Hello, Marie-Rose,' I said. Was that my voice, so choked with terror?

'Did you guess that I'd be here? I'd say you didn't, from your face.'

I must have shuddered at her touch. She must have known I was repulsed. Oh my God, I thought, the bangle. I hid the wrist that it was on in the fold of my petticoat.

'My face said that to you?' I croaked.

'It did for sure,' said Marie-Rose. 'Anyways, Bob always asks me to his parties. I couldn't miss the one for Frank.'

So it was Bob and Frank, I thought. She was right in front of me now, wedged between Frank and me. I set his present, a cookery book, down on the steps, put my hands behind my back, turned the bangle round and round, feeling for the tiny clasp.

'Caroline,' said Marie-Rose, 'why did you go through her things? Were you hoping to find something? Was that why you searched my room?'

She *knew*. But then, of course, she was a witch . . .

'What makes you think I searched your room?'

'The way you put her things back in. You're tidy, Caroline, like me.' She looked at me, all hurt and sad, as reproachful as the cow.

She's mad, I told myself again. *Mad*.

I was still trying to undo the clasp. At last I managed to unhook it. I tried to prise the bangle off and slip it into my shoulder bag. Instead, I lost my grip on it and it fell down the steps behind me.

Cursing silently, I muttered, 'Excuse me, I've got—'

But Marie-Rose had turned away to chat to someone. I looked around for the bangle. I couldn't see it anywhere. Please God, let no one tread on it.

My prayers were answered instantly. Francesca had picked up the bangle. I spotted her inspecting it, peering round to see who owned it.

'That's mine,' I said possessively. I snatched it from her hand and put it safely in my bag. Francesca looked me up and down, disliking everything she saw. She smiled at me triumphantly.

'You've cow dung on your skirt,' she said.

'Have I really? So I have.'

'You smell *horrible*!' she said.

Such a brat I thought she was. I could have boxed her shell-like ears and smacked that smirk right off her face.

She stared at me, a muscle twitching in her cheek, trying her best to hide her pain . . . No, I thought, she's not a brat. She's just a lonely little girl. Chastened, I saw an emptiness in her that mirrored what there was in me. From that void, our loathing of each other came.

I lost the urge to smack her. But I couldn't reach her either.

Was she right and did I smell? My skirt was certainly a mess. I groped for a tissue in my bag, wiped my skirt and made it worse.

Bob came down the steps and saw me. Awful timing. But he kissed my cheek and didn't recoil from the way I smelt.

'You're late. I thought you might have chickened out.' He picked up my discarded gift. 'Who left this parcel here?'

'Me. It was – it *is* a present for your father.'

He put his arm round my shoulder, guiding me from his daughter's wrath, away from his father and Marie-Rose, into the frosty drawing room.

It was crowded in there. A pianist was battling against the noise, playing songs by Percy French.

'I wasn't going to chicken out.'

Bob laughed. 'Good. What would you like to drink?'

His obvious pleasure in my arrival set the tone for the rest of the night. He stayed by my side as the party progressed.

'Great food. Great party,' people said, tucking into pepper tartlets, guzzling the sausage rolls.

I was still preparing for confrontation, hoping I would get the chance to have a word with Mr Studdart. But he was fenced in by his friends and I had to sit it out.

Every so often, through the crowd, I caught sight of Marie-Rose. But to my immense relief she seemed to be avoiding me.

Alice Egan and the others had come in from the garden too. Father Kavanagh was sitting at a small table where cups and saucers were set out, talking to another cleric.

'His Anglican compeer,' said Bob.

The Anglican priest, using a spoon and a sugar lump, was re-playing a game of cricket and trying to explain the rules.

'*Two* bails, did you say, on top?'

'Unless the wind is very high. Then you can dispense with them.'

Shortly afterwards, play was suspended and cheers rang out as a birthday cake with lighted candles on the top was carried in by Marie-Rose.

'Come on, Frank. Blow out the candles.'

More applause as the birthday boy obliged. Then a smiling Frank withdrew and stood over by the door.

My chance, I thought. I'll grab him now.

I stepped forward. Then Francesca made her entrance.

I heard Bob curse – 'Oh, shit!' he said – and saw Francesca in the doorway. She was wearing a wedding gown. Of course it was too big for her and she'd put the veil on crooked. She looked ridiculous, I thought. Ridiculous, pathetic and incredibly pretty.

'Was that her mother's dress?' I said.

Bob nodded. 'She's sending messages to us.'

'Poor little thing. She's all upset.'

'Little monster,' Bob retorted. 'I've had enough of all her nonsense.'

He strode purposefully towards the door. Following slowly, I heard him hiss, 'You're going straight to bed, my girl.'

'No, Daddy. Please. I want to stay.'

'Upstairs, quickly. Straight to bed.'

They were gone, the diminutive bride and her outraged papa. The crowd closed ranks and the party went on. Tomorrow, Francesca's statement would be discussed, her behaviour analysed in shops and pubs throughout the district.

'What do you think was in her mind?' people would be bound to say.

'Ah, sure, poor child. It's obvious.'

Poor little thing, I thought again. I lurked downstairs till Bob came back. Saw him peering round for me. Well, he'd have to wait a while.

I tiptoed quietly up the stairs. Paused on the landing. Heard her sob. I took a risk and didn't knock.

She was lying on the bed, face down, wearing just a pair of panties. Her head was covered by a pillow. But she'd hung up her mother's dress before dissolving into tears.

'Francesca?'

She tensed. In the silence that ensued, I risked myself a second time.

'You needn't worry that I'd come between your father and your mother. I understand how you must feel. You see, my mother also died.'

She didn't speak. She didn't move. But I knew she was paying heed to me. I felt my way towards the place where she was trying to hide away.

'It wasn't quite the same with me because I never knew my mother. And *my* father was in England . . .'

I launched into a monologue. I told her about Carrigrua. How I'd lived there as a child. What the house had meant to me and how I'd hated leaving it.

'When I went to live in England . . .'

By then, the pillow wasn't needed. She looked up from the crumpled sheet. 'How old were you when you left here?'

'Eight.'

'Poor you. But you've come back again,' she said.

The anger and sadness was gone from her now. She stared at me and rubbed her nose and brought me back to the vital point.

'Is my Daddy still as cross?'

'I don't know. I haven't seen him for a while. Do you want me to find out?'

'Maybe. But not yet,' she said. 'Look.' She pointed to a photograph. 'That's them on their wedding day. Don't you think she was pretty?'

'Very pretty. Yes, I do.'

'Daddy *said* the dress was mine.'

'Then I'm positive he means it. Listen, will you come and see my house?'

'Aren't there ghosts at Carrigrua?'

'Not inside the house,' I said, 'only outside, in the wood. And even then there's only one. People call her the Grey Lady.' I told her all about that story. I said that she, although a ghost, didn't frighten anybody.

'It was the house I thought was scary.'

'Carrigrua? Not at all. But when I was five or six . . .'

I made her laugh about the hangman. Then, because she was intrigued, I explained about the loft and about the clothes and shoes that Constance had abandoned there.

'Will you let me look at them?'

'Yes. But they're not in the attic now. I've brought them down to sort them out. I've turned one room into a fortress. I go and hide there from the builders!'

That appealed to her no end. She laughed, yawned hugely and settled underneath her bedclothes. Within minutes, she was sound asleep.

I tiptoed out – and found a spy outside her door.

'Bob. Have you been out here listening in?'

He pulled me to him. Kissed me gently. Then, taking my hand, he drew me along the corridor into a room overlooking the yard.

'My study. Hang on here while I nip down and find us both another drink.'

When he was gone, I spied as well. The room was functional enough. A table acted as a desk. A low sofa had been placed against one wall and bookshelves lined the other ones. The table was a mess, with pads and files all over it. How could someone work like that? With dust all over the computer?

187

Bob returned with wine and glasses.

'Sit down,' he said, chucking more files off the sofa and dislodging a Filofax. 'Oh, so that's where it's been all this time. I think the party's just begun. My father's down there, quite bemused.'

'I thought he was enjoying himself.'

'He is. Approval means a lot to him.'

'He's concerned about approval?'

Bob had drifted off again. I thought he wasn't going to answer but, after a long pause, he did so in a roundabout way.

He said, 'There was a period in his life when he felt – outlawed. It was a bad time. He was depressed. He sold the business. He . . .' Bob shrugged. 'Anyway . . .'

'I upset him. Did you notice? I can't imagine what it is. Can you make any sense of it?'

'It's nothing *you* have done, I promise.' He sat beside me on the sofa. 'Look. About Francesca. You were very kind to her.'

'Not so kind. We talked, that's all.'

'You were patient with her too. I'm afraid I got annoyed.'

'Aren't you rather hard on her?'

'Probably. It's just – I have a problem with Francesca.'

'What's the problem?'

Another of those lengthy pauses. Eventually, 'Do you think she looks like me?'

'No. Why?'

'You saw a picture of her mother. She doesn't look like Helen either.'

'What are you trying to say?'

'That she may not be my child. I'm sorry if that sounds melodramatic. I've never talked – I'm not sure what to say about it.'

'Just tell me what you think,' I said.

He took a deep breath. 'I don't want to speak ill of Helen. She didn't sleep around. We had a very happy marriage. But – we wanted children. We'd been trying for two years when we went to South Africa. We were getting quite disheartened.'

'Did either of you have a test?'

'No. We meant to. But we didn't. In Johannesburg, we said. But, once there, we were diverted. Getting to know the country. Meeting new people. We put off going to see a doctor.'

'Go on.'

'I was away a lot. My job played havoc with our life. We were always opting out. Saying no to invitations. Helen hated being alone so she started going to parties. Then she said that she was pregnant. I was over the moon about it. For her, as well as for myself. But when I think about it now, I realise she was less elated.'

'And?'

'Francesca arrived. She was lovely from the start. Amazing skin and lots of hair. I adored her. So did Helen.'

'So when did you become suspicious?'

'That's the point. I never did. Helen told me, Caroline.'

'She said Francesca wasn't yours?'

'She said she *mightn't* be my child. She didn't know herself for sure. At that stage she was very ill. We knew she wasn't going to live. I wasn't angry when she told me. In fact, it didn't seem to matter. It was such a brief affair. Nothing mattered very much except the state that she was in.'

Downstairs, a noisy sing-song had begun. A car had started up outside. It turned its headlights on our window.

'When did it begin to matter?'

'Gradually. I was numb when Helen died. I carried on with routine things. Decided we should come back here. Made the move. Got Francesca into school. She was insecure. She hung on to me a lot. She still does, as you've observed. I hate to say this, but it's true – the more she clings, the more I hold back from her, the more I think, have I been stuck with raising someone else's kid?'

The car outside was moving off. It was dusky in the study.

Bob said, 'Do you think I'm disgusting?'

'Not at all. Why should I think that of you?'

'I tend to think it of myself. Anyway, enough of that.' He got up. Turned on the central light. And then, 'What have you done to your skirt?' he asked.

Twenty

So now I was back to Norah again, hoping Mr Casey would know where it was she had been put. Another wait, five days this time.

Meanwhile, Bob went off to London. We didn't meet before he left but we'd agreed to get together shortly after he got back.

At Carrigrua, everything was taking shape. The work on the kitchen was almost complete. The upstairs walls had paper on them. The broken panes had been replaced. I thought we were getting places.

'About those books,' insisted Michael.

'I'm going to sort them out. I promise.'

It was not a job I relished. So many books had damp on them. But they were living things to me. I hated getting rid of them.

I put it off. I spun it out. But in the end I had to do it. I filled a dozen bags with books and took them grimly to the dump before returning to the house to repeat the exercise.

Once the higher shelves were cleared, I started working on the low ones. The books below were mainly reference, most of them of little interest to the women of the household. *The Irish Horse, A Walking Sunday, In the Neighbourhood of Dublin*, published 1921. I put them into the rubbish bag and attacked the shelves again.

Stuffed down behind a row of books I came across a plastic bag. A large bag, inscribed 'Todds of Limerick', the store that's owned by Switzers now. Inside the bag were other bags. And a property magazine, listing residential lettings in Richmond, Kew and Twickenham.

Odd. Very odd.

I scrutinised the other bags. Inside them were bras and nighties and a crazy pantie girdle with a Pop motif on it. The nighties were all short and frilly, low-cut ones with satin bows that drew attention to the bust.

I held one up against myself but it was too big for me. The bras were also much too large – size 34 and double D.

Whose could they have been? Not Olive's, I was sure of that. Apart

191

from being too big for her, the lingerie was much too unrestrained. Which ruled Constance out as well. And they weren't Clemency's; to judge by her dress and photo, she was as slim as I was now. That left me with Marie-Rose. Was the lingerie a gift Constance had acquired for her and then concealed behind the books?

Because it was wrapped in plastic, it was perfectly preserved. But the styling and the fabric told me that it had been purchased thirty years or so ago. Surely this was evidence that Constance had a troubled brain? Hiding presents behind books, forgetting them for thirty years, wasn't normal, sane behaviour.

'Ahem.'

'Yes, Sean?'

'Michael says you need to talk about those shelves you said you want.' His eyes fell on the underwear. His cheeks grew pink. He looked away.

'I'll just finish with the books.'

'I'll tell him that,' said Sean and fled.

My nutty aunt, I thought again. No wonder Marie-Rose was able to gain possession of her mind. But why would Constance rent a house, and in south-west London too?

Because she was deranged, I thought. What other reason can there be?

It was the morning of the twenty-seventh. Time I set off for my appointment with Terence Casey. Maybe he would have some answers.

'Will you be back before we go?' Michael asked, catching me going out of the door.

'I'm going to Scariff. Then to Ennis. I reckon I'll be home by four.'

'There's one last unit to go in. When that's fixed I'll need to know the way you want the shelving done.'

Anxious to be off, I said, 'We'll settle that when I come back.'

'The shelves are for your cookery books. I have to measure them, you know, to see how high we need to go.'

'I know. I'll have to get the books for you. They're up there somewhere in my boxes.'

'That space you wanted for the knife rack . . .'

'Yes.'

'And the rack above the sink, the one you want for draining plates . . .'

'Yes,' I said impatiently. 'But can we do this later?'

I got to Scariff slightly late but Mr Casey didn't mind. He was a middle-aged man with a bald head and a strawberry mark on one side of his face but, despite an unprepossessing appearance, he had the kind of confidence that rural people often have, from knowing where they stand in life.

He shook my hand. 'You came here for the funeral. I'm sorry that I wasn't there. My son got married that same day.'

I smiled and said I understood.

'What can I do now for you?'

'I'm trying to track down Norah Cusack. She used to work at Carrigrua. I'm told that she's been – put away. I think that means she's in a home.'

'Indeed she is. In Killaloe.'

'Killaloe? That's wonderful.'

'In fact it's really Ballina, across the bridge from Killaloe. We have her address in our files. She's in a private nursing home.'

'My Aunt Constance saw to that?'

''Twas sorted out for her already. Mrs Conroy made provision. Miss Cusack can stay there for life.'

'I might have known she'd think of Norah. Will you give me the address?'

'I will. My secretary will look it up and check the hours that you can visit.'

While she was doing this I asked what he knew of Clemency.

'Wasn't she the middle sister, the second one to die so young?'

'Yes,' I said. 'She drowned, you know.'

'I've been told that she was drowned.'

Told?

'Do you know any more about her?'

He shook his head regretfully. 'Not really. It was all before my time.'

Disappointed, I persisted. 'But you're familiar with our family affairs?'

'Yes. Of course. In terms of the documents that I hold.'

'Maybe they can tell us something. Oh, and another thing. I'd like to trace the other Conroys. Did you come across the others? We must have been a close-knit family, with the cousins getting married.'

'When did that take place?'

'Sixty years or so ago. Olive was a Conroy too.'

'You mean my client Mrs Conroy?'

'Yes.'

'But what gave you that impression?'

'I've always known that they were cousins.'

Silence.

'Is there something odd in that?'

193

Mr Casey said carefully, 'I was thinking, Mrs Tremain, what exactly were you told about Mrs Olive Conroy?'

He listened gravely as I explained. At the end his face was worried.

'Is there something wrong with that?'

'Just – I'm afraid it isn't true. She was not by birth a Conroy.'

I tried, and failed, to understand. Olive not by birth a Conroy . . .

'She *lied* to me?'

'She must have done.'

'But why would she have told a lie?'

'She would have had her reasons for it.'

'What reasons could she have?' I cried.

'The old ones. Shame and pride,' he said. 'She was illegitimate.' He mentioned Olive's maiden name. A stranger's name, in every sense.

I was bereft. Completely at sea. 'Are you sure that this is right?'

He was sure. Of course he was. He told me something else as well. That Olive's mother was a housemaid. 'We don't know who the father was.'

I said, 'I'm sorry but it's such a shock. I can't believe she was a liar.'

He must have thought I was naive but he tried to comfort me. 'The pressures on her would explain it.'

The pressures made no sense to me. Olive Conroy as *I* knew her was the soul of probity.

'Mrs Tremain?' The secretary was in the doorway. 'The nursing home is on the line. When do you want to see Miss Cusack?'

'When? Tomorrow if it's possible.'

She went out and returned at once. 'Tomorrow will be fine,' she said.

I thanked them for their help and left. Dazed, I drove away from Scariff.

She was not by birth a Conroy.

I don't remember going to Ennis. But I guess I must have done, and also to the antiques shop because, a week later, a stripped elm chest on chest with china handles and a four-door cupboard with a fan motif was delivered to the house.

Olive's mother was a maid.

It wasn't her humble birth I minded, only what she'd done about it. The expertise that she'd employed. The way she'd conned us. Conned *me* with her fancy airs. Her claim to be a different person from the woman that she was.

Olive the stranger. The never-known. But she, like me, had loved the house. That, at least, I knew of her. In other ways she might have changed, though to what I couldn't say, but Carrigrua was the same.

Carrigrua. My stabiliser and support. Steady as the very rock from which its name derived. Whatever else might change for me, I could depend upon the house.

So I told myself, going home. Going back, to look for refuge. To lose myself in restoration. To talk to Michael about shelves.

But Michael hadn't waited for me, and the lads had vanished too. It was only ten past four and the lot of them were gone.

I was furious with them. They'd all cleared off behind my back. Michael hadn't even finished putting in the final unit. Even worse, they'd eaten all the bread and butter – something that they never did when I was there.

Disillusioned, peeved and hungry, I went out in search of food. I parked the car near Michael's house and was accosted by his mother.

'Have they found her, do you know?'

I thought she meant have they found Norah. 'She's in a nursing home,' I said. 'I'm going to visit her tomorrow.'

'They took her to a *nursing home*?'

'They did. Of course she's very old by now. For all I know, she may be senile.'

Michael's mother shook her head. 'It's young Francesca that I mean.'

'Francesca Studdart?'

'Yes indeed. You didn't hear that she's gone missing?'

My stomach did a somersault. 'No. I've been in Scariff and in Ennis. How long has she been gone from home?'

'Michael says she went this morning. They're searching for her everywhere, Michael and the rest of them. I hear her father's wild with worry. It seems he had a row with her and afterwards she ran away.'

'Where are they then? Where did they go?'

'They've done the land by Rinskea House. The glebe house has been searched as well. She wasn't at the harbours either. They've gone off now the other way, along the road beside the bog.'

'She could be with a friend,' I said. 'She's only missing since this morning.'

'Ah, sure, but she's no good with friends. And she was gone before her breakfast. Her father found her room was empty. She maybe left when it was night. It seems the row took place last evening.'

I wasn't hungry any more. 'I think I'll go and help the search.'

'Do that now. And let me know when she is found.'

I drove to the road beside the bog. From the car I saw the crowd, split up into groups of four. There must have been a hundred people.

Children had joined in as well. Some men had brought sticks with them and slashed the grass as they walked through it.

I looked for Bob. Caught sight of him with Guard O'Hagan. Spotted Michael and the lads.

As I drove nearer, Bob turned round.

'Caroline. You haven't seen Francesca, have you?'

'No,' I said. 'I wish I had.'

'I went to Carrigrua first. But you'd already left for Ennis.'

'Do you think she hitched a lift?'

'I'm worried sick in case she did. I know the youngsters round here do it, but you never know these days.' He ran his fingers through his hair, every bit the frantic father.

'I hear you had an argument.'

'Yes. Last evening. All my fault.'

'What happened?'

'I'd only just got back from London. I promised I'd watch *Neighbours* with her but it's on so bloody early. I started working on my notes and I forgot what time it was. She was all reproachful with me. Said I didn't care about her. You know how it is with her.'

'So what happened after that?'

'Both of us were all worked up. I sent her off to bed again. I know – I *know* that I was wrong, but I got exasperated. I thought she was asleep up there. But she didn't come for breakfast and she wasn't in her bedroom. Then we found the front door unlocked. The thing is, she could have left the house last night after I had gone to bed.'

An awful thought occurred to me: Francesca walking in the dark all the way to Marie-Rose, the very person who had boasted of her friendship with the Studdarts. The fear that was stirred up in me came from the stories that I'd heard when I was a little girl. Tales of the kinkeshins – people who had evil power. Witches who would dope their victims. Cursing stones and stolen children . . .

'She may be somewhere fast asleep. Maybe in a barn or shed.'

'We've looked in all the barns and sheds.'

'Well, maybe—'

The green post office van pulled up and Roisin Ryan put down the window. 'I hear you're searching for Francesca.'

'We are. Don't tell me you have news of her.'

'I saw her earlier this morning, outside the gates of Carrigrua.'

'What time was that?' demanded Bob.

''Twas shortly after nine o'clock.'

'Was she heading for the village?'

'She was stopped outside the gates, as if she might be turning in.'

'On her way to Caroline. And Caroline was out, you see, so—'

'Did you search the wood for her?' I asked.

'Yes, we did, and the grounds. But she'd have seen your car was missing. Perhaps she went the other way, along the shore, towards Mountshannon. We didn't go in that direction.' Bob was all excited now. We beamed at each other, our hopes renewed.

I said, 'I'm sure that's what she must have done.'

'She's got to be there,' Bob declared. 'Let me round the others up and then I'll hitch a lift with you.'

'Don't call off the search just yet, just in case she isn't there.'

'No,' he said, 'I won't. You're right.'

Hating, but accepting this, he called and gestured to the others. They filtered back towards the road, getting into their cars or hitching lifts from people passing. Guard O'Hagan went with Roisin. Some got into Michael's lorry. Alice Egan came with us, bringing two young girls with her.

Back we went to Carrigrua, through the village, past the glebe house, which used to be the rectory, where the brothers who drowned had set out that fatal day.

Don't think of accidents, I said to myself.

All of us more cheerful now, we turned and drove into the wood, stopped in the yard and got out of the car.

The two young girls appraised the house.

'It's looking beautiful,' said one.

The other girl saw more than that. '*Look!*' she said, and tugged my arm. 'Smoke is coming from that window. Someone's up there, waving at us!'

'It's Francesca!' Bob exclaimed.

She was up there in the bedroom that belonged to Clemency. And smoke was coming from the window . . .

Bob was gone, inside the house and up the stairs.

I ran blindly after him. Halfway up I heard her shouting. 'Daddy, Daddy! Get me out!'

We were on the landing now, horrified by what we saw. More smoke – it was horrible – was puffing out beneath the door.

From inside Francesca shouted, 'Daddy. Daddy. There's a fire. I can't go out. It's by the door.'

'Don't go near the fire,' said Bob. 'Stay over by the window, pet.' He rushed back down the stairs again.

'Francesca,' I said. 'Please just stay beside the window. Daddy's going to get you out.'

197

'Get me out of here,' she wailed.

'*Daddy's* going to get you out.'

'You've got to let me out of here!'

But that was not Francesca calling. It was a voice coming out of the past.

'Let me out of here, you witch!'

I next recall being in the yard, watching Bob go up the ladder. There was the sound of breaking glass. Fragments fell like spiky hailstones.

Then, as two figures appeared on the ladder, shouts of triumph broke out around me. Francesca was draped across her father's shoulders, limp and lifeless, like a doll. As they got nearer to the ground, hands reached out to give assistance.

'Is she all right, the child?' said Alice.

'She's unconscious. Stand aside.'

Michael had removed his coat. He spread it on the cobblestones so Bob could lay Francesca down.

'She's inhaled some smoke,' he said. 'Has someone phoned the fire brigade?'

'Yes, I did,' said Guard O'Hagan. 'It should be here at any minute.'

Shortly afterwards, the Scariff fire brigade arrived. Six firemen leaped out, an oxygen mask was produced and held against Francesca's face.

'The ambulance is on its way,' the officer in charge assured us.

Meanwhile, smoke was pouring freely now from the window Bob had smashed. In an effort to assist, the crowd had formed a human chain, bringing buckets from the well.

'Stop!' The officer dispersed the crowd. 'Stand well back. We'll see to this.'

The firemen got to work with hoses. Cradled in her father's arms, Francesca regained consciousness.

'Daddy?'

'It's all over, little one. You're out. You're safe. I'm here for you.'

Then the ambulance pulled in. A stretcher was produced from it. Francesca was put on to it.

'I'll go with her,' Bob insisted, jumping into the ambulance.

The doors were shut. The siren sounded.

'Where are they taking her?' somebody asked.

'To the hospital in Ennis.'

She was out. She was safe. She wasn't crying any more. But, standing numbly in the background, I could hear those cries for help.

'*Let me out of here, you witch!*'

And with them, another voice, calling to me from the past.

198

'*You're staying there. I've locked the door.*'

The fire above was still being fought. I heard the sound of water too, and with it the roar of fire, like heavy rain and howling wind.

'*Let me out of here this minute.*'

'*You'll stay in there. You won't come out.*'

'Mrs Tremain?'

The firemen all wore yellow helmets but the officer's was white. All I could think of was colour and noise.

'*Please* move back a little further.'

Suddenly, there was an almighty crash and Alice Egan crossed herself.

'Mother of God, whatever is that?'

'I'd say 'twould be the water tank, falling through to the room below,' said the officer.

The room below was Clemency's.

'Keep back,' he repeated. '*We'll* put it out.'

In half an hour the fire was out but that was not the end of it. The firemen had to clear the debris, remove the ashes from the house – what had once been Olive's hats and those shabby woolly jerseys. And there was other trash as well. The remnants of a dressing table. The charred remains of that old bed.

The clearing job took three full hours. Several people asked me home, for food, for drinks, to spend the night.

I shook my head and thanked them all. I couldn't leave the house, I said.

So, in the end, they went without me and I waited in the yard until the firemen finished clearing.

'The house must be checked every few hours, Mrs Tremain,' the officer in charge informed me. 'We'll want to hose it down again.'

'I'll keep a watch on it,' I said.

'*You? You're* stopping here? You mustn't go inside the house.'

'I know. But I won't want to go to bed.'

They were kind, the Scariff firemen. They understood how people feel when their houses have been burnt. But eventually they left, to spend the evening with their families, and I was on my own again, sitting over by the well, remembering those cries for help.

Those cries had come from Clemency. I knew that now. I'd always known it. But I'd not acknowledged it. Not until tonight, when I remembered another night.

That night, there was a storm in Clare. The rain had pelted down on us. The wind had whined around the house, echoing the screams I heard. For I'd been in my room that night. I was cowering on the bed, just yards away from Clemency. I heard her scream and weep and shout. I heard her beating on the door.

And I heard a second voice, telling her to stop that bawling.

'You won't get away with it. It doesn't matter what you do. I've told you that you're not to go.'

Get away with what? I wondered. And where could she have planned to go?

But there was more than that to it. I recalled what else was said. The venom in the ugly words, and the shameful condemnation. I couldn't stand the things I heard. I couldn't face the implications.

Afterwards, the room was wrecked. I heard the sounds of that as well. And other sounds that frightened me. Animal sounds. The noises that a creature makes when it thinks that it is trapped.

I heard a window being smashed, followed by a peal of thunder. There was turmoil everywhere and I was sure that the *Tuatha De Danann*, the fairy people who lived beneath the ground, were about to rise from it.

I got out of bed and clambered on to the windowsill. I felt safer higher up. But as I huddled there in terror, the thunder roared and lightning streaked and I saw the rest of it.

Now, more than thirty years later, huddled up beside the well, I relived that night. I shivered as I thought of it.

'Caroline. What are you doing here all on your own?'

Bob had come to look for me. In his presence, I tried to adopt a normal facade and concentrate upon the present.

'Tell me how Francesca is.'

'They're keeping her in hospital but they say that she'll be fine. She's actually in quite good spirits. Just worried that you're cross with her.'

'Why should I be cross with her?'

'She came here to look for you. When you weren't home, she snooped around. You told her there were some old clothes stored away inside the house – in that bedroom, I suppose. She was curious – and hungry. She helped herself to bread and butter, thinking she'd make toast upstairs, light a fire in the grate. It's hard to believe the rest of it, but she says honey dripped on her. She got a fright and dropped the match.'

'She was right about the honey. You look done in,' I said to him.

'So do you. We need to sleep, the two of us. Come on. Let's get you out of here.'

I felt no fear of Bob that night. There was no room for fear in me. I was drained of all emotion. But I did have reservations.

'I can't go home with you,' I said. 'Your father mightn't fancy it.'

'We'll sleep on the boat instead.'

'I can't leave Carrigrua, Bob. The firemen said it should be watched.'

'That doesn't mean by you,' said Bob. 'I'll get someone else to do it.'

He prised me gently out of there and took me with him to *The Helen*. The someone else was rounded up to watch the house. I was given food and drink and Bob and I got into bed.

We did not make love. He simply held me in his arms and, though the thoughts I tried to banish did their best to batter me, his affection kept them from me.

I was the one who woke up first. Not because I'd slept enough but because someone tried to wake Bob.

'Bob,' said the someone. 'Bob, wake up. The hospital is on the line.'

Frank Studdart was standing beside our bunk. He didn't notice me at first, cuddled in there next to Bob. Then he did.

He gasped, his face a study in horror and shock. His reaction to my presence in his son's bed turned our night of tenderness into a louche, demeaning morning.

Twenty-One

On the way to Killaloe, I still felt his eyes on me. Little tart, I thought they said.

Francesca was well. The hospital had phoned to say she could come home.

'What time will you pick her up?' Frank Studdart asked Bob. 'They need to know. They're holding on.'

'Tell them I'll phone back,' said Bob.

His eyes averted from our bunk, Mr Studdart left the boat.

'I must go as well,' I said, wanting to get out of there.

In the car, it occurred to me that I should buy a gift for Norah, flowers and a box of chocolates. Peppermint creams were her favourite sweets, a passion she had shared with me and one that we'd indulged together at the cinema in Scariff. I was the one who was buying them now and the flowers would come from a florist's shop, not from the garden at Carrigrua.

The nursing home was a short distance outside the ancient town of Killaloe, itself the residence of the last High King of Ireland, Brian Boru, and the site of a monastery founded by Saint Lua in the sixth century.

A sign for Saint Flannan's, pointing in two conflicting directions, must have confused those who didn't know that Saint Flannan's Roman Catholic church stood in Main Street, at the top of the hill, and Saint Flannan's Protestant cathedral, with its magnificent Romanesque doorway, down at the other end of the town.

In that historic place, the High King had once assembled a fleet of three hundred boats to rout the invading Danes. But now only two old men could be seen in the town, sitting together on a bench, watching as the cars went by.

I drove over the thirteen-arch stone bridge that joins the county of Clare with the county of Tipperary. The bridge had its bloody history too. Four republicans were shot there by the Black and Tans in the early nineteen twenties. Their fingernails were pulled off first, or so Marie-Rose had said.

On the other side of the bridge was the little village of Ballina. The Leinstermen had lived there once, and lost their cattle to King Brian. Now, the houses of the affluent were lined up on the river bank.

It was the beginning of August, Lunasa, in pagan culture, when people used to sing and dance and party by the waterside. The farmers had brought in their crops but there was no festival to mark the end of harvest time, no one picking flowers and fruit as they would have done in pagan times, and no horses being swum to fend off the powers of evil.

I pulled into the grounds of the nursing home, an ugly one-storey building set between two broad oaks. As I turned off the ignition, dozens of small, white butterflies promptly fluttered round the car in a frisson of delight.

Inside the home, a white-clad nurse was expecting me.

'She's all dolled up for you,' she said. 'She was *thrilled* to hear you phoned. She's felt a bit neglected lately. Mind you, she does get confused. She couldn't work out who you were. But she'll be fine with you, I'm sure. Let me bring you in to her. Those flowers are just beautiful. She's going to be *delighted* with them.'

Made nervous by this chatter, apprehensive of finding Norah in a state of horrendous decline, I followed the nurse along a corridor into a room with pea-green walls.

In a high bed, propped up by three pillows, was a very old woman with a deeply lined face and sparse white hair on her pale-pink skull. She was asleep, her head slightly tilted to the left and her freckled, blue-veined hands relaxed on the snow-white counterpane, but the nurse insisted that she'd soon wake up.

'Sit down there so and wait for her.'

I collapsed into a dark-green damask armchair, wishing I could go to sleep too. The room was comfortable enough, the floor covered in a multi-patterned carpet which, although it set my teeth on edge, was new and soft beneath the feet. There was a small picture of a whitewashed cottage with a mountain backdrop on one wall and a china figurine on the windowsill. Someone else had brought in flowers, three large cabbage roses, and put them in a pottery vase.

Fifteen minutes or so ticked by. Maybe she would never wake but slip away from me into eternity before I knew that she was gone.

But then she gave a little shudder. Her head straightened up and her eyelids opened. It took another couple of minutes before she realised I was there.

'Clemency!' she said wonderingly. 'But they told me you were dead.'

'No,' I said. 'No, Norah. It's Caroline, not Clemency.'

'My lovely girl! You've come back after all this time. Come over here and let me kiss you.'

This was the welcome for which I had yearned. The tears were pricking at my eyelids as I went to let her kiss me. Her arms were frail, a pair of twigs instead of arms, but while their grip on me was feeble, the love in them was charged with power.

She smelt not of old age but of the shampoo that they'd used to doll her up.

'Sit down and let me look at you.'

I did so, fighting off the tears.

'Clemency,' she said again.

She might have hit me in the stomach.

'No, Norah. Not Clemency. *Caroline*. Don't you remember me?'

'Your voice is different, Clemency. You have an English accent now. Is that because you've been away?'

It's going to be hopeless, I thought, distressed. Her body's here but her mind has gone.

'Tell me, how is Constance keeping? She never comes to see me now. She used to come here all the time. But now it's only Marie-Rose, and she hasn't been for ages.'

'Constance is fine,' I said, unable to tell her that Constance was dead. At the same time I realised that if I was to learn anything at all from her, I'd have to play a part. To her, I was Clemency. However much I might dislike it, I must keep up that pretence.

'We're all fine at Carrigrua.'

She looked at me suspiciously. 'How can that be so?' she said.

I was beginning to run out of platitudes. I searched wildly for something to say. 'Why wouldn't we be fine?' I said at last.

She answered with surprising force. 'You know full well why that can't be so.'

Wherever I went a mist came up. Just now it would turn to fog.

I tried to break through the obfuscation. 'We *are* all right,' I lied again. 'You've only got to look at me.'

It was awful lying to her. She was too sincere a person, too loving, to be a victim of deceit. I badly wanted to own up. But I steeled myself against it, in the hope she'd tell me something.

When she spoke again she sounded cross. 'I don't know why they lied to me.'

'Lied? Who lied to you, Norah?'

'All of them. The whole lot lied.'

'What did they lie to you about?'

'About yourself,' she said impatiently. 'What else could it be about?'

'What exactly did they say?'

She ignored the question. Her eyes moved away from me. Her lips were pursed, as if in pique. 'They lied to me,' she said again.

'Tell me what they said,' I pleaded.

'You know full well, my pretty girl.'

'I don't. I promise. I've no idea what they might have said.'

'And why would *you* be nice to me?' She wasn't huffy now but wistful. There was a wobble in her voice. Her tired old eyes had tears in them.

I was a monster for plaguing her. But I did so, all the same.

'Why wouldn't I be nice?' I said, resisting the urge to hug her again, to wipe the sadness from her face.

''Tis surprising that you came. Does that mean you've forgiven me then?'

'Forgiven you?'

'I let you down. I know I did. I'll tell you now, 'twas my fault, pet. You told me not to breathe a word. But she got it out of me.'

I sat forward, excited now, aware that I was on to something. 'What did she get out of you?'

'She's that determined and that clever. I never meant to let it out.'

There was the sound of trolley wheels in the corridor outside. Teatime.

Aware that we'd be interrupted, I said quickly, 'I'm not blaming you a bit. But what did you say to her?'

Norah closed her eyes, as if to shut me out. She was quiet for so long I thought that she'd dozed off. I quelled the impulse to give her a shake, ashamed of myself for thinking of that, yet determined not to leave until I'd got the truth from her.

'Norah?'

The frail body gave a jerk.

'No,' she said, and I knew she wasn't sleeping, only hiding from the past. 'I didn't mean to let her know. You must believe me when I tell you.'

'I do, Norah. I do believe you. I just want you to explain—' I stopped, shocked by the distress in her. Her face was that of a very old ghost. Her hands were shaking on the counterpane, like dry leaves caught in an autumn breeze. Her voice was drowned by tears. They

206

welled up in her filmy eyes and filtered down her pallid cheeks. Horrified by this, I sat there dumbly, wondering how to rectify matters.

Norah buried her face in her hands. I got up and stood by her bed.

'Please, Norah. Please, please don't cry.'

Her fingers parted and through them the filmy eyes stared beseechingly at me. The eyes of an animal, trapped behind bars.

'Please, Norah—'

'What's the matter?'

It was the nurse who had shown me in. She was clutching a vase, presumably for the flowers I'd brought, but her mood had changed since our earlier encounter.

'What's going on in here? She's never like this. What have you done to upset her?' she demanded, eyes that were nearly navy blue spurting out two jets of rage. 'Ah, now, Norah, don't be crying. Sure, what need is there for that?'

'Nurse?'

But she had no time for me. 'You'd no right to get her into this state. You must go now, Mrs Tremain. You've been in here for far too long.'

'I'm sorry.'

'So I should think and all.'

'Norah? I'll come back in a couple of days.'

'Don't hurry yourself, will you!' the nurse exclaimed.

Bowed by remorse, I crept away from her disapproval. Like snowflakes whirling round the trees, the butterflies danced their lives away. But the temperature had dropped. I shivered getting into the car and quickly put the heater on.

I tuned in the radio. A U2 track blared out. I turned it off again, only to hear another refrain.

'*She got it out of me . . . I never meant to let it out.*'

As I drove through Ballina and over the bridge into Killaloe, the words went round inside my head. And my own words. '*What did she get out of you?*'

The two old men were still on the bench, taking stock of what went on. What did they know that I did not? What if I stopped and said to them, 'What do you know about my aunt?'

But that I might still get from Norah. I'd have to go back to the nursing home. I'd promised her I'd do that. In a couple of days, I'd said to her.

It would be easier to talk to her without the nurse I'd upset. She wouldn't always be on duty. I'd no way of checking her working schedule. I didn't even know her name. But it was Thursday now and the chances were that she wouldn't be working all weekend. I'll come back on Sunday, I said to myself. I won't phone first, I'll just arrive.

I went home, back to the ruins of Carrigrua. The walls were black and dripping wet, the brand-new paper falling down. All the floors were sodden too. It might have been a bog I walked on. The fire was out, no doubt of that, but Carrigrua smouldered still, in anger that it had been burnt.

The smell of scent was there no more. Instead, there was the stench of smoke outside the charred remains of what had been a bedroom door. Clemency had left the room. I knew that she was gone for ever, that her essence was cremated. In her place was desolation.

But that was where I went to stay. Where I hid away from Bob, and from my embarrassment. I pretended I wasn't in when he came to look for me. I lived and slept with the stench of smoke till Sunday came and then went back to the nursing home.

A younger woman with bubbly curls and a sunny smile had replaced the other nurse. She was humming a tune as I went in.

'Hello,' she said cheerfully. 'Who have you come to see?'

Her *joie de vivre* infected me.

'Norah Cusack,' I said quite brightly. 'If that's all right with you, I mean. I know she's frail. I should have phoned.'

'Ah,' she said. 'That's fearful sad. You've missed her by so short a while.'

'She isn't here? Where has she gone?'

'She passed away on Friday night.'

'She's *dead*?'

'Yes. It was sudden in the end. Are you related to her then?'

'In a way.'

'We didn't know that she had family. We were in touch with her friend all right. The one who's living at Mountshannon.'

'Miss Keane?'

'And there was someone else in Scariff. Her solicitor, I think. She never told us about you.'

'We weren't that close in recent years.' I wished that hadn't been the case. I wished that I'd reached out to Norah. Broken through the barriers that age put up, had her see me as I was, as Caroline, not Clemency. Instead of which I had deceived her. Taken advantage of her condition in my search for information. And meant to do the same again . . .

'I'm sorry for your trouble,' said the curly-haired nurse, trying hard to look grave, to superimpose sobriety on a face designed to smile.

I nearly said I was sorry for hers. Melancholy didn't suit her.

'Did she die in her sleep?' I asked instead.

'Well, she kind of slipped away. Not that she was in any pain. Only that she was distressed.'

My conscience stabbed me viciously. You see, it said, what you have done?

'What was she distressed about?'

'She was addled in her head. She was ninety-two, you know.'

'I didn't know she was so old.'

'She was alive in Easter Week! Anyway, as I was saying, she became a bit fixated. That old song was in her head. You won't know the one I mean. They didn't sing it in your day.'

I was confused myself by then. 'What song was that?' I asked the nurse.

For answer, she began to hum. 'I bet you don't remember that. My grandmammy sang it when I was young. I don't remember all the words, just—' She hummed again. Then she added the words she knew.

> *Oh, my darling,*
> *Oh, my darling,*
> *Oh, my darling, Clementine,*
> *Thou art lost and gone for ever,*
> *Oh, my darling, Clementine.*

She stopped and looked at me triumphantly. 'That was what she was on about. Clementine. I remember that because of the song.'

Conscience stabbed me a second time, digging the knife in that much deeper. I was weeping inside myself, not only for the loss of Norah but for the harm that I had done.

'I see,' I said. 'That's dreadful. Awful.'

'She didn't remember the words at all. Just the name of the girl in the song. And she put in another line, one that she made up herself. She kept going on and on about it.'

'What line was that?' I ventured to ask.

' "'Twas my fault, Clementine." She couldn't get it out of her head. "'Twas my fault, Clementine." She said it up to the very end.'

Twenty-Two

The trees in the wood were overgrown. From their interwoven branches, baby birds had learnt to glide since I'd come to Carrigrua. But I was confined in a nest made from loss and tragedy. I couldn't fly. I couldn't go on, as I knew I had to do if I wanted to survive.

But I had no more leads to follow. And around me there was havoc. The house was like a half-felled oak at which the high red wind had raged. I wept for the wasted effort and time we'd put into its restoration. I mourned the loss of the joy I'd known as the house came back to life.

'It's not as bad as you think it is,' said Michael, coming to work the following week as if there hadn't been a fire.

'I don't know how you can say that.'

'We could repair the roof for you. We could re-build the attic floor and lift the water tank back up. And the bedroom it fell on, that could be restored as well.'

'It would never look the same.' I was determined to be depressed.

'It didn't look so good to start with. I take it that you were insured.'

'I was. I am. But—'

''Tis a pity not to save it.'

I should have been enthralled by Michael's interest in the house. I couldn't summon up my own. I'm sure he thought I was a pain, the way that I responded to him.

'If you're sure that you can do it . . .'

'As I said, it's not so bad.'

He took over the project. You'd have thought the house was his, the way he spoke of saving it, the care that he put into it.

This time round, more men were needed. The lads were called in from the garden, and Ger's brother was recruited, the one who'd studied bees at school. Matt Murphy was enlisted too, to re-wire that section of the house that was damaged by the fire.

'It could have been far worse,' said Matt, intending to be reassuring.

211

'You only lost that little bed. You're lucky that the one with poles wasn't in the master bedroom.'

'I suppose I am,' I said, feeling anything but lucky.

Matt was all on for a chat while I wanted to retreat and take my fears inside a fortress. But there was nowhere I could hide. With all the extra men in it, the house felt much the same to me as Harrods does on Saturdays.

Thinking I should do some work, I took my paints and sketchpad out. But I couldn't settle down. I left my sketchpad in the kitchen and wandered aimlessly around.

Coming in to make a sandwich, I encountered Matt again. He was thumbing through my sketchpad.

'I see you've drawn the house in here. 'Tis just the way it is and all.'

I willed him not to hang around but he didn't get the message.

'You've even put the harbour in.'

I grunted and put on the kettle.

'And the Freeman 22.'

Ignoring that, I reached for bread. Got the butter and the cheese.

'It's rare to see one on this lake.'

'So I gather. Have you finished with the wiring?'

But Matt was not to be put off. 'The only one I ever saw was the one Frank Studdart owned. He had a Freeman 22.'

He had my attention now. *Frank Studdart* had a boat like that?

'A Freeman 22, you say? *He* had a Freeman 22?'

'I daresay there were others like it. But I never came across them.'

'When was that?' I asked, knowing that it would be *then*, certain that it was *the* boat.

'Thirty years or more ago.'

He lit a fire inside my head. I blazed with anger. Smouldered. Raged. Thinking all the while of Frank and of what he'd tried to hide. Thinking about Bob as well, and how he had lied to me. Bob had also seen that sketch. He knew who had owned the boat. Like Olive, he had lied to me. Dodged the questions I'd asked. Answered them with other ones. Asked *me* why I'd drawn that boat.

He had lied to me. And Matt had lit a fire in me.

I left Matt standing in the kitchen with the sketchpad in his hand. I rushed outside, into the car.

I took off with a screech of tyres. I drove too fast along the road that led towards the Studdarts' house, nearly hitting a farmyard dog, rehearsing my lines for the confrontation.

212

'Why did you lie?' I'd say to Bob. 'What are you trying to cover up? Whatever it is, I'm on to you.'

The broken gate had not been fixed. I pushed it open angrily.

Bob's car wasn't there. That made me madder still, set to take my anger out on his dishonest, heinous father.

Flushed with rage, I rang the doorbell. Was Mr Studdart in the house, peering from an upstairs window? When he saw that I was there, would he pretend he wasn't in? If so then I'd ring again, and do so till he answered me.

He came promptly to the door.

'Good afternoon,' he said politely.

Just for a minute, my anger went. I saw myself through Olive's eyes. This man was old, a gentleman. My attitude to him was wrong. I was being uncouth, I thought. I was stepping out of line. I was not being ladylike . . .

Then my anger was back again, winkling me out of the shell of the past into a less respectful present.

'May I come in and talk to you?'

Mr Studdart hesitated. But he had been conditioned too. 'By all means,' he said, and showed me into the drawing room – that cold, forlorn, unhappy room that cried out for a woman's touch. 'Please sit down.'

I think he knew what I was after.

He put a hand on the coffee table, his fingers splayed like half a star.

'I've come here about Clemency.'

He bent his head, surrendering, I thought triumphantly.

'I thought that might be why you came.'

'I know about your boat,' I said. 'That was the one the Guards found on the rocks off Holy Island after Clemency went missing. That's true, isn't it?'

'Yes, that's true. It was my boat.'

'I want to know what happened to her.'

'I can't tell you that,' he said.

'She was murdered, wasn't she? And you conspired in a cover-up.'

'No!'

I was determined to get at the truth, even if I lied myself. 'I know you did. I've proof of it.'

'That's not how it was at all.'

'I'm going to Dublin,' I said loudly. 'To tell the Guards there about it.'

'No!' Star-like hand on the coffee table.

'Then tell me what happened to her,' I said. 'Tell me about Clemency.'

'I can't.'

'I'll raise Hell for you,' I said. 'Hell for you, and Hell for Bob.'

He swallowed. Pleaded for mercy one more time, speaking only with his eyes. But I had no pity for him. I was ruthless.

'Tell me about Clemency.'

'I'll tell you what I know,' he said miserably.

He knew that the 5 p.m. Dublin to Limerick train would stop at Birdhill station, three miles from Killaloe, where Bea, his wife, had arranged to pick him up. He was a wine and spirit merchant. Dublin was the capital of the Irish wine trade and he went there fairly often to replenish stock, meet the main wholesale importer, and lunch with fellow merchants.

It was October. In his business, harvest time. In the taxi to what was then Kingsbridge and is now Heuston station, he was thinking about the high-quality vintage that was forecast out of Bordeaux. He was always thinking business. Bea said he was a workhorse, that he never seemed to rest. But Bea was a zealot too, involved with several charities and with Church of Ireland projects.

He was feeling pleased with himself. The vintage ports that he'd acquired were going to go up in value. But in weather terms Dublin had been rather bleak, with a biting wind and a heavy, leaden grey sky that he'd found a bit oppressive. He'd be glad to be in Clare where the wind would be blowing the autumn leaves and clothing the county in yellow and red instead of sombre pewter tones.

He arrived well in time for the evening train. He was never late – people said they set their watches by Frank Studdart's daily movements.

He found a corner seat and settled down with the *Evening Herald*. The train began to fill up. But nobody sat next to him and he was just thinking how lucky he was to have the seat all to himself when Clemency Conroy came up the aisle.

He'd known her since she was a child and watched her grow from a pretty girl into a beauty in her twenties. Yet he thought of her – on the rare occasions when he *did* think of her – not as a woman but as a girl.

She was quite smartly dressed in a lightweight suit with a bell-shaped skirt and matching dark-grey high-heeled shoes. But she didn't walk with confidence, as women who have lovers do.

'Hello, Frank,' she greeted him. 'Well, aren't I the lucky one, finding a seat beside yourself.'

She was a cordial, talkative creature and Frank, in spite of wanting

214

to read the paper, was happy enough to have her for company in the knowledge that she'd probably chatter all the way to Birdhill station.

She was carrying several bags, most of which he took from her and placed on the rail above her head. But she hung on to one of them, as if the contents were too precious to relinquish from her grasp.

'I've been doing Grafton Street.'

'So I see. Have you been buying gardening books?'

Clemency was an accomplished gardener who won prizes for her flowers. It was what she did all day – the Conroy sisters didn't work, or not for money anyway. According to Bea, the garden she had created up at Carrigrua House was really most unusual. All the flowers in it were red. Begonias and red-hot pokers. Stonecrop. Mallow. Dahlias. A bit too florid for Bea's taste but, all the same, a work of art.

'I did buy *one* gardening book,' Clemency said. 'But it was clothes that I was after.'

'Was your buying spree successful?'

'I've had *great* success today! I bought myself an evening dress.'

'Are you going to a dance?'

'Yes, the Clare Hounds' hunt ball. It's at Castle Oliver. I'm not that keen on going really. But my mother wants me to, in the hope I'll find a husband.'

Frank laughed. 'Don't *you* want to find a husband?'

'Not the sort that she would like.'

She'd seemed ingenuous till then. But her last remark was bitter and he detected anger in her. He decided to let it pass. Keeping things on a lighter level, he asked what colour dress she'd bought.

For answer, Clemency reached into the last of the plastic bags and drew out an evening gown. Rose-red, strapless, taffeta.

'It's beautiful,' he said politely. 'It will suit you very well.'

'Do you think so?'

Unconcerned by their fellow travellers' interest, she held the dress against herself. As she did so, everything changed. The neutral day, instead of being all washed out, was instantly infused with colour. Clemency, who was all in grey herself, came alive for him as well. He saw her in a different light, not as a rather coltish girl but as the woman she was meant to be.

As his perception of her changed, so did his attitude towards her. He thought how attractive she suddenly was, and how delicious it would be to kiss her and make love to her.

Clemency was smiling at him. How natural she was, he thought. How free from artifice. What fun. His was a rather serious life. He

215

enjoyed being with his son – Bob was nearly six by then – but otherwise his whole existence had been focused on the business.

As Clemency replaced the dress, folding it in tissue paper, Frank stared at his *Evening Herald*. He was over forty, he thought. Much too old for Clemency. Even if he were free. But of course he wasn't free. He had never been unfaithful. He was not disloyal by nature. He respected, *cared* for Bea.

Bea, though, couldn't be described as fun. Worthy, yes. A pretty woman. But they didn't laugh a lot.

What on earth was up with him, to be criticising Bea just because of this encounter? And what did he feel but a stab of lust, a heightened awareness of somebody else? Such things happened all the time. He was just a normal man, and Clemency was beautiful. That was all there was to it. A passing attraction, nothing more, and he'd soon forget about it. When he saw Clemency again – which, in spite of living near her, he very seldom did in fact – it might not even cross his mind. Nothing to worry about. Ships passing in the night – or people meeting on a train.

But their journey had just commenced. The train would take nearly three hours to reach Birdhill station. Clemency would get off there too. Who would be meeting her? A boyfriend of her own age? Why did he mind the thought of that?

He was being ridiculous. But it was disturbing, being so close to Clemency. He couldn't sit beside her all the way home with these notions in his head. He'd have to go to the bar instead. He'd have to tell her he was going or she'd think he was ungracious.

He started to explain himself. 'I think I'll go and have a drink—'

'I'm starving,' Clemency said at the same time. 'I haven't eaten a bite today. I think—'

They stopped, laughing rather nervously. Eating, he thought, would be something to do. Which meant that he would eat two meals. Bea would have supper waiting and he couldn't disappoint her. He wasn't even hungry now. Something light, he thought. An omelette . . .

It *wasn't* any better in the dining car, not the way the train was rocking. Sitting facing one another. Glasses sliding on the table. Hands that reached out to prevent them making contact by mistake.

As a distraction, he spoke of the boat he had recently bought. The pleasure Bob got out of it.

'He goes out *alone* in it?'

'No. He's still too young for that. We go together, all of us.' But that wasn't strictly true. Bea seldom came with them. She was frightened

216

of Lough Derg. Why had he said all of us?

'You must have a lot of fun. There's a harbour at our house but we've never had a boat. I'd love to learn to handle one.'

'You must come out with us,' he said. But, even as he spoke, he knew that any plan he made with her would be at a time when Bob was occupied elsewhere.

Before they got to Birdhill station, they arranged to meet again. An innocent plan ostensibly. A short cruise across the lake. He would mention it to Bea.

She and Bob were waiting for him. They were so alike, unmistakably mother and son, although, at five foot nine, Bea towered over Bob.

They waved as he got off the train. Clemency and all her parcels were already on the platform.

'Come and help me carry these,' he heard her calling out to someone.

The boyfriend? The sort of man that *she* would choose? Waving at his family, he was watching Clemency. And saw her meeting not a man, not a young potential rival, only pudgy Constance Conroy.

He knew he shouldn't be so relieved, so charged with joy at the sight of her. But he was. For him, that night, the grey sky had no lead in it. He didn't need to look at leaves to see the bright tones in the land. His world was colourful enough – because a woman had bought a dress.

The next step was not the seduction of Clemency but an exercise in self-deception. He wasn't going to make a pass. He might fancy her like crazy, but she wasn't keen on him.

Why should she be? he asked himself. Her only interest was the boat. He'd teach her how to handle it. Dream a little as he did so. And, afterwards, go home to Bea. Only one lesson, he said to himself.

But one lesson led to two and, after that, to several more. Frank went on deluding himself. The boating season would end soon. With the onset of November, the cruiser would be 'winterised'. That would be the end of dreaming.

The Clare Hounds' hunt ball was on 31 October, to coincide with Hallowe'en. Frank knew now that there was no other man in Clemency's life; that she had no specific partner in mind for the ball but was going with a party. She was driving to the castle, meeting up there with the others.

'Wearing your rose-red gown,' he said. 'I'd like to see you all dressed up.'

Clemency did not mince words. 'How could we work that?' she said.

'Come and see me on the cruiser.'

It was half-term. Bea was in Cork that week, visiting her brother's family. Bob had gone along with her.

'Before the ball or afterwards?' She laid it on the line for him.

'What time do you think you might get back?'

'I'll stay for dinner. Then I'll leave.'

It was a night for celebration. Snap-Apple Night, the children called it. In Cork, Bob would be having lots of fun, playing games with hanging apples. But it was also the Night of Mischief, when pranks were played and bonfires lit.

Frank waited on the boat, a glass of whiskey in his hand. Would she come, he asked himself, or would she stay on at the ball, monopolised by some young fellow?

It was a night for ghosts and goblins. For wicked fairies, like the *puca*, the Black Pig, and the *dallachan*, a horrid thing without a head, to creep out of their hiding places. Not that he, a Protestant, believed in myth and superstition. All the same, was Clemency all right, he worried, driving all those miles alone in her gorgeous evening gown?

And then he saw her car arrive and Clemency jump out of it. Obliging clouds had cleared the moon, and it shone directly on her, and upon her rose-red dress. Holding up the hem of it, she was running towards the cruiser.

He put down his drink and held out his arms, acknowledging only then what he'd known from the beginning, that they were fated to be lovers.

Of course, it wasn't a one-night stand but a full-blown love affair. Twelve months later, it was still going on. He was riddled with guilt, hating himself – and more in love with her than ever.

Clemency was more pragmatic. She saw their affair in romantic terms, their love as not exactly an act of God but something beyond their control.

She revelled in their secret meetings, on the boat and up in Dublin. She enjoyed taking risks. She told him that, when she was young, she used to climb the roof for fun. For her, the element of danger in their meetings, the constant fear that they might be caught, was a vital part of the magic of love, heightening its intensity.

He knew that there was speculation, that the eyes and the ears of their small community were alert to all intrigue. He wondered, too, if

218

Bea was suspicious of them. If she was, she didn't say so, but he thought she was withdrawn, more reserved than she used to be. She went to Cork more frequently.

Hurting Bea. Causing gossip. And he had another fear. What if Clemency got pregnant?

When she said, 'I'm going to have a baby, Frank,' it didn't come as a surprise.

Clemency was much more shocked.

'My mother mustn't know,' she said. 'She'd kill me if she heard about it. I'll have to go to England, Frank, and have the baby over there.'

They never thought about abortion. He never thought of walking out. Not on her. What to do was not in doubt. He'd have to leave his family. Live with Clemency instead. And he'd have to sell the business.

'Both of us will go to England. We'll get a place to rent near London.'

Clemency cheered up again. 'I think I'd like to live in Richmond. By the river. Maybe we could have a boat, or you could bring your own one over.'

It was nearing the end of October again. Bea said she'd go to Cork for Bob's half-term.

We'll do it then, the lovers said. We'll go to Dublin on the train and travel on by boat to England.

'We'll meet at Killaloe,' said Frank, still concerned about the gossip. 'You can go there in the cruiser and I'll drive down when Bea's gone.'

'Will you bring the cruiser over?'

'Yes. Once it's dark, I'll bring it round and moor it for you in your harbour. Get up early in the morning. Don't let anybody see you.'

'As if I would,' said Clemency.

Two more days went by, during which they couldn't meet. The night before they planned to leave, he took the boat to Carrigrua, secured it in the harbour there, did half a circle of the house and made his way across the fields until he reached the road for home.

It wouldn't be his home tomorrow.

He took a pill to help him sleep and didn't hear the storm come up. He woke, as planned, at half past five. Bea wasn't in the house. She must have gone to Cork already.

After the storm, the land had a weary, bedraggled look. The lake was calm, with no white horses. Good conditions for the cruiser. He imagined Clemency waking up and getting dressed. Any minute now

219

she'd be leaving the house. Sneaking quietly to the cruiser. Saying goodbye to Carrigrua.

It would take an hour for her to get by boat to Killaloe. Half an hour for him by car. He'd leave now. Be there, waiting when she arrived. She'd expect him to be early.

He waited for her for an hour, thinking she had overslept. Then he got more agitated. Another two hours and she still didn't come. He was frantic, waiting there, unable to make contact with her, disinclined to leave the car just in case she did show up.

At one o'clock he left a note, stuck it on the car for her and walked up to the hotel.

That was when he got the news of what had happened in the night. In the lavatory, he stood near a man he knew.

'How are you keeping, Frank? You didn't come by boat, I'd say.'

'There's not a ripple out there this morning.'

'Not like last night. I hear they've found a cruiser wrecked.'

'*Where?* On Lough Derg? Was there anyone on board?'

'I only heard they'd found a boat.'

The rest of his story was subdivided, partly drawn from his own experience and partly from outside information.

He went straight to the Guards. Had *his* cruiser been found wrecked?

When they confirmed the boat was his, he held on to the forlorn hope that the storm might have torn it from its moorings, carried it off without a crew, leaving Clemency at home, frustrated, but not overly concerned by the temporary setback, knowing he would work it out.

Instead, she was reported missing. The Guards searched the shore for her, and the islands in Lough Derg. Then they dragged the lake itself.

She'd never learnt to swim, he thought. She'd often mentioned that to him.

But *drowned*? *Dead?*

She couldn't be dead, he said to himself.

Bea returned from Cork. She was more withdrawn than ever and they hardly spoke that week.

The Guards came to question him but Bea didn't ask him why. Her clamlike attitude towards him added to the blurry nature of the days through which he lived.

Then, on the sixth day, the news that he was dreading came. A

220

woman's body had been found, washed up in the little bay, to the right of Carrigrua.

Clemency was dead. It should have been a time for mourning. For him to show that he was grieving. But he couldn't show the world how distressed he really was.

He didn't know about the suitcase Clemency had left behind. She had packed it before leaving. Inside it were her clothes for England, and her rose-red evening gown, and the diary that she kept.

But it wasn't on the cruiser. It was left at Carrigrua, and after they had found her body, Olive brought it to his house. She asked if Bea was at home, and then she gave it to his wife.

She said, 'This may be of interest to you.'

Olive must have torn the clothes, or slashed them with a knife, he thought. The rose-red gown was slit to pieces. All the clothes were ripped to shreds. But the diary was intact. He supposed that Bea read it. That what she learnt from doing so caused her subsequent reaction.

From then on she hardly spoke. She was in a trance-like state. She withdrew from Bob as well. She held back from everyone. They stayed in the house but they were never close again.

At some stage in that fearful week he found Constance by the gate. 'Do you have the case?' she said.

He'd hidden it inside the boathouse. 'Stay there and I'll bring it out.'

Her red-ringed eyes said she was sorry. Not just for her mother's actions but for *his* suffering. They didn't talk about it. Not then, nor in the months that followed. He left talk to other people.

Did Bea speak to other people, tell them that he'd been unfaithful? He thought she did, or else they guessed. He could read it on their faces.

But other people didn't matter. All that mattered had been lost. Clemency dead. Her rose-red gown ripped up like that, in a fit of savagery. He shuddered at the thought of it.

He didn't know, till later on, what else had happened on the night before they found the cruiser wrecked.

Twenty-Three

'What happened?' I said. 'What else do you know?'

Frank Studdart cleared his throat. 'I heard this from Marie-Rose. Clemency was in her room. Olive came and took the key. Then she locked the door on her. She'd found out about the baby. She told Clemency that she had disgraced the family. She couldn't live with me, she said, because I was a married man.'

But it was worse than that. Far worse. I knew, for I'd been a witness to it, out of sight and terrified. All along, throughout my life, I'd known deep down about that night. Known that Olive's was the second voice. That *she* had tortured Clemency. Tortured her with words, at first. Calling Clemency a slut.

A slut. *Olive* had defaced that picture. Ripped the front page from the paper. Olive. Not Marie-Rose, as I'd imagined, as I'd wanted to believe. And Olive, hiding from her own shame of illegitimacy, gave us our instructions not to speak of disgraced Clemency.

But there'd been more to it than words. The room reduced to devastation. And the blood marks on the sill.

'What else do you know?' I said to Frank.

He leant forward, forming a pyramid with his arms, holding his hands in front of his mouth, trying to hide his face from me.

He whispered – I could barely hear him – 'Isn't that enough for you?'

But I knew that there was more, and I thought that he might know even if he didn't say so. I was still suspicious of him. Suspicious now of everyone.

'I can't tell you more than that.'

He was worn out from talking to me. I had just enough feeling left in me to leave him and get out of there.

Driving away from the Studdarts' house, I asked myself repeatedly, what happened in that room? Asked the question I couldn't voice – did *Olive* murder Clemency? Wouldn't she have needed help to get the body down the stairs? Or had she managed on her own, charged with the superhuman energy that those who kill are said to have?

What did she do with Clemency then? Where did the boat fit into things? What else happened in the house? To my mother, Charity? Did she really did in childbirth, or did someone murder *her*?

I was sure that Olive had done it, that she had savage blood in her. And when I thought of her reactions, I thought about my own as well. How violent I had been after finding Sue and Leonard. The way I had lashed out at him, and how I had destroyed the bathroom.

Olive's blood was in my veins. I'd respected, worshipped her. Now I loathed her memory. And I hated myself. I hated what there was in me. I feared what might come over me, and what I might not be able to control. I understood now why, all those years ago, I'd turned down the offer of a two-man show and, with it, a career as a serious painter. That would have meant exposing myself, revealing what there was in me. I'd painted flowers instead – painted poppies out of fear. Pretended to be someone else – Caroline the Entertainer. Someone who was fun to be with while she hid her violent nature.

Only one other entity – the house, my beloved Carrigrua – understood what I was like: Olive cloned in brighter shades. Carrigrua had observed everything that she had done. Our lovely house had been abused, used as the setting for a horror film. No wonder it had called me back, said to me, 'But she and you are just the same, so you belong at Carrigrua.'

Now, even more than before, I wanted to be there alone. I didn't want the builders in it. I was suspicious of them as well, wondering what they might know. When I spoke to them, I didn't dare to raise my eyes in case they saw a madness in them. They *must* have thought I was mad, for being so furtive and unfriendly.

It wasn't possible to work – how could I paint poppies now, or any other flowers? So I took over from the lads, weeding and removing debris, thinking how the garden was when all the flowers in it were red. Till Olive took a hand in things . . .

'Quite Victorian, it was, when Mrs Conroy finished with it.' Another effort to delete the memory of Clemency.

Naoise Nolan trundled past, transferring rubbish from the orchard. Michael hadn't asked for him to help the others in the house. Each time he passed I could feel his eyes on me, but I took no notice of him.

I was dodging everybody. Still, two callers tracked me down. The first was Bob.

'Caroline, we have to talk.'

'You lied to me,' I said to him.

'What?'

'You lied to me about the boat.'

He sighed. 'I understand how you must feel.'

'You're despicable!' I said.

'Caroline, please—'

'We have nothing to talk about.'

'We need to talk. You know we do.'

'Keep away from me,' I said, even though he hadn't touched me.

He stood his ground. He tried his best to reason with me. I hurled accusations at him, a stream of invective that, in the end, made him furious as well. I was mad – paranoiac – he said, and couldn't I see that it wasn't like that?

I screamed at him to go away.

He relented. Became tender. Said he'd grown to care for me. That he'd be there if I needed him.

How could anyone care for me?

'Get out of here!' I shrieked at him.

'All right, I'll go. But remember what I said.'

Then, like Leonard, he was gone.

The second caller was Francesca. I opened the door and there she was, pulling at her T-shirt sleeve.

'Hello,' she said in a subdued voice. 'You must be raging mad with me.'

I wanted to reach out to her. Hug her. Tell her that she needn't worry, that I wasn't furious. But I couldn't reach out to anyone then.

'No,' I said. 'I'm not annoyed,' doing my best to sound off-putting, to push her away from me.

'It *seems* as if you are,' she said.

'I'm not. I just have things to do inside.'

'I didn't mean to burn the house. I've come to say I'm very sorry.'

I maintained my cold facade, and I hurt her in the process. She didn't know her wistful face nearly shattered my resistance.

''Bye so, Caroline,' she said.

Then she, too, went away, and only the builders and I were left. They waterproofed the roof, replaced the burnt rafters, put the felting in and finished off the battening process.

There was hope for Carrigrua. Not for me, but for the house. Just as I was thinking that, Michael said that they were leaving, that they had another job. They'd be back in mid-November. I didn't even try to stop them.

That was the darkest time. The house became a hermitage. And I couldn't forget those blood marks on the sill. When I was forced out to shop, I didn't talk to other people. When I saw someone that I knew, I quickly edged away from them or crossed the street with eyes cast down.

They were watching me, I thought. Nudging each other as I went by. What did they know that I did not? What knowledge did they have of Olive? Had they feared her all along, while I imagined they revered her? What would they think, they who lived beside the lake, if they knew I was like her?

I started avoiding the local shops. I took to going far afield to buy provisions for the house, and this was noted in the village. People there withdrew from me and I, in turn, was gruff with them.

The leaves were turning red and yellow. On the bog road, ferns as tanned as sunburnt bodies grew up higher than my waist. Dots of orange asphodels, purple ling, and tiny, cross-leaved violet heaths turned the stretch of peaty earth into one of Seurat's paintings.

Mist. The land and lake were swathed in it. When I drove in that direction, I couldn't see the Studdarts' house.

I was invisible, I thought. A person of inconsequence. But that was better, any time, than being a replica of Olive.

Sometime in that month, Matt Murphy came round to see me, holding out a piece of paper on which figures had been scribbled.

'I know I gave you a quote before. But I re-wired that whole top floor.'

'Did you? Sorry, but I didn't know.'

'More needed to be done than I told you early on.'

'What exactly are you getting at?'

Finding out what Olive was made me generally distrustful. I'd been too naive, I thought. Too easy to deceive. I needed to be on my guard when I dealt with other people.

Matt squirmed. 'That it's going to cost you more.'

'How much more?' I asked him coldly.

'Four hundred pounds in all. That would be for everything.'

I wrote out a cheque for him but I also let him know, by the coolness in my voice, that I thought he was a con man. He took the cheque but he looked hurt.

October fizzled out at last in drizzles of incessant rain. November the 2nd was All Souls' Day when, so Norah told me long ago, the dead would raise their coffin lids and climb unaided from their graves to spend the night in their old homes.

The skeletons of hungry trees were gaunt Giacometti figures. The shadows on the lake were black. Rivulets of silver water dribbled through the muddy fields.

Mid-November came and went without any news from Michael. It was December when he returned to Carrigrua, bringing all the lads with him – all of them except for Ger.

'Aren't you using Ger this time?'

'Ger has got another job. I'm going to bring in Naoise Nolan.'

'I don't want Naoise in the house.'

Michael scowled. 'Naoise is a powerful worker.'

'I'm not saying that he isn't. I just don't want him working indoors.'

'Mrs Tremain,' Michael said, 'I'm the foreman on this job. If you want me to go on, *I'll* choose who will work with me.'

I wasn't happy about that but, for the meanwhile, I subsided. It was getting near to Christmas. Leaves rotting on the grounds. Trees the bones of what they'd been. The colours faded from the bog. The land dressed all in black and brown.

More rain fell. The south wind whined and whipped the trees. Maddened by the wicked wind, the lake spat spume out on the shore. The weather went against the builders and held up the roofing work. The second phase of restoration entailed re-tiling and replacing the ceiling in the fifth bedroom, after which the whole house was to be redecorated.

Meanwhile, Naoise was indoors, putting up the ceiling joists. I couldn't stand his creepy presence. Michael said he worked so hard, but he always left a mess. He knew I was annoyed by that. I sensed him watching me overtly, smiling to himself as I walked past.

He, and those of the lads who remained on site, took a six-day break for Christmas, leaving me to speculate what the Studdarts might be doing.

I mustn't think about the Studdarts . . . And Christmas Day was nothing special. No reason to be sentimental. At Carrigrua long ago it was a religious day, a time for us to look at cribs rather than to eat a lot. The day itself had always dragged. I had not been given presents.

That Christmas Day was no exception. Cold and lonely. Horrible.

The next day was Saint Stephen's Day. That was when the Wren Boys came, chanting songs and banging things and holding up a stick or pole, to which a dead wren had been tied. This was an ancient custom, dating back three hundred years, to when Cromwell was in Ireland, storming towns and waging wars against his Catholic opponents. Irish troops had been approaching. Wrens had perched upon

227

their drums and the tapping sound they made had aroused the English soldiers.

'All our soldiers lost their lives,' Norah used to say to me. 'And that's why we hate the wren.'

But I didn't feel that way. I was sorry for the wren. It was the Wren Boys I disliked when I was a little girl. I didn't like them as an adult. I thought the custom would have died. But then I heard the old refrain.

> *The wran, the wran, the king of all birds,*
> *On Stephen's day was caught in the furze.*
> *Off with the kettle and down with the pan.*
> *Will you give us a penny to bury the wran?*

My antipathy returned. I opened the front door, intending not to reward the Wren Boys but to send them on their way.

There were three of them on the steps. They didn't look like boys to me but full-grown men in funny clothes with faces blackened to disguise them. The tallest one, who was holding up the stick, had put on an old straw hat.

'*The wran, the wran—*'

'Don't sing that song round here,' I said.

They stopped singing. Two of them turned round to go.

The third one, the one with the pole in his hand, took a step in my direction. He began to sing again.

'*The wran, the wran, the king of all birds—*'

'Go away!' I yelled at him.

He stopped singing. He laughed, and pointed the pole in my direction. They hadn't used a real wren, only a wooden simulation, but it was real enough to me.

I stepped back, shuddering, and the third man laughed again. There was something familiar about him. About his features. His mouth. The way he was enjoying himself, making such a fool of me.

I slipped inside and slammed the door, shaking more with rage than fear. The Wren Boy who had threatened me was Naoise Nolan in disguise.

'That's it,' I said. 'I've had enough. Naoise Nolan has to go.'

Michael thought that I was fussing. 'He only meant it as a joke.'

'Maybe. But I won't have him in the house.'

I got my way, and paid for it. A few days later, Michael took it out on me.

'I can't find another man to do the work that Naoise did. We'll have to wait till Ger is free.'

'When will that be?' I inquired.

'I can't tell you that for certain.'

Ger wasn't free in January. And February came in as well without a word from him or Michael.

It was very cold that month. Frost laid blankets on the land. The lake was layered with fine white ice. But then the weather became sultry. Dirty eiderdowns of cloud hung too low above our heads. The air about us was too warm and there was not enough of it. The countryside was holding its breath, waiting for something peculiar to happen. The animals felt much the same – the farmyard dogs were agitated.

In that odd, expectant climate, my own responses were quite primal. In the wood I saw a hare. Arrested in our tracks, we stopped, trying to make up our minds what we felt about each other. I wasn't overjoyed myself. Its coat was lovely, russet red, but I'd forgotten just how large and how feral hares can be.

Who had told me that the hare was the form a witch assumes? Who, long ago, had whispered to me, 'If a hare goes three times across your path there'll be danger up ahead'? Was it Marie-Rose or Norah? The words sent shivers down my spine.

Silly being upset by them. Simple people thought like that. And weasels can be witches too, and cats can also be demonic. I was all screwed up, I thought, overwrought and fanciful.

The hare, meanwhile, was also showing signs of fear – trembling body, twitching nose.

Poor thing. I'd just got over my gut reaction when someone threw a stone at it.

It missed the hare, but only just. Naturally, it fled in panic, zigzagging, the way hares do, to try to put you off their scent. It ran right across my path. Once, twice, three times . . .

So what? I thought. Relax, you fool. This is how a hare behaves. *That's* not the important thing. What matters is, who threw that stone?

Then I spotted Naoise Nolan. He was over to my right, sitting on a fallen tree, carving out a hurley stick from a branch he'd torn off it. I knew that he had thrown the stone. But his presence on my land maddened me in any case.

'What are *you* doing here?' I said.

He shrugged. 'Using up a broken branch. I'm not doing any harm.'

'You've no business being here.'

His eyes burnt with rancour and resentment. Dark eyes. Almost black, I thought.

'You'd better go. Otherwise I'll phone the Guards.' I knew I was being like Olive.

He stood up, stick and knife in either hand.

'And leave that stick behind,' I said.

'What good will it be to you?'

Good question. But I was being imperious.

'That's my firewood,' I insisted. 'And this property is mine.'

I thought it was touch and go, whether or not he'd use the knife. But he threw down the stick and strode past me towards the gates.

Anger carried me into the house. But I shivered again when I got inside, acutely aware of being alone. The fears I'd had of Marie-Rose I transferred now to Naoise Nolan. He'd seek revenge, I knew he would.

The next morning, I was woken by the sound of a gun being fired somewhere outside in the wood. I sat up with a jerk, wondering if I had been dreaming. I didn't hear the sound again, so I thought I must have been.

It was a curiously calm day, much too warm for February. But, because of the frost, the ground was hard. The herb beds were in need of water.

When I went over to the well, I saw a stonechat on the clothesline, a cheerful sight, a symbol of spring, with his smooth black head and his chestnut breast.

'Wee-tac-tac,' he called to me.

I might find his nest, I thought, if I searched the grass for it.

He watched me tugging on the rope, trying to bring the bucket up. It didn't move. I tugged much harder, and it did. But still, it was oddly heavy. I felt my face go red with effort.

Finally, the handle surfaced from the darkness and I reached out to grab the bucket.

The sight that met my eyes was terrible. I nearly let the bucket drop.

Gritting my teeth, I hoisted it over the wall of the well, set it down upon the cobbles, and stared sickly at its contents. It wasn't water that I'd drawn but a bucketful of blood. A dead thing had been put in it.

'Wee-tac-tac,' the stonechat called from his perch upon the line.

I was rooted to the spot, staring at that poor, dead thing.

Ears protruded from the bucket. Stiff, wet, russet ears, sticking up like bloodied knives from the body of the hare.

Twenty-Four

I fled. I can still remember running, not only from the thing that Naoise put inside the bucket but from all the horrors that had dogged my life since I'd first come home to Ireland.

I headed for the lake. Reached the harbour. Panting as if I'd run for miles instead of merely from the yard.

I was sweating. It seemed to me that I was observed, scrutinised by the countryside, watched by dozens of unseen eyes.

The air was thick. But the lake was placid and calm, smooth as jelly, a magnet drawing me out of the range of sadistic acts and the pain of recollection.

I've got to get away, I thought. I can't go back to the house just yet. Olive's there, or her spirit is, reminding me of what I am. And Naoise is lurking in the wood. I must escape the three of us.

I hadn't been out on the lake for months. I hadn't 'winterised' the boat – I'd left it tied up in the harbour – but, apart from mossy residue and a deposit of fallen leaves, it had survived my negligence. Fuel, I knew, was not a problem. I'd put diesel in the tank the last time that I'd used the boat. The season hadn't started yet. There were no cruisers on the lake and I could see no fishermen. But the water looked so tranquil. So tempting.

I climbed into the boat, untied the soggy rope, turned on the fuel tap and pulled the starter cord. The engine didn't start. I pulled the cord a second time and got no response from it.

I'd be trapped without the boat. Panic threatened. The low clouds added to the penned-up feeling. I *had* to get away.

I tugged and yanked at the starter cord. Then, when I least expected it, the engine throbbed into life and I was free, almost crying with relief.

Easing out from the harbour, I was seeking only the unique solace that the water can provide. I didn't have a destination.

As I puttered across the lake, the tensions of the day subsided and I became exhilarated. I was free, outside myself, sharing the world with swans and ducks. Safe from the madness of my life – for a little while, at least.

At the start of my journey across the lake, I thought of escape and little else. My passage on the peaceful water acted on me like a balm. But then the truths of the lake returned, and I began to think of Bob. Of our night at Gurthalougha, and the love that he had shown me. I hadn't seen him since September. Hadn't seen Francesca either. How were the two of them getting on? All the better, so I'd thought, for being without the likes of me. Yet was that the case? On the lake, I seemed to be another person. Not the one with savage instincts but a reasonable creature. Someone who'd been on the verge of loving both the younger Studdarts. Who might have brought benefits into their lives . . .

But I'd lost that chance for ever. It was pointless thinking of them. Thinking how it could have been.

A flock of cormorants had landed on a nearby outcrop. They clung to the black rocks with their webbed feet, their wings spread out as if to dry them.

I passed them by, steering no definite course just yet. A shiver of a breeze came up, so slight I hardly noticed it. I heard a heron calling out and then, just above my head, the rowdy sound of swans in flight. Higher up, there was a plane I couldn't see, hidden by the low-flying clouds.

I went on, losing track of time completely, forgetting it was early spring. Forgetting it would soon be dark.

The round tower of Holy Island came into view long before its land mass did. I wouldn't think about the boat which had foundered on those rocks. I wouldn't think of Clemency. But, when I drew nearer to the island, it somehow seemed appropriate to pay a silent tribute to her.

I slowed down, turned the engine off, and drifted in the shallow waters, lost in thoughts of her and Frank, and how their love affair had ended. I'd been hard on him, I thought. Too hard. Brutal in my selfish need to drag the story out of him.

The breeze, stronger now, tossed my hair across my face. I realised I was getting cramp.

I stood up, stretched, turned on the petrol tap and pulled the starter cord. Once again, there was no response. I was jerked back to the realities of my situation. The lake was no longer smooth. The wind was brisk now, from the west. It would take an hour, at least, to row home to Carrigrua. It would be night before I got there.

I turned the throttle full on and pulled at the cord again. The engine burst into life. But I'd left the boat in forward gear. It leapt forward, bucking like a flighty horse, hurtling me out and into the water.

The shock of it was punishing. Icy needles pierced my limbs. I sank, the water closing over my head, and re-surfaced as the boat, its outboard engine swinging wildly to one side, zoomed round me in a circle.

I nearly grabbed hold of it. But maybe there were saints at work, sending signals from the island, because just in time I recognised the potential danger of being swept in underneath that crazed propeller.

In England, I'd been taught to swim. I struck out for the shore, terrified that I wouldn't get out of the orbit of the boat before it came round again.

The wind was snagging at the water, making waves that carried me on. In that way I reached the rocks as the boat went roaring past. Dripping wet, but not too bogged down by clothes, I scrambled across the rocks, reached a carpet of leaf mould and grass and thankfully collapsed on it.

The boat was still careering round. I hoped it wouldn't hit the rocks. But I didn't really care. I was freezing cold, the temperature had dropped and a little light rain was beginning to fall. It was getting dark already. Was it later than I thought? I checked my watch to see the time, but it was no longer working.

I got to my feet. I'd have to find a place to shelter. The churches had no roofs on them but, on my previous visit to the island, I'd seen a workman's hut which I hoped might be unlocked.

To get to the hut, I had to follow the Pilgrim's Path, making my way from the church of Saint Caimin to the remains of a tiny chapel that was inside a small enclosure.

It is all so vivid still. The herd of cattle near the hut, watching me with liquid eyes. The lushness of their pastureland.

I reached the hut and there I found my luck had held. The workmen hadn't locked the door and to my amazement and delight they'd left their overalls behind. Dirty ones, but they were dry.

I pulled off my sodden garments and put both sets of overalls on. Then, shivering, I looked around the hut, thinking that I had no choice but to spend the night in it. There was no furniture. But there was a primus stove, a kettle, half full of water, and – wonderful! – a box of matches. The workmen had left tea bags, too, and some milk, though that was sour.

Resigned to going without food, I made myself a cup of tea. Then I heard a deluge starting. Raindrops beating on the roof. I went to the

233

door to see for myself what was going on outside. It was dark out there by then but an unearthly light, a scarlet glow, was shining on the ruined churches. If I'd judged them from their looks, I'd have thought they were on fire.

The sky was indigo, with blue and black and charcoal clouds moving fast across its face. Thunder rumbled in the distance. A single flash of lightning streaked across the bruised and angry sky.

And then it all came back to me. I was six years old again, sitting on the windowsill. I looked out as thunder rumbled and the trees began to shake and lightning streaked across the sky, lighting up the lake and garden. The fearful sounds that I had heard – the screams and shouts and other noises – had subsided this long while. There were no sounds now from Clemency's room, and I was sure that she was dead.

Death was not a stranger to me. People spoke about it freely. It permeated every story that had been passed on to me. I was seeped in sorrow and superstition, my world populated by a motley collection of phantoms and ghosts, some of them in human form, some disguised as cats or dogs. The sounds of the natural world – birdsong, the lake lapping against the shore, rain lashing at the windowsill – were intermingled in my mind with the wails of the banshee.

That same week, one of the kitchen cats had died. Though we called them kitchen cats, they weren't allowed inside the house. We had no pets at Carrigrua. Those animals that we had acquired – just tabby cats without names – were there to carry out a function, protecting us from rats and mice.

The dead cat was draped on the cobbles near the famine tub. It was wearing a frosty coat. I tentatively touched its fur. Finding it was stiff and heavy, I took it to the kitchen garden and laid it on the cabbage bed.

Stiff and heavy. Clemency would look like that, I'd thought. Limbs as rigid as the poker by the fireplace in the hall. Features frozen cold by death. Eyes like marbles in her head.

That night I saw her ghost. The spirit of Clemency, more substantial than I'd have expected in a person who was dead, appeared before me on the lawn. It wasn't dressed in gauzy robes the way that ghosts were meant to be, or in loose, white drapery, as the banshee would have been, but in trousers and a jersey.

My hands flew up to cover my mouth. I was terrified of screaming lest Olive hear me from her room and I end up a ghost as well.

The ghost on the lawn looked up at the house, as if to say farewell to it. It didn't see me perched up there. It didn't raise its hand to me.

Instead, it sped towards the harbour where, to my immense surprise, I saw there was a cruiser moored.

I raised the window and peered out, frightened, awed, yet fascinated. The wind was bawling at the lake. I thought it was the fairy wind, the red wind from the Otherworld, *an Gaoithe Moire*. Norah's wind.

The ghost had reached the harbour now. It must be going to board the cruiser, which had to be a fairy boat.

To me, saints and fairies were the same. They all lived up above my head and used different forms of transport, ranging from Cuchulain's horses to the very clouds themselves, on which the Virgin Mary stood when she was going up to Heaven.

It seemed quite feasible to me that Clemency would go by boat on her way to join the angels. That the wind would blow like that, to raise the fairy cruiser up. That it would fly above the lake and disappear inside the clouds.

Instead, the hands of the moon parted the clouds and the face of it lit up the lawn.

Across the grass a long, thin snake of a shadow slithered out of the silver birches. A woman was attached to it.

Olive, I thought, although I couldn't see her face. Olive chasing Clemency. But why? To stop her spirit going to Heaven? That had to be the explanation, with Satan at the back of it.

She must have shouted to the ghost. Or else Clemency's spirit, alerted by its guardian angel, became aware that she was there and swung round, just as Olive reached the jetty. She drew level with her prey, stopped, and they appeared to be conversing.

How tall Olive looked. Bemused, I thought that she had grown. The Devil must have stretched her out before she murdered Clemency so she'd work better on his behalf.

The conversation terminated. The ghost of Clemency turned away and took a step towards the cruiser. But it didn't board the boat. Its pursuer saw to that.

She sprang into sudden action, hitting out, raining blows at Clemency's ghost, forcing it away from the boat. The spirit tried to ward her off. But it was no match for a woman possessed, a woman, who, being in the Devil's grip, had been lent a wrestler's strength.

The woman struck the ghost again. Clemency kept going backwards.

The ghost tottered and, as the moon closed the shutters of the clouds, it stumbled and its arms flew out. Then, like a bird that has

235

been shot, it fell into the waiting lake.

It seemed to me that everything stopped. But surely that was not the end. Surely the saints would get to work and pull the spirit from the water.

The woman on the harbour must have wondered about that too, for she stood there for an age, waiting for their intervention.

The saints took no decisive action. But I thought they sent a sign to indicate that they were present, for violet lightning flashed again and showed me that the lake was rough, black as oil that had been burnt by Norah in the frying pan, but with flecks of white on it.

Eventually, the woman moved, went over to the boat and undid the ropes that held it. The cruiser moved out from the jetty, bobbing in the boiling oil. A huge wave broke across its bow, the wind saw red and roared at it, and I pulled the window shut.

I was an adult now. Standing there on Holy Island, I understood what I had witnessed. It wasn't *Olive* I had seen. It was another, taller woman.

Another woman . . .

Another memory. I was back with Clemency. In her car, sneaking home to Carrigrua after she had bought me sweets. Both of us in high old spirits. Until—

'Oh, shit, it's *her*!' Clemency said, getting all worked up about it.

There was a car parked near our gates, with a person sitting in it.

Her . . . She had a narrow, fine-boned face. Bob's face.

Bob and his mother had looked alike. Frank himself had told me that. And he'd told me something else. That Bea had been rather tall. Olive had looked tall to me when I'd seen her on the jetty. Only it wasn't Olive.

Bea Studdart, I thought. But of course, it must have been. Bea had the motive for it. And afterwards she was withdrawn. It must have been Bea, I said to myself.

And the ghost that I had seen? Who but Clemency herself, alive and heading for the boat, to stick to the plan she'd made with Frank.

I saw her in my mind again, as she paused there on the lawn. Had she been physically attacked in her room, or just verbally assaulted? Maybe she herself had wrecked that room. She was trapped there by her mother. She was in a desperate state, pregnant and in love with Frank, with whom she'd planned to run away. Perhaps, I thought, she just went wild. Tore the curtains in her frenzy. Ripped the pages out of books. Hurled the pictures to the floor. Smashed the glass and cut herself.

236

I could relate to that behaviour. I, who thought I was like Olive.

But Olive was a colder woman; she'd used words to show her anger. I should have looked to Clemency to find a replica of myself. Our features were the same, of course. But there was in both of us a passion that had been suppressed, until we had been driven crazy.

How did Clemency escape? I thought I knew that answer too. She had always been determined, much more so than I had been. And there was another difference. Love, to her, was linked to danger. As a child, she'd climbed on the roof for fun. As an adult, she'd climbed out of her bedroom window, worked her way across the roof and slid down the nearest drainpipe. Taking risks to get to Frank. To be defeated by his wife.

But *Olive* hadn't murdered her . . .

I was free. Released from the madness of the past.

Another kind of madness took hold of me. I left the shelter of the hut to confront the storm outside. Thunder growled as I emerged. Lightning tried its terror tactics. Rain tore at my tousled head. The red wind whipped against my face and brought the blood up in my cheeks. But I didn't mind a bit.

It was almost dawn when I thought of Bea Studdart in relation to myself, comparing my red jealousy to the passion that had fuelled her. In that demented state, *I* could have murdered Sue Wilkins had I been alone with her. But I'd been luckier than Bea.

Bea. Her face. The features that I still remembered, which were handed on to Bob and made me fear him later.

Bea.

The warmth of Clemency, her vivacity, her love for me, her image in the rose-red gown would remain for ever with me, along with the love I'd had for her. Yet I acknowledged to myself that, like all romantics, she had a callous streak, for she never thought of Bea except as a face inside a car.

Others must have noticed Bea acting out of character. Observed Frank with Clemency. Seen them cruising in the boat. There must have been a flood of gossip. Guard O'Hagan had confirmed it. No evidence was found, he'd said. *Nothing we could pin it on.*

So maybe they suspected Bea.

But why had people lied to me? And why had Alice Egan said don't mention this to Marie-Rose?

Daybreak. The sun steeling itself to confront the havoc of the night before.

Much resolved. The major things. But questions that remained unanswered.

And one person left who could help with that. But would that person talk to me or tell me that I had a nerve, after the way I'd behaved, to demand answers to my questions?

Twenty-Five

When the surprised workmen found me in their overalls the following morning, they took me in their own boat over to Mountshannon harbour. From there, I walked the short distance up to Marie-Rose's house.

The storm had scrubbed and rinsed the land and it had the subdued look that children have when their bodies have been washed. A tree had fallen across the road, and a house that I went past had a crooked chimney on it.

I'd barely reached the red gate when I heard the barking dogs. The back door opened and they emerged, bounding towards me with their tongues hanging out.

'Is that you, Roisin?' Marie-Rose called out.

'No, it's not. It's Caroline.'

She came out in her dressing gown.

'Caroline!' she said, surprised. 'Mother of God and all the saints, you're going to catch your death of cold. What have you been getting up to? Never mind to tell me now. Better go and have a bath.'

She ran the bath for me herself, putting oil and foam in it, and giving me a robe. When I was washed and dry, she made me sit before the fire and brought me breakfast on a tray.

It was only then, after I'd consumed bacon, sausage and black pudding and most of a loaf of her homemade bread, that I told her where I'd been.

'But what possessed you to go out? It's been raining cats and dogs.'

I'd forgotten Naoise Nolan. When I explained what he had done, Marie-Rose was furious.

'I'll settle that one's hash for him.'

'Why did he lay into me?'

'He's a vicious devil, that one. But the truth is, Caroline, the people round here can't stand snobs and he thinks that you're like Olive.'

'Is that what he said to you?'

'No, he didn't, but I heard it back.'

Which was fair enough, I thought. I'd been snobby with the lads. Done my Olive imitation. Traded on the Conroy name.

And who were the Conroys really but a group of different people who had lived at Carrigrua? The house wasn't built for us but for the Grey Lady's parents.

Still, that was neither here nor there.

'Marie-Rose,' I said, 'I need to ask you several things. But first I have to tell you something. I remember Clemency.'

'Why wouldn't you?' said Marie-Rose, unaware that I'd blocked out so many memories of the past.

'Olive wanted her forgotten.'

Marie-Rose picked up the tray. 'Are you sure you've had enough? I can easily make you more.' She was giving me the slip, just the way the others did.

'Marie-Rose, listen to me,' I said. 'I know Olive was a monster. I know most of what she did. I remember.'

'Do you?'

'I remember what she did to Clemency. Locking the door on her like that. And I know about what she told Bea Studdart.'

'It's better to leave the past alone.' Marie-Rose went through to the kitchen. I could hear her clattering about, sloshing water on to the pan.

I went and joined her at the sink.

'*Why* is it better left?' I said.

She removed her rubber gloves, slowly prising the fingers off.

'Marie-Rose? Tell me why it's better left.'

She dried the gloves with elaborate care, taking ages in the process. Then she said, 'You want to talk of Olive, don't you?'

'Yes, and Clemency as well.'

'I couldn't stand to talk of her.'

'You mean because you didn't like her?'

For answer she just shook her head.

'What then? Tell me, Marie-Rose.'

'I can't tell *you* what I think. 'Twould only be a shock to you.'

'Not now, it wouldn't be,' I said.

Marie-Rose took a deep breath and held it in while she was thinking.

'I won't be shocked, I promise you.'

She raised tear-filled eyes to me.

'It's Clemency,' said Marie-Rose. 'I always feared that Olive killed her.'

★ ★ ★

240

She took me on two journeys then, the first into her own mind, the other into Olive's.

Her own journey began with finding Norah, crying her heart out in the kitchen.

'What is wrong with you at all?'

Norah tended to annoy her. To the young Marie-Rose, Norah was a flutter-guts, fussing around inside the house, seemingly obsessed with dust, carrying out routine inspections every time a room was cleaned, never pleased with the results. Added to which, Mrs Conroy, who was hard on everyone else, had a chink in her armour where Norah was concerned.

But here was Norah, weeping torrents.

'What's up?' said Marie-Rose again, thinking someone must be dead.

'I'm fearful worried,' Norah said.

'Tell me what your trouble is.'

'I can't. It's not a thing to talk about.'

She's poorly, Marie-Rose decided. Maybe she is going to die. She didn't want to see her go. Irritating though she was, someone worse might come along.

'Does Dr Foley know about it?'

'Leave Dr Foley out of this!'

Having had her head snapped off, Marie-Rose abandoned Norah and went to clear the ashes out.

For the next few days Norah moped around the house, as miserable as January. Then, instead of getting better, she went to pieces altogether. The family had finished dinner. At half past nine Norah came into the kitchen, her face the colour of a leek.

'What is it?' Marie-Rose exclaimed.

Instead of answering the question, Norah burst into more tears and made a beeline for her bedroom. Marie-Rose washed up the dishes and turned up the radio; that way she wouldn't hear the sobs.

She was listening to the news when Constance burst into the room, just as traumatised as Norah.

'Can I stay with you?' she said.

What was the matter with everyone?

'Isn't it your house we're in?'

'Oh God!' Constance wailed. 'I don't know what to do about it.'

'You'd better have a cup of tea.' She didn't know what else to say. She'd worked for the Conroys for seven years but she wasn't close to them. Mrs Conroy made it plain that the staff should keep their

241

distance. *She* would be most upset if she knew where Constance was.

'You don't know what's going on.'

Well, that was true, thought Marie-Rose. Norah howling in the bedroom and Constance crying on her shoulder. What were the two of them on about?

'Would you tell me what's going on?'

The question released a torrent of words. Unlike Norah, Constance was only too willing to talk. Marie-Rose caught the gist of a story that explained why Norah, too, should have got herself worked up.

'. . . in the family way,' said Constance. 'Mother got it out of Norah. But he's married . . . going away . . . Mother's locked the door on her . . .'

'Ah, sure, it will all blow over.'

'No, it won't,' said Constance, weeping. 'Mother's going mad up there. I think she's going to kill my sister.'

'Don't be an eejit,' said Marie-Rose. She was not a histrionic. Life was bad enough, she thought, without adding drama to it. 'Drink the tea I've given you.'

Constance did as she was told. She was calmer afterwards, but Marie-Rose was getting tired.

'Aren't you going to bed?' she said.

'I'm not going up there tonight.'

'Then you'd better sleep down here.'

They lay head to toe in Marie-Rose's bed but they didn't get much sleep. The bed was only a single, and neither of the two was slim.

'I can't get Clemency out of my head. Do you think she's all right?' Constance fretted, several times through the night.

'She's getting more rest than us, I'd say!'

'Can you hear the storm outside?'

'Yes. Can't you *try* to go to sleep?'

At dawn, Constance slipped away. Marie-Rose got up herself and went to lay the breakfast table.

All the others came downstairs. Only Clemency was missing. Locked in her room, thought Marie-Rose, dishing up the breakfast eggs.

At ten o'clock, they were summoned to the library. Mrs Conroy's face was grim.

'I don't want my daughter Clemency's name mentioned in this house again,' she said. 'Is that clear to all of you?'

They answered automatically, no one daring to inquire the whereabouts of Clemency.

'Constance. Marie-Rose. Come upstairs with me.'

They followed her like little lambs. Was she going to punish them for having shared the single bed?

'That blue cupboard must be moved so it hides her bedroom door.'

They didn't dare to ask why the door should be concealed. Was Constance right? thought Marie-Rose. Was Mrs Conroy going mad? And where was Clemency, whose name was never to be mentioned? Dead, and behind the door? Was Constance also thinking that?

'Will you move the cupboard, please.'

They pushed and tugged compliantly until the door had been obscured.

'That will do,' said Mrs Conroy. 'Go along now, Marie-Rose.'

It crossed her mind to slip away and tell the story to the Guards. But they'd only laugh at her and say that *she* was going mad.

Then the Guards came themselves. An empty cruiser had been found wrecked. It was seen the night before, in our harbour, of all places.

'What boat is that?' asked Mrs Conroy. 'And who said that it was here?'

'A courting couple,' said the Guards. 'They were walking by the shore.'

'Trespassing upon our land. I know nothing of a boat.'

'But maybe, now, your daughters do.'

Constance, naturally, did not. And Clemency?

'Where is *she*?' the Guards asked.

When they learnt she'd disappeared, they began to search for her. Marie-Rose was still debating whether she should talk to them. Tell them all about the row that Olive had with Clemency. Tell them, too, about the cupboard . . .

But she should speak to Constance first, to see how she would feel about it, and she couldn't get to her. Constance went inside her shell. And there she stayed, in misery, till the Guards came again to say the body was washed up, along the shore from Carrigrua.

Clemency dead, as she had feared. But *in the lake*? Had Olive put her in the lake?

Constance thought she had for certain. On the night they found the body, Constance, being in need of comfort, sneaked downstairs a second time.

'My mother murdered her,' she said.

Marie-Rose believed her now.

243

After we had made more tea, Marie-Rose took me on the second journey, into Olive's early life. To the house where she was born. It only had the two small rooms and she shared it with her mother.

Olive's father lived in style in a fine hip-roofed limestone house set on the large estate that had been handed down to him. He shared it with his wife and sons.

Before Olive was conceived, her mother lived in that big house – she was a housemaid there – but after she had given birth she only went there once a week, to collect a sum of money from her former lover's wife. She took the child along with her, so Olive's earliest impressions were of the contrast between her home and the one her father owned. She didn't know he was her father. She never saw him, anyway. Only the house in which he lived, and the woman that he'd married. She was drawn to both. They were beautiful, she thought. The house with all the grand things in it and the flat-chested lady with her fancy frocks.

When her mother was too ill to make the weekly pilgrimage, Olive collected the money herself. She was eighteen by then and she knew the truth about her parents. She also knew she was very pretty.

That was in the nineteen twenties. Lawrence Conroy, who was injured in the war, was a guest at the estate. She met him when she crossed the yard.

The combination of her beauty and her tragic situation overpowered Lawrence Conroy. He was in pain himself, still shell-shocked and in need of nursing. When her mother died soon after, he employed her as a nurse.

Their marriage outraged all his friends. Lawrence said he didn't care. He thought he was a lucky man. To him, Olive was the epitome of feminine charm rather than a real person. He didn't sense the anger in her. He had to learn that she was cold, socially ambitious and determined to prove herself as the mistress of the house; that she kept up a masquerade while loathing what she really was.

All the while, her anger simmered. Lawrence might have drawn it out but he was too kind to do so. He went into himself instead, and sought solace in the bottle.

The other girls were more like him, being harmonious by nature. But Clemency was passionate. She had always taken risks. She was more provocative. She had acted like a slut, as far as Olive was concerned, and Olive's anger had exploded.

'But Olive didn't murder her.'

'How can you be sure of that?'

It was my turn to take Marie-Rose on the journey that I'd travelled.

I left nothing out of it, except for mentioning Bea Studdart. Why bring Bea into it? She was dead, like Clemency, and Frank had suffered long enough.

In my version of the story, Clemency was on her own as she reached the little harbour where the boat was waiting for her. The wind was tearing at her clothes, so she couldn't keep her balance. The harbour was being washed by rain and lashed by white-tipped, angry waves. So easy, then, to miss one's footing. Slip between the boat and land. Fall into the boiling lake. An accident.

That's what happened, I contended.

'Olive didn't do it then?'

'No.'

Marie-Rose was disappointed. I could hear it in her voice, see it written on her face.

'You should know the things she did.'

She told me about Olive's actions. Rounding up the photographs, removing them from frames and albums. Burning them. Except for one, which Constance found behind a chair.

'And even that was written on. Oh, she was a wicked woman!'

And then there was the case, she said, the one that Clemency had left, and the diary Olive read, which brought on another fit, so she'd ripped the evening gown and the other clothes as well.

'I know about the case,' I said. 'Frank explained what Olive did.'

'Constance kept the dress, you know. I have it still, beneath my bed.'

I kept quiet about that. Squirming. Waiting for her to say, 'Hang on a minute, Caroline. You searched my room when I was gone. You must have come across the dress.'

But she didn't. Something else was on her mind.

'I told people Olive did it,' she said finally.

'What?'

'I mentioned it to certain people. Just the odd few, Caroline. They might have passed it on to others . . .'

It was making sense at last, the way the people of the lake had reacted to my questions, their reluctance to discuss what had happened long ago, the sympathy they'd shown me, and the tears of Alice Egan. As I think I might have said, these are graceful, caring people. And Bob saying Alice had been right, that the past should be forgotten.

Now we had a debt to Olive, one that Marie-Rose had run up.

'You'll have to talk to them again. You'll have to say that you were wrong. That I've remembered certain things.'

She didn't like it, that was clear. But she was obliged to do it.

She said, 'It was *her* fault that Clemency died. *She* drove her to go out that night. She couldn't face her guilt in that. She couldn't stand to think of it. And that was why *you* had to go.'

'Me? What had *I* to do with it?'

'You and her looked so alike. You got more that way every day. And then you had a lot to say. You were Clemency again. And you were a torture to her.'

'That was all there was to it?' I hadn't failed the Conroy test. All that I had ever done was resemble Clemency.

'What other reason could there be?'

'You're right,' I said. 'There wasn't one.'

'She made your mother suffer too, being the bully that she was. She pushed her into your father's arms. They weren't suited to each other, he being kind of sober-faced. And Constance suffered, Caroline, not being pretty like her sisters. Olive made fun of her. But she was *lovely*, Constance was. I'm not the same since she has gone.'

Another spring. The country is sporting the national flag. The vivid green of the grass. The white mist over the lake and hills. The golden gorse, and daffodils.

White, sweet-scented flowers have come out on the blackthorn trees. Violets bloom on leggy stalks. Pilewort grows in matted clumps. Primroses spring out of the crinkled leaves that look like the skin of frogs. There are spiders in the bath.

The winter has been very wet. The children's graveyard has been flooded. Moss is rampant on the lawn. I have to find a scarifier. But I've pruned the flowering shrubs and we'll have strawberries in June.

Carrigrua hums with life, not because the bees are back but because we're all so busy. Bob is working in his study, the room where Constance used to sleep. I am painting in the basement – where she also spent her nights – preparing for an exhibition.

Francesca is preoccupied with the book that she is writing. She has found herself a plot. In her story, so she tells me, the Grey Lady's handsome lover doesn't die on the battlefield but comes back to marry her.

I, too, have made a comeback. Whitegate has forgiven me. Mrs O'Meara was the first to hold out the olive branch, by baking me another cake. I haven't told her I've found out why she hates the Keanes so much. Marie-Rose explained the problem.

'My father was engaged to her but then he opted out of it. It all happened long ago, but she's not got over it.'

I still don't know who mowed the lawn, only that I soon became, not an isolated snob, but a villager in spirit.

But that was then, and this is now.

'Caroline, Michael wants to talk to you.'

'All right, Ger. I'm coming up.'

I go upstairs and Bob emerges. His computer has packed up. He's working at a slower pace on his ancient Olivetti. It has tried his patience sorely.

'The noise up here is bloody awful.'

To think he used to frighten me. I have told him everything. He was shocked by what I said – how could it be otherwise? – but then when he, in turn, liaised with Frank, he confirmed what I remembered.

Bea, just before she died, confessed to Frank what she had done. How he survived I can't imagine. He was bowed down by guilt already and it must have crippled him.

I used to feel that way myself. Guilty about Clemency. Feeling that I should have saved her. As if the child that I had been could have helped the situation.

Clemency. The week she died, she went to Limerick. To buy clothes, said Marie-Rose.

Lingerie at Todds, I said. Bigger sizes, being pregnant. Therefore not for Olive's eyes. So she hid it in the library, in case Olive questioned her.

Bob has got a question too.

'When's this madness going to end?'

I was the one who comforted him. The one who said, 'I know how she must have felt,' when we talked about his mother, describing how it was for me when love pushed me to the edge and my husband overpowered me.

But that was then and this is now and I have another husband.

'You've got Tippex on your face.'

He groans.

I say, 'The builders will be finished soon. And you'll be pleased when it's all done.'

We had no option but to do it. Francesca has a lot of friends who sometimes stay the night with her. That puts pressure on the bathroom. We had to have a second one. So, you see, I changed my mind, and John O'Donnell was delighted. The obvious room to convert was the bedroom next to ours. Clemency had gone from it. But she's often in our thoughts, as I know she is in Frank's.

Soon – next week – the builders will have finished work and Carrigrua will be perfect.

To me, it's unsurpassable now. My classic, blue-grey Georgian manor, so graceful and so elegant in its robe of silver birch trees by the temperamental lake.

It was a symbol long ago of status and gentility. In Olive's time, a stylised and a sterile house. In mine, it is a dream fulfilled. A symmetrical vision of perfection, with a walled garden and an orangery, and a cobblestoned yard with a well in it.

And, the most important thing, it has become a home at last. A noisy place, filled with love and rowdy youngsters. Olive would have hated it.